THE ART THIEF

In the church of Santa Giuliana, Rome, a magnificent Caravaggio altarpiece disappears without trace at dead of night. In a basement vault of the Malevich Society in Paris, curator Genevieve Delacloche is shocked to discover that one of its greatest treasures has vanished. And in London the National Gallery's newest acquisition is stolen just hours after it was purchased for £6.3 million.

As three separate investigations get underway, Inspector Jean-Jacques Bizot in Paris and Harry Wickenden of Scotland Yard begin to suspect that what at first appears a spate of random thefts is nothing of the kind. Pursuing a dizzying trail of false leads, bizarre clues and double-crosses across Europe, the detectives' only chance of uncovering the truth is to band together to outwit an ingenious criminal mastermind with his own mysterious agenda.

THE ART THIEF

Noah Charney

WINDSOR
PARAGON

First published 2008
by Simon & Schuster
This Large Print edition published 2008
by BBC Audiobooks Ltd
by arrangement with
Simon & Schuster UK Ltd

Hardcover ISBN: 978 1 408 41393 7
Softcover   ISBN: 978 1 408 41394 4

British Library Cataloguing in Publication Data available

Printed and bound in Great Britain by
CPI Antony Rowe, Chippenham, Wiltshire

To my parents
James and Diane
&
Eleanor

Look deeper.

CHAPTER ONE

It was almost as if she were waiting, hanging there, in the painted darkness.

The small Baroque church of Santa Giuliana in Trastevere huddled in a corner of the warm Roman night. The streets were blue and motionless, illuminated only by the hushed light of a streetlamp from the square nearby.

Then there was a sound. Inside the church.

It was the faintest scream of metal on metal, barely perceptible in daylight, but now like a shriek of white against black. Then it stopped. The sound had been only momentary, but it echoed.

From out of the belly of the sealed church, a bird rose. A pigeon fluttered frantically along the shadowy chapel walls and swooped through the vaults and down the transept, carving a path blindly through the inky cavernous interior.

Then the alarm went off.

*   *   *

Father Amoroso woke with a start. Sweat clung to his receded hairline.

He looked at his bedside clock. Three fifteen. Night still clung outside his bedroom window. But the ringing in his ear would not stop. Then he noticed that it was not only in his ear.

He threw a robe over his nightshirt and slipped on his sandals. In a moment he was down the stairs, and he ran the few paces across the square to Santa Giuliana in Trastevere, which squatted,

1

like an armadillo, he had once thought, but now vibrated with sound.

Father Amoroso fumbled with his keys and finally pulled open the ancient door, swollen in the humidity. He turned to the anachronism just inside, switching off the alarm. He looked around for a moment. Then he picked up the telephone.

'Scusi, signore. I'm here, yes . . . I don't know. Probably a malfunction with the alarm system, but I . . . just a moment . . .'

Father Amoroso put the police on hold as he surveyed the interior. Nothing moved. The darkness sat politely around the edges of the church and the moonlight on the nave cast shadows through the pews. He took a step forward, then thought better of it. He turned on the lights.

The Baroque hulk slowly sprang to life. Spotlights on its various alcoves and treasures illuminated the empty spaces vicariously. Father Amoroso stepped forward into the center of the nave and scanned. There was the chapel of Santa Giuliana, the Domenichino painting of Santa Giuliana, the confessional, the white marble basin of holy water, the prayer candelabra with the OFFERTE sign, the statue of Sant'Agnese by Maderno, the Byzantine icon and chalices within the vitrine, the Caravaggio painting of the Annunciation above the altar, the reliquary that buried the shinbone of Santa Giuliana beneath a sea of gold and glass . . . Nothing seemed out of place.

Father Amoroso returned to the telephone.

'Non vedo niente . . . must be a problem with the system. Please excuse me. Thank you . . . good

2

night . . . yes . . . yes, thank you.'

He cradled the phone and switched off the lights. The momentarily enlivened church now slept once more. He reset the alarm, then pulled heavily shut the door, locked it, and returned to his apartment to sleep.

*   *   *

Father Amoroso bolted upright in bed, eyes wide. He'd had a horrible dream in which he could not cease the ringing in his ears. He attributed it to the zuppa di frutti di mare from dinner at Da Saverio, but then realized once again that the ringing was not in his ears alone.

Everyone must have eaten at Da Saverio, he thought for a moment, and then awoke more thoroughly.

It was the alarm, once again ringing violently. He looked at his bedside clock. Three fifty. The sun was still sound asleep. Why not he? He put on his robe and sandals and tripped down once more into the sleepless Roman night.

Father Amoroso, though rarely a profane man, muttered minor curses under his breath, as he fumbled with his keys, rammed them into the heavy wooden door, and pulled it open, leaning back on his heels for proper leverage.

This is supposed to be a church, not an alarm clock, he thought.

Inside, he spun toward the alarm on the wall, accidentally knocking the telephone out of its cradle. 'Dio!' he muttered, then thought better of it, and pointed up to the sky with a whispered 'scusa, signore. I'm a little tired. Scusa.'

He switched off the alarm, then turned to the church interior. The shadows seemed to mock him. He flicked on the lights with relish. The church yawned into illumination. Father Amoroso picked up the telephone.

'Si? Si, mi dispiace. I don't know . . . no, that shouldn't be necessary . . . just a moment, please . . .'

He put down the phone, and moved once more to the center of the nave. The tiny church gaped, huge and vacant, within the early morning darkness.

Nothing seemed amiss. This time Father Amoroso walked round the inside walls of the church. He moved along the worn slate paving, past rows of extinguished candles, carved wooden pews, and still shadowy alcoves hiding the figures of saints in relief or in oil. Everything was sound. He returned to the telephone.

'Niente. Niente di niente. Mi dispiace, ma . . . right, now it's four ten in the morning . . . yes, probably a malfunction . . . yes . . . later in the morning, yes. Nothing to be done until then. Thank you, good night . . . I mean, good morning. Night ended some time ago . . . Ciao.'

Father Amoroso looked with disdain at the alarm that had twice sounded for no reason, merely to mock him. Perhaps he should not have looked so longingly at Signora Materassi at Mass last Sunday. God has his ways. He would call to have the alarm system checked for faults later on. Perhaps he could still get a little sleep.

Father Amoroso switched off the lights. He ignored the smug alarm as he brushed out the door, locked it, and returned home to capture what precious moments of sleep he still could.

*   *   *

An alarm went off.

Father Amoroso jackknifed out of bed. But then he calmed. It was his bedside alarm. The time was seven, on a Monday morning. That's better, he thought.

The sun was present on the horizon and the day promised its usual Roman iridescence through the humidity of summer. He yawned thoughtlessly and stretched his fatigued arms cruciform. Throwing off his nightshirt, Father Amoroso waddled into the bathroom and emerged a new man, clean and fresh for a new day. He donned his clerical garments and made his way down to Santa Giuliana.

He was still ten minutes early. He was not required to open the door until the stroke of eight. The day was not yet too hot, and Father Amoroso decided to steal away for a moment. He slipped into the bar nearby and ordered a caffè. He admired the sunshine on the ancient paving as he sipped his espresso, standing at the bar. Locals passed in the street outside. The occasional tourist bumbled by, map in hand and camera at the ready.

He checked his watch. Seven fifty-seven. He drank up and crossed the square to his church.

With a pleasurable sense of leisure, Father Amoroso fumbled slowly at his keys and, finding the right one, twisted and tugged at the great wooden door. When he had it yawned sufficiently, he looped the metal catch to prop it open and allowed the still air trapped within to cool down in

5

the morning breeze that flowed without.

He entered the church and threw a look of disdain upon the alarm system as he passed. God, I'll have to have it fixed today, he thought, then realized his blasphemy and glanced up to Heaven for pardon. He shuffled across the floor to the church office, pushed aside the curtain that hid the door, and unlocked it. He turned and crossed to the center of the nave, stopping briefly to genuflect in front of the altar as he passed.

He was about to continue, when he saw it. He couldn't believe his eyes. Perhaps he was still asleep, he hoped. Then it sank in, and he stumbled backward, as he cried out 'Dio mio!'

The Caravaggio altarpiece was gone.

CHAPTER TWO

'But it's a fake.'

Geneviève Delacloche pinched the phone between shoulder and ear, and fumbled with the cord, which she had somehow managed to tangle round her wrists.

Her small office overlooked the Seine, with the yellow-gray stone medieval majesty of riverside Paris arched up on either side of the coral water. Her desk was overcome with papers that had, at one time, been put in precise order. Delacloche was of the hybrid sort of obsessive-compulsive who need a correct place for everything, but never actually keep anything in that place.

The prints on the wall were all the work of the same artist: Kasimir Malevich. They were of the abstract variety that drove mad those uneducated in art, with explicative titles such as *Black Square, Suprematism with Blue Triangle and Black Rectangle,* and *Red Square: Realism in Paint of a Peasant Woman in Two Dimensions,* the latter consisting, in its entirety, of a slightly obtuse red square on a white background. Wood-framed diplomas told of degrees in painting conservation and arts administration. On her desk lay a stack of monogrammed, cream-colored paper, with the elegant Copperplate-font words MALEVICH SOCIETY printed along the top.

Open on her lap, Delacloche held a catalogue for an upcoming sale of 'Important Russian and Eastern European Paintings and Drawings,' at Christie's in London. The catalogue was open to page 46, lot 39:

Kasimir Malevich (1878–1935)
Suprematist Composition White on White
oil on canvas
54.6 × 36.6 in. (140 × 94 cm.)
Estimate: £4,000,000-6,000,000

PROVENANCE:
Abraham Steingarten, 1919–39
Josef Kleinert, 1939–44
Galerie Gmurzynska, Zug, 1944–52
Otto Metzinger, 1952–69
Luc Sallenave, 1969
Anon. sale, Sotheby's London, 1 October 1969, lot 55, when acquired by present owner

EXHIBITED:
Liebling Galerie, Berlin, 1929, *Suprematist*

7

Works and Their Influence on Russian Spirituality, no. 82
Galerie Gmurzynska, Zug, 1946, no. 22

LITERATURE:
Art Journal, 1920, p.181

This painting is believed to be the first of Malevich's renowned and controversial series of Suprematist White on White compositions. It is considered the most important of the series . . .

'Jeffrey, I'm telling you it's a fake. Don't you tell me that I'm being severely French! I am severely French, but that doesn't make the issue go away. You're about to auction off a fake Malevich. I have the catalogue right here, yes. How am I so sure? I'll tell you how. Because the painting that you're planning to auction off is *here.* It's owned by the Malevich Society. I'm telling you, it's in the vault in the basement right now. Yes, that's right, three floors beneath my ass . . .'

*   *   *

Malevich strikes a balance between whiteness and nothingness, and he magnificently transforms this tense contrast in a contemplative meditation on inner tension. These works are wholly about feeling. Malevich has divorced himself from depictions of the everyday, of life and objects, and has honed his abilities into the projection of emotion. There is no right or wrong answer to the question 'What is this painting about?' The question is 'What

8

does this make you feel?'

'. . . Look, the painting has been in the vault for months now. I saw it there last week. We only very rarely lend it out for exhibition, so it's been locked away for ages. I don't know why you didn't contact us immediately . . . because of the provenance, well . . . I know you think that you are looking at it in your office right this minute, but I'm telling you, it has to be a fake . . .'

It is both revolution and ideology, abstract forms that may be appropriated by any viewer to his or her own end. Malevich frees his viewers from the shackles of iconography, and liberates them into a world of concentrated feeling. He did so long before such abstract works were popularized.

'. . . of course he did multiple versions of *White on White,* but I've only ever heard of two that are this large. All the extant versions of the painting are smaller, except for ours and one in a private collection in the U.K. But I recognize the image in the catalogue as ours. The provenance is all different, but if you're telling me that your own photographers took this catalogue photo from the original that's in your office, then it's a fake.

'Jeffrey, the Malevich Society's job is to protect the name of the artist. Just like if some fellow off the street wrote a symphony and called it a lost Beethoven, people would object, and the artist's oeuvre would be damaged. The same goes for this painting that must be forged, or at least misattributed.

'I recognize the painting, Jeffrey! How do I recognize it? I recognize it the way you'd know your wife if you passed her on the street. You're not married? Well, Jeffrey, I really don't care, but you know what I mean. When you've seen enough of these, especially of this particular painting, you get to know it intrinsically. It's my job to locate and protect every extant piece of art by Malevich. That's why I want you to withdraw this lot from the auction. I have my hands full hunting down forgeries, and it doesn't help when a high-profile institution such as yours is claiming that fakes are real . . .'

It is objective art, in that it does not rely on specialized knowledge for interpretation, as might a painting of a scene from classical mythology, which requires a recognition of the story in order to understand the action and glean the moral. It is a liberation from the excess clutter that impedes the path to pure emotion. It is an almost Buddhist focus, pushing aside the trappings of traditional paintings of things. It provokes.

For Malevich, the reaction was one of transcendental meditation and peace. But the painting is equally successful if it provokes anger in the viewer, who may say, outraged, 'How is this art? I could paint that!' In answer to this exclamation, if one actually sat down and tried to paint exactly this, one would find that it is impossible. The textures and tones, despite the monochromatic palette, are deep and subtle. Painting such a work is easier said than done. But in one's outrage, the painting

10

has succeeded. It provokes emotion. Suprematist art reaches for the stars and thereby creates a new emotional constellation that hangs in the sky for all to see and interpret as they will.

'Well, thank you, Jeffrey. Your English is very good, too. Yes, I know that you're English. It's a joke. Yes. Well, I had four years in . . . look, we're getting sidetracked here. I know the provenance looks good, I'm looking at it now. Well, I've not heard of all . . . no. But have you checked them all out? Well, what are you waiting for? I know you're busy, but if you sell a fake for six million you're going to be in a lot worse trouble than if you . . . Can't you just delay a bit, and I'll do the research for you? Well, if you don't have the authority, can I speak with Lord . . . it's not going to do any good. No, it's not my time of the month, I . . . but, I . . . yeah, well I hope you get royally fucked in the . . .'

*   *   *

'And this is the man we have to thank for the recovery of the stolen and ransomed portrait of our dearly beloved foundress, Lady Margaret Beaufort,' said the dean of St John's College, Cambridge.

He gestured to the elegant, trimmed, and gray-templed Gabriel Coffin, a smile in his eyes. The room in which he stood was a wide wood-paneled corridor, brightened only by candlelight bounced off polished silver sconces. The Fellows of the college assembled before him, each clasping tight a glass of preprandial sherry. They look like the cast

11

of a Daumier cartoon, thought Coffin. He stroked his close-cropped bearded chin, black speckled white.

'A renowned scholar and consultant to police on art theft, and a graduate of our own institution, he kindly volunteered his investigative services, when Lady Margaret went missing from the Great Hall. Of course, we'd all thought that those cads over at Trinity had had their way with her, but when it proved more serious, Dr. Coffin came to our rescue. Let us give him a hearty thanks, and then adjourn to dinner.'

*   *   *

The shudder din of voices and clinking cutlery whirled up from the long wooden tables and spun toward the dark-wood ceiling of the formal dining hall at St John's College.

Coffin stared out from the Fellows' Table, perpendicular to the long rows of students. Above his head, the large sixteenth-century portrait of the college foundress, Lady Margaret Beaufort, knelt in prayer. Was she relieved at her rescue? Back in her place, hung high on the wall. Coffin floated alone, adrift in a sea of conversation and laughter.

Waiters wove round the medieval benches full of students in suit-and-tie and academic robes. William Wordsworth, among other illustrious graduates, stared down inert from pendulous portraits on the wall, and donors proclaimed their gifts from coats-of-arms melted into the stained glass and branded onto the rafters.

Suddenly, Coffin heard a *clink*. What do I have that *clinks*? he thought. Then he felt his ribs nudged by a neighboring elbow.

He turned to the Fellow seated to his right, a toothless, red-faced old goat with a beard like a white sneeze. He was clearly on the losing side of the war for sobriety.

'You've been pennied, my boy!'

Coffin could feel the man's breath. 'I beg your pardon?'

'You've got to save the Queen from drowning. Bottoms up!' The Fellow gestured to Coffin's wineglass, at the bottom of which lay a one-pence coin.

Coffin rolled his eyes and downed his glass. The Fellow laughed and gave him an old-boy smack on the shoulder. When he had turned away, Coffin dropped the recently saved penny onto the Fellow's plate of bread-and-butter pudding. The Fellow spun around and his smile faded.

'Now you have to eat your dessert hands-free,' said Coffin, coolly. 'You know the rules. If I penny your plate without your noticing . . .'

The sounds of the hall nearly masked the ring of his mobile phone. Coffin lifted it to his ear.

'Pronto? Buona sera. I didn't expect to hear from you. What can I . . . Really? No, I can . . . I'll be on the earliest flight back to Rome tomorrow morning . . .'

Something had been stolen.

CHAPTER THREE

Geneviève Delacloche sat in her office with her stockinged legs slung up onto her desk. She had a fountain pen clutched between both thumbs and forefingers, and she was massaging it near to the point of breaking across the middle. Then her assistant brought in the coffee.

'Et voilà! I've never needed it so desperately, merci bien, Silvia. How much time before the call?'

'Only ten more minutes, madame.'

'Putain de merde,' Delacloche muttered. 'Ten minutes. Right. Just give me . . . just . . .' Her assistant knew and had already left.

Delacloche pulled out a cigarette, always Gauloise, and drew heavily on it. She gathered her thoughts as she stood, left arm across her chest, right arm at a right angle supporting the cigarette like a spyglass. Smoking helped her to see more clearly.

The president of the Malevich Society was away on business in New York. With a probable fake about to enter the market, they had to decide on the Society's next move. Delacloche sat, rolling her fingers along the cherry wood table. Before her lay a fat folder. She knew the decision that was needed. The president was their public face, a good hand-shaker and fund-raiser, but he knew little about art. It was up to her.

The phone rang.

'Alors,' she began, 'I've just spoken with that asshole, Jeffrey, at Christie's. He's not removing it from the sale. In fact, he's not taking us very seriously at all . . . I know that one solid claim that it is a fake should be enough to shut them down. The difficulty is that it is in no one's interest that this painting be found a fake . . . Right . . .

'The problem,' Delacloche continued, 'is one of

14

finance. Consider for a moment. If it gets out that this painting is a forgery, then a number of things occur. The benefit is for the Malevich name, and the name of justice. But the art world is rarely high and mighty when it comes to such things.

'But who is to suffer? The auction house looks the fool for vouching for a painting that turns out to be bogus. Their reputation, and specifically the reputation of this so-called expert, is tarnished. As we all know, the one thing that will ruin an expert's career is to be publicly fooled by a forgery . . . I know, that's why . . . yes . . .

'Remember the Getty affair, when their man claimed that several seventeenth-century Italian drawings that the museum had just acquired for millions were fraudulent. He even claimed to know who the forger was. And the Getty refused to acknowledge the accusation by testing the drawings. If they were indeed forged, then the Getty had just been screwed for millions. If they turned out to be legitimate, the scholar would have lost all his credibility. From the Getty's perspective, he was out to embarrass them, one way or another. And of course, all he wanted was the truth and a little justice . . . I know . . .

'And he was fired without anyone ever testing the drawings.' Delacloche tapped her fingers on her folder. 'So, that's what we're up against. Christie's has already put out the catalogue. That means they've told the world that this painting is a Malevich. Not only that, they have it estimated at four-to-six million pounds . . . How could they make such a mistake? It's simple. The provenance seemed . . . seems flawless. . . .

'I don't know.' Delacloche lit another cigarette.

'Of course, they won't let me research it, and they won't allow me to see the original documents. From the catalogue entry, I recognize about half of the places on the list. Some of the others are more obscure. It occurred to me that the obvious solution is that the image in the catalogue is incorrect, that there is a Malevich that fits this provenance but that it's not ours, and the photograph of ours somehow replaced it. But Jeffrey assures me that it is correct, and that the painting was on his desk . . . Well, we can only do something legally, to prevent them from selling it, if it's proven to be a stolen object . . .'

Delacloche was preparing the next cigarette for launch. 'The owner, who remains top secret thanks to Christie's anonymity policy, of course does not want to discover that his Malevich, and I use that in the loosest sense of the word, is a fake, because it will no longer be valuable . . . uh-huh. And if he's a criminal and knows that it's a fake, then he certainly doesn't want it discovered . . . right. And the buyers are such that they'd prefer, although they'd never admit this, to be blissfully ignorant of a fake than to have one fewer Malevich on the market to decorate their walls and adorn their pride. The discovery of a new Malevich on the market is a hot enough story that a world of the wealthy would be disappointed to see it melt away. So, Christie's would lose face and commission, the owner would have a valueless piece of canvas with paint on it, and the clientele would be heartbroken. It's no wonder Christie's isn't even willing to look into it.

'You'd think this expert would have been a capable enough man to investigate more thoroughly. But he's not a Malevich guy, he's a generalist in twentieth-century art. That means he knows shit-all about any one artist, like Malevich. You know how specific this sort of expertise gets. But you're right . . . he still should have taken an X ray, for instance. With my training as a conservator, that's the first action that came to mind. But scientific investigation is expensive, and faith is more highly valued than fact. The owner certainly wouldn't pay for it. Without good cause, Christie's wouldn't either. We all agree that our accusation is good cause, but there's another reason, airtight from Christie's perspective, for them not to investigate further: the provenance.

'It's only if provenance is shaky, or absent, that people look deeper. In this piece, it is unquestioned. This expert is the head curator of Russian and Eastern European paintings at Christie's. That means that he is in charge of everything to do with this upcoming sale. The catalogue has one hundred and two lots in it, and all of them have to be examined, estimates made, catalogue entries written, and so on. If the provenance of one piece checks out, it is highly unlikely that anyone in that office would give the piece a second look. Case closed, malheureusement . . .

'Uh, no. No, I don't think we should we go public with our accusation. It is most likely that it will jump-start interest, rather than scare people off. Buyers will believe the Christie's experts above other sources. Most of them are ignorant of the minutiae, and just happy to buy a recognizable name that they can drop in the Hamptons, or in St. Tropez. Museums want the real deal, but they

17

also want the flash of the celebrity name. They are better off with a small handful of renowned pieces, rather than rooms full of excellent examples of little-known artists. Your average public would flock to an exhibition that consisted solely of *Whistler's Mother*, before they'd grudgingly attend a museum full of Kusnetsov, Tatlin, Malevich, Kandinsky, and Chashnik and the history of Suprematism in Russia, in which you run the risk of actually learning something. No, museums want the big names to put on their ties and coffee mugs.

'Word will circulate, I am certain, about the questions we've raised regarding the painting. The buzz will draw out more bidders and voyeurs at the auction, and that will only add to the chaos, and the payoff for Christie's and their anonymous seller. That's . . . that's correct, yes . . . I think all we can do now is wait and trace. They're the ones who will get screwed in the end. If we involve the police now, then Christie's will crawl inside their shell, and if there's any foul play about, we risk scaring off the perpetrator. I will attend the auction and be sure to see who the buyer is. If it's a museum, then it will go public, but if it's a private buyer who will want to keep publicity under his control, I will need to be there to see for myself who is bidding. Otherwise the bidder, and the painting, could disappear from our radar.'

*   *   *

Delacloche leaned back in her chair. She had some more paperwork to do. The phone call had put her off her usual day's work. In addition to overseeing the care and upkeep of the Society's private

18

collection, she was in charge of investigation. There was an eighty-year-old in Minsk who claimed to have a letter from Malevich to Vladimir Tatlin, while in Lyon, a man wished to have the authenticity of a drawing, thought to be by Malevich, confirmed. That was just today.

Delacloche was exhausted. Her eyes scanned blankly around the room. Framed posters, diplomas, a black-and-white photograph of her as a newborn in her mother's arms, a Boston Red Sox World Championship pennant, a Whistler etching of old sailors in a tavern, empty coffee cups, a postcard of Boston Harbor at night, her silver Zippo lighter on the desk. She looked outside her narrow window. The azure sea of twilight floated gently on the tide of the evening breeze, above the darkening canopy of the city streets. I'm glad that the Malevich Society isn't in Russia, she thought.

She stacked the stray papers that had migrated on her desk into some semblance of order, ensured that all of the pens in her coffee cup were facing point-end down, and snapped shut her briefcase. Monday, mon Dieu. She closed her office door and stepped down the curling stairs to the ground floor.

Everyone else in the office had left. Delacloche continued down the stairs into the basement. She liked to find moments of quiet introspection to share with the artworks that it was her duty to protect. They could not thank her, but they did not need to. She punched in the code outside the vault door and inserted her key. Then the satisfying click, and the door swung open.

Inside the vault hung a phalanx of parallel-stacked metal grates from floor to ceiling, mounted on rollers, each no more than one meter away from the next. To the left were wide, shallow filing cabinets. They were filled with Solander boxes that kept out light and contamination, to protect works on paper, such as drawings and watercolors, and letters.

Delacloche turned right and walked to the end of the room, to the last row of movable wall. She leaned back as she pulled on the metal grate, and slowly the wall slid out toward her, with its cargo of framed Malevich paintings hanging loosely off either side. Once it was extended, she walked down to the far end, and scanned the titles. *White on White,* where is the *White on White*? Her eyes glided over the hanging works until she stopped.

The painting was missing.

*   *   *

Inspector Jean-Jacques Bizot was well into his third half dozen oysters, when the mobile phone, clipped between the bulge of his belly and the alligator gooseflesh of his green-tinged belt, began to buzz.

'L'enfer, c'est les huîtres,' he said, sliding a knotted snotty mollusk down his gullet.

'Let's hope not,' replied his dining companion, Jean-Paul Lesgourges. 'The Oyster Affair of '75 is not one to remember. I wonder if the plumber was ever resuscitated.'

It was well into the third succession of buzzes that Inspector Bizot noticed that something in the region of his loins was vibrating. But he attributed this to the aphrodisiacal powers of the bivalves of which he was in midconsumption.

All was going to plan, he thought, as he dreamt ahead to his liaison with Monique, or was it Mireille, at nine that night. It was not until the plate of asparagus descended from the hand of the waiter, like the hand of God presenting lusty fuel to Jean-Jacques' libido, that the phone began to buzz once more.

This time, Bizot could certainly feel something, as the vibration shimmied down the interior of his thigh. He cast a salty, bewildered glance at Jean-Paul Lesgourges, who was slipping the last slimy oyster between his equine lips. Lesgourges slowly noticed Bizot's gaze, and he returned it with a silent 'What?'

'Why are you rubbing me, Jean?'

'Me? Are you nuts? You've eaten too many oysters. I wouldn't rub you if you were a magic lantern with a genie inside, you great walrus!'

'Jean, I can feel you rubbing me!'

'Alors, laisse-moi tranquille et mange!'

Bizot and Lesgourges resumed eating, as the fourth and final round of vibrations alerted Bizot to his nether regions. His belly, weary of the unnoticed mobile phone, finally rejected and ejected it, popping the phone from its clip to the floor with the elastic projection of Bizot's folds of fat. The phone clattered to the restaurant floor.

Jean-Paul Lesgourges did not look up from the cutting of his asparagus. 'Something just hopped out of your stomach area,' he said, as he thought about his meeting with Angélique, or perhaps Mireille, scheduled for later that night. 'You know, the Emperor Augustus's favorite phrase was "faster than you can boil asparagus."'

'Fascinating, Jean . . .' Bizot, too, recognized

21

that something had fallen, but he was in a bit of a tough spot. The bulk of his stomach was wedged between his knees and the underside of the table. He could not see under the table, nor could he move at all, he now noticed, as he made an initial attempt to bend over and retrieve the fallen object.

'Il y a quelque chose de coincé dans le mécanisme,' Bizot grumbled, as he recognized the preposterousness of his situation. Lesgourges met his eyes and saw the beads of frustration on his brow. He opened wide his horse face in a crescendo howl that wept into laughter, as Bizot joined in, heart reddened by the two and a half empty bottles of wine that still stood on the table.

The laughter eventually attracted the attention of a waiter, but only after everyone else in the restaurant had stopped to turn and see the source of the cacophonic expulsions emanating from a booth in the back corner.

It was a sight to behold, the exceedingly reedy Jean-Paul Lesgourges, with putty-stretched cheeks that looked rouged, and a glassy cackle in his eyes, whooping with joy, as the puff adder Bizot, like a broken aqueduct, every facet spherical, rumbled mercilessly, the table and his knees pinching him in place, bright smile tears puddling up around his tiny, hidden eyes. His brambly peppered beard was a tangle of chin and leftovers, and bounced of its own volition, revealing his gummy smile.

It was some minutes before Bizot and Lesgourges stopped laughing enough for the waiter, who had bent and retrieved the fallen phone, to attract their attention sufficiently to return it to its owner. The other occupants of Restaurant Étouffe-Chrétien could not help but smile and laugh along with the infectious good nature and Santa Clausian demeanors of the two rollicking, incongruous gentlemen in the corner. Each table wished silently that they'd been invited to dine with that oddest couple, the burly bombastic cannonball of Bizot beside the candle-wax-dripped taper Lesgourges, both exuding the color red, as if they were Titian-underpainted.

Then Bizot saw the flashing message on his phone that indicated four missed calls. 'Putain de merde, ta gueule, vieux con, salaud.' He giggled as he checked his messages. 'Jean,' Bizot whispered loudly.

'What is it, Jean?' Lesgourges replied from the midst of a chew of asparagus.

'There's been a theft.'

'Sans blague? What is it?' Lesgourges was engrossed in his food and did not look up.

'That's when someone steals something.'

'Oui?' Lesgourges was elsewhere absorbed.

'From the Malevich Society.' Bizot struggled to pull a small black-bound Moleskine notebook from the breast pocket of his blue jacket. With one hand, he endeavored to unsnap the black elastic that locked shut the notebook. Failing to do so, he swung a stubby arm across his corpulence and snugged the phone between ear and shoulder. He opened the notebook and began to take notes, before realizing that he did not have a pen in hand.

'A pen! My kingdom for a pen! Jean, give me your damned pen.'

Still focused on asparagus, Lesgourges handed Bizot a butter knife, with which Bizot preceeded to write in his Moleskine notebook.

'Ça ne marche pas, Jean. Can I have a pen that writes?'

Lesgourges finally looked up and resumed his enthusiastic giggles, as he handed over a maroon Mont Blanc fountain pen from his pocket.

'J'ai dit,' Bizot continued, as his notes finally flowed out in ink onto the page, 'that there's been a theft from the Malevich Society.'

'What was taken?'

'A Malevich.'

'Really?'

'It's the Malevich Society—what else would they take?'

'Oh. I hadn't thought.' Lesgourges served some bacon-wrapped eel onto Bizot's plate.

'Hadn't thought. That I believe.' Bizot clicked shut his phone and stared down at his notes, which were scribbled beyond legibility. He shrugged.

'Eat, eat,' Lesgourges beckoned. 'You're nothing but skin and bones!'

'I'll give you skin and bones, you old donkey. There's a crime that's been committed.'

'Mmm,' replied Lesgourges. 'Shall we go investigate?'

'After dinner I'll check in with the officers on the scene. It's been secured, so we'll have a proper look round tomorrow. And what do you mean *we*? I'm the investigator. You're just an academic, and not a very good one either. The worst kind. What sort of academic has no degrees, and doesn't work in academia?'

'A rich one,' replied Lesgourges. 'If you have a château, you don't need a school, and if you have your own Armagnac vineyard, in Armagnac, then you don't need the cafeteria milk cartons.'

'You proud bastard,' Bizot grumble-smirked, 'I'll give you a bottle of your Armagnac up your . . .'

'I'm the only one licensed to distribute my Armagnac, Jean. But without my extensive knowledge of art, you'd be . . .'

'. . . a lot happier.' Bizot scraped the eel from his fingers onto his napkin, which hung, like a tie, from his neck. 'What do you know about art, anyway? I happen to know a lot more than you do about art, despite your little Modern art collection, and your backyard sculpture garden, and your . . .'

'. . . and my what?'

Bizot leaned in. 'Jean, you own the ugliest Picasso I have ever seen in my life.'

'Ah.' Lesgourges leaned back. 'But I do own a Picasso.'

Bizot thought a moment, then shrugged and returned to his meal. 'Touché.'

Lesgourges looked on at him. 'And what do you know about Picasso, anyway? You wouldn't know a Picasso if it walked up behind you and bit you on the ass!'

'Look, I know . . .'

'You *think* that you know. That's the worst kind.'

'Ah, eat your eel and asparagus, Lesgourges! I've put up with you long enough. Always wanting to tag along on my cases. You know I strictly work alone.'

'I've put up with you, Bizot, since I got you out of trouble with Hubert Pompignan, and I've been your guardian angel ever since. Eat more of the eel, it's good for you.'

'The Hubert Pompignan Affair took place when

25

we were eleven, and I'll thank you to stop patting yourself on the back about fading-ember glories. Pass the salt.'

'So,' Lesgourges smacked and dabbed his lips dry. 'I haven't anything better to do. Lost Maleviches. Are we on the hunt, or what?'

'As soon as I finish my meal. And dessert.'

CHAPTER FOUR

In Rome, the tiny church of Santa Giuliana in Trastevere was a nest of activity. The well-meaning, well-dressed Italian police swarmed the slate-paved square, and a crowd of Romans had found time during their lunch break to investigate the cause of commotion, had they missed it during the first day of investigation.

When word circulated that a painting had been stolen, from the altar, no less, people were more outraged at the principle of the theft from a church, than out of any particular attachment to the missing painting. There was no weight given to the fact that the painting was a Caravaggio.

Gabriel Coffin crossed the square and made his way toward Santa Giuliana, tapping his umbrella, which he carried despite the Roman sun, along the pavement as he went, alternating taps and swings with each step. Coffin slid through the crowd of onlookers, and past the Carabiniere guarding the entrance to the church.

Inside the church, several Carabinieri were wandering, pretending to look for something, while the priest, distraught and quick of breath, was speaking with balding and kempt Claudio Ariosto. Ariosto was one of the chief detectives from the Carabinieri's Unit for the Protection of Cultural Heritage.

The Caravaggio that had been stolen was a known quantity, unique, universally identifiable. It could not, therefore, be shopped by the thieves. It must have been stolen to order, either for an organized crime syndicate, as happened most often since the Second World War, to use as barter currency . . . or in the rarer instance, for a private individual who wished to possess it. It recalled the theft that prompted the creation of the Carabinieri Arts and Antiquities Division: another Caravaggio, *Adoration of the Shepherds,* stolen from a church in Palermo in 1969. It had been a thorn in the side of the department ever since, never found. From one Caravaggio to another. I'm sure that's crossed Ariosto's mind, Coffin considered. Wonder if he's more focused on retrieving this one, or if he thinks it's gone forever, like the Palermo *Adoration.*

Coffin scanned the interior as he took his first step inside. Three officers, one detective, one frantic priest, one missing altarpiece. Three flanking chapels on either side of the nave, each with a piece of art or relic as the focal point, chairs aligned in each, and empty prayer candles, one confessional booth, made of dark, oiled wood, much younger than the church itself, curtain in the front right corner must lead to offices, no holy water in the font, telephone beside the entrance, alarm keypad, motion sensors two feet off the ground along the periphery and across the altar, no locks on the ground-floor windows, not good, original stained glass of the Passion Cycle, but the

Way to Calvary window had been restored, none of the furniture out of place, plaster cracking in the inside of the dome, wax from the prayer candles recycled, church underfunded, Domenichino's *Santa Giuliana,* not his best work . . . Then Coffin took a second step into the church.

He met eyes with Ariosto and crossed over to him, hand extended.

'Buongiorno, Claudio. Come va?'

'Gabriel. Let me guess. You heard the word *Caravaggio* and sniffed us out?' Ariosto shook Coffin's hand in both of his.

'Actually,' Coffin began in mostly accent-free Italian, 'the company I work for now would prefer not to have to pay for this.' He gestured toward the vacant altar with his thumb.

'Insurance? Of course.' Ariosto looked momentarily concerned.

'Don't worry, Claudio. I'll stay out of your way. We both want the same thing. To see this altar filled again.'

'That's not what I was thinking. I'm just curious, although I know you're not supposed to say. But then, that's never stopped you before.'

'Well . . .' Coffin looked up at the altar, then down at the bewildered Father Amoroso. 'I really shouldn't say.'

'Suit yourself.' Ariosto, mildly displeased at the withheld gossip, resumed his usual habit of fiddling with the watch chain in his right jacket pocket. He was dressed, as always, in a gorgeously cut designer suit, offset by a necktie of a color that echoed, but did not overshadow, his shirt and jacket. 'Though they'd be fools if it were valued at more than forty million euros.' Ariosto looked up

28

from beneath his brow with a half-smile. He couldn't read Coffin's face.

Coffin smiled and shook his head. 'Do you have anything so far?'

'We've been looking since yesterday,' began Ariosto. 'But there's something missing.'

'I've noticed,' said Coffin. 'It's the altarpiece.'

'Very funny. How I've missed not having you with us. Are you still lecturing?'

'Yes. Can't keep my hand out of academia. And I need to come up with creative ways to supplement my income.'

'And your taste for collecting . . .'

'Guilty as charged.' Coffin twisted his umbrella beneath his hand. 'Do you mind if I . . .'

'Suit yourself,' Ariosto muttered. 'Nothing has been moved. But let us know what you find.'

'Of course.'

'We can help each other, I think.' Ariosto, fingers ringed, handed a folder to Coffin. 'We have fewer art thefts every year, but last year we still came in near twenty -thousand, and those are only the ones that are reported in Italy. I've got a lot to do, as you know. If you could . . .'

'Of course.'

Coffin took the folder and opened it. Inside were documents pertaining to the Caravaggio: color photographs, details of the back of the canvas and support, statistics, provenance. Unusually, in this case, the provenance was comprised of only one entry: one owner in the entire history of the painting's existence. The photocopy of a manuscript, dated 1720, a portion of which was highlighted, read: *Annunc. pict. Mich. Mer. da Carav. 120 d. 1598.* The sheet was an

29

inventory of possessions of Santa Giuliana in Trastevere, made upon the appointment of a new priest. An Annunciation scene painted by Michelangelo Merisi da Caravaggio had been purchased, apparently straight from the artist, in 1598 for 120 scudi.

Coffin wondered what 120 scudi would be today. Thirty years later, Claude Lorrain was earning the top wage for each painting, and would receive in the vicinity of 400 scudi. Caravaggio was no less acclaimed but was in constant financial and judicial straits, so this was a considerably cut rate. He must have needed the cash, and quickly, which explained the unusually small size of the painting in question. He fired it off for the money.

Coffin pulled one of the color photographs out of the folder. It was not a great Caravaggio by the artist's own standards, but miraculous by any other. There were Gabriel and Mary. The Annunciation was the moment in the New Testament when God sends Gabriel, the messenger angel, to visit Mary and tell her that she will bear the Son of God.

This moment, and the Crucifixion, were the two most commonly depicted in religious art, and the iconography was quite standard. Mary was shown as a humble, achingly young girl in prayer, often poring over a copy of the Old Testament. She is surprised by the arrival of Gabriel, beautiful and androgynous, who conveys the word of God, sometimes in the literal form of words or rays issuing out of his mouth. God the Father looks down from a top corner of the painting, and often shines a ray of light into Mary's womb. On occasion, a little baby Jesus or a dove may be seen sliding down the ray of light into Mary's stomach. I've always found that a little odd, thought Coffin. Looks like he's skiing. How could an as yet unborn baby know how to ski? The Son of God, presumably, is skilled in all winter sports, Coffin conjectured.

But this Annunciation scene, as with all of Caravaggio's paintings, differed completely from the iconographic norm. He was a stylistic pioneer of the Baroque. His paintings were incendiary, in both popularity and impact on every artist who came after him, as was his temper. He was forced to leave Rome because he had killed a man.

Coffin was not surprised to see that Caravaggio's *Annunciation* looked nothing like the traditional depictions. Mary's back was to the viewer, and she spun to look over her left shoulder at Gabriel, as he reached out to touch her. She had sensed the angel's presence, and there seemed to be some erotic charge between the two figures. This made sense, after all, for Gabriel's words are a sexual equivalent, leading as they do to Mary's impregnation. The look on her face had a coy startle to it, as if surprised by the appearance of her lover. Much of Gabriel's winged back was to the viewer, as well, and the scene was set against an amorphous black background, the chiaroscuro figures emerging into light as if from an inky sea.

It was clear that Caravaggio had spent less time on this work than he had on others. More of the background was simply painted black than in most of his paintings. In doing so, he had been able to avoid painting Gabriel and Mary from the waist down. The point of view put the focus squarely on the facial expressions, and left the viewer straining

31

to see more of the faces, which were partially obscured due to the odd backward positioning of the bodies.

Coffin noted the dimensions: 99 × 132 centimeters. Oil on canvas. No signature, of course. Artists rarely signed works until centuries later.

Then Coffin just stared. He locked his gaze on the photograph of the painting. Just as he did in museums, when examining a painting new to his eyes. He memorized it, drank in everything that it had to offer. He always began in the upper left corner and worked his way across and down. Paintings were meant to be read.

He handed the folder back to Ariosto.

'I'll just have a look around.'

He strolled down the aisle, between rows of pews, his umbrella clasped with two hands behind his back. He was in the habit of overdressing, and invariably in the same clothes: three-piece suit, Charles Tyrwhitt French cuff dress shirt. It was what he liked. He liked spats, though he did not often wear them. And bowler hats. And basset hounds. And eating lobster without utensils, while he ate chocolate bars with a knife and fork. And his James Smith & Sons mahogany-handled umbrella.

Coffin had long been nestled professionally amongst the art world's strange characters. Those in whom knowledge and passion are acute, and highly specific. But, Coffin felt, too often such scholars lost track of their own reality and plunged into the escapist world of focused expertise. For many tweed-and-bow-tied scholars, a vicarious life in 1598 in Rome, or in any other period for that matter, was safer and softer than the now. And this disregard for the trappings of reality led to unusual forms of dress, among other things unusual. Coffin self-consciously believed that he was one of them, but he preferred to limit his dealings to professional encounters and to socialize with a strata that seemed to him less novelistic. He played poker on alternate Tuesdays with a policeman, a plumber, and a mechanic—three of the most intelligent, yet least intellectual, people he knew.

Coffin noticed something. Down between two pews. A single feather. From a small bird. Gray. A pigeon? He was about to kneel down beside it but thought better. He slowed his pace, and then moved on.

Coffin paused for a moment. He looked up, then across to the ground-floor windows, then to the alarm modules, the motion sensors, then back to the windows.

He smiled.

*   *   *

The next slide clicked into place. The whir of the projector threw light through it, and onto the empty wall, producing an illuminated Jesus.

The office was overcome with books, books that crept off the shelves and seemed to run for the door, strewn as they were about the floor and furniture. Photocopied articles and pages of notes were tucked under and in anything and everything. Compared to this chaos theory of filing, the streets of London outside the window seemed a calm seascape.

33

A young girl in a black skirt and white button-down shirt sat on the edge of a green velveteen chair, the only portion unoccupied by papers.

'Professor Barrow, I've done the reading for tomorrow, and I'm still lost on this iconography stuff. All the medieval saints look the same, so how am I supposed to tell them apart?'

A white-haired, red-faced old man spun in his chair away from the wall and toward her.

'Do you mean to tell me,' he began sternly, then paused for effect, 'that you *did* your homework!?'

'Um, yes, sir.'

'Well, that's bloody brilliant, Abby! I never expect that any of my students do anything I tell them to, or listen to anything I have to say. This is indeed a joyous occasion. Good day!'

He looked over to the light pouring through his open window, then leaned over his desk and resumed work.

'But, Professor . . . about the saints?'

'What? Oh, right. Um, right. Let's see . . .' Barrow clicked the slides forward, and forward again, until a medieval Italian altarpiece slowly came into glowing focus.

'Take a look at this for a moment, and tell me whom you can identify.'

Barrow stood up, crossed around to the front of his enormous desk, for the most part buried in paper, and maneuvered around the vertical stacks of books that lay, like detonated mines, along the floor. He approached the window and looked outside. Then he quickly jerked back in.

He's still there, Barrow thought to himself. What the hell is he doing?

'Um, Professor, I can find Jesus and Mary, but

34

the rest of them all have the same beards and stuff.'

Barrow turned back to his student. His pure white hair was his own, but looked like a poorly made toupee. He seemed to sweat at all times.

'Right. Who are all these strange people carrying stranger-still objects? Now, you know that the only way to become a saint was to have been killed in some obscene and overly dramatic manner. The saints are traditionally identified by the object they carry, which is representative of the way in which they were martyred. A biography of the saints was written in the thirteenth-century by Jacobus de Voragine. It is called *The Golden Legend* and is the major source for iconography of saints. If we are to believe everything that Monsieur de Voragine tells us, then the only way to get into Heaven is to die a poor, starving virgin killed in an extremely unpleasant manner, but that's as may be. I'll give you a hint. If you read the Bible, *The Golden Legend,* and Ovid, then you can decipher most any painting in the Western canon.

'It can be rather fun to play the identification game. Who is who? Or *whom,* I can never remember. You need to know the story of martyrdom to unlock this riddle. And you are correct in thinking that I will test you on this, my dear.

'How was Saint Lawrence killed? He was roasted, without marinade, on a grill. So, he is painted carrying a grill. His famous last words: "Turn me over, I'm done on this side." Saint Sebastian? Well, it's a little more complicated with him. He was shot full of arrows, but he did not die, miraculously, so he was later clubbed to death, but he is traditionally shown with arrows sticking out of him. This symbolism is what we call *iconography*. You can begin to associate a certain saint with a certain object, so that object can act either as a stand-in for the saint, or as an identity badge.

'So, we've got Lawrence with the grill, Sebastian with the arrows, and Colonel Mustard with the wrench in the Conservatory. Are you getting the picture?'

Abby nodded, smiling, as she frantically took notes.

Barrow glanced at the window again.

'Abby, I've just noticed the time, and we've got to be at the National soon. Why don't you run along, and I'll just sort some things out.'

'All right, Professor Barrow. Thanks a bunch!' Abby left and closed the office door behind her. Barrow crossed to the window once more and looked outside cautiously.

Goddamn it, he thought. He wiped his bloodhound baggy cheeks with a purple bandanna from his breast pocket.

He laid his overcoat across his arm and left his office, closing the door behind him.

He paused by the exit on the ground floor. Through the glass doors and across the street, Barrow could see him. In a suit, wearing sunglasses. Just standing around. Probably wants an appraisal, he thought, bloody Americans. He often chose to forget that he was one.

Barrow walked past the glass door and through a corridor. He emerged from another exit, along the side of the building. The metal door slammed shut behind him, with a resounding clang that made him wince.

No matter, he thought. Cloudless blue shined above, as he stepped out onto the Strand.

At the front entrance to the Arts Building, the man in the suit checked his watch and stared in at the glass door. Then he lifted his mobile phone and dialed.

Barrow moved slowly, thanks to the limp that had plagued him since his hip surgery, two summers before. Crowds of people, tourists and businessmen, moved around him in the bright summer day. The sun beat down against his herringbone sport jacket, too thick for the heat, but he would not take it off. He thought of it as a counterbalance to the gross indecency of dress in the youth of today.

He passed by a window display and peered within, to examine a Verdi CD that had caught his eye. Then he saw the reflection in the window.

The man in the suit.

Barrow could see him standing on the other side of the street. What's he waiting for, he thought? If he wants me, why hasn't he approached? Barrow turned away and limped off along Upper St Martin's Lane, favoring his left leg since the surgery. The crowd of people grew denser as he passed the monument to Oscar Wilde, who lay smiling and smoking in his coffin.

A train must have just let out, Barrow thought, as a swarm of bodies emerged from Charing Cross tube station. He stole a glance at the reflection in another shop window. There was the man in the suit, again. Only this time, there was someone else with him. And they were both walking toward him.

CHAPTER FIVE

Barrow spun around and elbowed his way through the sea of people rising from the underground. Against the tide, he pushed down the stairs into Charing Cross station, which lay, labyrinthine, beneath Trafalgar Square.

Underground, Barrow stumbled his way down one passage, then another, until he reached a set of stairs. He surfaced by the foot of the monument to Lord Nelson, fringed by imperious stone lions, at the center of Trafalgar Square, and several hundred meters away from Oscar Wilde. He wove his way through tourists and pigeons toward the National Gallery.

As Barrow passed through the revolving door and onto the marble floor of the Sainsbury Wing of the National Gallery, he saw a cluster of his students, milling and giggling.

'Jesus, Mary, and Joseph, I'm over here, you toads! Kindly remove your minds from your trousers and the trousers of your neighbors, and think about art!'

He was at home once more, within the comforting walls of the museum. The students were almost incidental. They changed from year to year. But for Professor Simon Barrow, teaching was about communion with the art that he loved, and a new gaggle of students was merely an excuse to revisit old friends and unlock their mysteries.

'We will begin, aptly enough, at the beginning, and when we get to the end of the course, if anyone is still left standing, that is, we shall stop.'

Barrow mounted the vertiginous white stone staircase. The problem was that he tried to do so backward, in order to be heard by the group of twenty survey students trailing behind him, and he stumbled and fell on his posterior.

Barrow had turned many enrolled in the university's Survey of Western Art History course into art history lovers and majors, but it was early days into the semester, and affections had yet to be consummated. It was the flirtation period.

'Ladies and gentlemen, I am taking you on the Barrow high-speed tour of the greatest hits of the National Gallery. Please show requisite awe, veneration, and subsequent enlightenment.'

Barrow turned left at the top of the stairs, and left again into the rooms containing the oldest works in the National Gallery. His New England accent had long ago melted into fox-hunt British, so many years having passed since his necessarily permanent emigration to be with his kindred spirits.

'Let us begin here.'

He stopped in front of an enormous gold-choked altarpiece, perhaps twenty feet across and eight feet high, smothered in large figures of saints and assorted clergy.

'Before I launch into the talk that will change your meager lives, and for the better, I might add, let me set the scene. With your music television and action films and pornographic pictures and digital cameras, it is impossible for any of you to imagine what life was like before the printing press. But try, for God's sake.

'Imagine that you have *never* seen an image before. I know that's difficult to conceive, but most

39

medieval Europeans, without the large quantities of money required to commission art for themselves, would never have beheld an image. Without printing, every image must be handmade. Materials are very expensive, so the only art that exists is made on commission. Mirrors and glass are also very expensive. It is entirely possible that the only image you've ever seen as a medieval peasant was your own reflection in water.

'Imagine, then, that when you come to church, you are confronted with this!' He gestured toward the magnificent altarpiece, so large, and beaming with gold. 'The figures painted here may look two-dimensional to you, you dismal sheep, but imagine how realistic they would seem if you had never seen an image before. The awe that this must have provoked, the admiration for God and the Church, is astounding. So peel away your jaded egos, and bathe in this! Rising bollards, Tom! Stop looking at Sophy's breasts, and look over here!

'This altarpiece is iconographically exemplary. For those of you looking confused and drug-addled, the word *ikon* is Greek, and means "image." "Iconography," as Abby here can explain to you, is the study of symbolic images within art. There has always been a formulaic way to present the most common images in the Bible, and this is a painting of the Heavenly Choir.

'In early paintings, the most important figures were made larger than the rest, so we have Jesus and Mary, enthroned and clearly having taken their vitamins, in the center. Also, only divine figures were painted facing front, which is why only the big boppers, Jesus and Mary, are thus here. Now, who can tell me what the single most

40

expensive aspect of this painting is?'

Barrow looked out on a sea of confusion.

An anonymous response. 'Uh, the gold?'

'Uh, no, but that's exactly what I thought you'd say, so you've provided the perfect segue, thank you, Robert. What you are reacting to is gold leaf. The process is delicate. Sheets of gold are hammered to a width thinner than paper, so thin in fact that they would crumble if you touched them with a fat and oily finger. So, what did these brilliant medieval craftsmen do? They took a brush made with animal fur, and rubbed it in their own head of hair, creating static electricity. Using the static, they could pick up the sliver-thin gold leaf and press it onto the gessoed piece of poplar wood that would become this altarpiece, using an egg as glue.

'No, you turkeys! The most expensive aspect of this painting is the blue! You can always tell which medieval paintings cost the most by how much blue is in them. Blue was made from lapis lazuli, the philosopher's stone of alchemical fame, a pigment that was dangerously imported from what is now Afghanistan, and was the single most expensive thing one could buy during the Middle Ages. Artists did not go down to the corner store and buy tubes of paint along with their marijuana cigarettes and hair dye. Not until the mid-nineteenth century. Each artist ground his own pigments, dipped his brush in an open-cracked egg, dipped in the pigment, and went to work. This is tempera on panel. Almost all altarpieces are on large pieces of wooden panel, usually poplar wood, in Italian works. The wood is covered in white gesso ... remember that gesso is the white plaster-based preparatory layer painted between the support and the colored paint . . . then a drawing is made of the outline of figures. Then tempera paint is added.

'Not until the advent of oil paints, which we'll see in the next room, could true subtlety and layering be employed in the paintings. You slap on tempera paint, that's pigment mixed with egg white as a binder, and basta, you're done. Then a gilder would come in and add the gold leaf, sometimes using a tool to decorate with impressions. And, voilà, you have a very expensive work of art. These would exist almost exclusively in churches, paid for by wealthy patrons who were told that they could buy their way into Heaven, a practice which continues in American televangelism. You can read more about this in your homework, for which we'll be having a pop quiz tomorrow. Ask little Abby for help with iconography, as she will soon be supplanting me as Arts Department chair. Next painting!'

Barrow led his students into the next room.

Then he saw them.

It's those same turkeys, he thought. But now there are three. Are they procreating?

They were standing at the back of the room. One was on his mobile phone. A museum guard approached.

'Excuse me, sir. No mobile phones al—'

The man stared at the guard, who slunk away.

This has got to be my imagination, Barrow thought. I've seen too many movies.

Barrow tried not to glance over his shoulder, as the flock of students rumbled into the small peripheral room, containing arguably the single greatest, and most influential, painting ever made.

'Bow your heads, children. You are in the presence of majesty. Screw the *Mona Lisa,* screw Whistler and his mother, screw the *Water Lilies* and every other painting that you've heard of but know nothing about because it's famous for all the wrong reasons. This may be the most influential painting in the history of the universe!'

The students collectively rolled their eyes.

'Don't roll your eyes at me, you ignorant cows! I'm here to enlighten you and, damn it, you will be enlightened! This is *The Marriage Contract* by Jan van Eyck.'

'Never heard of him,' came an anonymous cry from the throng of students.

'Judas Iscariot! Dissension in the ranks. No, none of you has the cranial capacity nor the wherewithal to have researched on your own before starting my class. That is why I am here. Look deeper. I am your shepherd. And there are wolves about.

'Jan van Eyck was a painter, intellectual, and secret agent. Ah-ha! That caught your attention. You know James Bond, don't you, you movie-consuming capitalist wet dreams? Van Eyck worked for the duke of Burgundy, and was employed on numerous secret missions, as they are deemed in contemporary documents, on the duke's behalf. Not only was he the court painter, but he was an adviser and emissary. One of the first, dare I say it, Renaissance men. Although he did not invent oil painting, Jan van Eyck employed it to a perfection never before seen, and he influenced every artist who has come after him.'

'It doesn't look like a Jackson Pollock,'

muttered someone in the crowd.

'It doesn't look like a Jackson Pollock? You're right, but for the wrong reason.

'Ladies and gentlemen! Art repeats. The history of art is rife with allusion and self-reference. Art is cumulative. The most modern art comments upon, and reflects, everything that came before it. So, although this 1434 van Eyck does not look like a Pollock, Pollock would not exist without van Eyck, and every artist who came between them. Art that looks different is a reaction against, but it is nevertheless a reaction. I'll give you a train of for-instance.

'Ancient Greek sculpture influenced ancient Roman sculpture which influenced Cimabue who inspired Giotto who influenced Masaccio who influenced Raphael who inspired Annibale Carracci who taught Domenichino who worked alongside Poussin who influenced David who inspired Manet who was beloved of Degas who influenced Monet who inspired Mondrian who inspired Malevich who worked with Kandinsky who led to Jackson-goddamned-Pollock, thank you very much! Polydorus to Pollock in seventeen easy lessons.'

The students broke out into smiles and applauded.

'Thank you, thank you. I'll be here until Thursday. Try the meatloaf . . . Give me any two artists, and I can trace you the trail of influence between them. And you can too, if you pay attention, for bollards' sake! If you'll allow me to continue . . .'

Barrow trailed off, as he saw the three men standing across the doorway, the only way out of

44

the room.

'Let us first briefly look at this painting to the left. It is a portrait of the head of a man in a red turban. It is a self-portrait of Jan van Eyck.'

'I thought that only the divine were shown facing front?'

'Ah, good point, Lisa. Our friend Jan thinks quite highly of himself. He and another man, whose name should be familiar to you, Albrecht Dürer, were the two earliest painters to portray themselves in godlike poses. Portraiture before this point was done in profile, to mimic the portraits of Roman emperors minted onto coins. These full-frontal self-portraits have to do not only with ego, but also with the philosophy of Neo-Platonism. That's a reference to Plato. And this philosophy was hugely popular with artists of the Renaissance.'

Barrow's eyes still hung on the men at the back of the room.

'Dear God, where was I? Oh yes, Neo-Platonism. You'll have to forgive me, children. My train of thought is still boarding at the station. Briefly, Neo-Platonism suggests that art was the closest approximation to the perfection that must exist in Heaven, and that artists were therefore the conduit of a reflection, a shadow of the divine on earth. Raphael is the most obvious exemplar of this theory. In his biblical paintings, Raphael never portrayed any specific model, but instead assembled the most beautiful aspects of faces that he had seen into an ideal composite, one that does not exist, but that he thought echoed the perfection that must exist in Heaven.

'This is a roundabout way of saying that, while

45

van Eyck thought highly of his abilities, and rightfully so, there was also a legitimate philosophy percolating that said that artists were godlike in their ability to create. So, van Eyck is suggesting to us that he and God are not so dissimilar. And I'm sure his mother would agree.

'You'll notice some writing along the top of this painting. It is in Flemish, and says "As well as I can." Along the bottom is written *Johannes van Eyck me fecit,*" which is Latin for "Jan van Eyck made me." Van Eyck is showing off through his humility, telling the viewer, "I tried and this is the best I can do," knowing full well that what he'd done was superlative. What made van Eyck so great was his precision, and this was permitted by his use of oil paints. Tempera allowed for minimal layering, and so the colors look flat. Oil paints have a translucence that allows layer upon layer to be stacked and melted into one another. Tiny brushes were used, too, to allow for minute details. But it is the layering of paints that is key. Why do you think the *Mona Lisa* has an enigmatic smile? Because Leonardo could paint one layer with no smile, one layer with a little smile, one with a bigger one, one with a frown, ad infinitum, until he had something perfectly subtle and suggestive of all the layers beneath. There's no mystery to it.

'Look now to *The Marriage Contract.* It is a portrait of two people, Mr. and Mrs. Giovanni Arnolfini. The mister was an Italian cloth merchant living in Bruges, in what is now Belgium. He holds hands with his ball-and-chain, who is dressed in sumptuous green with fur trimming, clearly expensive. Mr. Arnolfini looks like a

46

toadstool, but it's not his fault, as hats of this type were popular at the time. The missus looks pregnant, right? Wrong! Sure she's got a big stomach, but look closer. Look closer. She has gathered up her copious dress in hand before her, showing off the cloth that was the source of her husband's wealth.

'Also, the ideal of beauty was different back then. We can see this in another work by van Eyck, called *The Ghent Altarpiece.* Incidentally, there is a medieval tradition in Ghent that, at the New Year, a bag of cats must be thrown out of a tower, but that's as may be. In *The Ghent Altarpiece,* there is a nude painting of Eve, as in Adam and Eve. Without any clothes to hide behind, we see Eve in all her glory. And she looks like a pear. She's got tiny little buoyant boobies stuck high on her chest, and an enormous belly. There's a Hungarian term for these perky little eye-gouging breasts, speermel, which I've always thought apt. The woman looks like a bowling pin. This was the ideal of feminine beauty in the Middle Ages. So, Mrs. Arnolfini is probably not pregnant, but is supposed to look fetching and fecund.

'There is more, so much more. During the Renaissance in the north of Europe, artists employed a technique with an intriguing name- disguised symbolism. Essentially, this meant allegorical iconography. Objects were placed in paintings that were metaphors or allegorical references to other things. I'll give you a simple for-instance. There is a piece of fruit, probably an orange, on the table below the window to Giovanni's right. Fruit symbolized prosperity and economic and biological fruitfulness. There is a dog on the floor between the couple. Look closely. Thanks to oil paints, and small brushes, and probably much squinting, van Eyck has painted every individual hair on this little dog, in an array of colors that cumulatively look highly naturalistic. The dog is the disguised symbol for loyalty.

'What else? See the statue on the wall at the back of the room? That's Saint Margaret, the saint to whom you'd pray if you're hoping to get pregnant. How do I know that this was not a shotgun wedding? Look at the top of the painting. There is a chandelier with one illuminated candle in it. If the candle were extinguished, then Mrs. Arnolfini is pregnant, and these two have already been married. But they are in the *process* of being married. Here's why . . .'

Barrow could not help but notice that the three men in suits had not moved from their positions blocking the door.

'There is a Germanic tradition that a candle be illuminated during a marriage ceremony, and placed outside the conjugal bedroom of the new couple. The moment the marriage was consummated, as in the couple had sex . . . see that got your attention . . . the parents of the couple would blow out the candle. Voilà, an extinguished candle means consummation, a lit one means they can't wait to hop in the sack.

'As an interesting aside, it's traditional in Annunciation scenes, that's when God sent the Angel Gabriel to tell Mary that she'd bear the son of God, during the Northern Renaissance, to show an extinguished candle in the room. This indicates that Mary is now consummated in mystical union with God, and she's pregnant with His baby.

'Disguised symbolism allows paintings to be read, like books, but first you must understand the code. Every painting in every museum in the world is in code. It is a riddle waiting to be unlocked. Some are more complicated than others. Paintings of the Northern Renaissance are the deepest encoded. They require specialized knowledge equating objects with ideas, and identifying saints with implements and stories. Some, like the beloved Impressionists, require almost no specialized knowledge to appreciate. They are merely objects of beauty. Others, like the Abstract Expressionists, require nothing. They are simply projections and provocateurs of emotion. But learn to read art, and it's like learning a new language spoken across the Western world. A dog may mean loyalty, but that is not self-evident. It is a specialized piece of knowledge. A guy with arrows in him is Saint Sebastian, so what does that imply? An old man with a beard and wings and an hourglass is Time. Personifications take the gender of the word they represent. "Time," tempus, is masculine, so the personification of Time is as a man.

'There are stranger examples. A parrot refers to an odd explanation of how Mary can be pregnant and still be a virgin. The rationale, if you can call it that, of some medieval priest. If a parrot can be taught to say 'Ave Maria," then Mary can be a pregnant virgin. And people seriously believed this, folks, just like you believe that smoking doobies and listening to Pink Floyd is the zenith of your vapid existences.'

One of the men at the back of the room was on his mobile again and was looking directly at

Barrow, nodding.

'Why is this painting called *The Marriage Contract*? I'll tell you why, because otherwise we'll be here all week. First of all, back in 1434, you did not go down to the mayor's office to sign a marriage license. All that was needed to get hitched was for you to hold hands with your girlfriend and recite a vow in front of two witnesses. We can see that the Arnolfinis are holding hands. They are also barefoot. What does this mean? Disguised symbolism? It means that they are on holy ground. But it's a bedroom. Yes, but they are in the midst of the ceremony of *holy* matrimony.

'Now, where are the witnesses? In turn, you should each look very closely. There is a convex round mirror in the center of the room. Convex mirrors have always been a staple of the artist's workshop since the Middle Ages. But what do we see *in* the mirror? Two figures. One with a blue turban, and one . . . with a red turban. Look to your left. Jan van Eyck is wearing a red turban in his self-portrait. Yes! Hallelujah! The curators of this museum are very helpful people. There are two witnesses shown in the mirror, meaning that they are standing where we are standing now, observing the scene. We, then, become the witnesses. Van Eyck's subtlety and skill are astounding.

'And, just in case you're not totally convinced, right in the center of the painting is a signature that reads "Johannes van Eyck was here, 1434." He has signed this painting as a witness. The painting literally *is* the marriage contract! Now, to the next room!'

On the way out of the room, Barrow walked in the midst of the crowd of students, who pushed past the three suited men. But in the doorway, Barrow felt his arm clutched.

'Professor Barrow. If we could speak with you a moment, please.'

'I'm in the middle of class, gentlemen. I'd be happy to meet with you during office hours . . .'

'Now.' Barrow felt his arm viced in the hand of one of the suited men, and something firm and metallic pressed against his back.

'Um, all right.' He looked around for a security guard. Of course there was none.

'Class,' he said nervously. 'Class, we are going to break early today. We'll resume the National Gallery tour next time. You may go.'

The students breathed a collective sigh of relief and dispersed. The three men surrounded Barrow and walked him toward the exit of the museum.

'Don't make any sound. You are coming with us.'

CHAPTER SIX

'It is my pleasure to present the first annual Giovanni Pastore Conference on Art Crime here at the Villa I Tatti, in Florence. This lecture series was endowed jointly on the part of Italian and American art detection institutions, to honor the current head of the Carabinieri Unit for the Protection of Cultural Heritage, who has served with dedication and success throughout his career.

'I am particularly pleased to introduce today's

first speaker. He is known to many of you who may have read his scholarly articles, but he is best known for his fieldwork in the recovery of stolen art. It is in that capacity that we welcome him today, to give a few introductory words to kick off the conference.

'Dr. Gabriel Coffin's resume is impressive. Grew up in Scotland, BA/BS Yale University, where he studied art history, engineering, mathematics, and also won a fine arts prize. MA at the Courtauld Institute in conservation of art, PhD Cambridge University in the history of art theft, then an MSc, this time at University of Edinburgh, in criminal forensics. Dr. Coffin worked for Scotland Yard in their Arts and Antiquities Division, before he worked as a special agent for the Carabinieri Unit for the Protection of Cultural Heritage.

'Dr. Coffin is the son of celebrated parents, who need no introduction. In addition to innumerable popular books on art history, including the international bestselling survey *Art of the Western World,* the work of Gabriel's father, Jacob Coffin, on the recovery and preservation of looted art during World War Two, was the subject of a recent feature film. His mother, Katie Williams, was one of the only female code-breakers to work on the Nazi enigma code during the Second World War. Both of his parents were remembered in a recent testimonial publication.

'Gabriel Coffin has lectured throughout Europe and North America, always in the language of the host country. He lives in Rome and now works as an art insurance investigator and freelance consultant on art crimes to police worldwide, in addition to his continued scholarly work and satisfying the constant demand for his entertaining and educational lectures. After these opening remarks, he will present a paper later in the conference on his contribution to the recent recovery of a stolen Michelangelo drawing. He is a man with many stories to tell, and we are honored to have him join us this evening. Please welcome Dr. Gabriel Coffin.'

The wood-paneled hall erupted in applause. Coffin approached the podium.

'Good evening, ladies and gentlemen. I'm pleased to announce that everything that Dr. Plesch said about me in her lovely introduction is true. However, she neglected to mention my Nobel Prize in chemistry and my fantastic collection of humorous corkscrews. But I digress. Already. This does not bode well. Perhaps I should begin.

'I thought that, by way of introduction, we might examine one case in particular that has plagued law enforcement officials. It provides a good subject to demonstrate the techniques that I use in investigation, techniques which are available to all but implemented by few. I speak of observation, looking in order to gather information, rather than merely looking. Look deeper. Observation followed by logical deduction leads to solution. You shall see.

'Let me paint you a portrait of the most successful unsolved art crime of the century. Then, together, we will solve it.'

*   *   *

'Might I inquire as to where I am being taken?'

Barrow was seated between two of the suited gentlemen, while the third was driving a dark Land Rover through the now rain-swept London streets, until so recently sunny.

'Our employer would like to speak with you.'

Barrow sputtered like a faltering motor engine. 'Well, he has a royally . . . cocked-up way of going about business. I have office hours for a reason, you know. There's a sign-up sheet posted outside my door . . .'

'Our employer is used to getting his way, on his schedule. I suggest that you indulge him.' The man looked straight ahead as he spoke, as did his colleagues.

Barrow did not recognize the route through London. They had left the center of town, out of Trafalgar Square and south, across the river, beyond Vauxhall, serpentine through an uncharted vacuum of industrial structures.

'You should all consider yourselves lucky that I am not one easily offended. I've decided not to press charges, nor to pummel you senseless, although I'm well within my rights to do both.'

'Stop being funny.'

'All right, then.'

Barrow crossed his arms over his chest and sat quietly until the car slowed to a halt outside a vast, anonymous warehouse.

'You're going in there,' said one of the men, as another locked onto Barrow's arm.

*   *   *

A sea of faces, like ripple-topped waves, stared up at Gabriel Coffin. 'Boston, Massachusetts. 1990.

At one twenty-four AM, the morning after the St. Patrick's Day revels, two men in police uniforms knocked on the side door of the Venetian-style mansion that houses the Isabella Stewart Gardner Museum. They said that they were investigating a disturbance in the grounds.

'Against museum regulations, the two guards on duty let them in. The guards were handcuffed, duct-taped, and locked in separate areas of the dark cellar. No weapons were seen or used during the heist. The two thieves were described as follows:

'Thief One: white male, late twenties to midthirties, five-seven to five-ten, medium build, dark eyes, black short-cut hair, wearing a dark shiny mustache that appeared to be false and square-shaped, gold-framed glasses, also probably false.

'Thief Two: white male, early to midthirties, six feet to six-one, one eighty to two hundred pounds, dark eyes and black medium-length hair, a black shiny mustache that appeared to be false, no glasses.

'You'd think false mustaches and glasses might be obvious, but perhaps not. The thieves stole carefully chosen paintings, ignoring many of high value, such as the Fra Angelico, Titian, and Raphael, but making off with Vermeer's *Concert*, Manet's *Chez Tortoni*, and Rembrandt's *Storm on the Sea of Galilee*, as well as five pieces by Degas, and a Chinese bronze beaker. They tried and failed to open a vitrine that contained a Napoleonic battle flag, and instead took the eagle-shaped fitment to the flag. Titian's *Rape of Europa*, arguably the most valuable painting in any

55

museum in the United States, was untouched.

'Other than a panic button on the guard's desk, the museum alarm was not rigged to trigger from the inside, only from external breaches. The thieves on their departure seized electronic video surveillance.

'The thieves were in the museum from one twenty-four to two forty-five AM. Current estimates list the stolen works at a total value of three hundred million dollars, but as with any estimation of price, it's fairly arbitrary, and could be much less, or much more, depending on the buyer, and the market in general.

'By 1997, the investigation had not progressed, and the museum raised the reward for the return of the paintings from one to five million dollars. Many false tips emerged, but one that sounded promising came from Boston antiques dealer William P. Youngworth III, then in prison. He had gained attention when he told a newspaper reporter, Tom Mashberg, that he and a colorful character, an imprisoned art thief named Myles Connor, would locate the stolen works in exchange for the reward, Youngworth's immunity, and his and Connor's release from prison.

'Youngworth's credibility was questioned, and so he arranged for Mashberg to be driven blind to a warehouse in which he was shown, by flashlight, what may or may not have been Rembrandt's *Storm on the Sea of Galilee*. Mashberg was later also given paint chips, supposedly from the Rembrandt. Tests showed that they were not from the Rembrandt, but may have been from the Vermeer.

'The U.S. Attorney's office demanded that one

of the paintings be returned as proof that the other works were on hand. When this did not happen, negotiations ended. Connor is now out of jail. All of the works are still missing.

'Now, what can we infer from the situation? A handful of basic things are clear, without any deeper involvement in the case. Imagine that we are fresh consultants working on the case for the first time. Trails have grown cold. But what can we say, based on the skeleton of facts with which I've just presented you?

'To begin with, the crime took place late into St. Patrick's Day. For any of you in the audience who are unfamiliar, Boston is a city on the East Coast of the United States, in the heart of New England, which boasts a very large population of Irish descent. St. Patrick's Day is celebrated with unusual vigor there, and that means that copious amounts of beer are consumed. If there is any day of the year during which the fewest people in the city of Boston have their best faculties functioning, it is St. Patrick's Day.

'This suggests a knowledge on the part of either the patron of the crime, or the thieves themselves, of the area. I say that the patron and thieves are different parties because almost every art crime is perpetrated on behalf of someone else, and every successful art thief steals on commission, as famous works of art cannot be sold on any open market, black or otherwise. Art crime patrons have vast wealth and do not need to steal for themselves. It's much like a clogged drain in the bathroom. Sure, you could perhaps fix it yourself, but why get dirty if you can afford to hire a plumber?

'I should make, now, a distinction which, too often, movies and fiction confuse. It is a rare occurrence that there should ever be a privately commissioned art theft. About eighty percent of all art crimes since 1961 have been perpetrated by, or on behalf of, international organized crime syndicates. In 1961 the Corsican Mafia began to raid the Riviera, stealing Cézanne and Picasso paintings in particular. This culminated in 1976, with the single largest art theft in peacetime history, when one hundred eighty Picassos were stolen from the Papal Palace at Avignon. This was also the first time of which we are aware that violence was used during an art theft. Organized crime's interest in art at this time seems to have been prompted by the television media's newfound love affair with announcing the prices for which artworks were selling at auction. And with organized crime comes the methods they traditionally employ, such as violence. Before this time, peacetime art theft had been nonviolent, gentlemanly, and dexterous. Almost admirable, as a feat of skill. But no longer.

'That is not to say that there are not still some private art crimes, and some collectors out there who wish to own a work of art, even through illicit means. And these instances must not go unstudied. But it is important to realize that they are the exceptions, rather than the rule.

'With organized crime now heavily involved in art crime, we should make a further distinction between the *patron* of a crime, as in the individual who orders the crime to be committed, in order to reap the stolen work or money from it, and an *administrator*-the individual who plans the crime and hires the thieves. Think of the administrator as the show-runner for a television program, while the patron would receive the "created by" credit—the former does all the work to make sure it runs smoothly and the job is done, the latter comes up with the concept and sets the ball rolling. When organized crime is involved, the administrator is part of the syndicate, and he hires thieves for a specific job. There usually is no patron, because for organized crime, an artwork is a commodity, like drugs or arms, so the selection of what to steal is based on feasibility of converting it into cash or using it for barter. There is no passion, only business.

'We can profile a patron. For the patron there is some element of self-completion in the acquisition of specific works of art. But for an administrator in a crime syndicate, art is an object equated with a certain value. The most important first step in investigation is trying to determine whether a specific art crime is instigated by a syndicate, for business, or by a patron, as a crime of passion. It is because I firmly believe that the Gardner case is a crime of passion, due to the selectivity of the thieves, that I suggest we apply this profiling analysis. But the thieves themselves, and indeed a middleman administrator were, I believe, members of a criminal syndicate hired by a patron to carry out his desire. Let us continue . . .

'The patron of the crime must have been a regular visitor to the Isabella Stewart Gardner Museum. People do not commission the theft of works of art they have never seen, or seen only once. They fall in love with specific works and wish to own them. It is a love affair. As you might pursue a beautiful woman whom you've seen on the street, art theft is the equivalent of seduction and conquest. Beautiful art, like beautiful women, provokes desire. A desire to possess and be possessed, a yearning to have created, a sense of peace and majesty, to hold this sublime proof of the existence of God, who must be great indeed to have created a thing of such beauty. In this manner, if you'll forgive the analogy, the patron is soliciting a prostitute; the beautiful whore is the work of art, and the thieves who provide her, the pimps. If you think of the art in terms of beauty bought-and-sold to the highest bidder, this analogy seems less ludicrous.

'So, I would suggest that the patron is familiar with the Boston area, and with the museum. The patron has visited the museum countless times. But it is dangerous to steal in your own backyard. I would bet against the patron still living in the Boston area. But perhaps someone who grew up, or attended university, in the area . . .

'I've never been asked to consult on this case, but if I were, there are some things that the police may, or may not, have already done, but that I would certainly put into action. One is a search for auction records of art buyers who grew up in the Boston area. This may sound like it would cast too wide a net, but the art world is small. I'd hazard a guess that there are fewer than twenty serious art collectors of considerable wealth who grew up in Boston and are still alive. This statistic is based on no research on my part, but the art thief is easy to profile.

'More than ninety percent of all criminal collectors are people of wealth and society, usually men, almost always Caucasian, who often have a hand in the art world at a legitimate level, and who have collected art legitimately, through galleries and auctions. They also feel some connection to the art that they steal, and it is the job of the good investigator to root out what that connection might be.

'So, in the Gardner Museum case, we're likely dealing with a wealthy Caucasian male, old enough to have made his fortune, say over age thirty-five, who grew up in the Boston area, probably does not live there now, and who has collected art legitimately.

'What has he collected? Well, let's examine what he chose to steal. This is a crime of love, not money. He ignored the Titian, the Fra Angelico, the Raphael. He could have had those, too. They were sitting on the walls right beside the pieces he took. They are of greater monetary value and prestige than many of the pieces he did want taken. So why not take them, as well?

'This man has morals, as much as can be said for a wanted criminal. I've always felt that there is an honor among thieves, a quiet dignity and elegance to a beautifully executed, nonviolent piece of clockwork thievery. The best thieves are honest and professional, never mistreating unless mistreated, cautious but never rude. High-class thieves are self-righteous; recognize their own value and the value of trust, even in crime. Of the thieves at Golgotha, the honest thief was saved. An honest crime is successful, because it does not stray from its purpose. Honest crimes are sleek and designed. They are a pleasure to watch, their profession an intellectual and physical chess

61

match. The greater pleasure still is cracking the hole in the clockwork mechanism, and that is why I love my job.

'But you must admire certain qualities of our theft patron. He is not gluttonous. He took exactly what he wanted, a prescribed shopping list, and nothing more. He liked Rembrandt, Manet, Vermeer, and Degas. Two French, two Dutch. He wanted a Napoleonic battle flag, and took a Chinese bronze beaker. He also is humane. The thieves did not carry weapons and did not harm the guards. They did not break the container that held the battle flag, giving up when they could not unscrew the hinges. They strove for grace.

'The patron. Let's profile his interests. It is safe to say that he has not bought a Vermeer legitimately, as there are only thirty-six known paintings by that artist, and they are all accounted for. Rembrandt and Manet would come at considerable cost. I would check the auction records for both artists. If he did, indeed, buy the work of such artists, it would be that much easier to tighten the noose around him because his income bracket would rise further. There are a finite number of people in this world who can spend millions on a Manet or a Rembrandt, and commission an art theft.

'The Degas works on paper intrigue me. They would normally be kept in special containers in the museum, filed away in Solander boxes for protection from light when they're not on display. They were on special display when this theft took place, and that is noteworthy. They are not on display regularly, so he may have requested to see them personally at some point, in which case his name would be in the museum records. But of the objects stolen, Degas pastels on paper are the most affordable, and so that is probably the best bet for something that he already collected.

'Question everything, trust nothing. In the words of my exemplar, Sherlock Holmes, "Eliminate the impossible. Whatever is left, however improbable, must be the truth."'

* * *

'In there?'

Barrow swallowed as he stepped out of the car, suited men on either side of him. He looked to left and right along the endless empty street. Warehouse canyon walls rose up and seemed to lean in. There was no one in sight, just a forest of metal and stone. Barrow stopped moving.

'Professor Barrow, this can be very easy. Or not. Decide now.' Barrow resumed movement.

One of the men entered a code into a panel on the outside wall, and a corrugated red metal gate slowly jerked into motion. Another dialed his mobile phone, and murmured only 'We're here,' before flicking the phone shut.

Inside, the men led Barrow past dormant wheeled and geared machines, like sleeping skeletons of iron dinosaurs in the inky sfumato warehouse darkness. They made their way to an elevator at the rear and climbed three floors.

The doors opened to reveal a hushed hallway, with offices on either side. There was a light seen through the glass in the office at the end of the hall.

'You go first.'

The men pushed Barrow out of the elevator and then followed behind him.

Barrow stepped slowly along the length of the hall, which seemed simultaneously to grow and close in around him. The illuminated doorway glowed through frosted glass.

The suited men stopped outside the closed door.

'I suppose you expect me to . . .'

The men stood cross-armed.

'Right.'

Barrow extended his hand toward the doorknob. His perspiring palm closed around the cool grip. He twisted. Barrow heard the latch click open. The door swung in.

Before him sprawled an office, decorated in somber wood panel and marble, a striking departure from the cavernous metal anonymity of the warehouse hull.

The only light in the room shone from a silver-necked halogen lamp, like a crane, on the mahogany desk. Black Mies Barcelona chairs sat in the peripheral haze behind a glass coffee table to the left, and a gold-framed Fauvist painting hung spotlit on the walnut wall to the right. Debussy was playing on a radio.

'Come in, Dr . . . Dr. Barrow.'

Barrow could not see the man sitting behind the mahogany desk, as the light cast forward, and he glimpsed the face in shadow. Only ironed-crisp cuff-linked wrists and the arms of a pale gray suit were visible. Barrow stepped forward slowly, and the door was closed behind him.

'You must forgive the intimidation. And the melodrama. I say forgive, but I retract neither the former, nor the latter. I know all about you, Dr. Barrow, and about what happened with the museum . . . in the United States. I have a business pro-proposition for you. You, of course, have the right to refuse, but it is not in your interest to do so. You will be rewarded for cooperation, or pu-punished for disobedience in this matter. I have read Pavlov . . .'

'But what is this . . .'

'Dr. Barrow, you are a renowned scholar of the history of art. I am in need . . . in need of your professional assistance.' He leaned forward severely.

'Would you like a cappuccino?'

*   *   *

'We're homing in on our target, but can do so further,' Coffin continued. 'The Degas and Manet, combined with the Napoleonic battle flag, suggest a French connection, a sense of patriotism. Sure, Vermeer and Rembrandt were both Dutch, but that seems incidental, as does the Chinese beaker, while the French pieces seem coincidental.

'Imagine you are about to commission this robbery. I would do what most shoppers would: browse the store. There is a strong possibility that the patron wandered through . the museum, gathering a mental "shopping list" of items that he wanted. And there had to be a reason for each. He's not able to show his prizes off to his friends. These are carefully selected objects of private admiration now. They're in his bedroom closet, under his sofa, behind the secret panel in the attic, in a safe-deposit box in a Swiss bank. If they are ever seen, then all is lost, as they are unique and recognizable. So, I say that this is a crime of passion, and there is something drawing our patron to these specific artworks. I infer that this patron has a French connection.

'What have we now in our profile? Caucasian male, aged thirty-five or older, grew up or lived in the Boston area, currently lives elsewhere, very wealthy, art collector, perhaps of Degas pastels, a family connection to France, moral and exacting, not gluttonous, nonviolent and intelligent, probably involved in the art world on some legitimate level, not interested in Italian art, and perhaps with some connection to Myles Connor and William Youngworth III, the men responsible for the most promising lead to surface in the case thus far.

'What we have accomplished in the last ten minutes is substantial. You all hold witness, I use no notes, I lecture impromptu, and together we have developed an impressive profile based only on logical deduction and observation, two characteristics in every man's arsenal. We should all propose ourselves to the Boston police as special investigators. We have profiled the patron with exacting measurements. We must also keep in mind the possibility of multiple patrons. Of course there will be anomalies inevitably that throw off profiles, but these discrepancies are few and far between. Just as ninety-nine percent of all serial killers have been Caucasian males between the age of thirty-five and sixty, quietly intelligent and reclusive, who have strained relationships with the women in their lives, art collectors are a finite and identifiable portion of the population.

66

'From within this incestuous circle of wealth and high society, art detectives work against criminals of infinite power and means, and some of the time, we are even successful. While most art crimes are perpetrated by organized crime syndicates, we must examine carefully incidents which suggest either a private crime, or a crime carried out by a syndicate on behalf of an individual who will end up with the stolen object. I feel certain that this latter instance is the case here.

'I hope that this brief case study has whetted your appetite for the rest of the conference. Thank you very much.'

The crowd applauded vigorously, as Coffin nodded in thanks and returned to his seat. The other presenters for the day's programming sat along the wall beside him, all faces that he knew well.

The conference host approached the podium once more.

'Thank you to Dr. Coffin, for that wonderful introduction to art crime and detection. Our next speaker is a renowned scholar from Florence, Professoressa Carrabino . . .'

*   *   *

As day outweighed the night and sank over the horizon, a train slid along its rail, like a drop of mercury in glass. Coffin sat on the train on his way back to Rome, his knee bent, chin on fist, in thoughtless reflection, as dimming blurs scuttled by the window and his sleepless dreaming eyes.

Across from him, a man folded his newspaper. Unsatisfied, he unfolded it, but the bends worked against him, and he began slapping the paper into form, muttering to himself. Coffin looked to the ringed finger on the man's left hand, and nodded indiscernibly. Beside Coffin sat the crisply halved, then smooth-quartered *International Herald Tribune.* To his left, a small girl sat on her mother's lap, absorbed in the fleeting images outside. The mother ran her fingers along her daughter's back, utterly absorbed in the girl's porcelain face, on which the sundown dance dappled.

Coffin looked away, lost into the window of the train. His job was to protect art from the wicked, the criminal. To hunt down thieves. But could there be a good thief? One thief had been saved. Up there, on Golgotha. If you sin and then repent . . . or if you steal for the right reason? His mind meandered.

He had been both honored and angered to be introduced that way at the conference earlier in the day. He had not been back since the funeral, not so long ago. Both of them. The day before his thirty-fourth birthday. He had found out the next day. Phone rang, he picked it up, and could hear only breathing in the receiver, followed by a slow inward breath, and . . . He did not miss home too much. Always preferred the Continent. The farthest north he'd been willing to venture was Cambridge, really. That seemed close enough. It might have been bearable, if only he'd had siblings. But, never a saint took pity.

He stretched his fingers. Empty. Oh, well. Maybe. Soon. There is nothing that cannot be *thought* into being. When one has too much time. Time is all the luck you need. I wonder what time it is? he thought. He tipped his wrist to read his

1920 Rolex watch with a brown band, which he'd been handed down for . . . oh, he didn't remember which birthday. That, and the mahogany James Smith and Sons umbrella that used to belong to his . . . well, those were the only things he allowed himself to keep.

Coffin fingered the nick on the underside of the umbrella handle. At least I can sublimate my obsessive-compulsive tendencies, he thought. He looked over to his newspaper and smoothed it once more.

CHAPTER SEVEN

The marble-white facade of the Malevich Society clung up, flanked between two buildings of considerably larger size, along the narrow street, rue d'Israël. Inspector Jean-Jacques Bizot considered that it looked like the last slice of wedding cake, as he walked up to the wooden brass-plated door.

He pushed, but it did not open. Then he pushed again, with similar results. Confused, Bizot pushed again. Then he knocked. No answer. Were they closed up for the evening? Bizot checked his watch. It was ten in the morning. He leaned his low center of gravity to gaze in through the window that trailed vertically along the side of the door. Someone was seated at a desk inside. Then they hadn't closed for the evening.

Bizot was about to knock again, when the door opened toward him. A young woman in a dark suit looked out. She was a full head taller than he, and much prettier.

'Monsieur?'

'Bonjour, mademoiselle, if you will permit me, my name is Jean-Jacques Bizot. I phoned earlier. I am investigating the theft of a work of art from these premises. I am with La Sûreté.'

'Ah, oui. Merci, monsieur, entrez, s'il vous plaît.'

She stood aside to allow Bizot to roll in. The ground-floor hall shone in white marble; gilt-framed mirrors and elaborate filigree stood in stark contrast to the framed Malevich posters on the wall. He admired the art on the walls around him. I should get some of these, he thought. Then he noticed that they were not posters.

'Bonjour, monsieur. I see that you are an admirer of Kasimir Malevich.'

Bizot swung his fat neck around, to meet eyes with the chest of a woman in a lilac blouse. Then he craned his neck up a bit more. She was beautiful, in a handsome sort of way, but probably the domineering type, he thought. Hair in a tight bun and all. Too much success and not enough sex will do that to a woman. Or so he had heard.

'My name is Geneviève Delacloche.' She extended her hand. A moment later, he realized, and shook it.

'Inspector Jean-Jacques Bizot, madame. I'm here about the . . .'

'. . . Yes, monsieur, I'm aware of the reason that I called you. It is most distressing. Shall I show you where it was taken, or . . . I'm sorry. Where would you like to begin?'

'Madame Delacloche, you are the . . .'

'. . . The vice president and chief investigator of the Malevich Society. It is my job to hunt down

70

forgeries and misattributions that might hurt the Malevich name. That's what I do, in the main . . .'

'And what else?' Bizot was fumbling once again with the elastic on his notebook, which kept snapping shut before he could get it fully opened.

'Would you like some help with that, Inspector?'

'What? No, no. Continue, please.'

'I'm also called upon to verify supposed works by Malevich, autograph manuscripts, and such. Shall I show you the . . .'

'And when was the last time that this piece, that has now gone missing, was seen?'

'It had been lent out to the Guggenheim in New York for an exhibition two years ago, and it had otherwise remained here. There was a scholar who came in to look at it a few months ago, but . . .'

'I will need all of the information regarding that inquiry, madame. Now, if you would show me the scene of the crime?'

Delacloche led him down the spiral stairs, whitewashed walls curling up as they descended, and the rail cast an iron shadow from a light below.

'You see, Inspector, a key and password are required to access the vaults down here. There are only three of us who have both. Myself, the president of the Malevich Society—he is away on business—and . . .'

'. . . and who?'

'The third is kept in a bank safety deposit box, along with the password.'

'And who has access to the safety-deposit box?'

'It's taken out under the Society's name, so it's just the president and myself.'

'So it's actually just two of you who have them.'

'Right. Sorry.'

'Let's go inside. Show me how it's done.'

They had stopped outside a brushed-steel door, with a panel of white numerical keys to its left, below which yawned a narrow keyhole.

Delacloche inserted a key and typed in a series of numbers. Bizot noticed that she shielded her fingers with the back of her hand, but he counted ten moments of pressure along the index finger. With each, the knuckle fell forward, and the ligament tightened and raised. This is pretty serious stuff, he thought. I can't even remember the three-digit code to my bicycle lock.

A metal sound came from behind the steel door, and Delacloche swung down the handle, pulling it open. Automatic lights flickered on inside. Bizot stepped in, careful to turn sideways a bit, to better fit through the door.

The room was long and narrow, and looked like the digestive tract of a computer. Vertical display walls on sliding rails were lined up, like loosely stacked playing cards. Paintings hung on either side of each, too many to count. At the end of the room, a black metal cabinet contained a tower of shallow drawers. For works on paper, he reasoned.

Delacloche had walked on ahead of him, down to the last of the display walls. She slid it out. The cross-hatch metal wall shivered to a stop inches before Bizot's corpulence. He took a step back, then wiped his brow, as he saw the slender Delacloche suck in her lovely chest to move between two of the sliding walls. Pale skin, dusting of freckles along the nose, watery blue eyes, tight black hair with a pencil stuck through it, and those thin-framed square metal glasses.

72

'It was right here,' she called, just out of sight down a valley of art and metal.

'Do I . . . I mean, must I join you in there, madame?'

'It's mademoiselle, and I think you can probably see from . . . wait a moment.' She pushed the wall out a few more feet, and it sank into locked position with a satisfying click.

Bizot surveyed the wall of abstract oil paintings, some framed, some merely hanging from their stretchers, like meat on hooks. A conspicuous space was empty. The note beside the void read '*Untitled Suprematist White on White*, 119.'

'That's the title and catalogue number,' Delacloche indicated. 'But we also found this.' She pointed to the dark all the way at the back of the room, between two tight rows of sliding wall.

'I suppose you expect me to . . .' Bizot began.

'I think you'll want to, Inspector. There's something down there.'

*   *   *

'Thank you for meeting with me, Claudio.'

In the heart of Rome, Coffin sat on the far side of the plain green metal desk, circa 1950, that rested alone in the middle of the undecorated office that had been occupied by Claudio Ariosto for over thirty years. Photographs of Ariosto in his official Carabinierie's uniform, Armani-designed, dark blue with red stripes, along the walls. Shaking hands with Mitterrand, Pope John Paul II, Berlusconi, his hero and boss, Giovanni Pastore; unveiling a recovered Perugino altarpiece at a press conference . . .

73

'Non è un problema, Gabriel. Come posso aiutarti?'

'Allora, it's about the Caravaggio.'

'I thought it might be. You don't come to visit.'

'I'm not usually invited.'

'Fair enough. Are you still living at Ninety-nine Via Venti Settembre? Above the Moses fountain?'

'Yes, well remembered.'

'Not an address easily forgotten. Now, Gabriel, what can I do for you?'

'I think that we might be able to help one another. We've both the same agenda. The gentlemen I represent don't want to pay for the missing Caravaggio, and you don't want that altar to remain empty.'

'This is all true. I'm surprised that the church could afford your insurers, or any at all, for that . . .'

'How is it going, incidentally . . .'

'I'll be frank, Gabriel. I've got a lot to do. Do you know how many cases are open right now? A flying shitload, that's how many. Just in the past week, we've had a marble hand from a second-century statue taken from a private collection in Umbria, and a sixteenth-century illuminated manuscript is missing from a rare books library in Calabria.

'I was just giving a talk to new recruits, and I dug up some statistics. Here they are. I mean, you know this stuff better than I . . . but since the Carabinieri Unit for the Protection of Cultural Heritage was founded in 1969 we've recovered 455,771 artifacts looted from archaeological digs, and 185,295 stolen works of art, mostly from churches and private homes. In addition,

74

investigators have unmasked 217,532 forgeries and brought charges against more than twelve thousand people. And that's just in Italy. In the year 2000, in Italy alone, Interpol counted 27,795 art thefts. By comparison, in the same year Russia counted 3,257 thefts. More than half of all stolen art is recovered in the country of the theft. So yes, my hands are rather full.'

Coffin smiled. 'The inevitable fate of a country that insisted on producing so damn many fantastic artists. Do you put some magical chemical in the pasta?'

'It's the foam in the cappuccino.' Ariosto permitted a tiny grin, then resumed with bombast. 'But that doesn't entitle every swaggering trust-funded trophy-hunter from New York to Tokyo to use my country like it's a supermarket. We've got a lot of agents now, over three hundred. That's compared to just eight working for the FBI, and six for Scotland Yard. But all our agents are in operation. The last thing we need is another theft, particularly of the magnitude of this Caravaggio. Most of what we work on would stay out of the headlines, and it's much better that way. It's different from when you were working here. One of our problems is that we are aware of so many more thefts, thanks to the mixed blessing of technology. For instance, a church in Lombardia that can't locate a Byzantine icon now has email to tell us about it. That's all well and good, but we're so vastly underfunded, the thieves are so vastly overfunded, and I don't have to tell you about Italian bureaucracy . . . I am Italian bureaucracy, so . . . To answer your question in the most roundabout fashion possible, non abbiamo trovato niente.'

'Nothing, eh? Well, things can only improve.'

'Very funny, Gabriel. What have you got for me?'

'One of my contacts has informed me that there is a certain unscrupulous character . . . a convicted art thief halfway through a four-year prison sentence, near Turin. Vallombroso is the name. Caught, not on the job, mind you, but as an accessory. It's pretty clear that Vallombroso is not the sort to have made a mistake, and was set up for that fall by the patron of the theft. Won't admit to anything, of course, but there are a number of missing artworks of great value to which this thief's name may be added as a primary suspect. Good, too. Smooth, intelligent, the right level of social standing to know too many of the right people . . .'

'Vallombroso. Valle ombroso . . . valley of shadows. I've heard the name before. Tell me more.'

'Allora,' Coffin consulted a file that he pulled from his briefcase, 'the file is limited on empirical, and heavy on circumstantial, evidence, as with any good thief. We do know that Vallombroso *could* have been the primary operative for at least eight unsolved art thefts, but there's never been any proof. The only possible perpetrator, but nothing to nail down an arrest, much less a conviction. Sign of a job well done. Age thirty-four, born in Amalfi, grew up in Naples, degree in engineering from University of Bologna, and then we lose track. Athletic, a gymnast and black belt in capoeira, strangely enough . . . speaks at least six languages. The family is believed to have a long tradition of

76

art theft, perhaps going back hundreds of years, but that's not been confirmed.'

'Sounds like a real nightmare.' Ariosto leaned back in his chair and lit a cigarette.

'It's true. The perfect thief. I thought you were quitting cigarettes?'

'I will, as soon as you leave. Any prior convictions?' Ariosto now leaned forward and rubbed his temples with a hand clutching cigarette between fore and middle fingers, as the smoke nimbled up.

'None. But, then, that's the point, isn't it?'

'Unfortunately.'

'There is one thing.'

Ariosto looked up. 'What?'

'In prison, there was a . . .'

'. . . what?'

'An incident. The warden records it as self-defense, but . . . Good behavior otherwise . . .'

'. . . keep on going, Gabriel. I'm listening. But . . .'

'You'll like this, Claudio. Some inmates picked a fight . . .'

'. . . some?'

'There were five of them. Guess how many were still conscious by the end of it?'

'Really?'

'Five of them, Claudio, all knocked unconscious and plastered around the room. Broken bones, traction. And guess who walked away from it without a scratch?'

'And the warden says that this was in self-defense?'

'Officially, yes. Apparently, some inmates took umbrage, but that was all they took.'

77

'Dangerous, too, Gabriel? You know what you're doing?'

'I know these people, Claudio. They are safe when treated well. They are distrustful, but that is because they work in an industry of double-cross. There's a code among professional thieves, the ones who view their work as an art form. They will be fiercely loyal, if it is in their best interest. We must only ensure that we remain Vallombroso's best interest.'

'We?'

'Trust me.'

'You think Vallombroso has something to do with this case?'

'Even better than that. My informant tells me that Vallombroso will take me to the Caravaggio. On one condition . . .'

*   *   *

Through tremendous strength of character, Bizot considered, he inhaled as much girth as he could, and crab-walked along the space between the rows of sliding storage walls. With a rocking motion, Bizot propelled himself, a sidewinder in the valley, away from the light. At the back, the concrete wall bore an inky scrawl. It's a good thing I'm neither claustrophobic nor scared of the dark, he thought, as perspiration tickled the back of his neck.

'May I have a light back here?' he croaked.

'Wait a moment.' Delacloche's footsteps echoed away and then returned. She handed a flashlight into Bizot's right hand. He thought for a moment. He exhaled accidentally, and his back brushed against a painting that hung on the wall behind

78

reful, please!' Bizot smiled
acloche, and compensated by
orward, bumping a different
l before him.
ed another moment. Then
He lifted his right arm over his
passed the flashlight to his left.
then flicked on the light. It cast
the cold concrete of the back
in what looked like red crayon,

CH347

ou suppose that means?'
nspector. I must tell you that I
ing straight since this occurred,
of letters and numbers means

o help.' Through magnificent
d his way out of the metal pinch.
more butter with breakfast, he
lf, but exertion restrained him
s see what we can do.'

*   *   *

we arrange for early release on
Gabriel. I've heard it before, and
And,' continued Ariosto, as he
ckled black leather shoes, inside
office, 'Turin is out of my
't know the people up there. I'd
re. The big man upstairs is not

79

apt to like the idea. A dangerous convict.'

'It was self-defense, Claudio.'

'And you're impressed by it. What makes you think that Vallombroso can provide?'

'I trust my informant and, as you know, art is a very small world. Art theft is even smaller. I'm told that this thief is truly excellent. There's one year and a half left on the sentence, and . . .'

'I've got one question.' Ariosto leaned forward in his chair. 'Will you take responsibility for this? I mean, I don't have the time or patience or men to spare on maybes. We'll be investigating, but my confidence in success is not high. If I make a phone call for you, you are accepting complete responsibility for the actions of this thief, and if someone pulls a trick, there's a run, or you're the one knocked unconscious and plastered around the room . . .'

'I understand. I have confidence in my informant, and good thieves are some of the most professionally honest people, when they stand to gain from that honesty . . . I know, Claudio. Give Vallombroso probation in my custody, and that altar will be filled again.'

'You realize that, if I can do this, and I say *if*, you'll have a time limit. They're not going to let a known art thief wander around indefinitely without . . .'

'I know. Trust in thieves, Claudio. Remember, one thief was saved.' Coffin clawed at his umbrella's mahogany handle from behind the desk. 'I think that it may take a thief to catch a thief. I think this will work, Claudio. I also think that, if it does not, we will never see this painting again. This is not a break-and-grab theft. This is not a car radio that's been stolen. This is obviously a well-planned commissioned art theft. As you know too well, most of these art theft cases now are perpetrated by international organized crime syndicates, who use stolen art to trade on a closed black market. If some millionaire wanted this painting, hired professional thieves through some series of middlemen, and now has Caravaggio's *Annunciation* sitting in his basement billiard room, that would be easier. We could reverse profile and narrow in on a suspect, get a search warrant, etc. But if the painting is just sitting in a warehouse, waiting to be swapped for x-amount of drugs or arms, only to be swapped again a few months later, never to surface . . . there is almost no chance of recovery. We recover most works when the criminals try to liquidate, sell the work and convert it to cash. If they never try . . . well, I'm afraid we may never see it again, once it is absorbed under the cloak of the syndicate.'

'If they got it out of the country, Gabriel. With lockdown and the country on alert, you cannot put a Caravaggio in your carry-on luggage and get by unnoticed.'

'Perhaps the thief lives in Italy?'

'Not if our profiles from the past half-century are accurate.'

'I think you're probably right. I can't imagine that an Italian would steal his own national heritage and keep it in his bedroom, next door to the scene of the crime. If this theft was as clean as it appears, then I'm sure they'll have thought of some way to get it out of the country. Put yourself in the position of the thieves. What would you do?'

Ariosto leaned back in his chair and swiveled

side to side. 'I'd box the painting up in some cargo shipment, a hidden panel in a case of wine or a false floor to a meat truck, some such thing. Why, what would you do?'

'Me? I would move to Italy. The food's better here, anyway.'

Ariosto smiled.

There was a pause, before Coffin continued.

'So, Claudio. Che ne pensi?'

*   *   *

One week later, Coffin stepped out of the taxi, at the entrance to the white-walled prison, on the outskirts of Turin. The sun was raw and dry, beating down without clouds to blunt it, and the grass that waved in the slow-moving breeze was like wheat. He checked in with the prison warden, who gave him the stern explanation on the maintenance of custody, and regulations for the return of the prisoner should the requisites not be met.

Coffin had been in custody of a criminal in a similar situation once before, with a convicted drug trafficker who'd once tried his hand at art smuggling and been caught in the act. A Swiss, Bertholdt Dunderdorf. Fifteen years of successful trafficking, and one art job found him behind bars. He'd been released in order to set up the patron of the crime for which he'd been caught. A little revenge backed the desire to be sprung from prison one year early. A familiar tune.

They'd almost succeeded, too. But Dunderdorf was still given his release, for cooperation and good behavior. Dunderdorf had been caught because he'd tried to rise beyond his means. Coffin had seen such things before. A criminal trying to raise his social status, who winds up unable to stay afloat in the deep end. Few were in the habit of failing with such panache as was Dunderdorf, but that was another matter.

That was the real problem with art crime. It was considered high class. At the top level of the caste system, art crime was socially acceptable, even thought of as prestigious and intriguing. It was the only serious crime for which the public tended to root for the criminals. But then, the public was not aware of how art crime funded more sinister crimes, such as the drug and arms trades, and even terrorism. The average citizen felt somewhat detached, and sometimes threatened, by fine art. It was considered elite and elusive, beyond their mental capacities, and therefore frightening to many. It was with some satisfaction that the public read about gracefully orchestrated art thefts. It was a combination of voyeurism into a glamorous world apart, and a satisfying jab at an institution that felt exclusive.

And the reward for the theft's patron was vast: to own a tangible piece of beauty. The punishment was that no one could ever know about the reward. The trophy that must remain in a black box.

Coffin stood outside the prison gate, looking up at the brilliant watery blue Turin sky. The warmth pressed down against his back, beneath his dark three-piece suit, and along his cleanly trimmed beard.

He twirled the umbrella within his palm. There was that feather-breadth nick on the underside of the mahogany handle that always drew his index finger. He checked his watch.

Through his tortoiseshell sunglasses, Coffin saw Vallombroso emerge from the prison, tall and slender, dressed all in black, squinting into the sunlight. She stood for a moment, bathing in the warmth.

'Buongiorno, Daniela.' Coffin smiled. 'Nice to see you. Where are we going today?'

'To London,' she said. 'For revenge.'

CHAPTER EIGHT

The main auction room at Christie's London was cacophonic. The maroon cloth walls were hung with abstract works by obscure Eastern European artists from the turn of the twentieth century, obscured further by the porcupine of bidders and onlookers. By Christie's standards, this was not a particularly important auction, although for the sake of promotion, all of their sales were labeled 'Important.' The most expensive piece in the sale was the Malevich *White on White,* selling for four to six million pounds. It would certainly attract attention and, judging by the crowd, already had.

The high rollers would bid through representatives: a gallery owner, perhaps a scholar or curator, professional buyers. Museums, too, sometimes hired professional buyers from among the intelligentsia of the art trade, rather than putting their own staff in the crossfire. Bidding was an art of its own. Sneeze at the wrong time, and you've spent another ten thousand pounds. It is all too easy to push the bid one or more steps higher than is comfortable for the budget. No one wants to show his cards too early.

If you can drive up the price of one piece, spending the money of an opposing bidder for a lot farther down the line, then so much the better, decreasing the opponent's pot. If you can distract, although considered foul play, that is done, too. There might be a team working for one buyer: one man bidding, one at the door, one observing from the front corner of the room, one on the street outside, all on mobile phones. Anything could happen, and had.

Delacloche sat at a good vantage point. If she turned to look over her shoulder, she could see the faces of the bidders. The auctioneer's podium rose up before her, with the screen behind it, painted in the Christie's deep maroon. Out from this screen would emerge the army of porters, in their white shirts and gray aprons with maroon lettering, carrying the pieces for sale. Delacloche's two favorite things mingled in the auction house: art and shopping.

Delacloche scanned the room before her. She made eye contact briefly with a handsome man standing far to her right and then looked away quickly. She opened the catalogue in her manicured hands and let flicker a short smile.

Delacloche remembered her first experience with fine art. Dressed in white with a blue bow in her hair, her tiny hand clasped inside her father's, she was led through the Musée Rodin in Paris. Her father had stopped in front of Rodin's *The Kiss*. He knelt to whisper to her. 'This is how I remember Mommy, Geneviève. If you ever want to remember her, too, just come here.'

85

The bidders were dressed in their best this evening. Auctions, almost exclusively Christie's and Sotheby's auctions to be precise, were places to see and be seen. They were social gatherings. Christie's was a moving museum, every week a different collection of artworks available for purchase on display on the walls, for anyone to see. But the event that was the auction, that was what kept such venerable institutions as Christie's in business, and fearless of such machinations as the Internet.

Those within the scope of private wealth who purchased art would invariably prefer to pay more to have bought a Renoir at Christie's than to have acquired it in any less distinctive manner. For sellers, the international nature of Christie's and Sotheby's made the world the buying pool and invariably would attract more attention, and higher prices as a result, than local auctions or fixed-price galleries.

The room was packed with people: greeting, milling, speaking, phoning, reading, plotting, calculating. Delacloche surveyed, looking for familiar faces. It was far easier to count the unfamiliar. There would be a couple of tourists who wandered in, having read that 'attending an auction can be a nice change of pace for a rainy day in London.' There were some of the less-preferable clientele: the gallery owners from up north who fancy themselves big shots; one or two Portobello Road junk salesmen who would prefer not to sell junk, or would at least like to balance the junk with real goods, to give their junk the illusion of value; private collectors, either new to collecting, new to London, or in person, when they're usually absentee or phone bidders. Delacloche knew how all this worked, from her two years working in the Twentieth-Century Paintings Department at Christie's Paris.

When the room was at capacity, and the crumble of mumbled voices was like sitting by the sea, the auctioneer stepped up to the podium. The crowd hushed.

CHAPTER NINE

'Sir, I think you should see this. We may have a situation.'

The fourth-floor computer terminus was the security nerve center of the National Gallery of Modern Art, in London, a half mile from the Christie's auction rooms. The room was ringed with computers and closed-circuit television screens. Two security personnel, including Jillian Avery, sat in black-suited surveillance. Jillian now called to her supervisor.

'There's a disturbance in the basement, in the utility room. We've registered some movement, but the closed circuit isn't showing anyone. See?'

Overnight security coordinator Toby Cohen leaned over Avery's shoulder as his eyes scanned her computer screen and skipped across to the CC-TVs on the wall. The TV screen showed an empty utility room.

'Anything on the nature of the disturbance?'

'A door is reading as unlocked. The main door to the utility room. Must have swung open. That's all we've got.' Avery clicked at her computer.

'What should we do?'

'Radio to Stammers and Fox. Tell them to check it out.'

Avery dialed into her computer and connected to the security walkie-talkie. She spoke into a microphone. 'Control to Security Two. Control to Security Two. Do you copy? Control to Security Two. Do you copy? Control to . . .'

'What's going on? What's wrong with them?' Cohen approached the computer.

'They're not responding, sir.'

'I know they're not responding.' He leaned toward the microphone. 'This is Control and Security One to Security Two, please respond. Control to Security Two! Where the fuck are they? Control to Security Two?'

'Shall we try Hammond and Hess?'

'Yeah, give me Security Three.'

Avery manipulated her computer.

'They should've been picking up on the Security Two line.' Cohen leaned forward. 'Control to Security Three. Control to Security Three, please respond. Control to . . .'

'Sir, look at the CC-TV.'

Avery pointed to the wall of monitors, which showed a selection of rooms in the museum, as well as corridors, entrance and exit points. Every monitor showed an empty room.

'There's no one there. None of the guards are there. What the hell's going on?'

Cohen stormed toward the wall of monitors.

'When was our last communication with a team?'

Avery checked the computer. 'That was twenty-three minutes ago.'

'Rewind the CC-TV screens.'

Avery typed and the monitors rewound. Suddenly guards flickered into focus.

'When was that?'

Avery scrolled down. 'That was twenty-nine minutes ago. Nothing after that.'

Cohen paced for a moment, then stared up at the monitors.

'Wait. Go back, and then let it run forward again.' Cohen stood cross-armed before the barrage of monitors.

'See,' he continued, 'they disappear. The guards don't walk out of the picture. They're there, and then they're gone. What the fuck's going on?'

'Sir.' Cohen crossed to Avery once more. 'We've got a disturbance again. Something's in the utility room.'

*   *   *

'Good evening, ladies and gentlemen, and welcome to this auction of Important Russian and Eastern European Works of Art. We begin on page six of the catalogue, lot one, a photograph of his sculptures by Constantin Brancusi, which you can see with the porter to my left. I have a bid for eight thousand to start, eight thousand to start. Do I hear eight thousand five hundred? Eight thousand five hundred, thank you. Nine thousand, the absentee bid, with me. Nine thousand five hundred? Nine-five? Nine-five? Surely, folks, nine . . . thank you, nine-five with the new bidder at the back. And I have ten thousand here in the book. Ten-five? Thank you, to the lady in the second row. Eleven thousand? I am out at ten-five. Still ten-five in the second row. A very lovely piece, excellent condition. Eleven . . . thank you, madam, eleven thousand with you now. Do I hear eleven-five? Are you out at eleven-five? I am selling at eleven thousand five hundred. And . . . oh, I see you, Jessica. We've got a new bidder at eleven thousand five hundred on the phones, thank you. Twelve thousand in the room. We've got twelve in the room, twelve-five? Twelve-five on the phones, thank you, Jessica. Thirteen? Do I have thirteen? No? I am selling, then, at twelve and a half thousand pounds to the phone bidder. And sold,'—the hammer came down with a bright wooden crack—'to the telephone bidder. If I could have the paddle number, one-nineteen, thank you, Jessica. Lot two . . .'

The auction fell into its rhythm, as the bidders fidgeted in their seats, flipped catalogue pages, and whispered among themselves. Above the auctioneer stood the price screen, showing the current bid value in pounds, dollars, euros, and yen. An auctioneer's assistant sat, elevated with a laptop computer, to the right of the podium. To the left of the auctioneer, a steady stream of porters carried out the objects for sale. Of course, everyone bidding had been to see the objects on public display during the last week, but this was a formality that Delacloche always enjoyed.

At the back of the room, a team of Christie's technical experts surveyed. They could see everyone in the room from their position. While there was nothing that they could do to intervene, they could identify the illicit goings-on that inevitably took place during the course of any given auction.

A glorious floral arrangement bloomed, preventing anyone from standing directly behind them. In the anteroom, a Christie's attendant sat behind a small desk, there to answer questions of the bidders and take paddle numbers for those who had purchased. Security guards stood on either side of the anteroom. Behind, the main stairway leading out to the lobby, and the street below, swept off into the evening.

Delacloche remembered her very first auction, in Paris. Not long after that trip with her father to the Musée Rodin. He had been crying, and he left the room when the painting came up for sale. Malevich's *Untitled Suprematist White on White*. It had been in her mother's family since it was first painted. Her father had wanted to keep it very badly. But financial circumstances, being what they were . . . They had made enough money from the sale to solve all of their problems, her father had said, and to send little Geneviève through the best schools, to university abroad, and to buy her a home. All this, for a piece of hemp canvas, painted all white by a Russian fellow about a hundred years ago. She knew that her father would have been proud to know that she studied Malevich, and followed the painting to the Malevich Society, which had bought it from them so many years before. Once she had the painting, hers to protect, she would not lose it. Not again. And now . . .

Delacloche flipped through the catalogue and turned to the faces behind her, as the auctioneer's voice rumbled. Raphael Vilaplana in the fifth row center, she thought. I'm sure he'll bid on the Popova in lot twenty. Bet he's got a buyer lined up already. Wonder how much he thinks he can get

91

for it? Delacloche knew, or had heard of, every expert or collector in the world of early-twentieth-century Russian painting. Recognizable names rose to the surface when stirred in the finite soup of the industry. In her analogy, she considered that collector and lawyer to the stars Thomas Frei would be a particularly large dumpling. The art world was small. Any specific period of art, and the world shrinks further.

A particularly bizarre and unattractive sculpture came up for bid. Dear God, thought Delacloche, that's awful. But, if one buyer thinks that shit is of value, and is willing to pay for it, then its value is as much as he's willing to pay. The trick is that if one person thinks it's great, then others follow suit. Delacloche smiled to herself as first two, then two more bidders, dove in after the sculpture.

'Fifteen thousand . . . thank you, ma'am, and sixteen with the gentleman . . .'

A four-year-old girl could sneeze on a piece of paper, and if someone loved it, and was willing to pay one hundred thousand pounds for it, then its value is one hundred thousand pounds, full stop. Delacloche flipped to the next page in her catalogue. But, she thought, if a competitor sees the sneeze, and most important hears the price, and wants one of his own, then maybe you get a bidding war, and up goes the value. Come to think of it, she thought, this is a brilliant idea. I should preempt Damien Hirst and corner the market on sneeze-related art. Next time my little niece catches cold . . .

The selling price has nothing whatsoever to do with the work of art being good or not. It has to do with what people are willing to pay for it at any given time. The auction house sets much of the value, when they put an estimate on the price. They set the estimates based on research of past selling prices for similar objects. If they give a high estimate, then buyers will think the piece more important, perhaps, than it is. But if they aim too high, the market won't bid. If they undervalue, the piece loses its cachet, but chances are more people will bid, get the momentum going, and they'll end up with a higher hammer price. It seemed to Delacloche that it was all too arbitrary. Maybe they sacrifice chickens and determine estimates based on the arrangement of the entrails. She smiled to herself.

What are they up to now? Lot 8, a small drawing by Kuznezov. He probably spent fewer than ten minutes on it, perhaps a sketch made while in the bath, some abstract design he thought up in a moment, then left aside, never taken up again. Maybe it was destined to be a monumental painting, the hub of his masterwork, but it never panned out. So here we are, left with a sheet of scrap paper, with some lines in pen scrawled over it. And it's quite lovely. It has interest, but no story behind it to up the value. It cannot be firmly placed in the context of the artist's oeuvre. But in the audience today, Delacloche looked over her shoulder, there are three bidders interested. And the estimate, she glanced down at the catalogue, three thousand pounds, is on the high side. Trying to jump-start interest in an easily overlooked piece.

'How much do you think it's really worth?'

Delacloche overheard someone speak behind her. Not a regular of auctions, to be sure. There is no such animal as 'real worth.' It does not exist. If someone says otherwise, they're full of it. Value is some number miraculously pulled out of the stratosphere. A combination of rarity, execution, perceived rarity and execution, number of buyers interested and their spending money, and how much the piece is propagandized. If it's got a color photograph in the catalogue, it will get more interest than a black-and-white, or no, image. A full page, maybe a two-page spread? So much the better. And for pieces like that Titian, sold not so long ago for thirteen million, that got an entire catalogue and sale all to itself, and was written up in international newspapers weeks ahead of time. So, the better question is how much would you, as an individual, pay for the piece, not what its value is.

In the auction room, the ebb and flow of the auctioneer's rhythm was in full swing, and there was little ebb. The auctioneer was skilful. His pace was leisurely, but he maintained the sense of tension that many bidders relished. Touristic onlookers were surprised at how calm and deliberate were the auctioneer's words, so unlike their only other exposure to auctions, which tend to be fire sales or cattle auctions. Auctioneers there speak at a rate of knots, unintelligibly, riling the bidders into a frenzy, those bidding unaware of what exactly they're doing, what they're bidding on, where they left their car keys, their mother's maiden name . . . A furious flurry of words with two intents: speed and disorientation. They have eight hundred steers to sell in four hours, and a confused bidder is more apt to spend than a thoughtful one.

This auction had none of the hectic edge, but it was an intense, focused experience. Hearts raced. It was like watching a thriller, suspense palpable whether or not one was bidding, or even knew the bidders. And this excitement was infectious.

The auctioneer enunciated, made everything clear, but never broke from his constant control of the situation. He never mentioned names of bidders, except those of his colleagues on the phone and presenting the objects for sale. There was never a moment of unintended dead air. Bidders were expected to be prompt, but they were never bullied. And it was nearly impossible to tell who was bidding. It seemed, to the untrained eye, that the merest flare of one's nostril, wink, or telepathic communion with the auctioneer, indicated intent. After one's initial bid was made clear, all subsequent bids for that same lot could be administered as subtly as one wished.

There were reasons for desired anonymity. For a private buyer, no one wanted any uncontrolled publicity around the purchase, nor did one want well-wishers, or dealers asking if they'd resell their new purchase. This was one of the reasons why Delacloche was sitting in the heat of things, taking note of every bid and, more important, every buyer. And why she attended every auction in which a Malevich work was to be sold. These objects could completely disappear after the sale. Melt into the distance, into any city or country house across the globe, traceless, unless the buyer wished to be known. Museums would want to know whom they should ask for loans. A losing bidder might want to try to broker a private deal. The press might wish to pursue the story behind a purchase of interest, or by the interesting. But the auction house code of honor protected the anonymity of both seller and buyer as much as either wished to be protected.

The gossip chain within Christie's leaked out, of course. When celebrities made a purchase, or attended one of the many parties and cocktail functions sponsored by Christie's, to keep the auction house firmly imbedded in the world of socialites, the staff talked about it. Delacloche kept in touch with a few friends within the auction world, as sources for just such information.

One sale she recalled, in particular, from her days at Christie's Paris. There were six major dealers in the Russians who had been in and out to examine pieces for an upcoming sale. They'd all looked at this sketchbook, with something close to fifty drawings inside plus notes, by Rodchenko. It was estimated conservatively at two hundred and fifty thousand.

They'd all shown significant interest, although they tried to hide it. She'd seen the Turkish bazaar dance of feigned disinterest so many times, it had become a formality. All six dealers should have been bidding on this sketchbook, competing against each other, driving up the price. It was clear that they were all salivating over it. But when the lot came up, there was one private buyer, and only one of the dealers, bidding. The book sold for one seventy-five, barely above the reserve price, below which it can't be sold.

Standing at the back of the room, observing the auction, Delacloche had figured out what was going on. But there was nothing anyone could do about it. She'd seen all six of the dealers earlier at the Red Lion around the corner, drinking pints and laughing. Then they sat together in the middle of the floor while the auction was going on, and none of them ever bid against each other. Yes, she knew exactly what had happened. The tidal swell of the auctioneer's voice woke her from her thoughts.

'Lot thirteen . . .'

CHAPTER TEN

'What do you mean that something's in the utility room? Why can't we see it?'

'I'm not sure, sir.' Avery's fingers fluttered across the keyboard, as Cohen's eyes rooted onto the utility room monitor.

Nothing moved. The room looked empty. So why was the motion sensor registering? And what had happened to all of the guards?

Cohen looked over his shoulder.

'Are we locked in here?'

'Sir?'

'Is this room secured?'

'No, sir.'

'Well, lock it! Lock us in now, damn it!'

Avery fumbled keystrokes, and the metal bolts on the control room door snapped into place.

'Secured, sir.'

'Now, what do we know? We've lost communication with all security personnel. Twenty-eight minutes ago, they all disappeared from the CC-TV. We've . . .'

'It's back again, sir. Something's still moving in

the utility room.'

'Keep trying to contact the guards. I don't like that we can't see . . . wait a second. What could cause both communication and video surveillance to . . . Call up the CC-TV from the disappearance again.'

Avery clicked keystrokes, as menus rose and fell on her computer screen. The monitors showed security guards in several darkened rooms of the museum. Then seconds passed, and the figures disappeared.

Avery scrolled forward and back, causing the guards to materialize, and vanish, in the monitors.

'Do you see that? Let the video continue.'

'I'm right with you, sir.'

The image blinked back and forth. There it was again.

Room 12. A dull cast of light from behind the doorway. Then a guard emerged.

But the light was still behind the doorway.

'The light from the guard's . . .'

'I see it, sir. The light from the guard's torch emerges from the hall. The guard turns into the room, then disappears, but the light is still in the hall. The video's been looped.'

'How the hell did someone do that?'

'The system must be broken. That's why we've lost radio contact, too. Someone's inside our computers.'

'Well, get them out!'

Cohen tried to breathe deep, remain calm under pressure, respond as he had been taught by his professional idol and old boss, Dennis Ahearn, director of security for all of the Tate museums. Ahearn runs an impregnable fortress. Do what he'd do, that's the ticket. Cohen crossed to the back wall and reached for the telephone. A direct line to the police.

'If we're cracked and cut off at our eyes and ears, then that means someone could be inside . . .'

'. . . the utility room.'

'But why the utility room? They could rip off any of the paintings, if the guards are . . . Oh, God . . .'

'We don't know that yet, sir.'

'I don't care, I'm calling in the police.' Cohen put the phone to his ear. He clicked the receiver again, then again.

'It's dead.'

*   *   *

The auction continued at its healthy clip. Lot 27 was approaching, and that was of interest. Delacloche looked around the room, as lot 26 crept up to the horizon. She rubbed her forefinger against her thumb habitually, and glanced down at her catalogue, creased open to the page. Lot 27. An all-white painting, school of Kasimir Malevich, estimate twenty to twenty-five thousand pounds. It looked, at a glance in the catalogue, exactly like the £4-6 million real Malevich. But then, Malevich had painted many similar white-on-white canvases. And all-white paintings have little room for variation.

It was listed as 'school of Kasimir Malevich.' The vocabulary of the tentative appraisal. It was so feared to mislabel, particularly to deem something the work of a famous artist, thereby increasing interest and value and status, and have it turn out not so, that auction house experts and museum curators had developed a specific lexicon of uncertainty.

'School of . . .' meant that the work was influenced by the named artist, in this case Malevich, and perhaps the work of a student copying the style of a master. 'Circle of . . .' would mean that the style approximated that of Malevich, but for various reasons was not considered to be his work. 'Attributed to . . .' would have meant that someone, at some point, thought that this painting was by Malevich but, for some reason, the Christie's expert was not comfortable or certain with the attribution, but didn't have a specific alternative to propose. 'Style of . . .' meant that it looks like a Malevich, smells like a Malevich, but who the hell knows. There were variations of these terms, but the principle remained steady: don't cry wolf.

'Now I have on offer a lovely painting, lot twenty-seven, listed as *Untitled: Suprematist White on White.* This is school of Malevich, ladies and gentlemen, no doubt inspired by the major work that we have upcoming. If you prefer not to spend in the millions, you can always buy this beauty and no one will know the difference. At least, we promise not to tell. A very nice approximation of the artist's work, a very large piece for the period. You get a lot of paint for your money, ladies and gentlemen. I have an opening bid of eight thousand pounds. Do I hear nine? Anyone? Nine? Thank you, nine to the gentleman in the middle. Nine-five with me. Ten? Ten, thank you, sir. Ten-five. Eleven? Eleven, thank you. Eleven-five . . .'

The bidding was between an absentee bidder

and a gentleman in a black suit with a red tie seated in the middle of the room. Delacloche did not recognize him. Each time he bid, he was raising his paddle. She eyed him suspiciously, then widened her gaze. There were two other men, similarly dressed, sitting beside the bidder. One was on a mobile phone, and whispering between it and his bidding partner. The one on the other side was scanning the room and kept crossing and uncrossing his legs. No one else seemed interested in this bastard painting. But these businessmen-types seemed bent on it.

Delacloche turned her attention to the painting on the maroon wall, indicated by the apron-clad porter. It was very large, perhaps the same size as the Malevich Society *White on White* that was missing. Yes, it was the same size. That means that it must have been directly inspired by the Society's painting. And now it shows up in the same sale. That's interesting . . . and a little odd.

Auctions were not meant to function like museum exhibitions, juxtaposing works of art in a scholarly manner as points of comparison. An auction was haphazard. There would be several per year featuring each category of work: books and manuscripts, Old Master paintings and drawings, silver, African, jewelry, furniture and decorative arts, sculpture, Victorian, British and Irish, and so on. Christie's would accumulate pieces of a type, in this case Russian and Eastern European paintings and works on paper, and auction them all in one sale. So, it was simply luck if two paintings that seemed to be connected to one another appeared in the same sale. Perhaps they came from the same seller? Maybe.

101

Or . . .

But why were these businessmen, clearly inexperienced in bidding, so interested in this piece? It would not be strange at all if there were just one of them. That could be explained. A new buyer who fancied acquiring a bit of culture, but new to the auction world. Moneyed but uncultured, perhaps. Maybe he even misread, and thinks this is a real Malevich. But the three of them sitting together, all cut of the same cloth, and on a mobile phone while bidding? They're not bidding for themselves.

'Seventeen-five with the gentlemen. I'm out, and we have seventeen-five on the floor. Lovely work here, ladies and gentlemen. You get a lot of white paint and canvas for your money. Excellent kindling in the winter months. I am selling for seventeen thousand five hundred pounds. Sold.' The hammer cracked down. The businessman on the mobile phone whispered encouragingly. Then he clicked his phone shut.

'Our next lot . . .'

Two of the businessmen, the bidder and the fellow on the phone, now got out of their seats and moved toward the back of the room, sliding through the accumulated crowd. Delacloche watched them disappear down the stairs. If they were asking about pickup and payment, they would have done so at the desk of the anteroom, not gone downstairs. More lots fell to bidders.

'Lots number thirty-one through thirty-three have been withdrawn. We therefore come to lot thirty-four, an anonymous Suprematist painting with an . . . unusual array of colors.'

My God, that's hideous, thought Delacloche.

'How much am I bid for this Suprematist work with an . . . interesting color combination? Can I start at fifteen hundred? Fifteen hundred. May I see your paddle, sir?'

What's he doing? Delacloche now noticed that the third businessman, the one still in the room, was looking harried and had tried to bid on this repulsive Suprematist painting. Her expression hardened. But one of his friends had the paddle. He was looking frantically for them, over his shoulder. Without the paddle, he was not a registered bidder.

'You must have a paddle to bid, I'm afraid. Anyone? I cannot sell for less than fifteen hundred. Thank you, sir!' The auctioneer betrayed his enthusiasm, as he pointed to a gentleman standing at the back of the room. Delacloche turned around to see who it was.

'Anyone else? Anyone? I am selling, then for fifteen-hundred pounds to the gentleman at the rear . . .'

A noise at the back of the room. Delacloche turned to look, as the two missing businessmen rushed into the auction room, their compatriot inside waving at them frenetically.

'. . . and sold.' The hammer cracked down. The businessman, now with paddle in hand, raised it violently in silent protest. 'I'm sorry, sir, the hammer had fallen. Sold for fifteen hundred. Lot thirty-four . . .'

The businessmen spun to the back corner, and fixed eyes on the buyer. He was graying, dark-eyed, and rough-shaven, in an open collared white dress shirt, blue sport jacket, and jeans. His face was down in his catalogue. He noted in pen.

103

Sunglasses clipped on brown alligator belt, mobile phone bulge inside jacket pocket, ringless fingers evenly tanned, oversize silver watch on wrist. The businessmen remained at the back of the room, eyes searching, for many minutes.

'Lot thirty-nine. The one you've all been waiting for. I'm pleased, ladies and gentlemen, to offer *Suprematist Composition White on White* by Kasimir Malevich. A substantial work, thought to be the first of his series of white-on-white canvases. This is the quintessential Suprematist artwork, of magnificent significance and on a magnificent scale, property of a gentleman. I'll start the bidding at seven hundred thousand. Do I hear eight? Thank you, madam. Nine? Nine with Caroline, on the phone. One million. Do I . . . thank you. One million in the room. One-one? One-one. One-two, thank you. One-three on the phone. One-four. One-five. One-six. One-seven. One-eight? Thank you. One-nine . . .'

Delacloche stared at the painting being sold. That is not the Malevich Society painting, she thought, and it is not even the painting pictured in the catalogue. She was a bit frantic, trying to keep track of all of the bidders. Someone's on the phone. I see a woman in the middle, in pink. Gentleman at the side, the one with the beard. Another at the back to the left. There are two near the front . . .

'Three million-four? Thank you. Back on the phone. Three-five? Three-five. Three-six. Three-seven. Three-eight? Three-eight. Three-nine? Caroline is out. And it's in the room with you, madam. Do we have four. Four? And . . . thank you, sir. Four-one? Yes, with you, madam, back to

104

you. Four-two. Four-three? Four-three. Four-four. Four-five. Four-six . . .'

Delacloche's mind ran hard. Looks like it's down to two, now. Delacloche's eyes swung back and forth across the room, in an effort to keep up with the calm, runaway-train pace of the auctioneer's words.

'. . . Five-two. Five-three. With you, madam. Do I have . . . thank you, sir, five-four. Five-five with the lady. Five-six. Five-seven. Five-eight. Five-nine. Six. We're at six. Madam, would you like six-one? We're at six. Would you like six-one? It is up to you, if you want it for six-one. I have an outstanding bid for six with the gentleman. Do . . . I . . . have . . . six-one? Six . . . thank you, madam. Six-two. Sir? Very well, six-three. Six-three with the lady in pink. Six-four? Sir? No? You're sure. The gentleman is out, then, and it is with you, madam, at six-three. Anyone else? I am selling, then, to the lady, at six million three hundred thousand pounds. Going once. And . . .'

*   *   *

'The phone line is dead, Avery! And all the guards . . .'

'Sir! We've got movement again in the utility room.'

'To hell with this. I'm going down there.'

'Sir, if the guards are . . .'

'I know. But fuck all if I'm going to stay locked up in here, like a bloody inmate in my own castle.'

Cohen unlocked the black steel cabinets that were bolted to the wall. The doors swung open.

105

He pulled on a bulletproof vest and strapped a gun holster to his thigh. He took a shotgun from the rack and pocketed some rounds.

'This fucker doesn't know who he's messing with.'

'Take this earpiece.' Avery handed Cohen a slim black headset. 'This will let us communicate directly, not via the computer.'

Cohen looped the communicator behind his ear, and the slender mouthpiece ran along his jawline.

'Avery. I want you to cut the security lights.'

'Are you sure, sir?'

'The hell yes, I'm sure.' Cohen reached into the cabinet, and pulled out night-vision goggles.

'That's a good idea, sir.' Avery returned to the computer.

This museum, like many others, employed low-powered red toe-kick lights to help guards navigate at night. This saved energy and limited the exposure of the paintings to harsh light. With a keystroke, the red lights that ran along the walls throughout the galleries hummed into darkness. The museum sat motionless, with only the blue of evening filtered in through the louvers and the windows.

'Lock yourself in, Avery. Don't open this door again.'

'Yes, sir. Good luck.'

'Fuck it.'

'Yes. Fuck it, sir.'

Cohen lowered his night-vision goggles and cocked his shotgun. Avery unlocked the door. Cohen exited and shut the door behind him. The metal bolts thundered back into place, as he stood in the hallway, absolutely without light.

106

CHAPTER ELEVEN

The hammer cracked down for the last time.

The auction continued. There was no tradition of putting the most expensive pieces near the end of the sale. It wasn't quite so theatrical. Nor would they be put first. Let bidders get into the flow, warm to the sale. Then, somewhere between the twentieth and the fiftieth lot, slide in the mother lode. The one-million Miró, the three-million Mondrian, the four-million Modigliani, the six-million Malevich, the seven-million Magritte, the eight-million Matisse, the fifteen-million Manet, the twenty-million Monet. The prices were arbitrary.

But, as Delacloche thought to herself, I always like to go through museums and play the pricing game. Can you quantify genius? Of course. You can quantify anything. But why does four million come to mind when I think of a Modigliani, and twenty million for a Monet? You begin to estimate by osmosis. I must have, some time in the last year and a half, seen or heard of a Modigliani selling for four million. But then, didn't I also hear of one of his paintings selling for eight?

Buying continued, but attention was focused on the lady in the pink suit and pearl necklace, with her whitening-blond hair done up in a bun with the chopsticks sticking out. Delacloche had recognized two of the bidders immediately. At the end of the field, it had come down to one private buyer and a museum. The private buyer, a collector with wide-ranging tastes who bought regularly, was of wealth and society, and he knew his art. The Swiss superlawyer Thomas Frei. The ideal Christie's client, from social, economic, and scholarly perspectives. As was the museum.

The museum was probably buying with private funds, as well. But in such a situation, Christie's employees will inevitably cheer for the museum. It meant that they, and the rest of the world, could enjoy the work at any time, that it would be cared for and preserved. That's not to say that it would be mistreated in a private collection, but chances are that the owner would not allow it out on loan, not for years, at least, so it might never be seen again.

Christie's needed the highest hammer price possible, and it all too often fell to uneducated private hands, so this purchase by a museum was a special treat. And it was bid upon by a known character in the London art world.

Elizabeth Van Der Mier, director of the new National Gallery of Modern Art, right here in London. Interesting, Delacloche thought. The museum director bidding herself, on behalf of the museum. With whose money, I wonder? Delacloche was straining to see through the gooseflesh of heads, to the well-kept woman in pale pink.

She was surprised, trying to piece things together. The Malevich *White on White* is an important work. It will drum up a lot of business for the museum. No doubt they'll have a special welcome exhibit for it in the next year, probably quite soon, to capitalize on the publicity. It tends to only be private buyers who don't want others to know what they've bought, except their society friends, of course. In this case, the more publicity, the better.

Her thoughts were interrupted when an old Christie's friend greeted her. Delacloche half-smiled and conversed in hollow phrases, as lot upon lot washed by. It was Jenny, or was it Jackie? From some department or another. Delacloche seized the opportunity.

'Tell me,' she said, 'was the authenticity of that Malevich, lot thirty-nine, ever brought into question?'

Her former colleague looked at her, smiled, and whispered beneath the din.

'It's in no one's interest to find the work inauthentic or incorrectly attributed. But, frankly, it *looks* right. All of us, we've noted that it just feels right. And the provenance is flawless.'

'Isn't it odd for the provenance to be so flawless?'

'It is, I suppose. But nobody wanted it to prove false. That's the real point. And it didn't look or feel wrong. The experts here, they trust their judgment based on whatever you'd like to call it, vibes or senses, over anything more scientific. You recognize authenticity like you recognize your friends. After you've seen enough, these artists and their offspring become more your family than your family. People can be tiresome.'

'Did no one question the provenance?'

'They had a lot to look at, in preparing this sale, I think. Why?'

'Nothing.'

'So if they get the vibe, and the provenance looks this good, then we thank our lucky stars and move on to the next piece. But you know all this,

109

don't you, Geneviève?'

'Think the museum will do its own investigation?'

'Not unless there's a damn good reason. They are more screwed than anyone, in the public eye at least, if they take home their six-million-quid Christmas present, and find that they've overspent by £5.95 million. Christie's will deliver it within the week. They'll give it a quick once-over in Conservation, maybe a clean and a new frame, then hold a press conference, announce an exhibition featuring their new treasure, and stick it on the wall, all within the month, at the latest. At least, that's what I would do. They'll get publicity: television, magazine, and newspaper reviews of the exhibition. It'll be like a new play has opened in the West End. It will bring in many thousands of visitors. They'll make *White on White* mouse pads and umbrellas. Everyone lives happily ever after. That is, provided this is the real deal.'

'So you're saying that not even the museum is going to check? Even after my phone calls and suspicions . . .'

'That's what I'm saying. Geneviève, no one knows about your phone calls and suspicions. Unless you tell them.'

'Right.' Delacloche paused. Her eyes scanned the room. 'What did the seller think? I don't think I ever heard who . . .'

'You know I can't tell you that. Come now. Some sellers are happy to let themselves be known, others I could slip you along the gossip chain. But some clients strictly request that their anonymity be maintained, and this is one. Only a few of us know.'

Delacloche looked away, and Jackie, or was it Jenny, patted her on the padded shoulder and slipped away into the crowd.

'Lot seventy-seven . . .'

*　　*　　*

Oh shit, Cohen reasoned, as he engaged his night-vision goggles. The hallway blurred from black to chemical green.

Let's go.

Cohen moved down the corridor, smooth until he crossed his left foot in front of his right, and stumbled. It had been a long while, and several centimeters on his stomach, since his training. Never anything quite so exciting as this.

Stay on your feet, you wanker, he thought. I bet this sort of shit never happens to Dennis Ahearn at the Tate.

'Control here, sir. Do you copy?' The sound in his ear made him jump back.

'Shit, Avery. You almost gave me a heart attack. Yes, I copy. Help me out.'

'You'll have to take the stairs down five flights. The elevators would reveal your position.'

'You're going to make me walk down five flights, are you?'

'I think it's advisable, sir . . .'

'Well, you're right. And knock off that "sir" shit. We're on a first-name basis right now, goddamn it.'

'Yes, sir.'

Cohen slipped along the hallway to the stairs, and carved his way down.

'The movement ceased in the utility room forty seconds ago, sir. But as much as I can tell, the door is still open.'

'Avery, how far into the system did this hacker cut? How come we can sense the motion but we've lost radio and video?'

'They got through the communication walls, but the internal alarms and locks are controlled separately, and those seem intact. That means that they can't take anything off the walls, unless . . .'

'. . . unless they cut off electricity completely . . .'

'. . . from the utility room.'

Cohen slid down the final run of stairs, to the basement floor. The gray metal door, green in his night-vision, lurked before him, leading into the utility and storage sectors of the museum.

He reached out to the handle and pulled.

'It's locked, Avery.'

'They must have gotten in through another entrance. I'm unlocking it now, sir.'

The tension in Cohen's arm relaxed, as the door pulled open. He stepped inside, and cushioned the door shut behind him.

'The utility room is around the corner. The door should be physically open, not just unlocked.'

'Right.'

Cohen cautiously stepped along the linoleum flooring, his vision a sea of bottle green and shadows. His shotgun was cocked and raised, breath came short and hot.

'I don't hear anything,' he whispered softly. No reply.

He was only a few steps from the perpendicular corridor, and the utility room along its left arm. His shoulder brushed the wall as he pressed his back against it, inches from the corner.

Gun first, he spun into the corridor.

Nothing. Just the quiet dark and iridescent monochrome of his vision. But at the end of the hall, the door was cracked open.

'I see it.'

Cohen moved smoothly toward the door. He could hear nothing but his quick-cut breath, and felt only the heat of perspiration beneath his Kevlar vest. The shotgun's weight felt good in his hands.

The door grew as he approached. The room seethed beyond. He was now only a few steps away.

'We've got movement in room nine, sir! Motion sensor has been tripped, and the laser wall in front of the paintings has been broken. They're upstairs!'

Shit shit shit shit shit shit shit, Cohen thought. They must've already been here. The utility room is just a diversion!

He spun away from the door and ran down the hall, back toward the stairs.

No more stealth now. They're going for it.

He charged up the back staircase.

'Room nine, still motion in room nine!'

'I'm almost there! Drop the security gates on both sides of the room. Drop 'em now!'

Cohen burst through the door to the main floor of the museum, as he heard the heavy steel gates fall shut several rooms ahead.

'Gates down, sir. The movement has stopped.'

'Light! Give me light!'

Cohen threw off his night-vision goggles, as the overhead lights flickered awake.

He ran through room 7, room 8. There was the steel gate that blocked entrance to room 9. He

113

approached the gate, shotgun first.

'This is security,' Cohen bellowed. 'Put your hands in the air and keep them there. Do not resist. Do not attempt any sudden movement.'

He swung up to the gate, and looked inside.

The room was empty.

'Sir!'

The sound came from behind him. Cohen spun around.

Four security guards, guns in hand, approached.

'Where the fuck have you lot been? What the fuck is going on?'

CHAPTER TWELVE

The waiter had just brought two plates of the eponymous dish at Au Pied de Cochon, as Jean-Jacques Bizot arrived, hot-cheeked and breathless. Jean-Paul Lesgourges did not pause to look up from his plate, as his nimble knife and fork sliced, with surgical precision, into the crackly skin of the pig's foot, pulling the knobby bones away from the succulent flesh.

'Et bien?'

Bizot did not respond, as he had his hands full trying to squeeze between a mirrored column and the overpopulated table behind, brimming with well-mannered children and obnoxious aunts, in order to reach his seat. Lesgourges looked up from his pig's foot with one eye, giggled silently, then resumed eating.

'I ordered for you, because the kitchen wanted to close,' he said. Bizot did not respond, as he was

114

attempting to pour himself over the armrest and into his seat.

'Jean, you have the grace of a wounded armadillo. Eat your piggy.'

Bizot, finally and firmly seated (he now noticed that he was wedged between and beneath the armrests), draped his napkin vertically down his chest and then horizontally across his stomach, took up knife and fork, and muttered in a puff of sweat, 'Bonsoir.'

'Bonsoir yourself,' Lesgourges replied, as he popped a curved knucklebone into his mouth, to suck it clean. 'So you wanted to eat late, because you had some business. A week into your investigation, and only now you let me in on the fun. Et alors . . .'

'A moment, Jean. Je mange, donc je suis. Stomach first, then mind.' Bizot began eating ravenously.

'As it was in the beginning, is now, and ever shall be . . . eating without end . . . amen.' Lesgourges intoned solemnly, before he gestured to the waiter for more wine.

In a matter of minutes, the brown-sugary skin and white meat of the pied de cochon had disappeared, and all that remained on Bizot's once full plate was a scattering of tiny gun-metal gray bones that shone, like ink, against the white of the plate below. With a daintiness preposterous to his circumference, Bizot dabbed the corners of his mouth with a napkin-tented finger.

'Are you going to tell me, or . . .'

'I will.' Bizot set down his napkin and leaned back in his chair. 'What do you want to know?'

'You overstuffed chicken, don't play coy with

115

me. On the phone, you told me about the investigation at the Malevich Society, and you said that there was a puzzle that needed solving, and that you'd wait to tell me in person, because it was more fun that way. Well, now I am here. And you have eaten . . .'

'Right.' Bizot smiled just enough for the wings of his beard to rise and fall. 'C-H-3-4-7.'

'Quoi?'

Bizot repeated. 'C. H. Three. Four. Seven.'

'That's the puzzle?' Lesgourges looked disappointed.

'That's what was written on the wall behind the sliding-wall thingy that the stolen Malevich was hanging off when it was stolen.'

Bizot fumbled through his trousers and emerged with a soft pack of cigarettes, bent and mangled. He drew one out between two stubby fingers. The end was broken and dangled by a sliver of rolling paper. Lesgourges started laughing. Bizot snapped off the broken end and lit his cigarette with a match from a book with the words 'Crazy Horse' printed on it, in pink cursive.

'Alors, qu'est-ce que tu en penses?'

'I'm not sure what to think.' Lesgourges leaned back and snapped open his silver cigarette case. His fingers rolled across the humpbacks of the row of ten thin black-cased cigarettes, each ringed with a gold band. The smell of clove wafted up from the case, and a sweet film clung onto Lesgourges' fingertips. He chose a cigarette and withdrew it. He conducted with his clove baton, as he spoke.

'It's not much to begin with, but the first thing that comes to mind is that it is a statement.'

Bizot looked up from the cherry of his mutilated

116

cigarette, then back down. 'That's what I thought, too.'

Lesgourges finally stuck the cigarette between his horse lips and lit it from his own matchbook, identical to Bizot's. 'The thieves wanted the Malevich Society to know . . .'

'. . . what?'

'Bizot, that's what I'm trying to work out. I'm thinking aloud. Silence et prépare-toi!' Lesgourges drew hard on his cigarette. The end smoked and crackled. He exhaled a sugarplum cloud. 'The thieves wanted to tell the Malevich Society that, one: they were able to successfully steal a painting from the vaults; and, two: the perpetrators were called CH347.'

Bizot stared for a moment, not at Lesgourges, but at the smoke dancing in front of him.

'You're a demi-idiot, Lesgourges,' Bizot confided. 'Half of your statement makes sense, and the other half . . . not so much. I agree that this crime seems like an act of ability, of puissance, not of the need to either own the painting or to sell it on. If not a statement, then why would they leave us any clue to work with? If they wanted to melt away into the night, never to be seen again, why leave a calling card? You are correct. This is a statement. But CH347 sounds more like a dishwashing detergent than the name of a perpetrator.'

'Perhaps it's a palindrome?'

'Quoi—743HC?'

'No, not a palindrome . . . qu'est-ce que je veux dire . . . an acronym.'

Bizot twirled the cigarette in place in his mouth, using his pointer finger and thumb. 'I was wrong,

Jean. You are a full-fledged idiot.'

'That doesn't answer the question about whether it could be an acronym.'

'No,' said Bizot. 'I was just saying that, on general principles. I can't think of any institution or terrorist group or . . .'

'What about a flight number?' Lesgourges tried, and failed, repeatedly, to blow smoke rings.

'Clove smoke is too thin,' remarked Bizot, 'as I've told you.'

'It's too bad the same cannot be said for you,' replied Lesgourges. 'As I've told you.'

'Ha. Ha. But that's not a bad idea. Except for the fact that it doesn't make any sense at all to write a flight number on the wall from which you just stole a painting.'

'Maybe the thieves were worried that they would forget on which flight they were planning to escape.' Lesgourges leaned over the menu. 'Do you want dessert?'

'I will check to see if there is a flight of that number. There may be some connection, but I wouldn't hold my breath. How about mousse au chocolat?'

'Hmmm.' Lesgourges turned to address the waiter. 'Deux tartes Tatin, s'il vous plaît.' The waiter shuffled off. 'You prefer tarte Tatin. What other options are there?'

'There was a crème caramel and a . . .'

'No,' interrupted Lesgourges, 'I meant other options for the CH347.'

'Right. Well, there's a chocolate cake . . .'

'Salaud! Je vais te frapper!' Bizot dodged Lesgourges' halfhearted attempts at stabbing him with a fork, his face turning bright red with laughter. Bizot's beard flopped up and down with his breathless expulsions, his upper body mobile while his lower half remained wedged between the arms of his chair.

'Calm down, Lesgourges.' Bizot regained his composure. '. . . We need to sort this out, but it's best to think on a full stomach.'

'How much fuller do you think your stomach could be?'

'We haven't had dessert yet.'

CHAPTER THIRTEEN

Elizabeth Van Der Mier got up to leave as the auction wound to its close. Christie's employees delicately attended to her, careful not to overstep, but present and helpful as needed. She disappeared with her entourage, which included two other museum representatives who had been lurking along the periphery of the room.

It was much like a James Bond film, Delacloche had always thought. The auction room full of high rollers, dressed for it, with wingmen stationed, and millions at stake. The prices had always struck her as outrageous, but to such an extent that they became inconceivable. This was toy money to these people who had it, and for those who did not, it was beyond comprehension. To drop hundreds of thousands of pounds on a whim, on a piece of wall decoration . . . so why was she in the industry? She loved the art, but also the world that rotated round it. She loved it all.

Van Der Mier was out of the building by the

time the graying gentleman who'd bought the ugly Suprematist work left the auction room. Delacloche waited a moment, then followed. The majority of the audience had gone and, although the seats were mostly full, the periphery was nearly vacant. Many of the paintings that had decorated the walls had been taken down to be stored, packed, or picked up by purchasers.

The graying gentleman approached the cashier.

'Good afternoon, sir. Paddle?'

'Well, I really shouldn't. We've only just met.'

'May I have your paddle number?'

'Oh. Certainly.' The gentleman slid his paddle across to the elegant, pearled young woman behind the desk. She opened a file and withdrew a form, which she prepared to fill out.

'Mr. Robert Grayson?'

'That's right.' His accent was American, but not offensively so.

'Lot thirty-four, anonymous Suprematist painting?'

'That's right.'

'How would you like to pay for your purchase, sir?'

'I think cash, if that's acceptable.'

'Of course, sir.' She began to fill in the form, glancing up briefly at Grayson, then down at his left hand. 'That's fifteen-hundred for the hammer price, plus seventeen-point-five percent commission for purchases under fifty-thousand, makes it a total of seventeen hundred sixty-two pounds and twenty-five pence. It is a very lovely piece, sir.'

'Thank you, darling. It's an acquired taste, I'll admit, and I seem to have acquired it. It will go

120

well with my curtains.'

'Yes, quite.' She laughed, unsure if it was a joke.

'Now, I'd like to have you bring me the painting. When should I expect it?'

'Whenever you need it, sir, it will be there.'

'I can be home tomorrow, Thursday, between nine and noon.'

'That will be fine, sir. Just fill out this form.'

Transaction completed, Grayson turned from the cashier with a wink, and he descended the grand staircase. The lobby sprawled out below, mingled with people conversing and admiring, congratulating and reading. The rack of catalogues of upcoming sales stood to the left of the stairs, small-linked gold chains locked between book and rack. There was the television, displaying the action in the auction room. There were books for sale, and the registration desk, where was seated yet another graceful woman, hair pulled back and clipped. That was affectionately described as the 'husband-catching' position for Christie's employees to hold—a chance to meet the influx of wealthy, and often single, gentlemen bidders, whose social standing, education, and tastes were self-evident from their presence at auction. But Grayson didn't know this.

He alighted onto the lobby floor, and his eye was drawn to one of the upcoming sales catalogues: *Important Nineteenth-Century Decorative Arts.* He approached it, when his path was barred.

'Mr. Grayson?'

'Yes. Do I know you?' There were three gentlemen in nearly identical dark suits standing before him.

'No, sir. We are fellow collectors and art lovers,

121

like yourself. We've seen you here before.'

'Is that so? Find anything you like today?'

'We did, as a matter of fact. We did make a purchase. As a matter of fact, that was something we wished to speak with you about.'

'Oh?'

'We wanted to congratulate you on your purchase of lot thirty-four. It's a very handsome piece.'

'Well, I . . . thank you. I think it's something of an acquired taste, but I seem to have . . .'

'The fact is, that we were rather hoping for the chance to bid on it ourselves, but we were out of the room when it came up.'

'Bad luck. Did you receive a phone call?'

'The fact is, sir, that we represent someone who would very much like the piece you just bought. He is prepared to offer you significantly more than you paid.'

'Is that right?' Grayson's eyes flicked around the room.

'That is correct.' There was a pause. 'I'm not going to be coy, Mr. Grayson. We are prepared to pay you ten thousand pounds for the painting that you just bought.'

'Ten thousand pounds?' Grayson smiled and leaned back. 'You must be mad. Do you know how much I paid for it? Fifteen hundred. That makes it . . . I can't even do the math, but that is many times the . . .'

'We know. It is of particular interest to us, and money is little object. Do we have a deal?'

'Thank you, gentlemen. I'm deeply moved. But the fact is that money is little object to me, as well, and my wife is going to love this painting. Good

122

day.'

Grayson brushed past the three men, and into the ever-growing crowd mingled in the lobby. The crowd closed up behind him, and the men watched through the field of bodies, as Grayson left the building. By the time they had reached the door, he had gone.

Delacloche watched this interaction intently. She stood in the lobby, straining through the crowd in search of Jeffrey, the expert with whom she'd spoken on the telephone. She wanted to ask him why the *White on White* that was presented as lot 39 was different from the one in the catalogue. Surely he was in the lobby. But she could not find him, or perhaps he ensured that she did not find him.

She spotted two former lovers among the pin-striped and French-cuffed. One mediocre, the other downright awful. The only two representatives of her brief forays into English lovers. Alas, the tentative and repressed make poor bedfellows. Her mental Rolodex flipped through faces, and the feel of hands. Rodrigo García and Marco del Basso blew all the others out of the water. She smiled to herself as she thought back. Those two could turn professional. Give me a Mediterranean any day.

The Christie's experts laughed and chatted with their clients, many of whom they'd known for many years, and with whom they had relationships outside the office. There were few enough collectors out there, particularly in any given area of interest. The best customers were repeat buyers, and the art alone could not ensure loyalty. Buyers wanted to buy from their friends, and it was part of the job of the Christie's employees to make and keep friendships with their clients. For some it might be considered a burden. But others thrived on it. It allowed one to live a very wealthy and glamorous life vicariously. Christie's experts might be invited to stay at the Tuscan villa of one client, eat at Taillevent with another, cruise on a private yacht in the Greek Islands, be given gifts of wine. It was all highly agreeable, particularly for those without a family, or for whom family life was not the blissful escape that it might be. For some, work was like a beautiful dream from which they did not wish to wake.

Delacloche knew most of the staff in all of the twentieth-century departments at Christie's in various countries. She'd encountered them in the past at sales, at exhibitions, and in academic settings. Everyone was a known commodity, and this walled world often became a hive of incest, both literal and intellectual. There was nothing quite so otherworldly as a scholarly convention among art historians. One brightly individualized character was one thing, but a room full of sixty, discussing and releasing their passions in alternation, was an event to behold.

Delacloche had seen many such sights. She surprised herself that she'd never slept with anyone on the Christie's staff. As far as she recalled. So she could not understand why no one was speaking with her. She stood in the middle of the lobby, as the insects buzzed around her in tones of gossip and praise, and wondered why.

Grayson sat in the taxi on the way to his St John's Wood flat. He did not see the black Land Rover that was following him back to his home.

124

CHAPTER FOURTEEN

'Explain this to me, from the beginning.'

The next morning, fresh off her triumphant purchase, Elizabeth Van Der Mier, director of the National Gallery of Modern Art, sat on the edge of her desk, arms crossed, looking unamused and wearing a black suit. Her whitening-blond hair was tied taut behind her head with a black ribbon, and her red lipstick was painted on with less than usual care. Her eyes punctured the night security staff, who sat in her wood-and-glass office. Four guards, one technician, one head of staff.

'At 21:22 last night, we registered a lack of communication with the security personnel,' Cohen began, sifting his hand through his thinning hair. 'We tried to radio in to them from the control room and received no response. We checked the closed-circuit TV monitors and could not find anyone. All the surveyed rooms and corridors appeared to be empty. We rewound the tape and found that the guards had been on video twenty-nine minutes earlier, but then disappeared abruptly from the screen. We later found that this was due to someone having tapped into our computers and looped the CC-TVs to broadcast the same recording of the empty rooms from earlier that night, on all monitors.

'Apparently, at this same time, the missing guards had been told by radio that there was a disturbance on the third floor. The two separate patrol teams were given different instructions and sent to opposite parts of the third floor. They were

125

addressed by a female voice that sounded like Ms. Avery, here. Avery noted that we had lost control of communications and video, but motion sensors were tripped in the utility room. I tried to phone the police, but the line was dead. Then I investigated, as I've told you.'

Van Der Mier tapped her left arm with her right index finger and bit the inside of her left cheek.

'What I don't like . . . ,' she began, '. . . where shall I begin? Someone broke into our computers. I don't like that. But then it appears that no one ever entered the building, which is strange. What was the motion in the utility room, and in room nine?'

'We investigated,' Cohen sighed, 'but found nothing. It appears that, while we thought that we were still in control of the internal alarms, they were actually being manipulated electronically through our computer system, from the outside. The hacker was triggering motion alarms in both rooms. We've found no trace of actual intruders.'

'The other thing I don't like,' Van Der Mier continued, 'is that there seems to be no rationale behind this attack. And it is an attack.'

'Sometimes hackers will break in, just to show that they can,' Avery suggested cautiously.

'That isn't good enough, my dear. An encoded museum security system is not Mount Everest, and I will not believe that someone with rather too much time on his hands climbed it simply because it was there. There was forethought and malice in intentionally separating both security patrols, and luring Toby into the basement, before tripping the alarm on the main floor to chase him back up again. What further pisses me off is that a thief

126

could have made off with a bundle of paintings last night, and whoever is behind this seems to want us to know as much, thanks to this show of power.'

She paced militarily in front of her desk.

'But a computer cannot carry paintings off the wall and out of the building. There must be a living, breathing human being in order to do that. And if the hacker can break into the system, then the hacker can put a person inside, and that is not going to happen.'

She stopped and stood straight.

'I want a complete overhaul of all the firewalls and codes, to block future access to our computers. Let us hope that this was an act of ability, a flexing of muscle, not an act of malevolent intent. But we will not allow this to happen again. None of you are to blame. You all acted appropriately. But I will caution you on one matter. Word of this must not circulate. The police are not to be involved. Nothing was stolen, and no one hurt. We can count our blessings for that. But we cannot afford the negative publicity that would come from such a breach in our defenses, nor do we wish to alert the criminal public to our vulnerability. We have just purchased a very important painting. Last night, during all of this mess, as a matter of fact. We will announce the acquisition at a press conference this afternoon. The painting will be the center of much positive publicity for the museum, and I have no wish to taint the exposure it will bring. So keep the events of last night silent. Thank you.'

*   *   *

The anonymous Suprematist painting, lot 34, had just been delivered to the St John's Wood flat of Mr. Robert Grayson. The raw-wood crate sat propped against his wallpapered hall, in the three-bedroom he occupied alone, for now. The luxury cars and bejeweled housewives of the neighborhood whirled by outside, as Grayson put on a Springsteen album.

There was one other piece of what Grayson would consider 'real' art on display in the flat. It was a Jasper Johns print of the American flag in an oversize driftwood frame, which gave it a rustic, Cape Cod, sea captain look, as he liked to describe it. The most widely sold print in history, he'd been told by the gallery owner. Other than that, his walls were sparsely populated with framed posters and photographs. A black-and-white of Ted Williams following through with his swing, as a catcher and umpire look on in awe. Jackson Pollock's *Lavender Mist* with the letters M-O-M-A printed along the bottom. A long, horizontal poster of Boston, seen from the harbor at night, in a silvery metal frame. A quotation printed in white on black, in cursive, italicized letters, that read 'Money and time are inextricably linked. You figure it out.'

Grayson was dressed in a collared green polo shirt with a small red polo player over the heart and khaki trousers. He held the endgame of a cigar in one hand and a glass tumbler in the other. He was wiggling to the music in an admirable, but failed, attempt at dancing.

His mobile phone rang.

'Hello? Oh, hiya, Charlie. Sure, sure. No problem. Yeah, so what've you got for me? I'll be on the flight that arrives JFK at eleven tonight, New York time. Yeah, have him meet me there, yup. Well, I've got the meeting downtown at ten, and a lunch with Harry Hancock at Union Square Cafe, at one thirty. Of course, I'm ordering the tuna burger. We should meet up for dinner, though. I'm only going to spend the one night, before I come back out here. I know it's crazy, but my workload is up my ass, and Manchester United are playing Liverpool, so I'd like to be back as soon as possible. You may say it's not real football, but I am enlightened. You can go shove your 49ers up your . . . what's that? No, that's fine. That won't be a problem. Gramercy Tavern at eight, sounds good. And I'll be swinging by Barney Greengrass just before Sal takes me to the airport on the way back. I'm going to smuggle some smoked sable back across the Atlantic. It's my only vice. That and cigars. And bourbon, yes. Well, so I have three vices. I'm sure you can think of some more, but that won't be necessary, thank you very much. Right, then, Charlie. I'll see you tomorrow afternoon. I leave in a couple of hours. Right, bye-bye.'

Grayson put down his mobile phone and crossed over to the wooden crate by the door. He knelt beside it and ran his fingers across the rough plywood.

*   *   *

'Greetings, and welcome to members of the press and public.' Elizabeth Van Der Mier stood in all her tall, dark-suited glory, behind a lectern in the Michael Marlais Lecture Hall at the National

Gallery of Modern Art. 'We are very pleased to announce the purchase of the most important Suprematist painting by the brilliant Kasimir Malevich, the first and largest in his series of *White on White* masterworks. It will have pride of place in our museum's permanent collection, but may first be seen in our upcoming special exhibition, entitled "What Is Not There: The Beauty and Eloquence of Minimalism." The painting will be unveiled at the opening of the exhibition. It is in the Conservation Department to be reframed, and then it will go on display as the centerpiece of the "What Is Not There: The Beauty and Eloquence of Minimalism" show. Until then . . .'

'Isn't it just all white?' whispered one member of the press to another.

'I think so,' came the reply. 'So what's the big fat deal, then?'

'No idea, mate. But I've got an idea what I'd like to do with the bird up at the podium, eh?'

'Too right. What's she talking about, then?'

'No clue, mate. Just take a photo, and let's grab a pint.'

A man at the back of the room smiled, unamused, as he overheard. He was wearing ironed-crisp, cuff-linked sleeves, beneath his well-cut suit.

*　　　*　　　*

Elizabeth Van Der Mier looked out over heads, cameras, and notebooks, surveying her fiefdom. This had gone very well. All the right people were here. This would be all over the magazines, newspapers, and newscasts. The icing was an

130

interview with her, scheduled for next week, to be featured in *Time Out* magazine. That would be seen by millions and ensure popular awareness of her exhibition, unusual for anything but the big-name monograph shows, or the Impressionists. People flock to shows called 'Vermeer,' or 'Manet's Paris,' or 'The Impressionists at Argenteuil,' but Russian art was too often overlooked. It could not be considered forgotten, because that would imply that someone had known of it, at some point. Now was its chance.

She did not see Delacloche, who sat at the back of the lecture hall, waiting.

*   *   *

Hours later, Robert Grayson sipped his bourbon, slung low in his business-class seat, thousands of feet above the Atlantic. He stared out the window into the spilled-ink sky, devoid of stars, obscured by a black-veil mist of impenetrable clouds. Before him, New York was bustling and bright-eyed. Behind him, London slept.

The National Gallery of Modern Art crouched like a great white moth on the south side of the river Thames. Swaddled in concrete and steel and glass, the London night bore a soft misty rain that ran like gauze over the hard surfaces. Dim yellow lights suffused from the ground around, casting shadows up along the walls. The windows yawned the darkness inside, as the paintings slept in silence. The illuminant sign on the front lawn of the museum hummed noiselessly.

Then all the lights went out.

CHAPTER FIFTEEN

'Are you fucking kidding me!?'

Toby Cohen screamed inside the control room of the museum, as Avery struck useless keys and threw her gaze across a matrix of empty screens, barely perceptible in the absolute, interior, windowless darkness.

'What the fuck is fucking going on in this fucking place!?'

'Sir, we've lost all power, including backup generators.'

'I can see that, Avery, goddamn it. Where are you, anyway?'

'One moment, sir.'

Avery fumbled through the palpable black of the room, then clicked on a concentrated beam of white light.

'Here, sir.' She handed Cohen a Maglite and clicked one on for herself. For the second time in one week, Cohen threw open the black steel cabinets and pulled out armaments. I'm getting too old for this, he thought.

'After we've just fixed the goddamned computer system so that it's hacker proof, something still goes wrong. Well this bloody technology can just . . .'

'That's the point, sir. This is not a computer failure, and this is not a hack. The new computer defense system is invulnerable. Except for one thing. It needs electricity.'

'They knocked out the power to the whole building?'

'That's the only way that the computers could be neutralized. And they'd have to cut the emergency generator, too. The whole area could be black, for all we know.'

'So somebody realized they couldn't break through our front door, so they walked around it.'

'It's the Gordian knot, sir.'

'I don't give a flying fuck what it is, but no one is going to steal from this museum while I'm on duty.'

'Are you sure they're going to steal something? Maybe it's a show of power, like the last time.'

'Why else would they be wanking us about, for Christ's sake!? Get me the boys on the radio.'

'The communications are routed through the computers, sir. But we do have manual walkie-talkies now.' Avery swung her light until she found what she was looking for. She clicked on the walkie-talkie with a hiss, and she pressed the button along its side. 'Control to Security Teams Two and Three. Do you copy?'

There was a long pause. Cohen stopped moving and listened, breath paused.

'This is Security Three, we copy.' Cohen and Avery exhaled, as the harsh, static voice came through.

'Security Two here—we copy, over.'

Cohen grabbed the walkie-talkie from Avery. 'This is Toby. Now what's going on?'

'Security Three here. We were on the second floor, making rounds, when the lights went off, all of a sudden-like. I'll be honest. I can't see a bloody thing.'

'Don't you fucking curse at me, Stammers! Let's keep things clean here, for fuck's sake. Security

Two, where are you?'

'Boss, we're on the ground floor, and we heard an explosion before the lights went out. It was muffled, though, so we can't tell where it's coming from. Felt like it was a big one.'

'What do you mean that it felt like a big one?'

'The floor shook.'

'The floor shook—that's just great.'

'What should we do now?'

'All right. Security Two, stay on the ground floor. Security Three, stay on the second floor. Avery and I will cover the first floor. I'll be on the night-vision goggles, but we only have the two pairs up here, so you'll have to use your Maglites. I want you to stay quiet and listen. We can't see shit, but we can hear it.'

Cohen clipped the walkie-talkie to his belt. He placed a handgun, through the dark, into Avery's hand.

'Sir, I'm not trained to . . .'

'Shut up. We have to contact the police.'

'But, sir . . .'

'Something's happening, Avery. Right now.'

'I know. But . . .'

'Don't give me any buts, I . . .'

'. . . the panic button is electric, and so are the phone and radios. Our mobile phones are in our lockers in the basement. We can't reach the police. We're trapped in here.'

'Then we'll have to break out.'

* * *

Security Team Three wandered through the silent halls, vacuous and full with the void of darkness.

134

The night was overcast and moonless. It appeared that the sky outside the windows had been blacked out, as well. No light shone in from any source. The only respite came in the thin, clear beams from the Maglites that flashed around the walls.

There were so many paintings, each one unable to defend itself, a helpless lamb, vulnerable. With the electricity on, there was closed-circuit surveillance, external and internal alarms, locks on doors, iron gates that dropped at exit points for containment security. Without electricity, however, there were no defenses but locks on the doors outside, and frames bolted to walls. That wasn't much. Museums don't anticipate attack, so there were only the six overnight guards. They hadn't even had time to reinforce, beyond computer firewalls, since last night's incident. Now the guards couldn't even see.

Guards Stammers and Fox walked through the dwarfing rooms, as their flashlights beamed over works of art they feared they could not protect. Like shepherds in a blinding snowstorm. The wolves could be anywhere, and there were too many sheep to defend.

Then they heard a sound.

'Did you hear that?' Fox stopped moving.

'Uh-huh.' They both drew guns.

There it was again. A footfall, perhaps. The guards turned around, then paused.

'I definitely heard that.' Stammers started toward the sound. It seemed to be coming from the next room.

Fox followed. 'That's room nine again, isn't it?'

'Yup.'

'Doesn't it feel like we've done this before?'

'Yup.'

They walked slowly forward, guns held by bent arms, lights cast along the floor.

'We can't close the gates this time.'

'I know.'

They stopped. The black air around them was submarine. The room gaped.

Then something ran out toward them.

A figure charged out of room nine. It brushed past Stammers and Fox before they could react. They spun and heard a voice.

'For fuck's sake, it's just us!'

Toby Cohen emerged from room nine. He shined his flashlight up at his own face, night-vision goggles tipped up on his forehead.

'Boo,' he said. Then he flashed to the figure that had run past, now standing in the room with them. It was Avery, also carrying night-vision goggles. 'I want Avery to get the police. Something's going down. I'm not going to take any chances. Let's get her out the door.'

They navigated through the cavernous rooms, until they reached one of the doors that led outside. What limited light there was leaked in through the glass front doors, locked and tight. Avery unlocked the door manually.

'Just reach the nearest phone, and then let the police in. We'll be inside and may not be able to hear you. And tell 'em to bring some lights, for Christ's sake.' Cohen held the door open for Avery, and she set out into the night. He closed and locked the door behind her.

'We're locked in, boys. Let's just hope there's nothing to be scared of.'

Across the Thames, several miles away, lay the St John's Wood flat of Robert Grayson. In the black basement of the building, the calm was broken by a muffled footfall. Then another.

The feet, clad in felt-wrapped shoes, crept along a corridor, and pushed open a metal door, soundlessly. Then a long, thin probe found a metal box mounted on the wall, and sank deep into its silvery keyhole. A minute later, the lock sprang, and the door rolled open. A thin-gloved hand fingered along the rows of fuses, until it found its victim.

A bright crash of glass fell through the cracked skylight, and down onto Robert Grayson's bedroom floor. It was followed by a black figure, who landed catlike on the ground, cushioned by muscled legs and skillful bend of knee. The alarm did not sound.

Without impediment, the figure strode into the living room, where an anonymous Suprematist painting slept in its protective wooden crate, resting against the wall.

A screwdriver flashed out of a holster strapped on hip, and the tight lid was unscrewed and removed. There, in the custom-made wooden box, sat the hideously ugly painting, lot 34. It was snug, surrounded by perfectly cut Styrofoam padding.

The figure drew a long, thin scalpel and pressed it into the flesh of the canvas. The blade ran along the outside edge, just below the nails that locked the canvas, spread tight across the wooden stretcher that gave it form. The canvas peeled forward off its stretcher, like dry skin. It was

137

carefully and loosely rolled, and placed in a black plastic tube that was slung over, and lashed tight, to back.

Climbing the rope that still hung through the shattered skylight, the figure disappeared into the night.

CHAPTER SIXTEEN

The museum guards wandered from room to room. Although in pairs, they might have been alone, for the tangible night sky inside the museum was carved into visibility only by the thinnest knives of their flashlights.

Cohen could feel the presence of the paintings around him, this hanging garden of cloth and wood and pigment and oil. He never understood the appeal of a mess of splotches or a black square, but he'd guard them with his life. And he never took the time to ask himself why. Perhaps because he feared that he could not come up with an answer, and that would plunge his life's work into nothingness. 'Avoid the void,' he had once heard someone say. If he allowed himself to think, well, that was not in the best interest of the working class. He knew that he was good at his job, and that was enough. He knew that he was valued by people far smarter than he, and that brought him some satisfaction. Why try to trick oneself into unhappiness, all in the name of thought? Did bodyguards have to love, and understand, the prime minister? No, they just knew that their job was to protect him at all costs. It was not for them, these existential conundrums. But, then, Cohen was not entirely sure that he knew what 'existential' meant.

The absence of light to his periphery was such that he could not even make out the walls. Whoever did this picked the right night, he thought. Overcast and moonless. A lonely soul bobbing up and down in a midnight sea, Cohen knew that ships were passing on either side, could feel them, but could not see. The sounds of this ocean mocked him, too, but did so with their silence. His ears awaited any sound, but none came to him, amiss or otherwise, to satisfy his hypothesis. This was an attack, he had been certain, a kidnapping. So why would the barbarians storm the castle for plunder, and then leave without a sound, without a coin to show for it? Was this yet another show of power? Twice in the same week. He engaged his night-vision goggles, and the black turned to green once more.

Van Der Mier had insisted that defensive walls be erected to block hacker access to the computer systems. It was now impossible, they had been assured, for someone to gain entry without a proper series of computer codes. But there was no defense for technology against the removal of its electric lifeblood, just as the mightiest armies would crumble, if the sky were stripped of oxygen.

It was such a simple way to disarm technology. Cohen felt embarrassed by his now-evident reliance on it. What if his night-vision should malfunction? He would be wading through an infinity of shadow, shadows cast without light, with only a spindly torch in hand, slashing through a jungle with a penknife, helpless to protect the inexplicable treasures that hung all around him, his only charge.

He had once read that the blind compensate by honing their other senses, such as hearing, to monitor their surroundings. It was with this in mind that Cohen had ordered his guards to tread lightly and keep off the walkie-talkies. It was unclear what sound he hoped to hear. Would it not be better to hear nothing, rendering this a false alarm? Not for him. But what? The sound of canvas cut from frame in a distant room? The tread of muffled feet on the wooden floor at the other end of the gallery? The museum had been disarmed with such elegance. It seemed ludicrous to assume that the theft itself would be any less graceful.

Cohen stopped for a moment. He stood in the center of a gallery, switched off his night-vision, and looked around. He saw nothing, of course, but he looked. His eyes pored through the thick fog blackness, this abyss in which he floated, aware of his grounding only through the feel of feet on floor. A meditative calm permeated the air. The museum, tomblike, deprived the senses. He was buried alive, yet breathed above ground. But his mind did not play tricks. Deep inhalation. He did not see what was not there. He simply did not see.

CHAPTER SEVENTEEN

Sonorous rumbles rolled forth from the open mouth of the sleeping Jean-Paul Lesgourges. His several gold-capped teeth glinted off the only light in his curtain-drawn bedroom: a shimmery sliver that knifed between two patterned curtains, from the street lamp outside. The telephone at his bedside had been ringing for several minutes.

By the third round of rings, Jean-Paul permitted one of his eyes to open and to stare down the villainous phone that chirped by his head. With his left eye still closed tight in hope of returning sleep, he extended his arm above his head, then down, then across, until it found the porcelain-white curve of the phone, which he dragged across the empty pillow beside him on his king-size bed. He eventually found his ear, beneath a hot tangle of sheet and pillowcase.

'Oui?'

The voice on the other end of the line came fast and sleepless. 'CH is the abbreviation for Chronicles.'

It was Bizot.

Lesgourges mumbled, 'Who is this?'

'C'est moi, Bizot! Tu sais bien que c'est moi, putain!'

Lesgourges rolled onto his back. 'Of course it's you, Jean. Who else calls me at . . . dear God . . . four in the morning. Now, what the hell do you want, so I can go back to sleep. I was dreaming of . . .'

'CH is the abbreviation for Chronicles.'

Lesgourges was silent.

Bizot continued, 'It's a book in the Bible.'

'Oh, right. Sans blague?'

'No, I'm not kidding, Lesgourges. I think that this may refer to a biblical quotation.'

'How the hell did you come up with that? I thought we'd decided it was a palindrome for . . .'

'I spoke with Geneviève Delacloche.'

'Qui?'

'The one with the beaux seins, the Malevich Society . . .'

'Oh yes.' Lesgourges yawned. 'You mentioned her.'

'Look, I'll tell you all about it, in person. Do you have a Bible?'

'What kind of a Catholic are you, Bizot, living in a house without a Bible? You should be ashamed of yourself. Were you raised by wolves?'

'So I can come over and use yours?'

'Oh, I don't have one. You'll have to steal one from a hotel. I think they have them in the bedside drawers . . .'

'I'm not going to check in to a hotel at four in the morning so I can steal a Bible. Don't you have the internet at your house?'

'Don't tell me that you're in so desperate a state that you're volunteering to sleep with the enemy?'

'As long as I'm not touching a computer myself, I can sleep at night. Feel no evil. You can do the touching.'

'I don't like the sound of that, but okay. Come over, Bizot. How long will you be?'

'Three seconds. I'm on my mobile phone outside your apartment.'

*   *   *

The police arrived at the museum before the creeping dawn. Thirteen minutes after Avery had left, six police cars screeched to a halt around the museum, and the building was surrounded. The police entered with large halogen flashlights and

142

panned through the rooms, now blue in earliest morning. Beams of light danced across the walls, over paintings still bolted in place. The guards were found, and each gallery on every floor was carefully scanned for missing works.

Nothing had been taken from the galleries. Cohen began to feel ashamed, and he was almost relieved when a broken window was discovered in the basement.

*   *   *

Lesgourges stirred the hot milk and dropped in purple-black pellets of Angelina's Chocolat Africain, dissolving the milk to a thick walnut richness. Then he slid the mug to Bizot, who sat on a stool in the glass-and-steel modern kitchen of Lesgourges' sleek apartment in the Sixteenth Arrondissement of 4 AM Paris.

'So I was interviewing this Delacloche about the case,' began Bizot, 'and I told her my idea about the writing on the wall turning the theft into a statement . . .'

'. . . my idea . . .'

'My idea,' Bizot resumed, 'and she thought that it was brilliant . . . so I asked her what sort of a statement the theft of this particular painting might make. And she told me a bit about it. Do you know about it, Jean?'

'I know . . . no, I guess I don't really know about Malevich.'

'Mmm, comme c'est bon.' Bizot sipped his cocoa. 'Well, I'll enlighten you. It turns out that the reason the painting in question is all white is that it is meant as the negation of the icon.

143

Malevich felt it to be spiritual, a better approximation of God than any formal image. Malevich thought that no formal image would do justice to portray God, so he chose an abstract one that suggested the idea of God to him. It removed things like iconography, which require specialized knowledge on the part of the viewer, in order to be understood. It's open to anyone. Malevich hung the painting in the corner to the upper left as you enter the gallery where it was exhibited. This replicated the place in a Russian home where an icon would hang. Instead of Mary and the baby Jesus, you get an all-white painting. Do you follow?'

'Want a cookie?' Lesgourges' attention was directed to a packet of madeleines that he was struggling to open. When he did, he dipped one of the firm almond cakes into his cocoa. 'This is going to be good. Like Proust, but more chocolaty.'

'Jean, were you listening to anything I just said?'

'Sure. White, God, chocolate. You should really try this.'

'It does look good, come to think of it.' Bizot dunked himself a madeleine.

'I'm not sure I follow you.' Lesgourges was dressed in his baby-blue pajamas, wrinkled with sleep, his little remaining hair a protruding shelf, perpendicular to his head.

'If the theft is a statement, then it must be a statement either for, or against, something. If the painting negates icons, then it goes against the church doctrine. So maybe . . .'

'I see. So CH347 could refer to a passage in the Bible, from the book of . . .'

144

'Chronicles.'

'Bizot, how did you think of which book it referred to? That's brilliant. So unlike you.'

'Actually, I had help with that part. I couldn't figure it out, but Delacloche suggested . . .'

'Did you call her at this time of night?'

'No, we spoke on the phone many hours ago. She'd been away on business, just returned. I was going to call you, but then I fell asleep. And then I was hungry, so I got a kebab behind St. Michel.'

'The stand near the movie theater?'

'Yes, that's the one. It's very good, although it usually needs salt.'

They sat in the kitchen in silence.

Eventually Lesgourges spoke. 'Shall we look for a Bible on the internet?'

'I suppose we should. We are godless men, aren't we?'

'Only if you believe that God has anything to do with the Bible. The computer's in the other room.'

Lesgourges sat before his computer, navigating inexpertly by mouse, with Bizot standing a safe distance back, arms crossed.

Bizot grumbled. 'I don't like anything . . .'

'. . . new. I know. This isn't new,' said Lesgourges. 'Computers have been around since before you were born.'

'Don't confuse me with the facts. I don't like them. I don't like anything smarter than I am.'

'But you like me.'

'Well . . . just do the typing, Lesgourges.'

'Right.'

The screen glowed the only light in the room, bathing the two men in a preposterous neon whiteness. They were reversed silhouettes, white

145

on black. Bizot's eyes lazily wandered the bookshelves. A thin film of dust caked most exposed horizontal surfaces.

'Do you own any literature?' Bizot asked.

'Of course.'

'These all sound like self-help books. I mean, *Life Is a Straight Line* by Macarena Plaza, *How to Find Things Very Interesting* by Alen Balde, *How to Find Everything So Great,* also by Alen Balde . . . mon Dieu . . . *Manual on Welsh Sexual Techniques* by Davyth Nelson . . .'

'It's not self-help. I got them in the philosophy section.' Lesgourges clicked away on the computer screen.

Bizot picked a book off the shelf. '*What It's All Aboot: Live Your Life the Canadian Way, Eh* by Andrew Hammond . . .'

'Will you stop fiddling? Here, I've logged on to the internet. What are we looking for?'

'What we need,' said Bizot, 'is a Bible . . . uh . . . what's it called when everything's linked up, you know, so you can look up one word and find all the examples . . .'

'A dictionary?' Lesgourges looked confused.

'No, not a dictionary. You know, where it lists . . .'

'A thesaurus?'

'No! Have you ever heard of a Bible thesaurus? What's the . . . we need a dictionary to look up the word for dictionary . . . ah! That's it. A concordance.'

'Oh, right.'

On the table next to the computer sat a framed black-and-white photograph of Lesgourges, with a full head of hair, his arms slung around a young

146

woman. The photo frame was dustless.

Lesgourges manipulated the keyboard with one hyperextended finger at a time.

'Now what do we do?' asked Bizot. 'We can just type in a passage name and number, and it will find it for us?'

'We'll never need to open a book again. What shall I enter?'

'Delacloche suggested that CH could be the abbreviation for the book of Chronicles. But 347 sounds like too many numbers for a chapter or verse. We should try all the combinations, and see if any of the passages make sense. Try,' Bizot considered, 'Chronicles, chapter 3, verse 4.' Lesgourges typed, and the screen stirred to action.

'This doesn't sound right.' Lesgourges read aloud: ' *"And the porch that was in the front of the house, the length of it was according to the breadth of the house, twenty cubits, and the height was a hundred and twenty: and he overlaid it within with pure gold."* We're looking for a clue, not instructions for do-it-yourself shed construction.'

Bizot rested chin on fist. 'That doesn't make any sense at all. Try the next one. Try Chronicles 3:7.' Lesgourges finger-typed, then spoke again: ' *"He overlaid also the house, the beams, the posts, and the walls thereof, and the doors thereof, with gold; and graved cherubim on the walls."* '

Bizot looked annoyed. 'It sounds like a magazine on interior decorating.'

'Could it describe a location?' Lesgourges lit one of his black, sweet cigarettes. 'Someplace that we're supposed to go, to find . . . uh . . . whatever it is we're supposed to find?'

'I can't imagine them leaving us clues as to

147

where we can retrieve the stolen painting. What would be the point . . . or can I,' Bizot whispered. 'If this is some sort of political statement, or show of power, then perhaps they don't want the painting at all. They just want to teach us a lesson, on our way to retrieve it. Like that case not long ago, where paintings were stolen from the Manchester Museum of Art, in England, and then they were found rolled up at a public lavatory nearby, unharmed. The thieves had just wanted to underline the insecurity of the system, and that too much concern is put on art, which the thieves felt was insignificant. Even the first Munch *Scream* theft, when the thieves left a note that read "Thanks for the poor security." If we're dealing with something similar, and we're meant to be taught a lesson, then the thieves may provide clues for us to follow. In that case, this may describe a place. But it doesn't sound like anywhere I know. The inside of a house painted entirely in gold, with baby angels carved into the walls? I don't know.

'Try the next one. Try Chronicles 4:7.'

Lesgourges resumed speaking through the lip-clench of his cigarette. ' "*And he made ten candlesticks of gold according to their form, and set them in the temple, five on the right hand, and five on the left.*" It could be instructions on direction, like a treasure hunt.' Lesgourges tapped his ash into a label-less, empty wine bottle. 'You know, take five paces to the right hand, then five to the left . . .'

Bizot nodded. '. . . add a pinch of salt, and bring to a boil . . . We would need a starting point, in order for these numbers to be directions. We can't walk five paces right, then five left, if we don't

148

know where to start walking from. There might be something in the numbers, ten, five, and five. But it's also possible that the reason that these passages don't make sense to us is not that we're misreading the clues, but that these may not be clues, at all. None have spoken to us as having an obvious connection. If we look too hard, we'll find that anything *might* pertain to the case. We could read the ingredients in a box of breakfast cereal, and if we try hard enough, we could apply it to this case. So caution, Lesgourges. We haven't run the gamut. Try Chronicles 3:47.'

The search engine whirred. 'That passage doesn't exist.'

'Then we can strike it from the list of suspects.' Bizot was fuming through his fourth cigarette. 'What's left? Is there a 34:7?'

Lesgourges typed. 'Here we are: *"And when he had broken down the altars and the groves, and had beaten the graven images into powder, and . . . ,"* shit, Jean, this is it.'

'What, what? Read it.'

' *"And when he had broken down the altars and the groves, and had beaten the graven images into powder, and cut down all the idols throughout the land of Israel, he returned to Jerusalem."* That's it, Bizot. What you were saying about the *White on White* being an anti-icon, negating the image of Jesus and Mary. It's a *false idol.* This passage is about the destruction of false idols. This isn't a political statement, or a flexing of muscle. It's a religious crusade, and Kasimir Malevich is the infidel.'

149

CHAPTER EIGHTEEN

It was not until the sun had fully risen that Elizabeth Van Der Mier arrived at the museum. In an elegant panic, Cohen thought. She restrained her anger as best she could, but only because she knew not where to thrust it. She would plunge it in to the hilt, but she needed a victim. Two attacks in two days. Glad I'm not to blame. Cohen shook his head.

The lights had gone out, an explosion had shaken the ground floor, a broken window, no electricity. With heavy lights, police excavated the smoky basement. The broken window was significant. The pane of glass missing was two feet square, large enough for a small person, or large person contorted. But there were no footprints to be seen.

The utility room was of particular interest. As the police led Cohen and Van Der Mier through the smog of dust particles, into the utility room, Van Der Mier saw the cause of the power outage. The control panel, which contained all of the fuses for the entire building, including the backup generator, had been destroyed. But the strangest thing was that it had been detonated while *inside* a locked steel cage.

'Mr. Cohen, would you care to explain to me how the hell that happened?' Van Der Mier's patience boiled.

Cohen and Van Der Mier were in the basement, when a police officer's walkie-talkie went off.

'Llewellyn to Jones, over.'

'What is it, Llewellyn?'

'I think that Ms. Van Der Mier should come up here.'

'We're down in the basement, looking around. We'll be up . . .'

'I think she should come here now.'

'What is it?'

'I'm in the Conservation Department . . .'

Van Der Mier slumped back, and was caught by a wall.

'Oh, dear God,' she whispered.

*   *   *

Inspector Harry Wickenden arrived at the National Gallery of Modern Art with a face only a mother could love. He carried an exceedingly large Styrofoam cup with a plastic top, which he removed to sip rhythmically, beneath baggy, dark eyes, and a brown sagging mustache, which hung down below his lips. His demeanor drooped, and his eyes seemed in a perpetual roll. He was very short, and he thumped along in orthopedic shoes that shuffled beneath a long khaki trench coat. His posture left something to be desired, as did his appearance, not unlike that of a basset hound. From behind his eyes, however, something flashed.

A police officer ran to meet Wickenden, as he entered the museum. 'Good morning, sir.'

'There is nothing good about a morning that begins before ten, officer. You'd think that the criminal world would have the decency not to burgle before breakfast.'

'Yes, sir. I'll take you up to the office of the museum's director, Ms. Elizabeth Van Der Mier.

She's not in a good mood, I should warn you.'

'Neither am I, but I paint on this rosy demeanor for your benefit. Take me to her.'

Wickenden and the officer worked their way through galleries, dim in the early morning light.

'We'll have to walk to the top floor, as the electricity is . . .'

'I've noticed the absence of light, thank you. Explain what is known, but not evident.'

They began the mount of the spiral marble staircase.

'Uh, right, we arrived around five in the morning, after having been called in by a security guard from the museum, a Ms. Jillian Avery. She'd been sent outside the museum to call us, because the electricity had been cut, from both primary and emergency power sources, neutralizing all communications and the security systems, all of which ran through the computers.'

'Technology will bite you in the bum, officer.'

'Yes, well . . .'

'You don't use one of those Palm Pilots, do you?'

'Uh, no, sir. I don't have . . .'

'That's good. A pen and paper can't delete itself. You may carve that on my tombstone.'

'Very well, sir. With the electricity out, the only defense was the locks on the outside doors. The overnight security captain, a Mr. Toby Cohen, ordered the remaining guards to disperse throughout the museum and listen for sounds of theft. They maintained contact through battery-powered walkie-talkies. They reported nothing, except an initial muffled explosion that shook the ground floor, and came as the lights first went out.

152

Other than that, nothing.'

'Sounds odd. That is my clinical diagnosis. But truth is stranger than fiction, I suppose. Nothing an author could contrive is half as bizarre as events that have truly happened. Don't you agree, officer?'

'Uh, yes, sir. We arrived and surrounded the building, for containment security. Then we swept all of the galleries, and found nothing missing. We went into the basement and found a broken window, but no footprints; and the cause of the power outage—the demolished remains of the fuse box, killed by explosive. But the wonky thing is that the explosion took place within a metal cage that's still locked.'

'A locked-room mystery? Perhaps it was worth getting up this early after all. Anything else?'

'Just Wednesday, a computer hacker had breached the system and manipulated the communications. It seemed to be a senseless act of capability, but it may be connected to last night.'

'Mmmph. Computers.'

'We also found what was stolen, sir . . .'

*   *   *

The sun spangled over the surface of the river Seine, with the yellow stone palaces draped in charcoal-colored rooftops, rising up alongside. Bizot was on his second pain au chocolat, as he turned onto rue d'Israël, and approached the narrow rectangular tower of the Malevich Society. Runt fingers crumbled crust across his jacket, as he dusted the oil and pastry from his good shaking hand.

153

He left an oily fingerprint on the doorbell and was soon greeted by the same breasty secretary. I'd like to work here, Bizot thought, as he stepped inside.

'False idols, what a load of crap,' Delacloche said in exasperation, after hearing Bizot's discovery. He looked nervously at her, then around her immaculately disheveled office.

'Do you mean you don't . . .'

'No, Monsieur Bizot, it's not that. I'm sure you are correct. It all makes sense. I'm just furious at ignorance. Why must the ignorant plague the informed? Cyclical poison. There's nothing so repulsive as violent ignorance wielded like a weapon. The idea that these philistines are capable of destroying . . .'

'I mean to prevent that from happening, madame . . . moiselle. If I may have your cooperation, I think that we can prevent any philistine . . . age.'

Delacloche bit the back of her fountain pen and leaned against her desk, with one leg bent against it. Around the office, each cabinet drawer and file was carefully labeled, handwritten in capital letters. But the papers were strewn all over the room to such an extent that one could not imagine that the files still contained anything at all.

'What we need, Mademoiselle Delacloche, is a starting point. And I think that it is somewhere here. We now have the motivation. The thieves may have made their point, but in doing so, they left us something to feed on. I think that we are dealing with a religious group, a violent one. Not in terms of bloodshed, but in terms of destructive capability and premeditated lawlessness.

Dangerous zealots. But this has, thus far, been conceived to a high polish. Such a clean crime.'

Delacloche offered Bizot a cigarette and lit one for herself. 'They've made their statement, but to whom? We've kept this out of the press. Who knows about it, besides you and I, and the others who work here at the Society?'

'They might have expected press.'

'Perhaps. But we shan't give it to them. Do you think they mean to destroy . . .'

'I'm not sure. It seems to be in no one's interest to destroy the work. It's like setting fire to a briefcase full of hundred-euro notes. We, as art police, rarely take seriously threats to destroy ransomed art. But what are the options, if not? One: they can keep it locked away. Two: they can hang it on their wall. Three: they can sell it. Given the motivation that we've determined, Two is not possible. That leaves One and Three. Any indication that someone might try to sell it?'

Delacloche looked up and to the right. She thought of Wednesday's day trip to London, then replied.

'No. I had thought they might, but . . . no.'

'We . . . I, think that this may be a political or religious statement, rather than a crime for profit or out of need. They can't sell it on any open market, so it would have to be sold to a private buyer who doesn't ask questions. That is where most art thieves are caught. It's not so hard to steal a painting, but it's very difficult to convert the painting into cash. Most illicit art fetches only seven to ten percent of the estimated legitimate value, and that is if a buyer can be found at all. So if they don't intend to sell it in the first place . . .'

155

'That makes more sense. In selling it,' Delacloche reasoned, 'they perpetuate its legacy. If their purpose is iconoclastic, if they want to bring down the anti-icon, then selling it to a buyer who will revere it as a great work of art . . . well, that would elevate it back to the status of icon. Anyone willing to buy it, in doing so, idolizes.'

'So that leaves option One: they mean to keep it locked away . . . or to destroy it altogether, both of which would accomplish the same end.' Bizot swayed on his heels, in thought. 'If they are indeed a violent religious group and aren't after money, then the risk of destruction becomes real.'

Delacloche was once again chewing on her pen. 'I'm a little nervous, monsieur, about the other Malevich *White on Whites.*'

'You have others?'

'Not here. But they were painted as a series. There are many of them, in museums and private collections around the world. One sold at Christie's the other day . . .'

'Wait, how many is many?'

'I have all of the extant ones filed here, but there may be more that we don't know of. I'm just worried that . . .'

'. . . they also might be in danger. I see.' Bizot paused for a long moment, taking in the gray carpeting. Delacloche interrupted.

'Monsieur?'

'I think we need to press on with concentration. I'll need your help, mademoiselle. The motivation is the key to solving crimes. There's no such beast as a motiveless crime, and the motive, once known, invariably leads to solution. The hardest part is past. What I need from you is point A. The start of

156

the trail. What did you find about the last person to request an audience with the *White on White*?'

Delacloche walked around her desk, mindful to step over the reams of paper strewn in neat stacks across the carpet. She sat in her chair and threw her black-stockinged legs onto the desk.

'His name is Christien Courtil. He's the curator of a gallery in Paris, near Invalides. It's called Galerie Sallenave. They specialize in Old Master prints, high-end stuff.'

'Isn't it odd, then, that he should want to see a Modern painting?'

'Yes, but he said that he was researching for a client.'

'That doesn't sound suspicious to you, mademoiselle?'

'Either everything, or nothing, in the art world sounds suspicious, Monsieur Bizot. It's like the weather in England. Either one carries an umbrella at all times, or never at all. But it is certainly worth looking into.'

'Who is the owner of the gallery. Not this Courtil?'

'No. He runs it, but it's owned by a vintner. He's from an old aristocratic family. They live in a castle in the southwest, between Biarritz and Pau. Independently wealthy, but he runs a couple of businesses: the vineyard around his family château in the south, the Old Master prints gallery here, in Paris, and he exports wine abroad, from other vineyards. His name is Luc Sallenave. He's getting on in years now. Must be nearly eighty. I've met him once, at a black-tie charity ball at the Musée Marmottan. He gives generously to support the arts. As far as I know, he collects only Old

Masters, and almost exclusively prints and rare books. A Malevich is certainly out of his profile. Maybe . . .'

'I think I know how to get audience with him. What is his address in Paris?' Bizot pulled out his Moleskine notebook and, with minimal ensnarement, unsnapped the elastic, and began to note.

'It's not listed, but I'm sure I have it somewhere. Give me a moment.' Delacloche rummaged a bit more, flashing through a file cabinet, until her fingers found their target. 'Here we are. His mailing address is care of the gallery, but it seems that he owns the whole building. The gallery is on the ground and first floor, but the second and third floors are one large private apartment. His primary residence is his château, but it seems that his pied-à-terre in Paris is directly above the print shop.'

'What's the address?'

'It's on rue de Jérusalem, number forty-seven.'

'You've been most helpful, Mademoiselle Delacloche. One last thing. I think we should check the safety-deposit box, and see if the password and the third key are still where they should be. Perhaps tomorrow morning?'

'Uh'—Delacloche scanned a finger over her calendar—'that should . . . that should be fine. We'll speak in the morning.'

'Very well. À demain.'

*   *   *

Outside, Bizot closed the door to the Malevich Society behind him. The new information shuffled through his thoughts.

Memory, he'd often liked to think, was like an enormous library of files and books in one's head. A memorial library not *to* someone, but *of* someone. He pictured his memorial library as painted a pale mint green, with file cabinets stacked to the rafters, higher than the eye could see. An enormous tapering ladder rested against one of the multitudinous walls of shelves and drawers, which encircled a small wooden desk, at which sat his mental librarian. Bizot imagined that his mental librarian was an elderly man, bent over and frizzle-white-haired, wearing suspenders and wool trousers hiked up above his waist, with a clerk's translucent green visor, and the stub of a chewed pencil behind his ear.

When Bizot wished to recall an obscure memory, the request would come over a loudspeaker. His librarian would grumble, surprised, and say, 'You want *what* now?' Then he would shuffle off to look up the request, mumbling curses under his breath, down one of the corridors of book stacks emanating, like sun rays, from the central desk and the librarian's rickety wooden armchair, the seat of Memory.

As Bizot reached the end of the street, he turned back to look at the Malevich Society. Then his sight caught on something. He did not register what it was, at first, but he knew that it was important. He stopped walking. He looked around.

The street was empty, save for a scattering of leaves tossed in the gentle breeze off the nearby river Seine. What was it that he had seen, that jogged him? He turned slowly in a full circle. Then

159

he realized.

CHAPTER NINETEEN

'The Kasimir Malevich *White on White* that we bought just two days ago and was sitting in the Conservation Room! Of course that's what was stolen! Fuck fuck fuck fuck fuck . . .' Van Der Mier paced back and forth in front of her desk, as Inspector Harry Wickenden, Toby Cohen, and an officer hid on chairs. 'It was the most prominent acquisition in years, the centerpiece of a huge upcoming exhibition, and . . .'

'. . . And you say that it's just white?' Wickenden fiddled with the pipe in his coat pocket, his nervous habit. He never smoked.

'Yes, Kasimir Malevich's *Untitled Suprematist Composition White on White,* which we just bought for £6.3 million. And of course they took that one, just my crap luck. The insurance was still being dealt with, for Christ's sake! The painting wasn't even bolted to the wall, it was sitting on an easel. The only defense to the Conservation Room is the alarm and the lock on the door, which doesn't work without electricity!'

'Why, Ms. Van Der . . . you know . . . ,' began Wickenden. 'Why was the painting in Conservation?'

'It was being examined and cleaned before the unveiling, as part of a high-profile exhibition that starts next month. The exhibition had been in the works for over a year, and we were hoping to . . . going to add this recent purchase to it. I mean,

160

think of the negative publicity. We've already had the press conference and everything.'

'I can't afford to consider your face, and the saving of it, Ms., uh . . .'

'Van Der Mier. Elizabeth Van Der Mier. It's written on this piece of plastic on my desk.' She indicated the nameplate.

'No matter. I shan't remember it anyway. Terrible with names. But I will find your painting. If you will cooperate with me during the investigation.'

'Inspector, have you dealt with art crimes before?'

'If you examine my illustrious career, then you will find that I have, ma'am. I am a member of Scotland Yard's Arts and Antiquities Division. I do not have an art-historical training, but that has not dulled my success rate, which is considerable. I have confidence, ma'am . . .'

'. . . But you haven't even heard of Malevich's *White on White* . . .'

'Advance knowledge of the artist is not requisite to success. I can, as they say in the industry, "look it up."' Wickenden spoke in a slow, monotone drone that quickly annoyed the frantic and neurotic, as in this instance.

'Detection is an act of problem-solving, not of scholarship,' he continued. 'Research may be one manner of detective work, but I deal with people who are alive, and think, and act as rationally as they are capable. Mathematicians don't need to know their multiplication tables. That's why there are calculators. If I need to do some homework on the art of Klezmer Malich, then I shall be happy to do so. Keeps the brain from calcifying, anyway. Or

161

I'll ask questions of an expert. In the meantime, until I find your painting, which I shall, if you'll just indulge me . . .'

Van Der Mier sat now, on the edge of her desk, arms crossed, unsure what to say. She finally settled on 'All right.'

'I think I shall take a tour of the facilities. Which way?'

Cohen stepped forward. 'I'll accompany you, Inspector.'

'No,' said Wickenden, 'I meant the toilet facilities. And some things, sir, are best done alone.'

*　　　*　　　*

Bizot stood in the middle of the street, staring at the street sign. Rue d''Israël. The address of the Malevich Society. Why did that give him pause? He could feel the coiling knot of inspiration. But what? Where was the connection? What had he just been discussing with Delacloche? Bizot tried to remember. He opened his notebook and scanned through. The address of the Galerie Sallenave . . . Rue de Jérusalem. What had the . . . and then it sifted into place.

'And when he had broken down the altars and the groves, and had beaten the graven images into powder, and cut down all the idols throughout the land of Israel, he returned to Jerusalem.'

'The land of Israel.' Rue d'Israël. 'He returned to Jerusalem.' Rue de Jérusalem. That was it. Bizot fumbled for his mobile phone and dialed.

'Jean, c'est moi. You're not going to believe this . . .'

*   *   *

'So that's as much as we know, so far, sir.' Wickenden walked a step behind Cohen, who now approached a closed blond-wood door with the words CONSERVATION DEPARTMENT stamped on its chest. There was a black box on the right-hand side of the door, with a small red-and-green light on its face. There was also a thin slot running vertically along its length.

Cohen pushed the door open. Wickenden looked surprised.

'Isn't there a lock . . .'

'. . . only with . . .'

'. . . electricity. Right. Why don't the doors default into the locked position? Wouldn't that make more sense?'

'Fire regulations. A fucking pain, if you don't mind my saying so.'

'I don't.' Wickenden didn't. They entered the Conservation Room.

The ceiling rose before them, as high as any of the galleries. The honey-colored wood-paneled walls were broken at regular intervals by large windows on one side, and hung canvases on the others. A door at the back of the room was labeled SCIENCE & TECHNOLOGY. The floor was dotted with enormous easels, some of them gripping works of art. One easel in the center of the room looked particularly vacant. On the floor beside it lay an empty wooden stretcher, the edges of the cut-away canvas still nailed in place.

'It was . . .' Cohen began.

'I know.' Wickenden nodded toward the empty

163

easel with three stools lined up before it. He shuffled slowly around the room, then merely stood still in its midst. He fingered the pipe in his trench coat pocket violently, as he calmly moved his gaze in horizontal sweeps, resting briefly on every object visible. His eyes caressed and digested the intricacies of shadow and shape. His breath came slowly, ruffling his low-hanging mustache tassels, which shook with each exhalation.

'What,' Wickenden asked, 'is in there?' He pointed to the Science & Technology door.

'That's, uh . . .' Cohen scratched his head.

'. . . And I can read what it says on the door. More explicative, please.'

'It contains the technical equipment employed by the Conservation and Restoration Department,' Elizabeth Van Der Mier said, walking through the open door behind them. 'I want to see what you find firsthand, Inspector.'

'Pleasure, ma'am.'

'I'll show you.'

Van Der Mier led Wickenden into the Science & Technology Room, windowless and dark. The police officer and Cohen spread flashlight beams, illuminating computers, filing cabinets, a microscope, an easel, and what looked like equipment best suited for dental hygiene.

'X-radiograph, ultraviolet light, black light, microscopes, chemical analysis stations . . . Everything we use for scientific analysis of artworks for the purpose of conservation. Thousands of pounds' worth of equipment, here for the taking. But it all looks intact.'

They withdrew from the room. Wickenden spoke. 'What strikes me as initially odd is the

164

abundance of stealables.'

'Of what?'

'Stealables, Ms. Van Dyke. Objects of value that would be easy to take. A gold ring on a bedside table is one example. A stack of fifty-pound notes wrapped in rubber bands inside the refrigerator is a stealable. A . . .'

'And a painting sitting on an easel in an unlocked room.'

'Precisely, ma'am. As are the hundreds of paintings, sitting on the gallery walls, that could have been taken. A thief without greed is a thief with a purpose. Focused, practical, intelligent, deliberate, moderate, clean. We've already a barrage of adjectives that radically limit our suspect pool. How many people do you know who would fit all of the aforementioned? I think that "clean" is the only adjective that I can apply to my circle of friends. And I myself do not claim to be possessed of that quality, in any great abundance.'

'I'm listening, Inspector.' Van Der Mier escorted the party out of the Conservation Room and toward the basement.

'It's commissioned; otherwise the thieves would have taken more. And the commissioner knew of your recent acquisition. And it's an inside job.'

'A what? Be careful, Inspector, before I start accusing my employees of being a party to this. Why do you think that it's an inside job?'

'I'll reserve absolute judgment. But the thieves knew that the painting was in Conservation.'

'But anyone could have known that it would first be in Conservation.'

'And why is that, ma'am?'

'Because I announced it at the press conference

yesterday.'

'Oh.'

Wickenden continued to walk, looking down at the floor. After a long pause, he continued. 'As I said, I shall reserve absolute judgment . . .'

In the basement of the museum, flashlights brightened the corridor that led to the utility room. Wickenden kept his eyes along the floor and walls. He stopped over the pool of broken glass. The open window, where the pane had been, sat over his left shoulder.

'Here we are.' Cohen reached out for the metal utility room door, then noticed that Wickenden was still back at the broken window, down the hall.

'Just a moment,' Wickenden mumbled. Van Der Mier tried to follow his gaze, but she could not tell what he was investigating so closely. Wickenden was muttering to himself. 'This thief or thieves knows or knew what he or they were or are doing.'

'What?' Van Der Mier struggled to see what had captured Wickenden's attention.

'Look at the glass that remains in the broken windowpane.'

Van Der Mier followed his finger to the top of the pane where, among the few remnants of glass still intact, a thin, clean vertical line could be seen.

'A glass cutter,' Wickenden made a cross-hatched wave with his still-extended finger, and giggled a bit. 'And watch your feet, Ms. Van Damme.' He crumpled over onto the floor, balanced on balls of feet. Wickenden ran his hands just above the tide of glass shards on the floor. Then he looked up to the windowpanes still intact. Then back to the floor. 'Why don't you have alarm glass in these basement windows?'

166

Van Der Mier looked at the windowpanes. They did not have the graph of black lines built inside the glass that would have triggered the alarm if the pane were shattered, and the lines broken.

'I hadn't even noticed, since I've taken over.'

Cohen approached. 'Allow me, ma'am. Inspector, I've been here since the museum was first established, for the past two directors before Ms. Van Der Mier took over a year and a half ago. The alarm glass is only on the upper floors, because the doors that lead from the basement to the galleries are locked from both sides. So you'd need security access cards to get up to the galleries, if you were to break in through the basement windows.'

'Unless, of course, you shut the electricity off first.' Wickenden buried his tongue inside his left cheek, as he often did when both thoughtful and annoyed.

'Right.'

'That's something that I suggest you address for future security concerns.' Wickenden stepped over the glass and toward the utility room, as he continued, 'There's no footprint in the glass.'

'How did they avoid disturbing it when they climbed in?' Cohen now looked at the glass once more.

'I have no idea,' said Wickenden without breaking stride. 'But I'll get back to you on that.'

Wickenden pushed open the utility room door and walked through.

'Don't you want to dust for fingerprints before you touch that?' Cohen asked from behind.

Oops, thought Wickenden, and then said, 'These thieves were too clever to leave prints, my

167

good man. They would surely have been gloved.'

The utility room was silted with dust, and fragments of metal scattered the floor. As flashlights cracked the darkness that was muffled only by a few thin strips of window, Wickenden surveyed the carnage. A once-proud steel cage, with links barely a centimeter apart, now lay mangled and twisted, blown open by what must have been a significant concussion. Cohen's light shone on the black void that once contained the fuse box.

'The problem,' Cohen began, 'is that the steel cage was locked, and the key to it is in the control room. So there was no way to get past the cage, and the explosive couldn't have been pushed through the cage links, as they're too small. Also, the fuse box is locked with a separate key that's also kept up at Control. That's two locked doors.'

'I love locked-room mysteries.' Wickenden's face was emotionless, but the space behind his eyes gave him away.

Treading cautiously, and tripping nevertheless, Wickenden threaded his way through the rubble, to the carcass on the wall that once was a fuse box. Wickenden ran his forefinger along the curve of the pipe in his pocket. His wedding ring clicked against the wood of the pipe. He craned his face right up next to the wall. Van Der Mier wasn't sure, but it looked as though he were sniffing.

'The explosive was placed inside the fuse box.' Wickenden spoke directly into the sooty wall, mere inches from his examining eyes.

'How do you know that?' asked Van Der Mier.

Without turning around, Wickenden pointed back toward the door through which they'd come.

168

Van Der Mier looked down at the floor by her right foot. There were the bent remnants of the fuse box door, the inside of which was charred.

'Which means,' continued Wickenden, 'that the cage was also breached. Now, how? With a key, or lock pick?'

A police officer picked up his walkie-talkie.

'Sam, can you check into the control room? We're keen to see if the keys to the utility room fuse box and the protective cage are still where they should be. And run fingerprints on that.'

'So . . .' Wickenden spun around now and raised his hand dramatically. 'What have we, thus far? A window broken with the help of a glass cutter. No footprints. An explosion from inside the fuse box, which was locked, and which, itself, was inside a locked cage. The electricity goes. The museum is disarmed and darkened. A thief or thieves slips or slip up to the Conservation Room, and make off with a recently purchased all-white painting by Kramer Malevitsky that was being cleaned, and which they knew was there. They escape with the rolled-up canvas, probably through the same window, without detection. Now, what's wrong with this picture?' He paused. 'Tell me again what happened two nights ago, with the thing with the computer thing.'

*   *   *

Later the next day, Robert Grayson returned home from his brief business trip to New York. When he opened the door to his flat and carried his suitcase into the bedroom, he found the skylight shattered, glass across the floor, and the

169

smell of night rain, which had fallen through the paneless window, onto his hardwood bedroom floor.

It was only after he'd called the police that he walked into his living room, and saw the open, empty wooden crate where once his new, ugly Suprematist painting had rested.

CHAPTER TWENTY

Delacloche and Bizot, like an icicle and the puddle below it, stepped out of the elevator, behind a bank clerk. She led them past a security guard, and through an iron gate, along a faded mint-green-carpeted hall, through smells of must and musk and dust, and dusk slowly rose outside the barred windows.

They turned to walk between two rows of identical metal boxes, each fitted with a small keyhole. The flow of cookie-cut containers made Bizot dizzy, and he wished that he had paused for a bite to eat en route. They finally stopped, and the clerk fitted her key into the box, sliding it out part of the way.

'Voudriez-vous l'examiner dans une chambre privée?'

Delacloche hesitated, then Bizot replied. 'No, thank you. We don't need a private room. We can look at it here.'

'D'accord. Appellez-moi quand vous êtes prêts à partir.' The bank clerk walked away, disappearing down a parallel row of shiny metal.

Bizot turned to the box before him. It was about

one meter long, one foot across and one deep. A sliding lid hid its contents. Bizot nodded Delacloche toward the lid, and she slid it open.

Inside lay neatly stacked files, a black briefcase, and a small safe with a combination lock. There was also a manila envelope, clasped with a red string. Delacloche reached for the envelope and unwound the clasp. She inverted it and the contents fell out into her hand: a piece of paper with numbers typed onto it, and one small silvery key.

'It's here,' she whispered, with a tone that Bizot read as both relieved and confused. 'What does that mean?'

'Permettez-moi, mademoiselle.' Delacloche stepped aside for Bizot, who took up the key in his short fingers. He held it in gloved hands, along its edge, up to the dull fluorescent light of the 1950s interior. Bizot rotated the key beneath the light. Then he stopped, suddenly.

'What is it?' Delacloche could not see what he saw.

Bizot turned away from the safety-deposit box, and walked over to an examination table, key in hand. He flicked on the lamp that sat on the table, and held the key up close to it. He rolled it around, to see it from all sides.

'Putain de merde . . . ,' he whispered.

'What is it?'

'Look at this.' Bizot moved aside, as Delacloche approached. She leaned in close to the lamplight and squinted down at the key held between Bizot's forefinger and thumb. He swiveled his wrist left, then right, then left again.

'The light,' said Delacloche under her breath,

171

'there's no light reflecting off the key. That means . . .'

'. . . that means that there's some substance on the surface of the key that should not be there. Something that has left a film, a residue, that's preventing the light from shining off the metal. An oily residue from . . .'

'. . . wax.'

'Good work, mademoiselle. Wax. Someone pressed the key into a block of wax and neglected to clean it afterward. This key has been copied.'

*　　　*　　　*

Harry Wickenden finished his pudding, as his generously proportioned wife, Irma, gathered the dishes.

'Do you want any more?' she asked.

'Nah.'

'Do you want any coffee?'

'Nah.'

'Tea?'

'Nah.'

'Right.' Irma shuffled into the kitchen. 'I might have a cup, then.' There was some clanging about, and sounds of rinsing, then the boiling hiss, then the pouring gurgle. The drop of milk, and the clink of spoon. The tap dry, rinse beneath the spigot, and thud of the stack to dry. Harry's tight shoulder twitched with each new sound. He gently pressed his closed eyes with his fingers.

He got up from his cracked vinyl chair at the kitchen table, pristine and clean as was the rest of the tiny flat in South London. He moved in his dilapidated slippers along the off-green carpeting,

172

as Irma loudly mumbled, mouth-filled, 'The apple crisp is nice.'

Harry climbed into his study, formerly the second bedroom of the house, vacant for many years now. He closed the warped door behind him, as much as it would close, then passed the faux-walnut bookshelf on his left, before he reached his felt-topped desk. It was the only one of the five rooms that Irma Wickenden allowed to contain dust and clutter, because she did not care to enter it.

Harry slumped into the chair behind the desk. He tried to throw his feet onto the desktop, but they failed to clear and fell back to the ground. He did not try again. His eyes glazed over the walls. A collection of faded photographs, pinned at top and bottom, and curled in on the sides. The yellowing triangled Tottenham Hotspurs banner. A stick-figure drawing of a house and three people, two large and one short, made in red and black crayon. The off-white porcelain pig with a coin slot on its back sat on top of the chest-height bookshelf, next to the dusty football trophy. One photograph was in a frame, but it was turned toward the wall. Their son had been only ten years old. But that had all happened many years ago.

'I'm going to put on the telly,' came the voice from the far side of the wall. Wickenden dragged the rubber band off the manila folder that occupied pride of place on his desk. He gently spread the lips apart, to reveal the case. He cracked his knuckles one by one. His nose twitched in the still, dusty air. The sun had fully set outside the small window behind him. The phone rang.

'Telephone, dear,' came the shout from the next

173

room. Harry picked up the line.

'Yup, it is. Nope. Yup. Nope. Nope. Yup. That's right. But isn't there someone else? I'm up to my arse in . . . Really? Disarmed alarm. Is that so? You're kidding. Suprematist? Like the . . . yeah. What's the name? Robert Grayson. And the address? Right. No, glad you called, Ned. I'll check it out in the morning. Right, first thing. No, it could be. Could be. Can't hurt. Give my best to . . . you know. Ta.'

He returned the receiver to its cradle.

Harry sat for a long while. Then he reached out for one of the pipes on his desk, a gnarled, dark, woody one, and began to fondle it.

He sat for a while longer, staring indirectly at nothing in particular.

*   *   *

Early the next morning, the doorbell rang to the flat in St John's Wood.

Robert Grayson, wearing only his navy-blue terry cloth robe and a coffee cup in hand, opened the door. In the hallway stood Gabriel Coffin and Daniela Vallombroso. Robert gestured them in.

'I was wondering when you'd get here,' Grayson said. 'Now what the hell happened to my painting?'

*   *   *

Several hours later, the doorbell rang again.

Robert Grayson, now bathed and clothed in a white T-shirt and blue jeans, and with coffee cup in hand, opened the door to his St John's Wood

174

flat. In the hallway stood a slightly hunched, short man, dressed entirely in shades of brown, who seemed in need of an increase in tire pressure. Grayson stood there for a moment, before he spoke.

'I'm sorry, I don't have any spare change.'

'Pardon?' The deflated figure in the doorway looked confused, but did not seem drunk. Grayson reciprocated the confusion.

'My apologies. May I help you?'

'Are you the American, Robert Grayson, the occupant of this flat?'

'No. I killed and ate him. The remains are in the refrigerator. I was just defrosting lunch, if you'd like to . . .'

'Jokes aren't funny.'

'That depends on who's telling them.' Grayson paused. 'And if there are any moose in the punch line.'

There was a long pause.

'I'm going to assume that you are Mr. Grayson, and that I don't like you. But that's as may be. Did you, or did you not, have an anonymous Suprematist painting stolen from the premises?'

'Oh, yes, yes I did.'

'Then you are, in fact, Mr. Grayson.'

'Yes.'

'Mmmph.'

The brown man pushed past Grayson, into the flat.

'I am Inspector Harry Wickenden of Scotland Yard's Arts and Antiquities Division. I was contacted by the police after they took your information yesterday, regarding the theft. I'm here to help . . . believe it or not.'

175

Grayson closed the front door slowly. Wickenden, full steam ahead, was already around the corner, and headed for the bedroom. Grayson followed.

Wickenden stood in the bedroom, his neck craned up to the skylight.

'Excuse me, Inspector. I'm sorry, I do appreciate your coming. But before we proceed, could I just see your . . .'

Without turning around, Wickenden extended his left hand back behind him, at the end of which was held his identification.

'Right. Coffee?'

'No, Wickenden. Now, where was the painting?'

'In the living room. I'm honored that Scotland Yard would take this robbery so seriously, but frankly, don't you people have better things to do? I mean, this painting cost me just fifteen hundred pounds. I make that in a couple of hours. Is there some other reason why Arts and Antiquities is interested in this?'

They walked into the living room, Wickenden in the lead. 'I'm not at liberty to say.'

'That sounds like a yes, Inspector.'

'Was anyone in here before me?'

Grayson tried to see what Wickenden was looking at. He could not make it out.

'No, why?'

'Are you sure?'

'Well, I . . . I mean, the two policemen came when I called to report the theft.'

'Is that all?'

'Oh, and the investigator from my insurance company.'

'So quickly?'

176

'I called the company as soon as the piece went missing.'

'It's Sunday today.'

'I'm a good client.'

'I'll bet you are. Let's go over what happened.'

Grayson spoke from the kitchen. He was making a sandwich. 'I gave a full report to the police.'

'Humor me.'

'All right. I came home from a brief business trip to New York and found the skylight broken open. The painting was gone from inside the transport crate, canvas cut out of the wooden canvas-holder thingy. But nothing else was taken, nothing disturbed. I noticed that my alarm clock was flashing. The policemen told me that the fuse had been cut to my apartment.'

'I know. That's why the alarm didn't go off when the skylight broke.'

'But how did the fuse get cut?'

'That's a good question, Mr. Grayson. I'm working on it. What can you tell me about the painting?'

'Not much. Hey, can you smell this mayonnaise?' Grayson leaned over the island that separated the kitchen and living room, brandishing an open jar. 'It's been around awhile, and it smells kind of funky. What do you think?'

'I don't eat mayonnaise. And it's called "salad cream." About the painting?'

Grayson stuck his nose in the jar, shrugged, and began to spread its contents on two slices of wheat bread. 'I don't know anything about it. I bought it on a whim. I paid just about the lowest a guy can, at a Christie's auction. I kind of liked it. The colors

177

were maybe a bit funny, but it had something, I don't know. I didn't do any research, if that's what you mean. Why, do people think it's worth more than I paid? As far as I know, it's anonymous, painted around 1920 or so, Russian, in the Suprematist style. But you know all of that. Should I have turkey or ham?'

'Turkey. Do you have any idea who might have known that the painting was here? If, as you say, nothing else was taken, then the thief or thieves wanted only that. That means they knew what they were looking for, and were not greedy.'

'Who would commission the theft of a fifteen-hundred-pound painting that everyone but me thinks is hideously ugly?'

'I didn't say anything about commissioning, Mr. Grayson. What makes you suggest that?'

'Well, if I was going to steal a painting, I'd hire a professional to do it for me. But if I were going to the trouble to steal a painting, I'd certainly choose something more exciting than an anonymous Suprematist that costs less than a night at the Ritz.'

'Yes. You're right, I'm sure. Who would have known that you'd bought this work?'

'Well, anyone who was at the Christie's auction. Some of my colleagues in the States. Come to think of it, there was something funny at the auction. Might be connected. Can't believe I didn't think of it sooner. As I was leaving the auction house, these three guys, business types, stopped me. They were perfectly polite, but it seemed like they were trying to intimidate, you know? Anyway, they said that their employer had wanted them to buy the painting I'd bought, and they hadn't been

178

able to bid, or something. They offered me ten thousand pounds for it, on the spot. I told them that the money wasn't an issue, and I liked the painting, so I'd keep it. Frankly, I thought they were playing around. I can't imagine wanting to pay that much for any piece of art, much less what I'd bought.'

'I'm glad that you remembered the incident. You are not an art collector, Mr. Grayson?'

'Me? No. I've got some vintage photos, but that's about it. No, I like some things, and I don't understand much of any of it. I know what I like, and I liked this one. But if the bidding had gone much higher, I would've been happy to let it pass. I like the thrill of the auction, more than what you get to take home after it.'

'Would you recognize the three men who accosted you?'

'Gosh, I'm not sure. I guess I might. I didn't look too closely at them. They were all dressed just about the same, and they didn't have any features that really jumped out at me. I don't know, maybe.'

'Right, Mr. Grayson, thank you for your time. I'll leave you to enjoy your turkey and salad cream sandwich. We'll let you know if we find anything. I hope that your painting may be restored to you.'

'Me too. Thanks for coming by. Boy, this country sure is something, when they'll send out a big-shot detective from Arts and Antiquities for a nothing little painting like that. I sure appreciate it. I'd really like to get it back.'

Grayson waved good-bye to Wickenden and closed the front door. He turned and walked back into his flat, throwing his uneaten sandwich into

179

the rubbish bin as he passed.

CHAPTER TWENTY-ONE

Harry was hunched over the remnants of his corned beef and cabbage. Irma cleared the last of the dishes. She reached in for his plate.

'Still eating.'

'Oh. Sorry, dear. Would you like some pudding?'

'Nah.'

'Tea?'

'Nah.'

'I think I'll have a cup.'

Irma moved the plates into the sink and wiped down the counter twice. Switched on the spigot, poured in water, clicked kettle, water hissed, into pot, steep, splashed in milk, into cup.

Harry was in the study and heard nothing. There was a knock at the study door. Harry looked up from the open file. The door creaked open a short way. Irma, tea in hand, peeked in.

'How's the case coming, dear?'

'Fine.'

'Think I'll watch the telly.' Irma withdrew from the threshold and pulled shut the door behind her.

Harry looked over at the rotary telephone that sat on the corner of his desk. The sounds of BBC *Ground Force* emanated from the other room. Harry turned to the folder and picked up a pipe, which he rubbed between two fingers.

Irma was giggling to herself, as Charlie, Alan, and Tommy remade the garden of an unsuspecting victim. Irma's face was rounded with the blue light of the screen. The teacup was nestled in the pink robe on her copious lap.

'Irma?'

Harry was standing in the doorway. Irma didn't say anything.

'Could I . . . I'm having some . . . Could I watch with you, for a tick?'

'Of course, luv.' She patted the green corduroy sofa pillow beside her, and lurched herself over a bit. Harry sat, arms crossed.

The credits ended. Irma got up and switched off the television. She returned to the sofa. 'So?'

Harry hadn't moved. 'I'm having a . . . if we could maybe . . .'

'I'll put the kettle on. How about some leftover spotted dick?'

'Nah. Ta. It just helps me to . . .'

'. . . I know. I'll just nip into the kitchen to grab myself a piece.'

Irma was off, rooting through the refrigerator. Harry put his slippered feet on the coffee table.

'So, a few days earlier some computer hacker broke into their system . . .'

'. . . You always warn people off computers . . .'

'. . . I know, and to top it off, they had all their internal communications linked through the computer, and all the security functions. I mean, I was in the WC, and a computer flushed for me as soon as I stood up. You may as well lop off my hands, as I won't be needing them anymore.'

'You always said . . .'

'. . . I know, thank you very much. Does anyone listen? No, I . . .'

'I do.'

181

'. . . Then they found that the motion detectors were being manipulated by this computer hacker. I mean, what was wrong with card catalogues? You can't hack up a card catalogue!'

'Hack *into,* dear.'

'So I arrive at the museum after their second crisis of the week. The first one they didn't report, of course. Can I have a spot more tea?'

'Surely, luv.' Irma poured a fresh cup, milk first.

'Ta. Then they call in the infantry when the electricity gets cut the other night. They had beefed up the security *inside* the computer, but not out! Would you believe it? So all of a sudden the power goes out, which eliminated the fancy computer and the telephones, so they had to run one of their men out to get us. Then they notice that a painting by Kamiser Malich is missing, one they just bought for six million quid, I might add. And all these pearl necklace types are bobbing round the museum, looking distressed, and there's me in the loo with an automatic flushing machine, I tell you. Well, turns out that someone blew the bollocks out of all the fuses in the building, and had planted the bomb inside the closed fuse box, which was inside a steel cage. Slipped in and out through a broken window in the basement. And that about sizes it up.'

'Anything else, luv?'

'Not sure if it's related, but Ned called me with a theft from a posh flat in St John's Wood. Wouldn't have called me in, but it was a Suprematist painting, same style as the one from the museum, and also bought at the same auction. And the electricity to the flat had been switched off, which rings a bell. What do you make of it?'

'Which part is giving you particular grief?' Irma sipped her tea and ate her spotted dick.

'Well, I don't like how easily security measures are neutralized, but that's not my job, I guess. Mine is not to prevent, it is to cure. But this theft is so specific. Nothing taken but this one, new acquisition. So, tomorrow I'm going through the Christie's surveillance videos, to see who was at the auction. I'd guess that it was an interested, moneyed party in attendance at the auction. Maybe they lost to the museum, or didn't want to pay the full price. Thieves cost less than the art they steal. Why didn't the thieves steal the first night, when they had control of the computers? Why did they wait until the electricity was out, a day later?'

Irma sipped. Then she put down her cup, only to pick it up again. Then she sipped once more. 'It's the Maginot Line. They circumnavigated the defenses, instead of confronting them, luv. Went round.' Irma rolled the letter r, like a Spaniard. She was silent for a moment. 'When did you say the stolen painting was purchased?'

'What? Oh, last Wednesday night, the auction was.'

'And when did the computer thingy happen at the museum?'

'Last Wed— Irma, you're brilliant.'

*   *   *

Dim fluorescent lights whirred far overhead. The periphery of the hulking warehouse was in shadows, and night waited patiently outside. What little light that was provided by the selected

183

fluorescents revealed five figures.

One of them, Professor Simon Barrow, was dark- and red-eyed and wore pajamas beneath his overcoat. Two stood with their arms crossed, bulges over hearts beneath jackets, on either side of the one formally dressed figure. He stood tall and well-postured, flaxen hair fading into white, in a blue pin-striped suit, with ironed-crisp cuff-linked wrists. The fifth figure was a woman. She wore blond hair tied up in a bun, and a white lab coat. She sat on a stool, with her back to the four men. There were also two canvases, resting on easels, in the room. The woman in the lab coat was bent over one of them.

Barrow squinted. He had not had time to put in his contact lenses. Then he remembered his glasses, in his overcoat pocket, which he slipped on. His world blurred into view. Barrow did not expect what he saw.

What the hell is going on? He thought. Then he spoke. 'What the hell is going on?'

'Pa-patience, Dr. Barrow.' The flaxen man spoke with a cool, aristocratic British accent. 'All will be revealed. Literally.'

*   *   *

'So the computer hack was preparatory for the actual theft. The painting the thieves wanted to steal was not yet in the museum!' Wickenden was standing now, dancing, in the loosest sense of the word, in his slippers.

'That's good thinking, Harry. How about some spotted dick?'

'Yes. Pull it out, Irma. This calls for

celebration.'

'The next question is, it seems to me, at what time was the computer hashed . . .'

'. . . I believe the term is "hacked," dear . . .'

'Pardon—of course you're right. I'd like to know if the . . .'

'. . . if the painting was purchased before or after the computer was hashed, of course! They'll be about the same time on the same night.' Harry took a forkful of spotted dick and swallowed it dramatically, giggling as he did so. 'The organizer of the theft must have known that the museum was going to buy the painting.'

'Or he was at the auction, and watched the museum buy it. Otherwise, it implies that the . . . Harry, you don't think the auction was rigged, do you?'

'Do I?'

'No, I shouldn't think so.'

'Probably not, Irma, but I leave no stone unturned.'

'You said that the fuse box in the utility room had been exploded open from the inside?'

'That's right.'

'And the computer picked up movement in the utility room during the night it was hacked, last Wednesday?'

'Aye. Wait a second! That would explain it. The explosive was planted during the first breach, but only detonated after the painting was in the museum, ready to be stolen!'

'You're quite sexy when you're on the case, Harry.'

'Ta, luv.'

185

'The other night you said that you needed me to identify a . . .'

'A moment, Dr. Barrow. Pa-please continue, Petra.' The blue-suited man gestured to the woman in the lab coat. Barrow could not understand. He had never before seen the two paintings that stood on easels before him.

One was a hideously ugly abstract Suprematist work.

The other was all white.

'I'm just telling you, I don't know anything about these. I'm a seicento man. An Early Modernist. I don't know anything after 1800. I don't even know what day it is.'

As Barrow spoke, one of the flanking men answered a mobile phone and handed it to the gentleman in the blue suit. Phone in hand, he walked out of sight, melted into the colossal darkness of the warehouse.

Barrow turned his attention to the paintings before him. One was truly atrocious, a diseased mess of incompatible colors that suggested very old cheese. To Barrow, it looked to be early twentieth century, Suprematist style, Russian probably, somewhere between 1915 and 1930. That was as much as he could muster. He could not see what Petra, in her white lab coat, was doing to the lower left-hand corner of the canvas.

The other painting was completely white. Not white on white, Barrow thought, recalling the recent, highly publicized sale at Christie's of a famous painting by Kasimir Malevich. This painting was just plain white.

On longer inspection, Barrow found the cause of this appearance. The top layer of paint had been removed from the canvas, revealing the raw gesso beneath: the preparatory white mixture of plaster and glue that is put on canvases as a base layer, before the real painting begins.

The top right corner of the gessoed canvas was a slightly different shade of white, and had a texture to it. The painting, it seemed, had been white in its completed state, but it had been scraped down, and only one corner of the original work remained. But why?

Then Barrow saw what Petra was doing. On her lap, she held a small tray containing jars of chemicals, brushes, and palette knives. Barrow leaned to see around her. Whatever chemical she used, it was dissolving the paint on the surface of the ugly Suprematist work. The lower left corner was now exposed, revealing smooth black paint beneath.

It was a hidden painting.

Barrow stood there, in overcoat and pajamas, realizing to what he was a party. Chemicals had dissolved most of the ugly Suprematist painting. It was being worked from the bottom up, revealing the treasure beneath with aching slowness.

The bottom half of the painting was black. A smooth, unpainterly shade. Evidence of brushstroke had been painted out, so the darkness was velvety, and coated the canvas like night water. There seemed to be the torsos of two figures, but they had not been painted from the waist down. They seemed to melt away into the amorphous black background. Then the base of a wing emerged.

187

Barrow pieced things together. He took the handkerchief out of his overcoat pocket and mopped his matted white brow. The cuff-linked gentleman returned. His face betrayed anger. Taut hands ran through his yellowy locks.

'Ap-pologies for my absence. Business.' He spoke, then whispered into the ear of one of his associates. Barrow barely caught some words: 'I'm so sick of these fucking games . . . look up . . .'

The man turned to Barrow. 'I presume that you've deduced why I woke you so abruptly this evening. Your judgment is invaluable, and you will be rewarded for the inconvenience.'

'I can't believe this.'

'Imp-pressed or distressed, Dr. Barrow?'

'A little of both, I think. I've not quite decided yet.'

The last portions of paint flaked off the canvas, and the hidden painting was now fully revealed. A young woman in blue, surprised by a winged figure behind her. She turns, her neck gently curved, her pale skin and brown teardrop eyes sublime and graceful.

Barrow wiped the back of his neck and his cheek. He just stared at the canvas, unsure as to what he should do. The handkerchief was damp. He clutched it inside his pocket, feeling the wet against his slick palm.

'How did you get it?'

'Now, now, Doctor, you're not being pa-paid to provide questions. Only answers.' The gentleman paused, significantly. 'I've consulted extensively, Dr. Barrow, and you are generally considered to be the world's foremost authority on Baroque Roman painting, the Caravaggesque, and the

Caravaggisti. Your colleagues have written of your pre-preternatural sense for correct attribution. I am no scholar, but neither am I a fool. I am concerned that I have not been fairly dealt with. I need an authentication.' He crossed his arms over his chest and drummed his left forearm with a flurry of right-hand fingers.

Barrow felt his heels fall out from under him, as he stumbled backward a moment. His fists were tight thrust into both pockets. His breath came short.

'Relax, Dr. Barrow. I'll only shoot you if you lie.'

Barrow knew the answer, but did not know what to say. His dilemma was not moral, but corporeal. His full mind whirred in vacillation. Then he chose the truth.

'I'm sorry. It's a fake.'

*   *   *

The gentleman waited a very long time, before he spoke.

'You are certain?'

'No question. I'm sorry.'

'So am I, Dr. Barrow. May I ask how you can be certain, so quickly?'

'I'm sorry, I knew before she had cleared all the paint off.'

'How?'

'Would you recognize me?'

'I see. You did not, then, pre-presume your answer before corroboration?'

'Look, I told you! I'm . . .'

'. . . sorry. I know. You may stop your ap-pologies. I'm not going to shoot you. The

189

explanation doesn't matter, right now. At least, you're not the one with explaining to do. Give me the phone.'

One of his burly accomplices handed over the mobile phone. He dialed. As the phone rang, he waved his hand in dismissal. 'Take Dr. Barrow back to his home.'

The two silent associates walked Barrow out of the warehouse cavern. Before his egression, Barrow heard a few words spoken into the telephone. 'There's nothing under the one I bought, just plain white gesso. There was a Caravaggio under Grayson's painting, lot thirty-four. But Barrow said it's a fake. Of course, I believe him, why would he lie? Well, we may know who pa-painted it, but there's not much we can do now. No, I don't think we should confront . . . Not yet. I'll think of something. But we still need him for the . . .' And the door slammed shut.

Barrow was outside, as he had been not long before, on the street, in the midst of a canyon of anonymous warehouses. In the aquatic night, the reflected blue sheen of the metal buildings seemed like great sea turtles floating in a darkest trench, leagues deep. Barrow had not noticed that one of the men with him had left, and now pulled up in the black Land Rover. Seems to be my mode of involuntary transport, he thought. The door was opened for him, and he entered. During the ride home, the front-seat passenger turned around and presented Barrow with a fat white envelope.

'With compliments and appreciation,' said the anonymous henchman. 'You will be called upon at least once more. If you inform anyone about this, you will be killed. If you continue to cooperate, you will receive more. On behalf of our employer, we apologize for the threatening and melodramatic way in which you have been treated. We also apologize, in advance, for future such situations. That was a joke, Dr. Barrow.' The man wasn't smiling.

Barrow opened the envelope. It was stuffed full of cash in large denominations. Barrow mustered an upturn of lip.

*　　　*　　　*

Bizot hunched over his desk. A gauze of lamplight spread over him, as the rest of the office lay dark. The Formica tabletop bore the crushed-ash remains of old, unswept cigarettes. A plain black ashtray was overfilled and brimming with thin, white, stubbed-out carcasses of thoughts long past.

Bizot stroked down to the southernmost tip of his scraggly graying beard. He looked over at the framed photograph perched on the edge of his desk. First mother, then father the following year. Empty wheelchairs and leftover oxygen tanks, still full. He glanced to his own cigarettes piled into a barrow in the ashtray. Now he was alone. The burden of care gone, replaced by the hollow weight of their absence. Too much, now too little. It was their time, he supposed. But when would it be his? He looked away. Then back. Then down to the open file between his elbows, bent in support of his weighty chin.

A pile of closed files was stacked to his left, and the junk-shop-recovered radio on a shelf across the room sung a treble-topped twangle of some piece or other of classical music. Bizot didn't listen. He ran his eyes over page after page, and noted in his Moleskine journal, until the last page of the last file was folded over and shut. Bizot pushed it forward, spilling a few loose ashes from the cigarette fossils onto the pages. He didn't bother to blow them clean. Bizot slouched in his chair, the foam beneath his generous posterior exposed in places, and flattened beyond form. He slung his foot up onto his chair. His elbow rested on his knee, his chin in his palm, head in hand. He tongued the current cigarette to the left corner of his mouth and tilted his notebook to better read. The page spoke up to him.

Luc Sallenave was the thirteenth comte de Vieuquont and inhabited the eponymous château, built by his ancestor, the third comte de Vieuquont, in the fourteenth century. He was a Knight of the Order of St. John, an honorary position in current times, but a post held by countless prominent figures throughout history, from Diego Velázquez to Paul I, emperor of Russia, to Caravaggio, since the inception of the order in the eleventh century. He was also a Freemason, always highly suspect. Every president of the United States had been a Freemason, and the Masonic symbol of the eye inside a triangle adorned the American dollar bill, so rooted was this secret cult organization in positions of world power. The eye in the triangle could be found haunting the background of works of art throughout Western history. It meant that Sallenave could move and shake, and probably did, in subterranean circles with roots that sprang into powerful trees aboveground.

Sallenave was an avid collector of butterflies, as

192

well as Old Master prints and rare books, particularly those printed before 1501, so-called incunabula. He had a buying record with all the major auction houses, but nothing that he was on record of having bought dated from after around 1700. He owned a small army of Rembrandt etchings, as well as Dürer, Goltzius, and very early religious woodcuts. He bought books, none of which Bizot recognized, but the number and prices were impressive, beyond what he could fathom. Bizot did feel intimately connected to Sallenave in one way: he had gotten drunk, on many occasions, on Château Vieuquont wine.

But Bizot had circled only one cluster of notes: Luc Sallenave's charitable donations. As far as Bizot could tell from the tax write-offs, Sallenave had given enormous sums of money, every year on file, to several known Christian organizations that may, or may not, put money to charitable means. They were the institutions that were known to lean to the far right, more political than ecclesiastical. They wielded the cross, rather than paid penance to it. Bizot circled these donations. His pencil ran heavy around them, and around again. One of the institutions listed was unfamiliar to him. Le Pacte de Joseph. The Brotherhood of Joseph. Its address was listed, without a number, as rue de Jérusalem. The same street as Sallenave's gallery.

That's enough, thought Bizot. On verra. We shall see.

He looked over to the desks of his coworkers, adorned with monogrammed coffee mugs and framed photographs. Then he stood up, switched off the desk lamp, and walked home.

*   *   *

A throbbing ring. Jean-Paul Lesgourges fumbled to turn on his bedside light, knocking over a clock and an empty glass. He pulled the telephone to his ear.

'Jean.' It was Bizot. 'Jean, I . . . I just . . .'

Shudder—breath silence.

Lesgourges sat up in bed. 'It's okay. I'm here. I'll be right over.'

CHAPTER TWENTY-TWO

New morning filtered through the windows, refracted and broke over the warm, still bed. Soft cotton covers soaked the heat. As the light crept toward the headboard, the blankets stirred.

Coffin squeezed open his eyes. Whiteness burst through the windowpane. He rolled to his right, and graced his arm over her. She was warm and soft, like the sun and the blankets. She leaned in and kissed him.

'Buongiorno, bello.'

'Buongiorno a te. Come va?'

'Bene, con te, tesoro. Dobbiamo andare subito?'

'Non ancora. È meglio dopo. È troppo comodo a letto.'

Coffin nestled in close to her lips, and parted them with his.

'It's like a conjugal visit, isn't it?'

Daniela laughed. 'It is a conjugal visit.'

'All the benefits of married life, without the muck.'

'Why must there always be muck? It's rather like slogging through sandy seawater.'

'You have a delightful turn of phrase, Dani.'

'I got a lot of reading done, in there. Nothing much else to do, waiting for you to . . .'

'I always keep my word. If someone plays honestly with me, I'll never break it. And for you, especially . . .'

Coffin ran his hand along her stomach, down over her hipbone, and softly clasped her thigh.

'You did work out in there, though. These are stronger than I recall.'

She threw him over onto his back with a smile, and climbed on top.

'You're so confident in your memory?' She pressed her legs tight around his waist.

'I'm impressed.'

'And you've gotten a belly since I saw you last.'

'Well, I . . . um, yes, perhaps.'

'I still like you.'

'I'm glad. What's for breakfast?'

'Oh, am I making you breakfast, now?' Coffin rolled her over onto her back, her black curls cascading over the white pillow.

Vallombroso laughed. 'You know I could kick your ass.'

*   *   *

The bacon sizzled in the pan, next to two sunny-side eggs. Coffin wore his bathrobe and nothing else. He wielded his spatula. 'It's all in the wrist,' he said.

'What the English eat for breakfast is just revolting.'

195

'What do you prefer? Pasta?'

'Don't be silly, Gabriel. Although I wouldn't put it past me.'

'Easy or hard?'

'What do you think?'

'No, I mean the eggs.'

'Doesn't matter. I'll like it any way you do it. Everything you do is just right.'

'Now see,' said Gabriel, 'that's what I think, too.'

Daniela picked up the newspaper from the kitchen table at which she sat. She looked out the window. 'It was bright and sunny ten minutes ago! What's wrong with this country?' Thunder echoed in the distance.

'Tell me, Dani, did you play any chess while you were, you know . . .'

'No, because I knew you would ask, and want to play with me once I got out, and then I'd have to put up with you when I beat you!' She giggled and poked at Coffin with her fork.

'Fair enough,' Gabriel said. 'I am rather rusty. Been awhile. I stopped playing when I beat that computer game you bought me, where the animated pieces fight each other.'

'Your parents would be very proud.'

Coffin looked down at his plate. Daniela picked a piece of bacon off it. She looked into his eyes, then down quickly to the newspaper in her hands. 'This headline reads that murder rates have gone down thirty percent this year, but the subheading says that shootings have increased. You know what that means, don't you?'

'What?'

'It means that there are just as many criminals,

196

but their aim has gotten worse.'

*   *   *

The empty plates were pushed aside, and the coffee was leaned over.

'Vuoi ancora del caffè?'

'No, grazie. Abbiamo qualcosa da fare, no?'

'Sì. I have to make a few phone calls, and then what shall we do before this evening?'

'This will all be sorted soon, won't it? I mean, we're on the right track.'

'I promise.' Coffin poured himself another cup of coffee, putting his feet up on the chair in front of him.

Vallombroso stood up. 'I'll have a shower.'

Coffin smiled. 'Don't bother dressing afterward.'

*   *   *

Warm lashes of rain pelted the dirty glass outside the Wickendens' ground-floor flat. Silhouettes huddled by, shoulders pinched to raise coats in defense, but the rain was inescapable. Most of them turned to look into the mustard-colored kitchen and saw Harry Wickenden eating a piece of blackened toast with marmalade, the sort with the little bits of orange peel mixed in, wearing his tattered baby blue bathrobe that he refused to retire.

Harry hated being on the ground floor, 'the fishbowl,' he called it; the subject of inadvertent, mindless gawking streetwalkers. He'd considered buying one-way glass, but deemed this option too drastic and obvious an avoidance of the more logical cure: moving. But Harry, and particularly Irma, was possessed of inordinate inertia, and the only event that could drive him to move elsewhere, was if his current residence burned down. For Irma, the inertia was physical, not mental, as she could not imagine walking all the way to the store, and then walking home *up stairs.* And so, the Wickendens had maintained residence at 82 Ferraby Rows, Flat 1A for twenty-seven years, the next February 18. All the while, curtains had never occurred to him, but might have if he had given them enough thought.

Harry looked down at his toast, then up at the window. A rain-slicked, stick-thin boy of ten or so was looking in at him, a nearly translucent red cotton jumper pulled up over his head. Perhaps I should blacken the windows, thought Harry, knowing that nothing was the most he was likely to do.

Irma was slicing at her second plate of eggs over-medium, bacon, and tomato. Her small eyes shone from under gray bangs, several decades out of date, and caught and refracted the light from the fluorescents overhead, which ricocheted off the silverware. Harry's gaze, meanwhile, slung heavy on his face, remained fixed on the minute sawing of his wife's knife, an act which annoyed him daily, and which he'd never once, in thirty-two years, articulated to her with any greater eloquence than a roll of his eyes, never noted by Irma.

Without looking up from her plate, she said, 'Why don't you just give the medicine a try, then?' Silence. 'Dr. Wild thinks that they might help you.'

198

Silence. 'Can't hurt.'

'Could.'

'Well . . .'

'I don't need . . .'

'Of course not, but . . .'

'I don't want . . .'

'I know, luv.'

For the next seven and a half minutes, Harry looked through his wife's slicing.

Then the phone rang.

Wickenden picked up the phone on the third ring, as always.

'Yup. It is. Oh, you've got to be kidding me. Bloody hell. I'll be right over.'

*   *   *

Wickenden mounted the front steps of the National Gallery of Modern Art. The sun was unusually bright and blinded off the avalanche of white marble steps. He was met by Elizabeth Van Der Mier.

'Can you bloody-well believe it?'

Wickenden looked up through the glare. Van Der Mier was haloed in brilliant light, like a nimbus. 'I can,' said Harry. They walked into the museum.

'My grandmother taught me a word for this: chutzpah.'

'I don't know what that means, but I know what you mean,' Harry said, trying to keep up with Van Der Mier's long-legged gait. 'I can't say that the thought didn't cross mind. This means that it may not have been stolen on commission, and that makes my job much more difficult.'

'Because it eliminates . . .'

'. . . eliminates motive for choice of object stolen. Anyone could have learned of the purchase, and known that the Malimich painting was in Conservation, since you were so good as to announce it at the press conference . . .'

'. . . don't give me flack, Inspector, I . . .'

'. . . and that would diminish the percentages on a profile fitting the criminal.'

They wound down a gleaming hallway and stepped into the elevator.

'So,' continued Wickenden, 'how much did they ask for?'

'Six-point-three million.'

'That's not a coincidence.'

'I know.'

'Not good.'

'I know.' Van Der Mier tapped with her foot as the elevator ascended. Wickenden noticed the lights and the movement of the elevator. The electricity had been restored.

'That further suggests,' he droned in his usual tone, 'an uncommissioned crime, perpetrated perhaps by professional thieves, but not by experienced art thieves. Probably part of a larger organized crime syndicate. Come to think of it, it's the worst amount they could have possibly asked for, from my perspective. It shows that they . . . no. It *suggests* that they have no idea of the actual value of the piece, so they wind up asking exactly what you paid for it, a number that the press have touted about.'

'The theft was too professional for amateurs, surely, Inspector.' The elevator dinged, and they stepped into Van Der Mier's office.

200

'True.' Wickenden sat down. 'But experienced art thieves don't steal for ransom. It's dangerous, uncertain. There's no guarantee that the money will be paid. Then they've risked for nothing, and they're stuck with a painting that they don't want. And any idiot with a toe in the black market knows that you can't shop around high-profile stolen art. No, it's got to be professional thieves, but without a connection to the art world. They would have been commissioned by someone who knows what they were doing, but the sale fell through. That's the most likely scenario now. You don't steal to ransom. Their Plan A failed. Now ransom is Plan B. Ransom takes all the fun out of crime.'

'Well, I'm sorry to spoil your fun, but frankly, I don't give a flying fuck. What am I going to tell the trustees? What do you do with ransom demands? Do you respond, or what?' Van Der Mier sat behind her desk to give herself, in her time of confusion, an illusion of authority.

'We can call in more troops from the office. But the more pertinent question is, do you want to pay it?'

'Of course not.'

'I mean, given the situation.'

'It's not my money. I'll have to pose it to the board of trustees. I can call an emergency meeting, if you think we should consider . . .'

'. . . consider all options, Ms. Van Der Pfaff. If you ignore completely, then the painting will be retained by the thieves, disposed of in some way. I'd always call the bluff that they'd destroy it. Makes no sense to anyone to destroy it. The valuable object is gone, and it can't inform on you, the way a kidnap victim could. They want the piece

201

off their hands. It can either go back to you, or disappear. If you respond and offer to pay, then you will probably get your painting back. My bosses don't want me to say that, but I'm playing straight with you. Probably . . .'

'Probably?'

'Consider that the thieves cannot dispose of it in any way other than ransoming it back to you, or hanging it in their living room. They want the piece off their hands, like I said. It's burning. The theft was well considered, but ransom, by nature, is not. We're not dealing within the art sphere, or the thieves would have known better. Or something well planned fell through. Commissioned art theft is the only way to play the percentages.' Wickenden paused. 'Could you raise the money?'

'I don't know. The museum can't budget it, certainly, not after the auction purchase. We'd be relying on private funds. The board might feel obliged, to save face. I appreciate your keeping this out of the public eye . . .'

'. . . as much as we can, for now. Though gossip is a boat full of holes.'

'Yeah, well . . .'

'So . . . may I have something to drink?'

Van Der Mier looked surprised. 'Oh, uh, certainly. What would you like?'

'Do you have any green tea?'

'Pardon?'

'Green tea. Good for the blood. Stimulates the brain. It's green.'

'Oh, right. Well, um,' she pressed the intercom on her desk, 'Sarah, could you bring in some, uh, green tea for Inspector Wickenden? Cheers.'

They stood in silence.

'What did it sound like?'

'Pardon?'

'The ransom demand. What did it sound like?'

'The call came in soon after I got into the office this morning. I don't have caller ID here. Sarah patched it through. It sounded like a man's voice, but it was far too low . . .'

'A voice concealer.'

Van Der Mier looked suddenly pallid. 'This is real, isn't it? I mean, it seemed sort of like a bad dream, like something I was floating through. But this is real. It's like in the movies.'

'I'm afraid so. What did he say?'

'To leave the light to my office on overnight tomorrow, if I wanted the painting returned, and he would contact me. That was it. He was on the phone for less than a minute.'

'Are you sure that it was real?'

'You mean, like, a crank call? Not enough people know about it, I hope, for that.'

'If you wanted to stall for time, to raise the money, we could ask for proof of possession,' Wickenden offered.

'How would I contact him, though,?'

'I'll be honest, ma'am. I'm good at the detecting part, but I don't deal well with ransomers. I've encountered this twice before, and most recently we called in someone who knows much more than I.'

Van Der Mier paced. 'You don't inspire confidence, Inspector.'

'I just want to be straight with you, ma'am.'

'I'm just wondering . . .' Van Der Mier walked behind her desk and began to flip through files that splayed at incongruous angles on her desk of

203

glass and perpendiculars. She looked up at Wickenden. He was fingering something in his pocket, looking down at the floor. 'Do you know the director of the Yale British Art Museum, Inspector? No? She's a school friend of mine, and we've kept in close touch as we're both in the art world, you know. Well, they had a painting go missing a few years back . . .'

Wickenden pricked up. 'I never heard . . .'

'That's the point, Inspector. They didn't want news to get out, even within the law enforcement community. Someone tried to ransom a Joshua Reynolds back to the museum. The painting was insured, and there was a top insurance investigator on the case who got it back for them. News never surfaced, face saved, everything. I'm wondering if we can call in this fellow . . .'

'The Yard will provide everything that . . .'

'This is nothing personal, Inspector. This is trying to push the fan out of the way before the shit comes flying in, if you'll forgive the expression. I appreciate your honesty in your strengths and weaknesses. It takes a strong man to ask for help. Here it is . . .'

Van Der Mier extended an ivory business card toward Wickenden. He took it as if it were a precious metal. He looked at the name on the card. Van Der Mier thought she could detect a ruffle in the corner of his mustache. But perhaps it was nothing.

'Look, I'll yield to whatever you suggest, Inspector. But I don't want this publicized if we can help it. Everything's been very discreet, and if we can keep it that way, well, we'd all be grateful. A private tragedy is one thing, but public is far worse.'

Wickenden was still looking at the name on the card.

*   *   *

Gabriel Coffin and Daniela Vallombroso were just finishing their sticky toffee pudding at Rules restaurant, when Coffin's trousers began to vibrate.

'*Daniela . . .*' He kicked her under the table.

'Ma, cosa?'

'Oh,' he said, 'scusa.' He reached into his pocket and retrieved his mobile phone. 'Sì? I mean, hello? Oh, Ha . . . Harry, it's been ages . . .'

Daniela looked around the room. It was a horror vacui. Not an empty space in sight. Every piece of yellowy wall was covered in a painting, watercolor, taxidermied animal head, *Vanity Fair* cartoon, plant, quotation, or otherwise Victorian vertiginous excess. Waiters in white shirts and black vests roamed, trays balanced precariously but with utmost precision. A maître d' surveyed and picked up every instance overlooked by staff. A dropped fork, a low water glass, a new order, where is the restroom, cognac, please. The circulation of activity was mesmerizing, yet it was meditative to be seated looking at it as it transpired around you, in the soft cocoon created by great restaurants. However many hundreds of diners, you were made to feel as though you were the only one that mattered. And there were few better than London's oldest restaurant, Rules.

'. . . I hadn't heard. Just got to London, actually. But that's incredible. Or more so, as you've been able to keep it out of the media. That's understandable of course, but easier said than done. No, I haven't been professional for some time, now. Getting on in years, I suppose. No, didn't think you'd ever stop. I'm just in London to give a lecture, actually. Yes, tonight. At the Courtauld Institute. That's what keeps me off the streets, still. And I'm on a bit of a holiday. I have to go back to my old haunts, whenever I'm in town. At Rules, right now. Yes, have you ever . . . oh, well you must make it sometime. Really? Well, I suppose . . . yes, I think that would be all right. Why don't . . . listen, can you meet me after the lecture? Then we could go somewhere and speak privately. Right. From five to six, so . . . oh, that would be . . . lovely. Cheers, see you then.'

Coffin clicked shut his phone and sat for a moment, staring at the stuffed, severed head of a dik-dik that smiled upon the wall.

Daniela leaned in. 'Allora . . .'

'You are absolutely not going to believe this . . .'

CHAPTER TWENTY-THREE

'I finally got through to Sallenave's household, but I'm afraid the news is not promising. Have you tried the pear?' Lesgourges and Bizot sat on the banks of the Seine, beneath an inviting sun. Lesgourges' legs hung down toward the muddy green water, while Bizot's legs rather extended horizontally. They consumed tiny boules of Berthillon ice cream.

Bizot replied through a chocolaty beard.

'Mmmph.'

'It's good, you should. It's like eating a pear.'

'Mmmph.' They sat in silence for a moment, digesting their discussion.

'So, the bad news,' Lesgourges continued, 'as far as the case is concerned, is that Luc is ill. He's taken to bed, and has not been out of the house in some time. Christien Courtil is at the château with him. I spoke to Luc's secretary, but he was reticent. He's half Austrian, of course.'

'Oh, God.'

'I know. But he and I have always been mutually respectful. It's been a long while. Last time I was at Luc's château was six or seven years ago. We'd talked about exporting my Armagnac abroad, but he was asking a small fortune, and I prefer to keep my nectar exclusive, anyway. But I couldn't get any more information out of the secretary. Not sure how serious, but at Luc's age . . . Anyway, it must be pretty bad, if Courtil flew down there to be with him. Maybe even last will and testament . . .'

'Right. So that means that Courtil is out of town, and the Galerie Sallenave will be closed.' The last of Bizot's ice-cream cone disappeared into the vacuum amidst his beard. 'I think I should pay a visit to the gallery. I have enough to get a search warrant.'

Lesgourges looked disappointed. Bizot paused, before continuing. 'Are you coming along, then?'

*   *   *

'. . . Which is another one of the many dangers of the art market. The best forgers are those within the art world. Because of an intimate knowledge of

207

the methods available, not only for forging, but also for the detection of forgery, conservators are popular suspects. It is their job to authenticate works of art and sift out the fraudulent. Skilled and knowledgeable about the most advanced detection methods, they are in a perfect position to exploit the weaknesses of their own industry.'

The fourth-floor lecture hall of the Courtauld Institute in Somerset House in London, with its sloped maroon seating, was filled with bright-eyed students, most of them either pearled and feminine, or gay. The majority sat at attention. Others took notes, or perhaps sketched, in their notebooks.

'Logic is a greater tool in detection than extensive knowledge of art history. Scholarly knowledge can only help, and will speed the process, but anything may be looked up these days, and experts may be consulted on specific matters. Let us use your abundant knowledge, then, and piece together how the master forger succeeds and, thereby, how we can catch him.'

Harry Wickenden stood in a corner at the back. He had seen Gabriel Coffin twice before and met him only once. He had been surprised at Gabriel's apparent recognition of his name and voice. Perhaps his reputation preceded him, more so than he'd imagined. Or perhaps Gabriel was just polite.

'Let us take a painting, for example. Why would a forger choose a painting? Surely there are easier pieces to forge? A drawing has fewer dimensions, requires only the ink and the paper. We will discuss the forgery of drawings in a moment. But for now, let us consider a painting. An inherent difficulty is that most of the famous artists have been extensively catalogued. Their works of art known to be extant are in identified locations. So, a forger needs either to paint an invented, anonymous artwork, or to research works by known artists that are listed as "lost." Both methods have worked, but the second is better. Can you guess why?'

The first time that Wickenden had seen Coffin was at a lecture, much like this one, given at the Victoria and Albert Museum, in South Kensington, nearly ten years ago, when Coffin was newly a professor and Wickenden was in his midforties. He attended, back then, out of enthusiasm and interest. Both had dwindled, insofar as his extracurricular attendance was concerned. He could muster fervor only in the heat of the hunt, and he had noticed, to his own dismay, that his taste had blunted for extramurals of any sort.

'The success of any work of art that is being sold, is the provenance. If the documented history of any given artwork is solid, its authenticity will not be questioned. The soundest provenance would be a signed contract from the artist, selling the piece to the family of its current owner, with a price indicated and both parties undersigned. If I were to buy an original artwork today, for example, I would save the contract, which would become the provenance for the piece. Through centuries, few artworks have such tight provenance, but you'd be surprised at how much has been preserved. Art has always been recognized as of great value, and documents relating to artworks and transactions are often saved. One of the dangers of the present is that computers eliminate the paper trail that is so important to historical research. It is too easy to delete relevant documents, or lose them in the depths of a computer.

'But I digress. If a forger can find documentation of a missing artwork, for instance a Michelangelo drawing that is not extant, but that is mentioned in an extant letter, then the forger essentially is matching an artwork of his own creation to already existing provenance. That whets the excitement of scholars, who are all too-often so eager for a new discovery, that they will overlook details and look too hard for corroboration of hypotheses. In this way, a keen scholar can fall into the forger's hands, and aid in the crime unknowingly.'

The V&A lecture had been on art theft, as well. Seemed to be this fellow's specialty. But Harry had heard of Coffin, and they'd crossed paths professionally, as well. Coffin had been involved behind the scenes in stopping the attempt to ransom Edvard Munch's *The Scream,* the first time it had been brazenly stolen in front of rolling CC-TV cameras from the National Gallery in Oslo, Norway. The whole job had been caught on video. Two men leaned a ladder up against the side of the museum, climbed in a window, and walked away with *The Scream* under one of their arms. All on camera. Of course, no one had been looking at the monitors in security, so they got away, for a while. It was an amateur job, Soviet bloc mafia types who'd pounded their way into the museum and had no sense of the art world. They'd been caught, needless to say, soon after ransom demands were made.

'So, the best sort of forgery, and I mean "best" in the sense of having the greatest chance at success, requires airtight provenance. The better the provenance, the less the artwork will be scrutinized before it is deemed legitimate. But a forger cannot survive on provenance and hungry scholars alone. Let us use, for an example, a small, an anonymous Italian medieval panel painting. Forging is like cooking. You need to know the ingredients to produce a dish before you start to cook. What are the ingredients of such a painting?

'Well, to begin with, what is the support? Are we making linguini or capellini? It's either canvas or panel, and in this period, it would have almost exclusively been a smooth poplar-wood panel. But it has to be wood that can be dated back to the period of the painting forged. There's the rub.

'"What's the medium?" is question number two. Is it pesto or bolognese? You'll have to forgive my simplistic analogies, but I promise you, they stick. You'll leave this lecture tonight, and you won't be thinking to yourself, "Did he say poplar wood or pear wood was the most common support for medieval religious painting?" You'll have an inexplicable craving for pasta, and find yourself thinking about forgeries in the midst of your penne all'arrabbiata. The medium? If it's early enough, and style would suggest that, then it would be tempera paint. Now, Renaissance and Early Modern paintings are more difficult to forge than Modern. Can you guess why?'

Wickenden was trying to place Coffin's accent. It was neither here nor there, with an American tone mixed with the received pronunciation accent

211

taught to British newscasters and foreign actors playing Brits. Wickenden could usually tell a lot about a man's history from his accent, but this one had him at a loss.

'It was not until the nineteenth century that artists bought premade paint. Artists cooked up their own paints in their studios, which meant that every painter had a slightly different recipe for each color. In order to accurately forge any painting before this period, the forger needs to know the composition of that specific artist's colors. And these colors have to be reproduced from scratch. The materials are available. As basic as it sounds, an egg is cracked open and dipped into, to form the bonding element in tempera, and then mixed with a raw pigment, such as lapis lazuli, for blue, or sepia, made from squid ink, for a burnt orange umber. But, the organic materials in the paint must be carbon datable back to the correct century.'

Wickenden's second encounter with Coffin in person had been in the line of duty. Coffin, at least some time ago, had worked for the Carabinieri. There was a case across borders, and the Carabinieri had always been willing to work with law enforcement from other nations. Harry admired them for that. In his experience, Scotland Yard had always been more isolationist. Maybe it's the whole island thing.

'This necessary chemical knowledge allows us, the hunters, to narrow the profile. The requisite intelligence, in the sense of specific knowledge and general brain power, can drastically limit the number of suspects. In simple terms, there are fewer smart people out there than there are

212

dummies, and that can be to the advantage of law enforcers. It is not easy to forge well. It is quite miraculous, in fact, that criminals are willing to attempt it, and are actually successful. Success truly requires a willingness and complicity, however inadvertent, on the part of the victim. Close scrutiny will root out the inevitable flaws in the forger's armor. It is my opinion that, if a forger's work is perfect, then he deserves to get away with it. But I've never come across a forgery that approached perfection. Those deceived inevitably look back upon it with self-derision, for having been taken in by what is, in the light of day, clearly fake.

'Once you have the ingredients, you need the artistic skill to reproduce masterpieces in a convincing manner. The artwork has to be convincingly "aged." A story concocted as to how it was "found," that links to its provenance. Then, the entire package, product, provenance, and story, must be *believed by someone.* It is a long and winding road.

'Other art forms are easier to forge, you may think? The components may be fewer, but this does not necessarily make them easier. One must also think of value. It is in no one's interest to forge a Piranesi print. That is not to say that it's not been done, but the potential return, in the low-thousands-of-pounds range, is probably not worth the effort required. You've got to match the ink, find paper of the period. So, while the requisite components, just period paper and ink, are fewer, so are the rewards. Good forgery is a high-cost endeavor.'

Wickenden's department at Scotland Yard had

been tracing a stolen set of pre-Columbian figurines, which had gone missing from the home of an aged collector. They were so small that the six figurines could fit into a travel toiletry kit, and had. The suspect, a Milanese, was thought to have fled to Rome, and the Carabinieri were contacted. Gabriel Coffin, as a Brit working with the Carabinieri, was the primary liaison and had exchanged many phone calls with Wickenden. They'd met in person only once, just before the arrest. But Coffin had earned a reputation as a consultant in recent years, since his young retirement from active duty with the Carabinieri. He couldn't be more than forty, Wickenden thought, young bugger. It was in this informal capacity that Wickenden planned to speak with him. He did not like being told, or rather *suggested,* what to do by Van Der Mier. But he recognized a good idea when it was forced on him.

'Needless to say, the world of master forgers is minuscule. The best develop reputations, and are often, but not always, caught. When they are, it is usually not due to their own mistake. Hubris seems to be the only consistent chink in apprehended master forgers.

'As I am already running long, I shall give you a brief, real-life example of a master forgery. It involves the Getty Museum, and the reputable Colnaghi Gallery, revenge and disgrace.

'The story begins when this master forger had stumbled upon a drawing in a flea market, which he'd purchased with the hope that it might be more valuable than the price indicated. He had no specific idea as to what it might be, but he took the chance. He brought the piece in to Colnaghi on

Old Bond Street, one of London's oldest and most renowned art dealers. An expert there said, yes, this is worth more than you paid for it, and said that Colnaghi would buy it for two hundred pounds. A significant profit, the man accepted the offer, and walked away pleased.

'A week later, he was walking down Old Bond Street once more, and stopped by the window of Colnaghi. He found that the drawing he'd sold was on offer. For sixty thousand pounds. He was furious, and he decided that a subtle, artful revenge would be sweetest and could turn lucrative. He taught himself, based on no prior experience, to forge drawings. He was an intelligent man, with considerable artistic talent, and he read his way into master forgery. He bought sixteenth-century books of low value, to use their pages as support for his forgeries. He studied the drawing styles of Italian artists of the period. He melted down the ink from the books, to provide fuel for his drawings. And he created his first piece of forgery. A friend posed as a seller and contacted Colnaghi. They said that they'd be happy to look at the piece. The friend brought the drawing in and professed to know nothing of the artist, but it had long been in his family. Colnaghi experts identified the piece as by a known sixteenth-century Italian artist, and offered to buy it for over one hundred thousand pounds. With this success, a forger was born.

'Over the next decades, the master forger, who has since been caught, claims to have made, and sold, hundreds of fake Old Master drawings through Colnaghi. Colnaghi did not suffer fiscally, and it was only the forger's sense of satisfaction at tricking these so-called experts, that repaid his efforts at revenge. But his own bank account was nicely lined by his handiwork, and Colnaghi became his primary financier. He avoided detection by changing the identity of sellers, and by copying, with an equal degree of skill, a wide variety of different artists. The degree of his success was only brought out in a plea bargain while he was imprisoned, and that is when his name became synonymous with success in this crime of utmost proficiency.

'The Getty Museum purchased several drawings from Colnaghi that one of their own curators later accused of being forged. With millions of dollars' worth of crow to eat, the Getty denied the allegations of its own scholar and refused to test the drawings. The curator even believed he recognized the hand of the forger, as that of the then-deceased Colnaghi revenger. But the Getty refused to budge. The curator was fired, disgraced for having made a public accusation of counterfeit that was never substantiated. Blacklisted, he was not hired again within the art community. He now works abroad, under a different name . . .'

Wickenden's mind began to wander. He'd heard the story before. Colleagues had put the forger in prison. His gaze wandered to the backs of heads arranged in front of him. So many blondes with their hair done up. Not that he minded.

He snapped awake at the applauding audience, as they slowly skidded into silence when Professor Sheila McLeod approached the lectern. Wickenden had seen her before and always quite fancied her.

'On behalf of the Courtauld Institute of Art, I

would like to thank Dr. Coffin for that fascinating and insightful lecture. Next week, we will have Professor David Simon, an internationally renowned scholar of Romanesque architecture and sculpture, lecturing on his extensive work at Jaka Cathedral. Thank you.'

The students murmured their way out of the lecture hall. Coffin exchanged words with McLeod and, out of the corner of his eye, saw a droopy-looking man standing, wilt-shouldered, near the back of the room.

When most of the crowd had gone, Professor McLeod was still standing with Coffin. Wickenden nodded from across the room, but Coffin didn't see. Harry pretended that he had a crick in his neck. Finally Coffin met his gaze, and Harry approached.

'Inspector. Good to see you again.' Coffin extended his hand, which brushed Wickenden's, making the latter jump. Wickenden was unused to unannounced human contact and trespass on his personal space. He looked at it for a moment, then clicked, and shook it. Coffin's grip was firm. He was dressed in an Italian-cut black suit, wearing a starched, blue-collared dress shirt beneath it.

'Dr. Coffin.'

'Please, it's Gabriel.' He turned to McLeod. 'We're old friends from work. Back when I was a Carabiniere, if you can believe it. Harry, I've got to go and have drinks with the students for just a moment. Will you join me? Hope you don't mind.'

'I, uh, no, that's fine.'

'Lead on, Sheila.' Gabriel and Harry followed Sheila out of the lecture hall, down the gently wound stairs of the academic portion of the

217

Courtauld Institute. Out in the courtyard at sunset, the lights of the belly of Somerset House burned a gentle white, casting vertical shadows and a glaze of coral blue over the pale gray stone. The iridescence phosphoresced through the spouts of water from the fountain.

They entered the gallery across the way, up the torqued stairs that Rowlandson had caricatured. On the top floor, a small, faceted gem of Impressionist and post-Impressionist artworks dotted and bejeweled the walls. Students mingled, never straying too far from the wine served on the landing. Coffin wandered through the galleries. Manet's *Déjeuner sur l'Herbe*. Daumier's *Don Quixote*. Monet, Cézanne. He sipped his wine. It tasted of tannin and sulfide.

'They'll feed anything to students,' he said. Harry half-smiled, then retracted, as Coffin looked away. 'I love Degas,' he continued. 'Scholars say that his pastels of women bathing are misogynistic, because he posed them in awkward positions. Rising from the bath, or drawing a comb through long red hair. But I've always seen them as longingly in love with the subtle machinations of the female body.'

'Hmmph,' said Wickenden.

'You're not a fan, Harry?' Coffin moved into another room.

'I chase criminals, Dr. Coffin. I'm smarter than they are, and I like that. Whether they've stolen a car, a bag of money, or a piece of cloth with some paint on it, it doesn't matter to me. I like to solve the puzzle. I like understanding. But the money involved in this industry gives me indigestion, and I can't tell a Degas from a Manet from a fancy I-

218

'don't-know-what. I don't mind any of it, but that's about as much enthusiasm as I can muster. Thankfully I don't have to be an enthusiast to do a damn good job at my profession, which I do. I admire skill at the game as, it seems, do you. What the game is, checkers or chess or burglary, I don't give a flying . . .'

'I used to play chess,' Coffin interrupted, his gaze lost along the gallery walls. 'Quite a bit, when I was younger. Ah . . . I think you'll find this interesting, Harry.' Coffin gestured toward two paintings on the wall, black voids in which floated a pattern of shapes and colors, like a suspension in ink. Harry reined up beside Coffin, a full foot shorter, and more musty.

'Now,' continued Coffin, 'this painting on the left is an original by the Russian Wassily Kandinsky. He, like his contemporary countryman, Kasimir Malevich, used abstract painting as a vehicle for the concentrated projection of spirituality. He painted what he found spiritually moving. And it is worth millions. But here's where it gets interesting. This painting on the right . . .'

'It looks the same to me.'

'That's right, Harry. It does. But this painting on the right is a modern replica, worth a few hundred quid, perhaps, if that.'

Harry looked from one painting to the other, then back again, and again.

'Now that's amazing, Doctor. I have to say, that's something I really admire. Like I was saying, displays of skill . . . ability, no matter the . . . now, how did you know that this one on the right is a fake? Looks exactly the same.'

Coffin smiled, and pointed to the wall. Beside

219

the painting on the right, hung a sign that read REPLICA. Harry flashed and recoiled a very brief smile.

'Look deeper. Observation, Harry. We can make a conscious choice to *see,* not just to look at. Passive versus active viewing. Observation and logical deduction, the . . .'

'. . . two tools that everyone has, and no one uses. I heard you lecture, Doctor. There's a lesson in there, somewhere . . . But at least you practice what you preach. I've been saying for years that I must cut down on my caffeine intake, but I'm still at ten cups a day. Abstinence gives me indigestion.'

In the next room, Coffin stopped for a long while. Harry's eyes were down at his feet, but he looked up when he saw Gabriel's stop.

'Manet's *Bar at the Folies-Bergères.* Is this not the best thing ever?'

The unusual placement of the negative threw off Wickenden. He didn't quite know what to say.

'I just love it,' Gabriel continued. 'She looks so sad. But so much more.'

A female student giggled her way over to where Coffin, McLeod, and Wickenden stood, goaded by her friends. 'Professor Coffin?' Gabriel always liked it when people called him that. 'If you were going to nick one of the paintings from this museum, which would it be?'

'Lucy Jarvis, that's not a very nice . . .'

'No, it's all right, Sheila. I think that's an excellent question, Lucy. I often like to play that game when I wander through museums. But I play it in each new room.' Coffin leaned his chin on fist, an art historical reference, as he surveyed the

220

room. 'But an easy decision. I'd take that one.' He pointed at the Manet.

'Why?' Several other students had gathered around, after refilling their glasses. Wickenden wasn't sure if he was annoyed, or just curious. He decided he was curious.

'It's a self-conscious masterwork. Manet knew that this was his big bopper, painted just before he died. The scale shows its importance. And the subject is of the zeitgeist. The woman stands, facing straight out at us. She looks sad, frightened, but there is more to her gaze. The *Mona Lisa* can go screw herself, as far as I'm concerned.' Giggles from the students.

Coffin continued. 'The woman is a bartender at the nightclub, the Folies-Bergères. See behind her? The club was two stories tall, with an open theater space in the middle, where acts could perform. In the top left, you can just see the legs of an acrobat on a trapeze. I know they look blurred, but the figures in the audience are identifiable, real characters from late nineteenth-century Paris.

'Now, we can see that the bartender has been approached by a gentleman in a dark suit and top hat. He is set off at an angle. But how can we see it? Surely, he is in front of the woman, standing where we, the viewers, stand. It is because everything behind the bartender is a mirror reflection. You can see the subtle lines of light refracting off the mirror's surface, all over the backdrop.

'The gentleman wants something. Is it a drink? An orange from the bowl at the bar? A Bass ale? You think I'm joking, but see that brown bottle with a red triangle insignia? That's right. Good

221

product placement.

'Perhaps he wants a drink. But more likely, he wants sex. That's right. She's a prostitute. Prostitution was different back then. That period saw prostitution as a norm. Gentlemen had mistresses who would accompany them socially, often as much like a geisha service as cash for sex. A woman might become a bartender at establishments such as the Folies-Bergères, in order to meet clients.

'But what is going through this woman's mind? Stare into her eyes. She has just been solicited. She needs the money but hates what she has to do for it. Perhaps she has a child to support. She is torn. She needs a client to provide, but she cannot abide her life. Yet she cannot see escape on her horizon. Others tell her that she has a good job, in a good position. The men she meets are wealthy and clean. She has a salary to supplement her true profession. She inhabits the heartbeat of the world of Parisian society, its whirl of art and literature in the late nineteenth century. The Folies-Bergères, Moulin Rouge, Toulouse-Lautrec, Émile Zola . . . But don't you have the sense that she'd rather be a quiet housewife? Rather an Emma Bovary than a Nana? Yes. I'd take that one. But then, it wouldn't be here for all of you to enjoy.'

The students just stood for a moment. Lucy spoke.

'Wow. I would just take the one nearest the door.' Everyone laughed, except for Harry. The students mingled a bit longer.

Wickenden wandered the rooms, past Kandinskys, Fauvists, Rousseau, until Coffin finally caught him. 'How about we adjourn for a

222

proper drink?'

They descended the torqued staircase, and out into the cotton London night.

'I didn't know you were a Manet scholar,' Harry said.

'That? Oh, I don't know any more about Manet than a survey student. That impromptu lecture was based solely on logic and observation. You know, at Yale University Medical School, there's a required course in which students visit the Yale British Art Museum, and do clinical diagnoses of people in the paintings. They have tests in which a student is given thirty seconds to look at a painting and then must describe it in as much detail as possible, or diagnose the depicted figure. That's brilliant. Logic and observation are two universally possessed tools that no one realizes they have.'

They turned right along the Strand, past the Royal Courts of Justice, and left. Soon they came to the hushed seclusion of the scarcely traveled street behind the Royal Courts.

'Here's my favorite pub in the city. The Seven Stars. It's usually teeming with lawyers, but despite that fact, it's a wonderful escape.'

Wickenden had not been. He favored the Coach & Horses across the street from his flat, and felt it a trespass to drink elsewhere. But, when in Rome. He glanced in the long, horizontal vitrine that ran across the stomach of the windows of the Seven Stars. It was lit in an umber glow, more like sepia, Harry thought. And full of strange objects. A stuffed owl. A horse's skull dressed in tortoiseshell glasses and a judicial wig. The battered black sign, with seven gold stars, like asterisks, swung in the mild wind.

Inside, Coffin bought two pints of best bitter and carried them carefully to the table beneath the yellow poster of a lawyer film starring Peter Sellers. 'It's good to hear of your work, Harry. Word travels around the business, as you no doubt know. You have quite a reputation for no-nonsense success. In fact, I've not heard of a case that you haven't solved.'

'There are some that I consider disappointments. I've been fortunate. I've always retrieved the art, or the thief, but occasionally only one of the two. I've never come up empty-handed.' Harry sipped his beer, moistening inadvertently the droopy tassels of his mustache, and surveyed the pub. Long and thin, like a galley kitchen, the round-rimmed glasses on the balding bartender, a sextet of lawyer-types laughing and standing by the bar.

'Your career with the Carabinieri was very impressive, I must say.'

'Oh, I've done well enough. But that life was too much for me, to tell true. I had too many other interests, and to be good at that job, it was consuming.'

'Didn't I read that you were a boy chess champion?' Wickenden maintained a steady lack of eye contact as he conversed.

Coffin leaned back and smiled. 'Parents' pipe dreams. But yes, sort of. I prefer to dwell in the present.'

Wickenden could see he'd made Coffin uncomfortable. 'You've done very well. Highly recommended...'

'My few triumphs were part of group efforts. But you usually work alone, don't you?'

'I . . . prefer. People are a pain in the ass.'

'L'nfer, c'est les autres.' Harry didn't know what that meant. Coffin continued. 'Think you'll retire soon? You're nearing retirement age, aren't you? Should get a nice package and put your feet up.'

Harry looked into his pint. 'Well, I've been younger. But no. What the hell else am I going to do? I've never before excelled, and never will after. Live out what you're good at, and contribute while you can. And then . . . well . . .'

'I understand.' Coffin sat back. 'That's why I'm still in the lecture circuit. It doesn't pay enough of the bills, I can tell you. I need to think of all sorts of creative ways to supplement my income. But, like you say, if you do something well, then it's a crime not to do it. Most of the time.'

'I was thinking, uh, Gabriel . . . The last time I worked with you . . . there was that bafflingly inept burglar, small potatoes, who wanted to raise his status on the criminal food chain. It sounds a bit familiar to the case I'm on now. I could use . . . well, I'll tell you about . . . I mean, I was wondering what happened to . . .'

Coffin smiled and shook his head. 'Ah, Dunderdorf. He's one not easily forgotten. It's funny you should ask. Good story. He's been in and out of prison, always on a small sentence . . . that much you know. But, I'm afraid we won't be seeing him for a few years, now.'

'Oh?' Harry sipped beneath a frothed mustache.

'You're entirely correct, he was trying to eat above his social status, an Untouchable reaching for Brahmin, and it wasn't meant to be. But his latest caper was too delicious. He was intent on making his mark on the art world, and he certainly

225

has, although not quite as he'd hoped, I think.' Coffin leaned forward. 'He'd decided that there's no glory in stealing a painting or sculpture. That had been done.'

'So, what did he do?'

Coffin smiled. 'He tried to steal a room.'

'Pardon?'

'He tried to steal an entire room, in one fell swoop. Out of the Philadelphia Museum of Art, in the United States. There's an installation of a room brought over from a house in Holland . . . seventeenth-century Haarlem, a Vermeer-style drawing room, with all the original inlaid wood panels, a chandelier, coffered ceiling, furniture . . . a bed, for God's sake . . . He tried to nick the whole thing at once, lock, stock, and barrel. It was made all the more amusing by how concerted was his effort. Needless to say, it was ill conceived and ill fated, so you can cross him off your suspect list. But I'm sure we've not seen the last. I hope not. I rather liked him.'

They sat for a moment in silence, broken only by intermittent sips of beer.

'Now, how can I help you, Harry?'

CHAPTER TWENTY-FOUR

The boardroom in the National Gallery of Modern Art was a cacophony, every seat filled and occupied by a loquacious, well-dressed figure. A guard outside the door closed it carefully and stood at watch.

It was after working hours. The majority of the

museum staff had long ago returned to their homes. The white oak round table in the center of the room was ringed with the board of trustees in twelve chairs, the museum director, and other powers-that-be. Inspector Harry Wickenden and Gabriel Coffin stood at the back of the room.

As the door knocked shut, Elizabeth Van Der Mier stood and addressed the assembly.

'Thank you all for coming on such short notice, and at this . . . inconvenient hour. This is a crisis meeting. I've spoken with each of you individually, to inform you of the situation. We must now, collectively, decide what to do about it. I'd like to introduce to you some . . . professionals, who are here to advise and help us through our . . . situation. Inspector Harry Wickenden, of Scotland Yard's Arts and Antiquities Division, is in charge of the case, and has been most helpful and understanding in keeping this out of the media thus far. His men are up in my office at the moment, in . . . anticipation of an incoming phone call. And we have someone joining us in an . . . advisory capacity. This is Dr. Gabriel Coffin, formerly of the Carabinieri, and a renowned expert on art crimes.' Van Der Mier now took off her black horn-rimmed glasses. Beads of sweat coagulated at her temples.

'So we're all on the same page, here are the facts. Last Wednesday night, while we were at the auction purchasing the work in question, our computer was breached, and control seized, externally, of our communications and security systems. Thanks to Inspector Wickenden's detection, we are aware that during the computer hack, the utility room was breached and an

227

explosive placed inside the fuse box.

'On Thursday night, the explosive was detonated, and our electricity was knocked out. During the blackout, our new £6.3 million purchase, the Malevich *White on White,* was stolen from the Conservation Department. It was the only object stolen. It had been recently delivered by Christie's, after I had made the purchase, on the museum's behalf. The painting was insured by Christie's until successful delivery. We are currently in debate with our insurance coverers, as to whether the Malevich was covered at the time of theft or not. As you can imagine with insurance companies, the answer will probably be not.

'The painting spent only a few hours in the museum before the theft. It was in Conservation to be cleaned and reframed, but the examination had only just begun. With electricity, the painting and museum would have been perfectly secure. In its absence, as a fire precaution, internal doors default into the unlocked position. Therefore, all doors were open at the time of the theft. The fuse box is locked, and protected further by a steel cage. There is still question as to how the thieves initially breached these defenses. Inspector Wickenden continues to investigate. But our focus must now turn to the ransom demand that I received yesterday. I'll yield the floor to Inspector Wickenden.'

Wickenden groaned up to the podium and addressed the assembly without ever raising his eyes from the floor.

'Thank you. Yesterday morning, Ms. Van Der Mier received a phone call patched into her office, from an anonymous person whose voice was concealed electronically. It sounded like a man, but technology leaves the gender in question. The voice demanded a ransom of £6.3 million, in exchange for the safe return of the Malevich painting. Ms. Van Der Mier is to leave the light on in her office overnight tonight, if the demand will be met. If not, she was informed that the painting would never be seen again.

'There are a number of components that allow us to profile the ransomer, who is most likely also the thief. Unfortunately and paradoxically, the clues make the search more difficult. The demand for £6.3 million, the exact cost of the painting, shows a lack of imagination and forethought in pricing the ransom, that suggests an unprofessionalism, or an inexperience in the art world. It also suggests that the thieves developed the heist plot after they knew of the museum's purchase, and knew of the likelihood that the painting would be in the Conservation Room, after it was announced at the press conference.

'Investigation has shown, however, one very interesting piece of information. Last Wednesday night, the computer was hacked *before* the museum purchased the painting.'

There was a stir of discussion within the room. Van Der Mier looked nervous.

Harry continued above the din. 'Please, a moment longer. This fact leads to one of two conclusions. One: The thieves were planning the heist, and later chose to steal the Malevich as a crime of convenience, because it was neither in a vault, nor bolted to the wall, and they knew of the monetary value. The other possibility is not so nice. It may mean that this was an inside job.'

The room gushed once more. Van Der Mier stood up and took the floor. 'This is merely a possibility, my friends. But this, along with the wish to avoid publicity, is a reason most of the museum staff are not present at this meeting. Only museum staff and board members would have known of the museum's intention to buy the painting, and of the high price we were willing to pay, in order to claim a centerpiece for our upcoming show and help to publicize it. In theory, only a few staff members were aware, but I am not naïve enough to think that word does not leak. Gossip is a boat full of holes. But that is the situation, as it stands now. We must decide how to deal with the ransomer. I open the floor.'

'I'd like to hear what Dr. Coffin thinks on the matter.'

A voice spoke from the crowd, and all eyes swung to the trustee standing in the corner, wearing the light blue Tyrwhitt shirt, a gray vest, and with a matching gray jacket slung over his akimbo arm.

Coffin stepped forward. 'I have had some experience in such matters during my professional career. I do not wish to sway the congregation when it is not my money at stake. But it is my belief that the surest way to get the stolen object back, however unpalatable it may be, is to comply and pay the ransom. You must do so, however, in such a manner that the ransomers feel safe, and that you can be certain of having the painting returned.

'These ransomers are scared. Inspector Wickenden is correct in saying that the evidence suggests that the thieves are not veterans of the art world, and this may very well be their first art theft. They want to get rid of the painting. They did not steal it for decoration. They want cash. Consider the options. If you do nothing at all, ignore the request, they will probably try to contact you once more, press the issue. They are, if you'll forgive the expression, shit out of luck, if you do not want to pay them. If they don't have a backup buyer, and try to find a black market for it, law enforcement will track them down. So, they will either keep the painting or destroy it.'

The assembly did not like this idea at all, and the voices began to rumble. A voice from the back of the room called out, 'Suppose we offer the ransom and trap the thieves?'

'If you lead the ransomers to believe that you will accept their proposal, but plan to double-cross and have the police lying in wait . . . well, let's just say that the percentages don't favor success. The ransomers will have to make a gross error that will lead us to them, in order for the police to apprehend both them and the painting. A failed attempt at capture will certainly result in the disappearance, and possible destruction, of the Malevich. I think that it is safer to use the theft as our indication of the criminals' ability, rather than the ransom price asked. The theft was beautifully executed. It leads me to believe that those involved would not err in the ransom stage of operations, despite their inexperience with the art world.

'Obviously the best end that can come of this is to have the police find and arrest the thieves, and retrieve and return the painting, unharmed. But unless the criminals make a mistake, the advantage is theirs. The questions, I believe, are do you want

231

the painting back, and do you have the money for the ransom? If the answer to either question is no, then problem solved. You can ignore the ransomer, and hope the police track him down, or you can try to draw the ransomer into a trap, helping the police. But you run the risk of the destruction of the Malevich or, more probably, its disappearance indefinitely. If the answer to either question is yes, then . . . you can hope for an arrest, but I think that the ransomers have you by the . . . upper hand.'

Coffin stepped back from the hushed table. He mouthed to Wickenden, who nodded. Coffin exited, as he heard Van Der Mier's voice rise, the door closing gently behind him.

*   *   *

'. . . I understand that you'd like to be kept informed of the progress of the investigation, Mademoiselle Delacloche, and, as I've said, I will keep you abreast. You've been most helpful, thus far. But I'm not obliged to say any . . . I understand, of course. I can only tell you the old news, not the current, if anything is in a precarious, and easily compromised position. Right. Of course, of course. That's fine. Au revoir.'

Bizot clapped shut the mobile phone, and tucked it into the holster on his belt, below his considerable circumference.

'We'll have one cheese fondue, and one meat, s'il vous plaît. And two white wines.'

The waiter, abrupt and brusque, draped in a squirrel-tail gray mustache that drooped down either side of his chin, rendering his jawline

232

invisible, spun off to the kitchen.

Bizot sat on the long bench that comprised one wall of Refuge des Fondues, behind and beneath Sacré Coeur, at the foot of Montmartre. Every inch of the walls, benches, tables, and chairs was covered in carved and penned graffiti. It was not so much encouraged by the management, to carve one's name on any available surface, but it was frowned upon if one did not. Bizot's name could be found beneath the second table on the right, as one walked through the door. No one sat in the chair opposite him. In the back left corner of the tiny restaurant sat the owner and friends, who resembled remarkably the cast of an Astérix and Obélix cartoon, Bizot often thought.

The waiter arrived with two baby bottles full of white wine. Bizot lifted one and suckled at the silicone nipple. Always something strangely soothing about this, he thought. Then the rainstorm outside flew in with the swinging door, followed by lanky Lesgourges.

'Je suis comme un mouchoir déjà utilisé.' Lesgourges smiled as he sat down, wiping the rain from his shiny forehead, dripping on the wooden floor. He drank long from the baby bottle, with a slurping sucking sound that made the restaurant turn to see what was the matter. Bottle half drained, he slammed it down on the table, and the diners resumed their own interests.

'You're always late,' complained Bizot.

'And you're never on time,' Lesgourges replied, wringing out his sleeves. 'That's why we get along . . . and one of the many reasons why you never married.'

'It's sad, but true. The news of today, besides

my having ordered for us, is that the man I had planted to survey Galerie Sallenave has intercepted something. Something very interesting.'

'Is it Morinière?'

'Quoi?'

'The man staking out the gallery. Is it François Morinière?'

'Why does that matter? What does that have to do with anything?'

The fondue arrived, a cauldron of bubbling cheese with the perfume of must and cold dark caves emanating from the Emmenthaler, beside a basket of bread, apples, and grapes.

'Nothing, but he's a very good cardplayer. I like him.'

'Well, it is him. Don't you want to hear what was found?'

'Mmm.' Lesgourges mumbled through a mouthful of cheese, the tail of which still clung to the edge of the cauldron.

'Since Christien Courtil has been in the south with the ailing Luc Sallenave, there has been no activity, and the gallery has remained closed and dark. The first and second floors of the building, too. Post has been slipped through the mail slot at the gallery entrance. No one has tried to get into the building.'

'You need to make an appointment in advance to shop there,' Lesgourges said, with a dramatic gesture of his fork.

'Quite. So, no one has tried even to approach the building. Until earlier today.'

The waiter arrived with hot oil and a plate of raw meat. Lesgourges looked up at Bizot. 'Je t'écoute.'

'I'm glad that someone is listening to me. My man, Moriniére, watched from his car.' Lesgourges gestured as if to interrupt, and Bizot silenced him with a preemptive raised finger. 'It's a Renault . . . and saw some fellow in a dark blue coat with the collar turned up, and his face shielded with an umbrella. This homme en bleu stood in front of the door for a moment, then walked off. Briskly, I am told.'

Lesgourges plopped some meat into the bubbling oil. 'Was it the postman?'

'No, it was not the postman! That's the point. Only the postman has been to the gallery in the last four days, except for this man in blue. In fact, the salient characteristic of the past four days is that only this one person, other than the postman, has come to the door. And he left something.'

'Wait.' Lesgourges swallowed, without chewing sufficiently. 'Was it raining this morning?'

'No.' Bizot harpooned through the oil.

'Then why was the man in blue carrying an open umbrella?'

'That's a stupi— that's a good question. Maybe it was preemptive.'

'What do you mean?'

Bizot ate. 'Whenever anyone asks, "should I bring an umbrella today," the inevitable reply is "if you bring one, it won't rain, but if you leave the umbrella at home, it is certain to rain."'

Lesgourges laughed. '*I* never say that.'

'Well, then you are *un weirdo*. Umbrellas are like people in the art world, Jean. Either you always bring one with you, or you never bring one with you.' Bizot stabbed another piece of meat from the oily depths.

'That doesn't make any sense at all.' Lesgourges looked annoyed. 'Did you read that somewhere? You know how bad you are at remembering memorable quotations.'

'The umbrella thing doesn't matter, does it? I don't care why he was carrying an open umbrella when it wasn't raining, and you won't either, when I tell you what he left.'

'Et alors?'

'So now you want to know . . .'

'Only if you want to tell me. You don't have to.'

'Of course I want to tell you! When this man in blue had disappeared around the corner, Moriniére approached the door. At first it didn't seem like there was anything different. He was about to return to his car, when he saw something.'

'What did he see?'

*   *   *

Two hours later, the doors to the boardroom pushed open, and the trustees filtered out. Shaken, tired, they were relieved, but frustrated by their forced complicity. As they bottlenecked through the door, they shook hands and grasped shoulders with Lord Malcolm Harkness. He nodded sternly in reply.

Wickenden walked into Van Der Mier's office. Van Der Mier sat behind her desk, facing out the bay window, her back to the door. 'So now I do what?' she asked. 'Wait for him to call, or . . .'

'It's understandable that you're upset, Ms. Van Der Mier.' Wickenden's voice was gentle and firm. 'But you've been promised the money, now. We'll just have to handle it in a way that ensures the safe

236

return of the painting. And we're here to help you do that. Men will be posted in your office. In the meantime, I will continue investigations. It's never too late to nail them, even after the painting is returned. Now, tell me a little something about Lord Harkness.'

Van Der Mier turned around in her chair. 'Malcolm's been a board member since just before I took over. He's from a very well-respected family, England's ancien régime. A castle and everything. His father, Lord Gielgud Harkness, was a trustee before him, highly prominent and beloved. They've been patrons of the arts for decades. Have quite a collection themselves. Two of his family's pieces are on permanent loan in the galleries downstairs. The family Bible, a rare printed sixteenth-century number with illuminations, was the centerpiece of an exhibition at the British Library. They've an eclectic collection but always make it available to museums for short loan. A family of ideal patrons. Malcolm's no exception.'

'Does he have this kind of money to throw around?'

'I've no idea. But he wouldn't volunteer it if he didn't have it. In the past, his family has always been very generous. He's been a quiet board member while I've known him, but generous with his time, anyway . . . I'll tell you what I think. I think that Malcolm would like to establish his own presence as a patron of the arts. His family has the reputation, but he'd like to secure himself a spot. Live up to his father's legacy. Word of what's happening will circulate among the friends of the trustees, and those are the ones who matter to

Malcolm. In offering to pay the ransom out of his own pocket, he secures his position in society, establishes a personal foothold as a great patron. He's buying social standing. Not like he needed any help, with that last name . . . but there's nothing wrong with his motives. He's doing a very good deed, and one that won't be publicized, so it is more out of goodness of heart than most.' She paused. 'What does he do? Cut a check?'

Wickenden continued his vigilant surveillance of his shoelaces. 'I'm sure that the ransomers have a plan. The days of briefcases full of cash are over. I would guess that they want the money deposited in a numbered bank account, and as soon as they have confirmation that the cash is in there, they'll hand over the painting.'

'I see. Unless they don't.'

'The question is, Ms. Van Der Mar, do you want to try to ambush, or do you just want to pay the ransom? This is your decision. We can follow you in unmarked vehicles, we can hook you up with microphones. It might work, and it's what I'm told to recommend to you, in the name of justice. But it does run the strong risk that the deal will turn sour, and you end up without the painting and, the danger is, without the money, too.'

'No. I understand your position, but if Malcolm Harkness is going to pay £6.3 million out of his own pocket to retrieve this painting, there's no way I'm going to risk it. And you can believe me, once this painting is back in our hands, a guerrilla army couldn't steal it away.' Van Der Mier paused. 'I should tell you, Inspector . . . I've spoken to one more source, at the suggestion of Dr. Coffin. I'm happy to yield to authorities greater than myself,

238

in matters of investigation. An expert has agreed to come and advise us. She is a specialist Malevich conservator, and investigator for the Malevich Society, in Paris. Her name is Geneviève Delacloche. She'll be the best authority to confirm authenticity when we have the painting back, and she also has the best knowledge of collectors and criminals with an interest in Malevich. We, or perhaps I should say *I,* need all the help I can get.'

Harry stood in silence.

That night, Elizabeth Van Der Mier left her office light on. In the cool watery evening, her window glowed like a ship ablaze on a vast twilight sea.

* * *

'So our man, Morinière, at the gallery,' Bizot leaned in, then back quickly, as his beard had floated precariously near to the hot oil fondue. 'Alongside the door, he saw . . . a mezuzah.'

'What?'

'One of those Jewish thingies.'

'What Jewish thingies?'

'You know, those Jewish thingies that you hang in the doorway. It's a decorative tube that's supposed to contain parchment with a prayer written on it. Keeps away evil spirits, or something. I know . . . I had to look it up today.'

'Jean, there is no way that Luc Sallenave is Jewish, I can promise you . . .'

'I know. Neither is Courtil, neither is . . . anyone. That's what is so interesting about it. Morinière realized this, as well, when he was on the scene, which is why he thought to look inside.'

239

Lesgourges' eyes betrayed his enthusiasm. 'He looked inside the mezuga?'

'Yes. Neither he, nor I, nor anyone who had been on the scene had noticed it, because we had never stepped into the doorway, always just looked at the door from a distance. When the officer touched the mezuzah, he saw that the top was partially unscrewed.'

'This is unbelievable.' Lesgourges shook his head, then raised his hand and called, 'Hey, can we get some more wine here?'

'So Morinière unscrewed the top, and there was a piece of paper rolled up inside. Not old and brittle, but new. He took it out and photographed it, before replacing it, so our surveillance would not be . . . you know, surveyed. The mezuzah is a message conduit. Very clever, really.' Bizot reached into the breast pocket of his tweed jacket and drew out a photograph. He slid it across the table to Lesgourges.

'This is what was found inside. What do you make of it?'

Lesgourges looked down at the photograph. It was of a piece of printed paper. 'It looks like a page from the Bible.'

'Tu as raison. It is. Look closer.'

Lesgourges bent over to examine. It was a passage from the book of Isaiah. He began to read aloud: *'"They that make a graven image are all of them vanity; and their delectable things shall not profit; and they are their own witnesses; they see not, nor know; that they may be ashamed. Who hath formed a god, or molten a graven image that is profitable for nothing? Behold, all his fellows shall be ashamed: and the workmen, they are of men: let*

240

them all be gathered together, let them stand up; yet they shall fear, and they shall be ashamed together . . ."'

'Keep reading,' Bizot encouraged.

'"*The smith with the tongs both worketh in the coals, and fashioneth it with hammers, and worketh it with the strength of his arms: yea, he is hungry, and his strength faileth: he drinketh no water, and is faint.*" Ah, this part is circled: "*The carpenter stretcheth out his rule; he marketh it out with a line; he fitteth it with planes, and he marketh it out with the compass, and maketh it after the figure of a man, according to the beauty of a man; that it may remain in the house.*" What does that . . .'

'I have no clue. But it's a clue.'

'I know it's a clue, but . . .'

'I haven't gotten that far. That's why I need your help.' Bizot smiled and took another sip of wine.

'You do?' Lesgourges sat up. 'You do.'

'Look,' Bizot said. 'It's obviously a communication, and we don't know of what, or from whom. But it's conspiratorially secretive. Like a spy movie. Which means the communiqué is important to the recipient and the communicator. I think that we need to look around the gallery, and perhaps this message will become clearer.'

'Has the warrant been approved?' Lesgourges asked.

'Just this morning. I've been thinking about this all day. What is the nature of this quotation? It's from a passage about craftsmen who should be ashamed of making an image that will become a false idol. That much sounds familiar. The portion that is circled, Isaiah 44:13: "*The carpenter*

241

stretcheth out his rule; he marketh it out with a line;
he fitteth it with planes, and he marketh it out with
the compass, and maketh it after the figure of a man,
according to the beauty of a man; that it may remain
in the house." It's about a carpenter practicing his
art . . .'

'Jesus was a carpenter.' Lesgourges looked
pleased with himself.

'That's true, But so was Jesus' father figure,
Joseph. And, as I mentioned to you, we've learned
that Luc Sallenave has donated a considerable sum
of money to an organization called . . .'

'. . . the Brotherhood of Joseph.' Lesgourges'
light turned on.

'The address of which is the same street as
Sallenave's gallery. It's all rather a snug fit.'

'It certainly is,' Lesgourges echoed. 'I'm not
even hungry for dessert.'

'Come *on.*'

'Well, we could at least look at the menu. So,
you think we'll find the stolen painting somewhere
in the Galerie Sallenave?'

'Or in the apartment above it,' said Bizot.

'If you were to wager, what would you guess
we'll find?'

'Berries in crème fraîche . . .' Bizot scanned the
menu, then looked up. 'Well . . . let's think about
this. *"The carpenter stretcheth out his rule. He
marketh it out with a line."* A carpenter is
measuring and marking wood to be cut. A woodcut
print maybe? That's if the solution is a pun.
What's the next line? *"He fitteth it with planes, and
he marketh it out with the compass."* If it's literal,
then perhaps there is some structure made from
wood that contains the Malevich painting. Maybe

242

it's hidden in a garden shed, or in a false wall, but for the word *"compass."* It must refer to something measured and made from wood, planed flat, then measured with a circle from a compass.'

'It could be an outhouse.'

'Then, *"and maketh it after the figure of a man, according to the beauty of a man; that it may remain in the house."* So the wooden construction is shaped like a man, and this is what allows it to remain in the house.'

'What about the *"beauty of man"* bit?'

'That I cannot figure out. I'm also not sure what might be made of wood and shaped like a man. I thought of a sarcophagus, but that would be slightly conspicuous.'

'What do you think the communiqué is for?' Lesgourges asked. 'Do you think that the thief has hidden the painting somewhere, and is informing the patron of the theft about its location?'

'I haven't thought that far ahead, Jean. My brain is very small, and I can only solve one puzzle at a time. But the solution to one inevitably lights up clues to the others. In my career, as you'll want to note one day, when you become Bosworth to my Johnson, the domino effect has been my guiding principle. It makes no sense to speculate too long on things about which one is insufficiently informed. It leads to a lot of mental exercise that may prove fruitless, and I am inherently lazy when it comes to mental exercise.'

'And physical.'

'So I will only tackle the problem at hand, and solve the next one as I come to it. I hope you're taking notes.'

'Aren't investigators meant to think moves

ahead, like a chess player, to outwit the criminal? Like Sherlock Holmes and Miss Marple?'

'Do I look like Sherlock Holmes?'

Lesgourges looked Bizot up and down and across and back again. 'You look more like Miss Marple.'

'Ha.' Bizot coughed. 'Ha.'

'Maybe if you wore one of those floppy hats with the flaps hanging over your ears. . . .'

'Maybe if you drank a tall glass of shut-the-hell-up . . .' Bizot grumbled, then noticed that the waiter had been standing beside them for some time, ready to take their dessert order. He seemed somehow entranced by their conversation, his eyes glazed above his coonskin mustache. Bizot continued, 'So I don't know what we'll find, but I know where we need to go to find it, whatever *it* is, and then we'll sort it all out when we get there. So there.'

Lesgourges looked up at the waiter. 'Des profiteroles, s'il vous plaît. Do you think it will be hidden? The Malevich?'

'Undoubtedly.' Bizot paused. 'Des profiteroles pour moi, aussi.'

'I certainly hope so.'

'It's all a lot of fun for you, isn't it, Lesgourges? You realize this is my job, don't you?'

'Oh, stuff it. You love every minute.'

Bizot crossed his arms above his stomach. 'I suppose I do. As long as there is time for dessert, no job is too large.'

Lesgourges grinned his equine grin and leaned back in his chair. 'There's always time for dessert.'

CHAPTER TWENTY-FIVE

The next morning, Van Der Mier's office was flooded with bodies. Harry Wickenden directed four officers, who prepared the telephone to receive the ransomer's call, in hopes of tracking it. Wickenden had enough experience with such matters to know that the best they could hope for was an error. Any criminal worthy of the name would anticipate the phone trace. A fish that knows a lure from prey, knows enough not to bite. But to err is human, and hope is buoyant.

'Do you think they'll call soon?' Van Der Mier didn't like all this activity inside her nest.

An officer, who sat in front of a laptop, responded. 'We'll wait as long as it takes, ma'am, not to worry.'

That's what I was afraid of, she thought.

An hour and a half later, and Van Der Mier was trying to get some work done. With at least two officers present at all times, and the pressure of the situation at hand, it was difficult to stay focused. Through all of this, she had a museum to run, and had to make the public feel that nothing was wrong. There was a stack of loan requests to consider. MoMA wanted a Picasso, the Tate Modern down the river was assembling a retrospective and wanted a Barbara Hepworth sketchbook, and the Vigeland Museum in Oslo wanted a clay mock-up for one of Vigeland's monumental outdoor sculptures, which was in the National Gallery of Modern Art's collection. There were three years' worth of upcoming exhibitions to plan, letters to write, loan requests to be made, publicity, a curatorship to be filled. Van Der Mier sent a few emails, met with the Contemporary Drawings curator, did some paperwork. She did not touch her phone, but could not keep her eyes off it for long.

And then it rang.

The two officers in the room snapped to attention and met Van Der Mier's worried, questioning gaze. One of them whispered into a walkie-talkie, while another sat down in front of the laptop and put on headphones. By the third ring Wickenden and two other officers had swept into the room, and all put on headphones. Then Wickenden nodded to Van Der Mier, who picked up the phone.

'Hello?' The officers hung in wait, exchanging glances and checking the tracing and recording monitors. Wickenden silently encouraged. They waited, as Van Der Mier listened, the receiver to her ear.

'Oh, for Christ's sake! No, I don't want to go to lunch!' Van Der Mier slammed the phone down. Perspiration beaded, like tears, along her neck.

'What . . . was that?' Wickenden and her officers stared.

'That was the director of marketing! She doesn't know about the . . .'

'I see.'

'Sorry, I'm . . .'

'No, it's all right. Believe it or not, you're calmer than many I've dealt with.' Wickenden sat down, eyes still on Van Der Mier. 'Well, if she didn't know about the theft yet, she's probably suspicious that something's up now.'

Van Der Mier slumped into her chair. As her posterior touched the leather of the seat, she heard a *ding*.

'Oh, you're not going to believe this . . .' Van Der Mier was staring at something on her desk. 'A motherfucking email. Jesus H. Christ.' She was almost smiling. Almost. Wickenden was not.

The officers gathered around the back of Van Der Mier's enormous glass-and-mahogany desk, and collectively peered at her laptop screen. Van Der Mier double-clicked on the new letter.

'How did they get an email address with our domain?'

'Must have set it up when they hacked you last week, in anticipation,' said an officer, hoping to be helpful.

'They have a goddamned sense of humor, don't they?' Wickenden did not.

To: Elizabeth Van Der Mier
elizabeth.vandermier@ngma.org
From: Kasimir Malevich
malevich.white@ngma.org

Thank you for excepting our ransom offer. You will transfer £6.3 million into a numbered bank account, as listed below. On Saturday, at 10 in the morning, one museum representative will go to a location that we will specify in a future contact. We will then tell that representative where the painting is hidden, and you will be free to retrieve it. Do not bring policemen with you. Tell the policemen reading this email that we will not tolerate interference. We will not

247

strike again. We will keep our word, as long as you do. Cor 13:7

If the money is not in the account by the end of the Friday workday, then our offer will not stand, and the painting will be destroyed.

Then we will steal another one.

Thank you for cooperating, and have a nice day.

'Those cheeky monkeys,' whispered Van Der Mier. Wickenden eyed her expression, somewhere between a laugh and scream, perhaps a little of both, on the inside. 'Did you notice that they spelled *accepting* incorrectly. Or, rather, they used the wrong word. They wrote "excepting." That's odd. And it's so polite.'

Wickenden's mustache crept into the faintest smile before drooping once more.

'Like a student's request for an internship,' Van Der Mier mumbled.

'Harry, what do you make of this?' an officer asked, holding up a printout of the email.

Wickenden took the paper in hand and moved with it around the room.

'So much of this suggests art-world amateurs. Highly intelligent, skillful, low-class amateurs. It all profiles into expert thieves from outside the arts, trying their hand at art theft. They've clearly considered carefully how the ransom exchange will pan out. But the price choice and the misspelling, and the tone . . .'

'Is it possible that they're just very polite?' Van

248

Der Mier spoke in a joking manner, but the question was genuine. She gained confidence, and continued. 'I mean, who's to say that ransom notes must be matter-of-fact and brusque.'

'Don't forget that they do threaten. Destruction and future thefts . . .'

'Yes, I noticed that, Inspector. That part puts my knickers in a twist, but I have to say that I have trouble wholly hating these people. They put the art into art theft.'

'And the theft,' remarked an officer.

'I just wish that I was not their victim. Then I might admire . . .' Van Der Mier stared out her bay window across the London skyscape.

'The word choice error is . . . what? Carelessness?' Wickenden was very still. 'It's almost too much.'

An officer offered: 'It could be a red herring.'

'You think so?'

'I mean, all of these profiling characteristics that we're pointing out, they could be plants, meant to lead us to the wrong conclusions.'

'I don't know,' answered another officer. 'I don't think so. They've done such a bang-up job with the theft, and keeping their distance with the ransom and all . . . To divert the profile seems like an unnecessary precaution.'

'I don't hear enough hate in your voices, lads,' Wickenden cautioned. 'Don't go soft on me. We're out to nail these wankers. I don't find the way they mock us endearing. One way to look at this letter is as polite, good-natured criminals who are just out to make some dosh. But I see it as taunting, and I don't bloody-well like it.' He was looking at the printout. 'It says "Cor 13:7." What the hell is that supposed to mean?'

Van Der Mier crossed to him, and looked at the handout. 'Cor 13:7 . . . that looks like a . . . is it a ref . . . is it a Bible reference, chapter and verse?' She looked around the room, at a series of blank faces. 'Doesn't anyone go to church anymore? Jesus H. Christ!'

Wickenden scanned the officers in the room. 'Can you find us a Bible?'

A few minutes later, an officer reentered the room, a Bible in hand.

'Took long enough. Where did you find it?' Wickenden asked.

'Stole it from a hotel across the street.'

'Right.' The officer handed it to Van Der Mier, who opened to the index at the front. Van Der Mier ran her finger along the soft paper.

' "Placed here by the Gideons." Well, they won't miss it.' Van Der Mier smiled. 'Ah, Corinthians, of course. What is it? Thirteen-seven?'

Wickenden looked up, then read from the printout. 'Thirteen-seven.'

'Right.' Van Der Mier cascaded the skin-thin fresh white pages. 'Chapter thirteen, verse seven . . . oh, that cheeky . . .'

'What is it,' Wickenden approached, and looked over Van Der Mier's shoulder. ' "*Now I pray to God that ye do no evil; not that we should appear approved, but that ye should do that which is honest, though we be as reprobates . . .*" what the . . . Must be a group of religious zealots.'

'Do you think it's a right-wing religious group?' Van Der Mier began. 'I mean, Malevich's *White on White* was famously iconoclastic. It was made all white, in fact, to negate the icon. When it was first displayed, it was hung in a high corner of the room, the traditional place where Russian families would keep icons, old paintings of Mary and Jesus. Replacing Mary and Jesus with a white painting is the ultimate in iconoclasm. Maybe it's a statement against that iconoclasm.'

'Maybe,' said Wickenden, 'but they're still asking for money. These ransomers are asking for cash, and lots of it. But it certainly does skew the profile.'

'If you don't mind, Inspector, let's call in the Malevich Society expert, Geneviève Delacloche, so she can examine the painting when we get it back. And I'd better keep Lord Harkness abreast.' Van Der Mier picked up her phone, which caused all of the surveillance and tracing instruments to whir into action. Van Der Mier rolled her eyes and dialed.

CHAPTER TWENTY-SIX

By ten on Saturday morning, Portobello Road was choked. A blitz of stalls and wares and buyers, wanderers, tourists, everyone and everything, a claustrophobic vastness, a joyful mess, a bargain-hunter's dream, a boiling pool of treasures buried amidst the vertiginous jungle of crap. It was said that absolutely anything could be bought, and had been bought, at Portobello Road.

For those gawk-eyed tourists, with Hard Rock Café shirts and broad mindless smiles and brass voices, it was a spectacle to behold. They, in turn, were hungrily beheld by the stall-lurking sellers. It

251

is true, there were bargains to be had, but there were also buyers to be had.

The true treasures were off the main road. Portobello Road itself suffocated with stalls dripping junk. Although there probably were many illicit goings-on, most of the fleecing was gentle and benevolent. Truth was not volunteered, but neither was it maliciously avoided. If someone asked, they would be told that the eighteenth-century map of England that they admired was a photocopy of an original that would have cost many times more than the £25 asking price. But many buyers, tourists in the main, did not bother to ask, so the seller did not bother to tell.

When Van Der Mier had come to London for the first time, as a young girl, her parents had taken her to Portobello Road. She vividly remembered playing 'I Spy' with her father and brother, and was jaw-dropped at the list of objects spied. One in particular, a blackface minstrel monkey lamp with a base made from antler, ingrained in her mind as strangest of all. Portobello Road had been something of a fantasy world to her. Frightening for the swarms of bodies, in which a child could easily get lost, but not so foreign; extraterrestrial in a way that inspires awe, not fear. The smells recalled: damp and mothballs and mildew and old books and metal polish and bodies and sunlight and beer and coffee and yellowing lace, and summoned flashbacks of her study of Proust in Professor McCatty's class at university.

She had once concocted a story, never written. She'd imagined that somewhere, in the deepest, darkest heart of the Portobello Road moonscape, amidst the endless clutter and saturated tabletops, a booth lay in wait. This booth consisted only of a table, with just one object on it. And for whoever approached the booth, the object on the table was the one thing that they had been looking for. The man behind the booth had a red-and-white goatee and a silvery glint in his eye. The price for the object was always just a little more than the buyer had on him. So, the seller would be more than willing to barter a deal . . .

She'd been to Portobello Road only a handful of times, as a child. Her Dutch father was an attorney who was renowned for his work in the War Crimes Tribunal, and split time between London and The Hague. Her British mother had brought up her and her brother at home, spending summers in Holland, and the rest of the year in Kent, a short commute from London's center, but very much in the countryside. But from an early age, Elizabeth had been to boarding school in America, and to university there. She'd returned only ten years earlier, to accept a lucrative curatorial position, and had remained ever since.

The few trips to Portobello Road were fresh in her mind, as she now walked the endless road, full of things that no one really needed but nevertheless convinced themselves to buy.

Van Der Mier's educated eye could now separate the wheat from the chaff. It was unlikely that one would find anything of great value, and the sellers knew more about their wares than buyers hoped, but good prices were assured, haggling welcome, and jewels to be found within the sand. She skimmed over photocopies, shined-up silvery steel, homely antiques, wormy books, and latched on to original prints, silver objects, and crisp, dry tomes. To a trained eye, promising objects are nimbused.

Van Der Mier checked her watch: 10:03. Her mobile phone was still on. Good. Why hadn't they called?

She wove through a forest of people, padded along the gray pavement, with the sun glinting off car tops and crates of silver, the sound of hundreds of voices like the shudder of wings.

The phone rang.

'Yes?'

It was Wickenden. 'We just got the email. The money has been confirmed. The painting is inside one of the arcades, one with a green door, on a corner. The message says that the painting's in the basement, across from a bear.'

'A bear? As in . . . a bear? Do you think that's a joke?'

'I don't know. There can't be a . . . what do you think it means?' There was a pause, and the sound of voices in the distance. 'None of us have ideas, for the moment. Stay on the line, though.'

'Don't worry, I will.'

'You'll like this. They sign off the letter with "best wishes."'

'Cheeky bastards. How do you read this politesse?'

'I think that we're dealing with a handful of wankers.'

'Ah.' Van Der Mier was two long blocks into Portobello Road, the crowds increasing in density. Stalls on both sides of the street narrowed the pedestrian way. She felt the claustrophobia of dense bodies below an open blue sky.

Wickenden continued. 'Do you know the arcade they mean? With the green door?'

'I do. It's got two levels, so the basement direction makes sense. It's just up ahead. Do you think they misspelled "bear"? Or meant "bare"? After the last message, I wouldn't put it past them.'

'I don't . . . no, we think . . . that wouldn't make any more sense, but I . . . ah, who the hell knows?'

'I know how you feel.'

'Sorry, Ms. Van Der Mer. It's just that, if someone acts logically, then you can think logically and anticipate and solve. But if you don't trust them to be logical . . .'

'Then all bets are off. I agree. What a pain in the ass.'

Van Der Mier stopped in front of an ornately carved doorway, painted mint green, which stretched wide, like a great yawning mouth. She recognized the location. The true deals to be found were in the warren of indoor stalls, off the touristy road, like mine shafts running into a mountain. It was easy to lose oneself, retrace steps, vision blurred by watches, cigarette cases, pewter mugs, and blackface minstrel monkey lamps with a bases made from antler. Van Der Mier smiled to herself, briefly.

'How should I go inside?'

'It just says that it's in the basement. Is there more than one entrance?'

'If I remember this place correctly, there are several. It's like a beehive. I'll just try one and see if it leads to stairs going down.' The mobile phone pressed to her ear, Van Der Mier entered.

There were no stairs in sight. Booths oozing

books and knickknacks on all sides, but no stairs. People brushed past, laughing and talking. The dizzying array of passersby, and excess of objects, disoriented. Mixed with nerves, Van Der Mier felt light-headed. She chose a direction and walked it. Meters farther on, she turned left, and a trident of paths opened before her. She looked back and could no longer see the door through which she'd come.

'I think I should have brought some yarn, or a GPS tracker, or something . . . hello? Hello?' Her phone had cut off. She looked at the monitor. No service. Then she looked up at the ceiling. She made a mental note to switch to a new phone server.

The middle path seemed as good a choice as any. She wound along it, and was confronted only with more options, none of them down. She met eyes with a woman at a stall, selling delicate costume jewelry from a glass vitrine.

'Do you know how to reach the basement?'

'I've no feckin' idea, luv.'

'Well, thank you, anyway. Do you, by any chance, know where someone might be selling . . . a bear?'

'The stalls change each week, luv, so I've no idea. But bear baitin' is illegal, so I'd watch who you ask.'

'Right. Cheers.'

'It's no trouble at all, dear.'

Van Der Mier spun down another corridor rife with shops. She looked at her phone once more. Still no service. People stood all around, but no basement in sight, and no bears. A line from Coleridge came into her mind. She felt thirsty.

Elizabeth looked up to her left. There was a small, creamy porcelain statue of a saint. Apt, she thought.

She hadn't remembered her past trips to Portobello Road Market as quite so labyrinthine. Perhaps it was because she had never been looking for anything particular before. It's best to visit without an agenda. The more specific the object desired, the more frustrating the visit could become. Better to wander aimlessly. That's when you don't get lost, she thought. It's only when you've a place to be . . .

She stopped at another booth to ask for directions.

'Oh, sure. The cellar's that way. You go to the end of the walk, turn left, go a few paces, but not down the long way, just the short one, it's a little hop to the right, then a jog a few paces, past a point where the paint is sort of peelin' down off the ceiling like, and it's just on your left. Can't miss it.'

'Right . . .'

Van Der Mier followed the directions as best she could. End of the walk. Left turn. A few paces farther. A corridor opened up before her, but she did not follow it. Instead, she curled to the right. About a meter along, she saw something strange on the ground. It looked like piled clips of white paper. Then she looked up at the ceiling. Flakes of paint dangled precariously overhead. Damoclean swords. She looked to her left. There were stairs leading down to the dark.

It looked as though no lights were on at the foot of the stairs. Van Der Mier stared down, as if at the edge of a precipice. Perhaps a dim light below, but she saw no movement. She checked her phone once more. Nothing. She stepped down.

As her eye level descended, the gauzy fog of the sparsely lit basement sifted into view. There seemed to be but one fluorescent light, which flickered menacingly, creating the illusion of a mist in the cellar below. The wooden stairs creaked, precarious, under Van Der Mier's heel. When she was low enough to see what was in the cellar, she nearly fell over.

At the foot of the stairs, Van Der Mier slipped and barely caught herself. Through the sputtering fluorescence she saw, bathed in the dim, aquatic light, an enormous roaring bear. Its teeth and black gums bared, clawed arms open wide, it towered up, head against the ceiling. It was stuffed, of course. Van Der Mier managed a nervous laugh.

Well, that's a bear, she thought. Her eyes adjusted to the middling light, and she saw a feast of horrors before her.

The booth at the foot of the stair looked like a Victorian nightmare natural history museum. All manner of taxidermied creatures, in horrible unnatural poses, lurked in the pall. A stuffed leopard, the skeleton of a baboon, a series of shrunken dried monkey heads on a table, a skeletal bird on a perch inside a birdcage, a human skull, the whole skin of a crocodile, giant shark teeth, a long snakeskin, a tray of impaled butterflies.

That's ghastly, thought Elizabeth. Then she noticed that every frightening creature had a price tag attached to it. Who would want to buy any of this? Like the set of a Vincent Price picture. But I

258

have found a bear.

'Careful of the step, luv.' The sound of a voice nearly made her fall again. She turned to see a toothless, gray old woman, sitting on a milk crate, in the cast of a shadow. She wore a ratty blue wool sweater, and a patchwork skirt that barely covered her bony, bent knees.

Jesus, thought Van Der Mier. She looks like she should be mixed among the dead animals. Then she heard a voice from above.

'Hey, honey, I've found more stalls! Come and take a look. Wow!'

An American accent screeched down from the stair top. It was soon followed by a pale-legged man in khaki shorts and a T-shirt that flowed down his thighs, cinched in by a purple hip pack. He wore a neon-green baseball cap with a mesh back, that was tilted at a forty-five-degree angle above a balding pate. Sunglasses swung from a yellow string around his neck. His face beamed with glee.

'Well, darn, if it isn't dark down here. What the heck happened to your lights . . . oh, my sugar jets!' He leapt back in surprise when he saw the bear growling at the foot of the stairs. 'Nearly gave me a heart attack. Ginny, there's a bear down here!'

'What's that, Ted?' An airy sparrow voice leaned down the stairs, followed by a wildly overweight woman in a flowered blouse that was several notches too tight. 'Ooh. I see.' She tried to step daintily off of the wooden stairs and slipped. 'Oh, my.' She was sizing up the bear, or perhaps vice versa.

'Look over here, Ginny. There are some paintings. This one looks real good.' They drifted

259

toward the old woman's stall. She smiled up at them from her milk crate.

'Sorry about the light, dears. It's been flicking about all day, and there'll be no one to change it 'til Monday. I think I'm the only one who's opened up today. I see you all like Herbert. That's what we call the bear. Jim Boylan runs that booth, but he's not come in today. Herbert's been with us for over a year now. Can't seem to find him a home.'

'Well, we'd take him, sure enough, ma'am,' said Ted, 'only he wouldn't fit in my suitcase.' He and Ginny started giggling in brazen tones. 'Hey, Ginny, look at this one . . .'

Van Der Mier tore her eyes away from the canopy of horrors and walked past the other cellar stalls. There were only four of them. The owners had clearly drawn the short straw in the selection pool. The basement felt blue and submarine, as she scanned the stock of each booth. They were all paintings down here, except for the stuffed monsters behind her. Van Der Mier did not want to look upon them again, but could barely resist. She shivered and walked on.

A host of nondescript amateur oil paintings in bombastic frames hung on the stall walls. Could the Malevich be hidden inside one of these booths? Rolled up in a corner? God, she thought, I hope it wasn't rolled tightly. I'm going to have them killed if that painting cracked. Three booths yielded no immediate answers, and Van Der Mier turned to the old woman's stall, where the Americans were giddily fondling artworks.

As she turned, Elizabeth thought that she saw the old woman staring at her. But when she looked

260

down, the sorry toothless creature who sat all bony on the milk crate was talking with the Americans, her back to Van Der Mier.

'I like that one, Ted. It'd go well in our kitchen.'

'Nah,' replied Ted. 'It's just all white and clumpy. Heck, I could do that for you, with the stuff I got in the garage.'

'I know, but it matches our walls. I read that you're supposed to match the art to the wall color, or something.'

'I'll paint you one when we get back.'

'Okey-doke.' They waddled away from the stall, and slowly back up the stairs, which groaned under Ginny's heft.

When they had gone, Elizabeth felt the palpable quiet, amidst the dark hum of the single fluorescent, and the silent breathing smile of the old woman. Then she registered what the Americans had been saying.

She moved to the center of the old woman's booth. It consisted of three sides of a white square cage, on which hung countless gold-framed paintings of all sizes. In the middle, on a stretcher, but the only one unframed, was a painting that was white on white.

Van Der Mier reached out and lifted it off its hanger. She looked at the edges of the canvas, where it had been stapled to the wooden stretcher. The staples gleamed. She saw that the canvas was unevenly taut, with a small ripple along the bottom left. As if it had been affixed to the stretcher in a hurry, and recently. Then she looked at the painting.

That's it, she thought. That's it.

'Ya like it, luv?' The old woman glared up at

261

Van Der Mier, one eye squintier than the other.

'Ma'am. My name is Elizabeth Van Der Mier, and I am the director of the National Gallery of Modern Art, here in London. This painting belonged to the gallery and was misplaced. I'm here to retrieve it. Can you tell me who gave it to you?'

The old woman looked suspiciously at her. 'I can't say. My husband runs the business most of the time, and he must've got it during the week, as it's new. Ya like it?'

'Yes, but . . . is your husband . . . no, doesn't matter. Thanks.' She turned to leave, painting in hand.

'Excuse me, miss. That's ten pounds.'

'What?'

'The painting you're walking off with. It costs ten quid. Cash only.'

'But you don't seem to understand. This is the property of the National . . .'

'Look, luv. I don't give a flying monkey's arse if it's from King Tut's tomb. That sticker on the side has got a ten on it, and that means that my Roddy wants ten quid for it. If you want it, then you're welcome, but . . .' She held out her up-cupped palm. She wasn't smiling anymore.

'You've got to be kidding . . .' Van Der Mier mumbled to herself. She looked at the painting, looked at the old woman, then thought about the stairs. She put down the painting and reached for her wallet, cursing under her breath.

Elizabeth opened her Bottega Veneta wallet and flipped through her bills. Oh shit, she thought. Then she looked hopelessly at the old woman.

'Look,' she said. 'I can't believe it myself, but I

262

only have a fiver on me. If you just . . .'

'I'm not that nice, luv. Look, I can see you drive a hard bargain. I'll give it to you for nine.'

'Nine? But I just told you, I only have . . .'

'Like we all haven't heard that one before. Come now, nine's a good price. That's a bloody big painting for nine quid, and if Roddy knew, well . . .'

Elizabeth stopped listening, as she rifled through her wallet, checking the coin purse, then the credit card slots.

Nothing.

She thrust her hands down tight-fitted pockets. Her right front, left front, right back, left back. She felt something there.

She pulled out a scrap of paper. On it was written 'Pick up dry cleaning 2:30.' She threw the paper down, and reached back in. There was something else. She opened her fist.

It held another five-pound note.

She looked skyward, mouthed a thank-you, and looked back down, hard, at the old woman on her crate.

'Here,' she snapped, thrusting the two fivers into the wrinkled, waiting hands. She picked up the painting and turned.

'Don't you want your pound change, then?'

'No, I don't fucking want my pound change!'

'Thank you, then. Have a nice day.'

Van Der Mier quickly looked back over her shoulder. The old woman was neatly folding the two fives, quietly humming to herself beneath her patchy white hair. No way, thought Elizabeth. She walked out of the cellar.

Once outside again, Van Der Mier flipped open

her phone. Service, at last. There were three new messages. She knew whom they were from. She dialed.

'Ah, Inspector, it's me. Yes, I know. I went indoors and lost my service. You wouldn't believe . . . yes, I have it. Looks unhurt. It's been rolled and newly stapled to a fresh stretcher. But I think it's okay. Call Conservation, and see if the woman from the Malevich Society, Geneviève Delacloche, has arrived. I'm coming straight back.'

CHAPTER TWENTY-SEVEN

Elizabeth Van Der Mier, Harry Wickenden, Geneviève Delacloche, and the museum's chief conservator stood in the Conservation Room of the National Gallery of Modern Art, trying not to recall that this was the painting's second visit. The two guards posted outside the room hoped to ensure that it would leave only on more appropriate grounds.

The painting sat on an oversize easel. Wickenden thought that it looked smug. Delacloche considered that it exuded an air of relief, or perhaps it was she who did. The conservator, Barney, couldn't wait to get his hands on it, as it had slipped through them merely a few days before. Elizabeth looked concerned but tried to mask her disquiet.

'I think we can get started,' said Van Der Mier, who did not know what to do with her hands. She turned to Delacloche. 'Thank you for coming, Ms. Delacloche, under these . . . less than ideal circumstances. You can understand why we prefer to keep the museum staff out of this for the time being . . . in case, well, in case anyone is involved. So we've had to look outside for expert advice. We appreciate your help and expertise. You come very highly recommended.'

'I'm happy to help, if I can,' she replied.

'Can't wait, myself,' said Barney, approaching the canvas. 'Don't see any obvious damage.'

'Do you suppose there'd be fingerprints on the stretcher?' Elizabeth asked.

'We can check,' said Wickenden, 'but these blokes have been too smooth to leave fingerprints now.'

'Right. And that creepy old woman probably got her paws all over it. That was monumentally bizarre.'

'Did the woman know where her husband had acquired the painting?' asked Delacloche.

'Nothing useful like that, I'm afraid.'

'It couldn't be . . .'

'She didn't look like the art thief type. She didn't look like the breathing type, either. You should have seen her. All bones and kneecaps . . . what's the matter, Ms. Delacloche?'

'It's just . . . I . . . it doesn't look right.'

'What do you mean?' Elizabeth seemed worried.

'What do you mean?' Wickenden seemed worried.

'Huh?' Barney didn't hear.

'I mean, it just . . . it looks good, but I . . . something's wrong.'

'Can you be more descriptive?' Elizabeth perspired.

'It's just a vibe you get . . . I'm getting,' Delacloche continued. 'It looks like the original, but . . .'

'It's white,' Wickenden spit, 'of course it looks the same!'

Barney stood up. 'There's a reason that I have all of these brilliant, expensive gadgets. Let's play.' He crossed to the door marked SCIENCE & TECHNOLOGY and entered. The sound of rummaging followed.

Delacloche continued. 'The one at auction looked authentic, as if it were a different painting by Malevich from the same White on White series. But it was not the one Christie's had photographed in the catalogue. But strange that I should never have seen it before. I've seen every extant Malevich. So the one at auction must have either been a newly discovered White on White original, one not listed in any literature, or an excellent fake.'

Elizabeth's mind was elsewhere. Wickenden tried to read it. The first hint of concern about the authenticity of this piece set her imagination in motion, and led it to places she'd preferred to deny the privilege of possibility. What made her so certain that this was the original painting? The painting had been stolen before it could even be checked properly by Barney and his team.

Van Der Mier would not recognize an original from a copy herself. Not a Malevich. She had her degree in twentieth-century American painting. If it were a Pollock or a Close or a Fish, then perhaps she'd have the visceral reaction.

There was a term for someone with this *almost* preternatural sense for authenticity. Almost. The

266

extreme knowledge of a specific artist's style and canon, known as 'connoisseurship,' had been taught widely, but these days it was a rare commodity. It was this rarity that, in Elizabeth's belief, had led to its veneration. Those who did not understand that intimate degree of knowledge possessed by traditional scholars, mistook connoisseurship for divination. Those who could identify authentic works at a glance were popularly referred to as 'divies,' for their apparent powers.

But Elizabeth, never one to fall back upon a New Age, mystical explanation, knew better. Perhaps the last bastion of taught connoisseurship was her postgraduate alma mater, the Courtauld Institute. Their method of teaching reminded her of a story she'd once been told.

In ancient China, a youth was apprenticed to a master jade smith. The master's jade jewelry was coveted, and he was considered the greatest artisan of his time. The apprentice was thrilled to have been taken under this master's wing, and he eagerly anticipated his first day of learning the art.

On the first day, the master approached the youth.

'Put out your hands,' he said sternly.

The youth obeyed. Into his hands, the master placed a small piece of jade. It was beautiful, smooth and green, like coral beneath the sea.

'Now,' said the master, 'I want you to examine this piece of jade very carefully. It is real. It should be taken in with all senses. I will come to get you at the end of the day.'

The youth was disappointed at his assignment but approached it with intensity. He rolled the jade in his fingers, looked at it from all sides,

267

listened to the sound of his fingernail against it, even smelled and tasted it.

At the end of the day, the master returned. He saw that the boy had been diligent, and he congratulated him.

The next morning, the youth was eager for his next assignment. But when the master approached him, he handed the boy a different piece of jade.

'I want you to examine this new piece of jade very carefully. I will come and get you at the end of the day.'

'But . . .' The boy tried to protest, but was silenced by a hard stare.

'If you wish to learn from me, my son,' said the master sternly, 'then you must do exactly as I say. Follow my instructions, and you will succeed me as the greatest jeweler in the land.' The boy obeyed.

For one year, every morning the boy was given a different piece of jade and was left alone to examine it all day long. Though frustrated, the boy was still honored to be apprenticed to such a master, and he deeply wanted to learn his art. So he did not complain, and did as he was told, diligently inspecting each new piece of jade.

One morning, the master approached the youth and placed a new piece of jade into his outstretched hands. As the master turned around to return to work, the boy spoke.

'But, Master,' he said, 'this piece of jade . . . it's not real.'

'Ah,' said the master. 'Now you are ready to begin.'

Elizabeth had heard that story at her matriculation to Courtauld, and it had stuck with her ever since. It embodied the culture, that had become a cult, of connoisseurship. True connoisseurs knew an infinite amount about something minutely specific. Connoisseurs, like Geneviève Delacloche, were a dying breed.

Barney had been dancing his way around the canvas for some minutes, before he turned around. 'You're right. There's something wrong. The paint's not old enough.'

'What do you mean?' Elizabeth snapped out of her reverie. 'It's not 1918?'

'Try a few days.'

'Are you kidding me!?' Wickenden was not pleased. Unlike Delacloche and Van Der Mier, he had suspected nothing.

'I don't think it's even pure oil paint. Something else mixed in. I'll have to run tests to say anything more, but . . .'

'Are you kidding me!?' Elizabeth was at a loss.

'. . . but I think that we should take an X ray. It'll take some time, but we have the facilities here, so . . .'

'Do it. Do it now, Barney.' Elizabeth Van Der Mier stood very still.

Wickenden tried to read her eyes. Somehow, she had known. Or had she? It was easy to impose prescience, in retrospect. But this was too much to bear. If this was not real, then she had lost not only the museum's money, but a fortune from Lord Harkness, which he'd been kind enough to provide out of his own goodness and pocket. And all for the recovery of a fake. But the question remained: was what the museum had bought at auction fake all along, or had it been swapped for a fake during the ransom? Wickenden nodded to himself.

'Ms. Delacloche?' Elizabeth repeated,

awakening her from a stupor. 'You say that you were at the auction. The painting I bid on . . . was it . . .'

'I don't know. I've been trying to visualize it. But . . . it must have been. I mean, I just *knew* that this was the wrong . . . I just . . . I mean, the one at auction looked authentic, but it was not the same one that was pictured in the catalogue. But it did look authentic, a different painting from the same series, also by Malevich. And then . . . I guess it might have been switched between the time it was purchased at the auction and when it was delivered here. But that would imply impropriety on the part of Christie's, and I can't imagine . . . I'm just . . .'

'All right. Let's sit down and have a cup of tea and sort this through. Barney, call us when you're ready.' Elizabeth led Delacloche out of the room.

Wickenden was still confused, unsure as to whether or not he was angry. He seemed in a perpetual state of indigestion. 'Are you trying to tell me that this is not even a Malevich, much less the original?'

'Looks more like a Benjamin Moore.'

'Is he an artist?'

'No, that's a house paint company.'

'That's not funny!' He stormed out of the room. Barney shrugged. Glad it's not my six million, he thought, as he went to work.

*   *   *

In Elizabeth Van Der Mier's top-floor office, tea was just brewing. Delacloche and Wickenden sat on the Mies van der Rohe Barcelona chairs in the corner of the office. Elizabeth poured the tea,

270

without inquiring how much milk, and passed it around.

'Is there . . .' she began, '. . . is there anything we could have done differently . . . Inspector?'

Wickenden was silent for a moment. 'No. They had us by the bollocks, and that's that.'

'I wouldn't blame yourself. It was a very difficult situation . . .'

'. . . But it's my job to work it out, for Christ's sake . . .' he trailed off. 'I mean, they were good. They did everything perfectly. We never saw them, never had actual, direct contact with them. Never even near them, as far as we know.'

'They had us by the bollocks and dragged us around as much as they liked. I just can't help thinking,' continued Elizabeth, 'that there might have been a way to better ensure that we'd gotten the right painting back.'

'Or that you started out with the right painting.' Delacloche spoke. 'Something was going on during that auction . . .'

'I wouldn't have minded the whole damned thing so much if we'd gotten the painting back.' Elizabeth sipped her tea. 'I'd applaud having been bested by skillful criminals. One has to marvel at exceptional ability, in any field. But this . . . this removes any of the fun . . .'

'What's fun about it?' Wickenden moped.

'I know what she means,' said Delacloche, her voice drifting. Wickenden saw that she and Van Der Mier made eye contact. 'But to be denied surrender even after you've admitted the superiority of the opponent . . . It is cruel and greedy. I can understand the profession of theft. If it is a means to earn a living, however distasteful, I

271

can understand that. But to keep the stolen painting even after the ransom is paid—it's like shooting someone after he's voluntarily handed you his wallet and pleaded for mercy.'

'Aren't you both being a little heavy-handed about this? It's not as though someone's life were lost.' Wickenden sat up now, as he spoke. 'I'm displeased because I was tricked, but it's just a piece of canvas with some white paint on it. I mean, it's just white!'

'And you're just a man with a droopy mustache,' Delacloche snapped.

'What does that have to do with . . .'

'It's the same thing. Your comment is just as useless. Don't denounce what you don't understand, simply because you don't understand it.'

'A moment.' Elizabeth stood. 'The more I think on it, the more I believe that we're dealing with criminals from outside the art world.'

'But they kept the painting,' Wickenden gesticulated. 'What do you think they're going to do, stuff it up their attic in a pile of mothballs?'

'Something like that.' Elizabeth began to wander the room. 'Remember the Bible quotation. I think all of this may be more of a statement, rather than a financial opportunity. Maybe both, but just think about it. We buy the painting for £6.3 million. There's much fanfare and publicity. We don't even get to put it up, before it's stolen. The ransomers ask for the same price we paid at auction, then they return a fake that, *to them*, is just the same as the original. They have no sense of the value of the original, and are trying to tell us that we should not either. They want us to conclude that money should be better spent than on a piece of canvas painted white, as Inspector Wickenden so bluntly put it.'

'I think you may be right,' muttered Delacloche, still staring off. 'Or, they want to mock Malevich's iconoclasm, and are saying that we should go back to the graven image, in this godless time. That, of course, implies that they know the history of art, and is contradicted by their choice of ransom price. They may be religious zealot terrorists. I hate violent ignorance, particularly when it's evangelical. Why do people feel the need to inflict their opinion on others?'

'This is just . . .' Wickenden gazed into his teacup. '. . . it's just . . . I'm sorry. I can't say anything more right now, I'm just . . .'

'It's all right.' Elizabeth put her hand on his shoulder. He shivered away from the contact. 'No one could have predicted this.'

'It's just that I . . .' It's just that I can't stand being fooled, and it's never happened before, Wickenden wanted to say but did not.

'Well, I really appreciate your coming down to advise, Ms. Delacloche. I wish that we had met on happier terms. Give my regards to our mutual friend, and tell him how much I appreciate the recommendation. Now, I haven't a goddamn clue what I'm going to say to Lord Harkness. Sometimes I hate this job.' Elizabeth sat down at her desk once more. Then the phone rang. She picked it up.

'Hello? Oh, hello, Barney. We'll be right down.'

CHAPTER TWENTY-EIGHT

Bizot and Lesgourges and two officers sat in a gray van down the street from the Galerie Sallenave, on rue de Jérusalem. They could see the entrance to the gallery in their rearview mirror. They heard a van door slide shut somewhere in the street behind them. Three figures entered the frame of the mirror, then disappeared down the alley alongside the gallery. Bizot looked both ways along the length of rue de Jérusalem, then whispered, 'On y va.' The four men exited the van and crossed the empty street.

Galerie Sallenave was a four-story neoclassical building, thoroughly renovated with modern features. In addition to the alternating peaked and rounded pediments above the windows, and the volutes rolling out of the eaves beneath the canopy of slate rooftop, a new front door, made of a solid block of maple ringed in steel, and surveillance cameras revealed the present day.

Bizot led his officers along the alley to the left of the gallery, and around to the service entrance. Lesgourges followed, dressed enthusiastically in a khaki trench coat purchased expressly for this occasion, collar turned up and Vuarnet sunglasses on, despite the overcast sky.

The service alley was dull gray paved, and flanked with neatly aligned rubbish bins. Lesgourges nudged Bizot. 'Jean, where is the advance party?'

Bizot responded with a violent *shhh* of finger to lip. 'Tu vas voir.'

One officer watched the entrance to the alley, while the other pushed through the service entrance door. Inside, the advance group was just closing their briefcases. There was an elevator to the left, and a door to the gallery on the right.

Bizot whispered to Lesgourges. 'They've picked the lock, turned off the alarm, and they'll loop the surveillance so it never sees us.'

'That was fast. How do they do that?'

'I don't . . . don't ask stupid questions.'

'Okay.'

'And don't touch anything.'

'Did I touch anything?'

'No, but just don't.'

'Do I look like I'm going to touch anything?'

'Just . . . *shhh.*' Bizot turned on his flashlight and walked past Lesgourges, who was still marveling. The other officers spread out through the ground floor.

The gallery was stark and white. Ornamental features, dentillation and marble fireplaces, were allowed to shine as the only decorative elements of the otherwise empty rooms. Each room was small and intimate, the whitewashed wood panels broken only by periodic prints, on display in simple, understated black frames, a switched-off spotlight aimed at each. Light from flashlights in hand flickered around the dim rooms. A thin film of cloudy sunlight filtered in through slats in the closed window shutters and the particles in the air.

Lesgourges could not see his reflection in the glass protecting each print. Nonreflective, ultraviolet-protected glass, he noted. Like he used to frame his prints, and to protect his Picasso, in Armagnac.

Each print had a small piece of wall copy beside it, merely a label, without explanations. Lesgourges recognized some of the names, but his art-historical knowledge stemmed from only periodic bouts of autodidacticism. Goltzius, Marcolini, Rembrandt, Dürer, Wierix, Piranesi, van Veen . . . He had heard of Rembrandt, Dürer, and Piranesi. Not that he could identify any of them by sight, necessarily. The others reflected some sort of mental echo, but its decrescendo was too distant to bear meaning.

The prices listed did trigger something in Lesgourges. It was admiration. Admiration for a knowledge of the material foreign to his own, for having the ancien régime taste and money stained with blue blood, for the Sallenave name. It was Lesgourges' father who had earned his way, and bought their château and vineyard. Sure, Lesgourges had more money than many Old World aristocrats, but they had what he could not buy.

And so he had taught himself, as best as he could, as much as he could. But he was still having to try, while they all seemed to do, effortlessly. Lesgourges caught up with Bizot in the third display room.

'Jean,' said Lesgourges, 'have you seen anything that looks promising?'

'Pas encore.'

'Me neither. There are prints of Jesus, but none of Joseph, so far. I don't see any carpenter shops, or sarcophagi, or outhouses, either.'

'Courage, mon ami,' Bizot said, his eyes ever cast along the walls. 'When we see it, we will know. Whatever it is.'

The ground floor circumnavigated, Bizot and

Lesgourges moved upstairs. The first floor was one large, open space, with a glass desk in the corner, and the walls covered by substantial tapestries, also for sale.

Bizot approached the desk. It was immaculate, its contents perpendicular to one another, everything in blacks and grays. Bizot nodded in approval. With a gloved hand, he flipped through the address book, black leather bound, on the table. Alpers, Bonavita, Chetcuti, Danks, Esterházy, Frei, Grayson, Hancock, Inzaghi, Janot, Kuznezov, Lalani, Marlais, Nikolova, Oyeyemi, Peretti . . . He closed the book.

'This doesn't look promising,' said Lesgourges, who was standing in the center of the room, hands on hips, while officers examined around him.

'I want to see the apartment up . . .' Bizot was interrupted by a shout.

'Ici, j'ai trouvé quelque chose!' Bizot crossed the room. An officer was kneeling before one of the tapestries.

'Qu'est-ce qu'il y a?' Bizot stood beside.

'There's a false wall behind this tapestry.'

From what Lesgourges could see, Bizot's outline standing behind the tapestry looked like a misshapen plump lump of clay caught under the smooth-flowing fabric. Bizot was a buttress beneath the enormous tapestry that covered a wall of the first floor of the Galerie Sallenave. Beneath that tapestry, whitewashed wood paneling ran the length of the wall, but there was a discernible rectangular outline. Bizot scanned his flashlight along the thin shadow that revealed, tracing the false piece of wall.

'Let's get this open,' he said.

Two officers approached with tools. One prepared to insert a screwdriver into the gap and pry, but his elbow glanced the wood, and the panel sprung open.

Behind it was a safe.

'Putain de, merde, salaud, mon Dieu . . . ,' Bizot muttered with pleasure.

'Qu'est-ce qu'il y a?' Lesgourges fumbled his way behind the tapestry.

'A safe.'

'Hmm.'

'What do you mean, hmm?'

Two of the officers made eye contact.

'I just mean,' Lesgourges replied to Bizot, 'that it's interesting.'

'What's interesting? What could be more interesting than this!?'

'Well, did you notice the content of the tapestry that you are under?'

'No.'

'Hmm.'

'Don't *hmm* me! What is it?'

Lesgourges crossed his arms. 'It's a copy of the tapestries designed by Bronzino for Cosimo de' Medici.'

'And?'

'They show scenes from the life of Joseph.'

'You mean . . .'

'Not that Joseph. The Old Testament Joseph. With the brothers and the coat and the dreams and Pharaoh, and that stuff. But it's still a Joseph.' Lesgourges was pleased with himself.

'Hmm,' Bizot replied.

The safe occupied all of the niche in which it sat, about one meter square, and quite deep.

Lesgourges leaned into the niche.

'I know the safe brand,' said Lesgourges, who always relished the moments when fortune made practical his trivial knowledge. 'It's a Cobb-Hauptmann.'

Bizot nodded, impressed, then turned to look from Lesgourges to the safe. It had the words *Cobb-Hauptmann* written across it, in small silver script.

'You've been marvelously helpful, as usual, Lesgourges. You have truly mighty powers of perception.'

'Always glad to lend a hand.'

'Does the brand name of the safe mean anything to you?'

'It's the same safe that I use at the château. An alarm goes off if you enter the incorrect combination twice. It has a seven-number code. Right, right, left, left, right, left, left. It's the best model available. And no one's stolen anything from mine, yet.'

'Isn't that because no one has ever tried to rob you?'

'Perhaps. But maybe no one has tried to rob me, because I use a Cobb-Hauptmann safe.'

'Sir, should we . . . ,' an officer interrupted.

'Yes, we should,' said Bizot, relieved. 'Anything, yes. We've got safe experts, Jean. Go amuse yourself.'

Lesgourges stood for a moment, then slunk away.

Bizot examined the safe, as officers took photographs. Apart from the monogram, the safe front contained a brushed-steel handle, and one centrally located combination-lock dial, bearing

279

numbers zero through fifty.

Bizot pulled out his notebook.

*   *   *

Lesgourges had wandered back downstairs. He followed the murmur of voices through three rooms and back to the point of entry. Several of the other officers had unlocked the elevator to the left of the entrance. They gathered their tools and entered. Lesgourges increased his pace and joined them in the elevator, just before the doors slid closed.

The elevator was barely large enough for two, and Lesgourges' presence as the fourth occupant did not endear him to the other riders. It was not the first time that Bizot's strange and cumbersome friend had accompanied. Talk among the officers questioned the usefulness and practicality of what Bizot described as a 'specialist assistant.' The doors opened on the second floor, and the elevator occupants were released.

A palatial apartment spread out before them. A wealth of architectural features, stylishly selected, adorned every aspect of the modernized interior. Subtle track lighting contrasted with the white neoclassical interior. Granite flecked with quartz reflected off the tabletops, and the floor had been replaced with white maple. The walls were hung with prints, much like those in the gallery downstairs, but without labels and prices, and some in dramatic frames. Directly across from the elevator was an intricate giltwood frame, Baroque and winding and elaborate, like a decorative tangle of thorns, or a gust of waves reaching out from the sea. It contained no picture. Just the empty wall through the middle of the frame.

What a brilliant idea, thought Lesgourges. I must get one of those for home.

The officers spread out to photograph, and Lesgourges roamed without aim. He was struck, seized by a fit of interior design envy. His feet moved him into the kitchen, which bore a sparkle and polish of factory newness.

Damn, he's got a Viking professional line stove, thought Lesgourges, adding to his mental shopping list. And his refrigerator is the size of my bathroom. Merde.

*   *   *

'There's something else in here, sir.'

An officer called to Bizot, who spun and quickly returned his attention to the safe behind the tapestry.

'What is it?'

The officer leaned in to the niche and cast his flashlight on the wall immediately beside the safe. Something was written in chalk. Bizot could not make it out at first. He squinted, and the characters took shape.

He sighed. 'Well, I'll be . . .'

*   *   *

Lesgourges turned down a corridor lined with identically sized prints, three on each side. Each print was framed in the same way, and had a swan-neck light curling out of the wall above it. Rhythmic hanging, thought Lesgourges. Then he noticed the content of the prints.

Each print showed the exact same scene: the descent from the cross. Jesus, slumped and lifeless in the arms of Nicodemus, is lowered from the cross. Viewed from a distance, the figures are a sketchy silhouette of fired-off lines, a web of ink up close, a block of ink from afar, masterfully done. But each print bore a slight tonal variation from the others, ranging from a light gray wash, like mist descended, to an oppressive, cavernous darkness. Different states of the same etching, thought Lesgourges. Even more valuable. Then he noticed the signature in the bottom right corners, which read: *Rembrandt.*

Still no carpenters, Lesgourges noted. Beyond Jesus, of course. Wood and nails of the cross? Ironic that the tools of a carpenter should be used in the carpenter's execution.

There was a closed door at the end of the hall. He opened it.

A metal skeletal spiral staircase led to a landing on the next floor. The wall behind the tight-wound stair was all frosted glass, and let enter bright light, despite the cloudy day outside the Galerie Sallenave. The filtered sun threw the stair in a silhouette that resembled a torqued strand of DNA. Lesgourges climbed to the third floor.

The entire third floor consisted of one master bedroom. The vast open space was disconcerting. Lesgourges considered himself an agoraphobic sleeper, and could not be comfortable unless he could feel the walls around him. This room was a vast, oceanic nothingness. A void with rafters and skylights, flooded with concentrated beams of external light. The only subdivisions in the room

282

came from Oriental area rugs and one Chinese screen, painted with cranes and temples. Lesgourges moved to the center of the room, where sat an enormous bed, four-poster and antique cherry, strangely floating in the otherwise modern interior, a ship at sea.

Lesgourges' daze was limitless. He could not have anticipated the tasteful modernity of such an ancient family name. So much of his effort had gone into affixing a sense of history to his modern prosperity, seeking a ground for his wealth in an appropriation of false past. He had a predilection for Modern art, certainly, but that was a matter of personal taste. When new visitors came to see his château in Armagnac, he told them that the medieval portraits on the wall were of his ancestors. They did not need to know, he reasoned, that the portraits had been purchased by his father, along with the property.

But Sallenave, Lesgourges wondered, Sallenave has such an ease, a sprezzatura. He is the ideal courtier. His nobility is intrinsic, and so he can drape himself in this purple cloak of tasteful modernity, make a cocktail of past and present, the cream of both.

Lesgourges shook his head.

*   *   *

'What do you make of it, sir?' asked the officer.

Bizot smiled. 'It's another reference to a line in the Bible. I'm beginning to sense a theme.'

The officer's torch illuminated a small circle of wood on the right side of the safe. Written in white chalk were the characters: *PS7115*.

Bizot shook his head. 'Thanks to magnificent foresight on my part, I actually brought a Bible with me. Stole it from a hotel.' Then Bizot remembered that it was not the officer who was privy to that joke. Bizot's fat fingers fluttered through the small, wafer-paged Bible, the text showing through the paper, making it nearly illegible. He found what he was looking for.

'I'm getting good at this. Psalms, chapter 71, verse 15. *"My mouth shall shew forth thy righteousness and thy salvation all the day; for I know not the numbers thereof."* Those fuckers.'

'What does it mean, sir?'

'It's mocking the fact that we don't know the combination to the safe, *the numbers*. We are definitely meant to be on this trail. The painting must be in there.'

'Should we confiscate the safe, sir?'

'No, we'd need a different warrant for that. Take too long. They've led us this far. They want us to find the painting. That means that the combination is here, somewhere. We've just been too blind to find it.'

Lesgourges allowed his thoughts to move. The vacuity of the master bedroom, seeming never to have been inhabited, highlighted its few prominent features, like braille raised on paper. Three framed prints caught his eye. They hung on a large swath of wall, all to themselves. Like the prints downstairs, they bore identical frames and lighting devices. Only these prints were infinitely more intricate. Lesgourges recognized them immediately.

They were, perhaps, the three most influential prints in Western art history, certainly by the most influential printmaker. Albrecht Dürer's *Saint Jerome in His Study, Knight, the Devil, and Death,* and *Melencolia I.* Dürer's so-called master prints. And, of course, Sallenave had all of them, in perfect condition. God, Lesgourges thought, I hate him.

He examined each print. Such a marvel of engraving, he thought, the lines so tightly woven and spaced. Lesgourges had seen the engraving process and knew how difficult it was. Tremendous physical force was required to push the metal burin into the flesh of the copper plate, digging out metal with metal, before ink flowed into the resulting grooves, and the plate was run through a press, and the image transferred onto wet paper. Not like Rembrandt's etchings, a technique more akin to drawing. Not that they weren't impressive. But Dürer's ability to coax delicate detail from a medium that required brute strength in addition to sleight of hand was unimaginable.

Saint Jerome sits in his study, the bottle-light flowing in from the windows to his right. He leans over intently, writing his famous translation of the Bible from Greek into Latin, the Vulgate. Above him on the wall: an hourglass, a cardinal's hat, candles, prayer beads, and more. A gourd hangs from the ceiling, above a sleeping dog and lion, friend to Jerome, who removed a thorn from its paw. A precariously balanced skull stares out from the windowsill, where books, pillows, and discarded slippers rest, as Jerome cannot, until he completes his calling. A crucifix on the desk reminds him, should he tire, that he must complete his translation. In case we were uncertain of his sanctity, a halo of light surrounds his head.

285

In *Knight, the Devil, and Death,* three figures move from right to left, perhaps toward the fantastical castle on the hilltop, in the distance. The knight smiles ever -so slightly, much of his face hidden by his helmet, his armored body supported by a mighty horse. He is a warrior who has survived many combats, but two phantoms are forever at his shoulder. Death, bearded and skeletal, with a snake-entwined crown, mocks the knight, holding aloft an hourglass to indicate that, despite his battle skill, his time is inevitably finite. Behind the knight walks the Devil, a hybrid monstrous horned goat, with owl's eyes and talons. Is he ready to snatch the knight's soul the moment Death permits it? Is the knight evil, or is it merely evil to have killed others, no matter the name or cause? Lesgourges had read once that the knight was the ideal Christian soldier, who does not fear Death and the Devil because God is with him. Whatever, thought Lesgourges.

Perhaps the least explicable, *Melencolia I* contained a multitude of details that seemed to lead to no clear explanation. An angel sits in brooding thought, her head leaning on her left hand, a compass in her right. Beside her, a putto sits on a stone-cut wheel, his back to an unidentifiable stone monument, from which hangs a balance, an hourglass, and a bell. Strangest of all is a square cut into the monument, divided into sixteen smaller squares, each containing a different number between one and sixteen, in no apparent order. A ladder leans against the monument, with a dark sunburst and rainbow, perhaps a comet or solar eclipse, over a seaside town in the distance. In the foreground, along with the angel, there is a geometrically cut multiangled stone, a hammer, a starving dog asleep, a sphere, a piece of wood, four used nails, a saw, pliers, a plane for shaving wood . . . Lesgourges could not even identify all of the objects.

These works were clearly full of symbolic meaning. He had once heard someone mention that *Melencolia I* contained a key to Masonic mysticism, although he had heard many things that sounded more conspiratorial than art historical. Still . . .

He paused for a moment. Wait, he thought. No. But . . .

He looked back at the engravings. A hammer, a plane, a compass . . .

*   *   *

Bizot and his men had swept the first three floors for clues. Bizot had a full notebook, and the interiors were well documented in photographs. Now to check the top floor, he thought, and then sort through all that we've gathered. We found the safe. Now we just need the combination.

Bizot had just reached the top of the stairs, when he heard Lesgourges shout.

'Jean! Jean! I think I've got it!'

*   *   *

'I do not believe it! That is amazing,' Elizabeth whispered, as she stood alongside Barney, Wickenden, and Delacloche in the museum Conservation Room, staring at the X ray that mocked them from its perch on an easel.

Hidden beneath the white surface lay an underpainting. Elizabeth could not, at first, process what she was seeing. It looked as though an angel, with its back to the viewer, was startling a young woman, who craned her neck around coyly to see her gentle assailant. Delacloche recognized it immediately.

'Holy flying shit,' she said. 'That's Caravaggio's *Annunciation*.'

'The painting that was stolen last month?' Elizabeth had read about it, and it was much spoken of, at luncheons among the art literati. But it was the furthest thing from expectation, that it would appear *underneath* this stolen, and apparently fake, Malevich.

'Did Malevich underpaint?' Wickenden asked politely.

'Not with a Caravaggio,' replied Barney.

'How is that possible? To paint over something without ruining it?' Wickenden inquired.

'It's quite simple,' began Barney. 'It's what we do, here in Conservation. The watchword in art conservation these days is to never do anything to a painting that you can't undo. That's one of the reasons why the field is now called conservation, and used to be called restoration. We try to prevent future damage, and leave the original intact as much as possible. Today, less is more.

'In the past, restorers would repaint without documenting their actions, would edit out bits they didn't like, change a color here and there, and otherwise ruin. In Bronzino's *Allegory of Love and Lust,* for instance, a restorer painted out Venus's nipple and tongue, and added a fern to cover Cupid's ass, because when it was acquired, in the

288

Victorian period, the head of the National Gallery thought it was too naughty.

'But these days, we record every change we make, and we use paints that can be removed without damaging the original. The addition of chemicals to the paint we make to restore makes them constitutionally distinct enough from the original paint, that they can be removed with chemicals, while the original is left untouched.'

'So, you're saying that you can remove this white painting on top, and expose this angel painting underneath, without damaging it?'

'Sure. Just give me some time.'

Delacloche had been thinking the whole while. 'If that is really what it looks like, I mean, the stolen Caravaggio, then we're going to need to ID it.' She took a breath. 'This is just too bizarre for me to process.'

'Do any of the museum staff know enough about Caravaggio?' Wickenden asked.

'No.' Delacloche was biting the flesh of her thumb. 'We need an Early Modernist. Ms. Van Der Mier, do you know . . .'

'Simon Barrow.'

'Oh, of course,' said Barney. 'He's perfect. Can you contact him?'

'Yes,' Elizabeth replied. 'I can. Barney, can you have this stripped and revealed by tomorrow morning?'

'I'll have to make sure of the constitution of the top-layer paint. It could be easy and can take a few hours. But if the paint on top is too similar to what is beneath it, it might be a very slow process. Weeks, rather than hours. I'll see—and I'll let you know what I can do.'

'Good. Thank you, Barney. I'll see if Professor Barrow can come by tomorrow morning. If he gives a positive ID to the Caravaggio, then we'll have to return it to the church from which it was stolen. I don't know what the hell is going on, but we'd better contact the Carabinieri, and . . . and this has turned into an enormous bloody mess.' Elizabeth was breathing harder now. 'And I have to call . . . Lord Harkness, and then speak to the board. Any of you are welcome to shoot me now.'

'I'll call the Carabinieri,' said Wickenden. 'This case just got a lot more interesting.'

'It was interesting enough before,' Elizabeth said, as she walked toward the door.

Barney spoke: 'Why would the ransomers keep the stolen Malevich, but give us back the stolen Caravaggio? The Caravaggio is worth maybe ten times more than the Malevich. Unless, maybe they didn't realize it was under this white piece of crap that they gave back to us? But then, who painted over it?'

'This is too much for me to process right now.' Elizabeth massaged her temples. 'Let's make our phone calls and reconvene tomorrow morning, first thing. A whole lot of shit is going to hit the proverbial fan tonight.'

*   *   *

Encroaching night dimmed the city to blue, as Elizabeth's phone rang. Her office hung like a lamp in the cobalt. Windows allowed the evening to drift inside. Elizabeth could have looked out onto the city of London: St Paul's Cathedral under white floodlights, the cradled luminosity of

Somerset House. But Elizabeth Van Der Mier's eyes were shut. She did not hear the first ring and only picked up on the second.

'Yes? Oh, Geneviève. Thank you for . . . that would be good, if you could come by again tonight. I'm glad that you thought to call me here. Can you . . . all right. I'll see you soon.'

CHAPTER TWENTY-NINE

Bizot and Lesgourges stood in front of the three master prints, on the bedroom wall on the third floor of the Galerie Sallenave. Bizot stood to Lesgourges' right and, from the other side of the room, they remarkably resembled the lowercase letter *b*. Both leaned in simultaneously to examine the third engraving.

'A hammer, a plane, a compass . . . all tools used by a carpenter.' Lesgourges could not believe his own words. 'What's the quotation, again?'

Bizot was dumbstruck. He fumbled to open his notebook and flipped to find the passage.

'*The carpenter stretcheth out his rule; he marketh it out with a line; he fitteth it with planes, and he marketh it out with the compass, and maketh it after the figure of a man, according to the beauty of a man; that it may remain in the house.*'

They looked from the rough-scrawled text in Bizot's hand to the engraving on the wall and back.

There was a long silence.

Bizot stroked his beard. 'I'm certain that this is it.'

'It's certainly the only thing I've seen that seems

to connect with the passage.' Lesgourges observed the sober reverie of the moment. 'Of course this proves all our presuppositions wrong, but . . .'

'This must be right. Do you see what I see?'

Lesgourges looked at the engraving. Then he looked harder. Then he observed.

'I do.'

They were both staring at the same thing: a square containing sixteen smaller squares, each small square containing a number between one and sixteen.

'The combination is somewhere in there.'

Silence.

'Jean,' resumed Bizot. 'I think you did it.'

Bizot and Lesgourges stood, arms crossed, brows knit, eyes squinting, necks leaning in.

'God, I hate numbers. My brain doesn't function in rational terms,' said Bizot. 'The answer must be there. We're staring at it, hidden in plain sight. Those bastards have handed us a puzzle.'

He took a deep breath.

'Let's start from the beginning.' Bizot extended his diminutive legs in front of him. 'Alors . . . et puis ensuite . . . What do we have? A four-by-four square of sixteen total smaller squares. Each of the smaller squares contains a number, from one to sixteen, not in order. Reading from left to right, the top row contains 16, 3, 2, 13. The row below it: 5, 10, 11, 8. Below that: 9, 6, 7, 12. And the bottom row contains 4, 15, 14, and 1.

16	3	2	13
5	10	11	8
9	6	7	12
4	15	14	1

'We need a total of seven numbers, each between zero and fifty, for the combination to the safe. Now what?'

Lesgourges looked up and to the left. When in thought, he often put his right pinky finger inside his right ear. It was his Think Button, as he liked to say. He was pressing it.

'My guess is that we are staring at the seven numbers we need. We just don't know which seven. There is some pattern, some order in which you are meant to read the numbers in the square. For instance, if it was a simple pattern, like two diagonals, then the solution might be . . . let me see . . . 3, 11, 12, then 16, 10, 7, and 1. Or if it's meant to be a serpentine pattern, then perhaps the combination is 4, 9, 5, 16, 3, 10, 6. But combinations of seven numbers in a four-by-four arrangement are unsatisfying. It's not clean, while all of these other clues have clicked nicely into place.' Lesgourges stopped speaking and began to mouth the numbers that passed through his head. 'Bizot, do you think we should try to figure this out now? I mean . . .'

'I considered that. It would be easier to think from the office, and we could call more people in on it. But it was hard enough to get the search warrant, and if we leave here with no hard evidence, just an art-historical treasure hunt, then we may have missed our chance. By the time we got another warrant, if I could convince one out of them, then Courtil would be back from the south. To come here again would risk tipping the thieves, and then they might disappear. They may want to prove a point, and we may retrieve the painting,

293

but they're political thieves, not martyrs. They're not going to want to be caught. I think we should test our mettle here. There must be some unifying principle. Otherwise we're grasping at straws. Based on the other clues, the answer should be obvious, right on the surface. We just don't know how to look yet . . . what? Jean, what is it?'

Lesgourges was staring at the square.

'Tu as trouvé quelque chose, Jean? What is it?'

Lesgourges smiled. 'Give me . . . just . . . one . . . moment.'

Bizot looked from Lesgourges to the square, and back. 'Qu'est-ce qu'il y a?'

'Look at the top row of numbers.'

Bizot leaned forward and squinted at the numbers before him: 16, 3, 2, 13.

'Do they have something in common?' he asked, impatient. 'What am I supposed to do with them?'

Lesgourges' excitement bled through his words. 'We've been staring at the stars, without seeing the constellations. It's simpler than we thought.' He paused, and touched his finger to his lips, then shook his head with a smile. 'Add them.'

'Add them?'

'Go ahead.'

Bizot mumbled to himself. '16 plus 3 is 19, plus 2 is 21, plus 13 is 34.'

'Now the row below.'

'5, 10, 11, 8 . . . 5 plus 10 is 15, plus 11 is 26, plus 8 is 34.'

'And the next.'

'9, 6, 7, 12 . . . 9 plus 6 plus 7 plus 12 is . . . 34.'

Lesgourges shook his head once more. 'It's about *how* you look. Now the vertical rows.'

Bizot counted in whispers. 'They all add up to

34.'

'It's so obvious, once you stop staring and start looking. I think we're on to something.'

Bizot could not believe his mind. The solution was so simple. He had been thinking too much. He pinched shut his eyes, to reclaim objectivity. While they were closed, an idea came to him.

'Wait a moment.' Bizot's gaze fixed on the engraving. 'The rows and columns of four numbers all add up to 34 . . . But look at the numbers that are in clusters of four. Like at the bottom left. 9, 6, 15, 4. It also adds up to 34. Look, there's another one. Right in the middle: 10, 11, 6, 7. 34. The sum of any four contiguous numbers is 34. We've discovered our number.'

'The only problem,' began Lesgourges, 'not to deflate . . . is that the combination we're looking for requires seven numbers.'

'Merde,' Bizot considered.

'Is it possible,' began Lesgourges, exceedingly slowly, 'that a further clue is in the passage from the Bible? A clue that we didn't realize was a clue, but might make sense now?'

Bizot flipped through his notebook. 'There must be . . . I mean, thirty-four . . . but seven numbers . . . here we are. We've been given three biblical quotations. There was the one written next to the safe, that sounds the most promising. I thought it was just meant to mock us, but maybe . . . here it is: Psalms, chapter 71, verse 15. *"My mouth shall shew forth thy righteousness and thy salvation all the day; for I know not the numbers thereof."* Wait, could it be the chapter and verse numbers of each quotation?'

'No. The Cobb-Hauptmann safe dial only has

numbers zero through fifty, so Psalms, chapter 71, won't work.' Lesgourges stuck his finger back in his ear. 'That passage doesn't sound like it will help us.'

'Malheureusement. The next passage was the indicator of this engraving. Isaiah 44:13: *"The carpenter stretcheth out his rule; he marketh it out with a line; he fitteth it with planes, and he marketh it out with the compass, and maketh it after the figure of a man, according to the beauty of a man; that it may remain in the house."'*

'That was just meant to bring us here. Doesn't sound promising, either.'

Bizot flipped back farther in his notebook. 'The first quotation, the one we began with, was 2 Chronicles 34:7: *"And when he had broken down the altars and the groves, and had beaten the graven images into powder, and cut down all the idols throughout the land of Israel, he returned to Jerusalem."* That doesn't . . .'

Lesgourges grabbed Bizot's arm. 'Hold on, Jean.'

'What?'

'What did you say were the chapter and verse?'

Bizot glanced at his notebook. 'Uh, chapter thirty-four, verse seven.'

Lesgourges met his eyes. 'Thirty-four: seven.'

Bizot's mind opened. 'You have got to be pulling my . . .'

'It makes sense, doesn't it?'

'We've got to try it,' Bizot snapped shut his notebook.

'But if we get it wrong, won't the alarm go off?'

'Come on, Lesgourges, you froggy genius!'

They dashed downstairs, retrieving the other

officers as they went.

*   *   *

Jean-Jacques Bizot, Jean-Paul Lesgourges, and five officers stood nervously in a preposterous-looking clump beneath a tapestry, on the first floor of the Galerie Sallenave. The false wall yawned wide and confronted them with the big silver safe.

'If you get it wrong twice,' cautioned Lesgourges, 'the alarm will go off.'

'We only need to get it right once,' reasoned Bizot, disguising the crack in his voice. The safe seemed to stare out at them. Bizot reached his fat fingers toward it.

'Inspector Bizot, are you sure about this?' asked an officer.

Bizot withdrew his hand. 'Sure, I'm sure. I'm pretty sure. I . . .'

'. . . Now I'm certain.' Lesgourges interrupted, an ever-broadening grin spread across his long face.

'Et alors?'

Lesgourges swung his head from side to side. 'Just look at the monogram on the safe.'

All eyes turned to it. In thick silver script: *Cobb-Hauptmann.*

'Now,' resumed Lesgourges, short of breath, 'what was written on the wall of the Malevich Society?'

Bizot linked eyes with him, and smiled. '*CH347* . . . I cannot believe it.'

'Cobb-Hauptmann, *CH,* and the combination: *thirty-four* dialed *seven* times,' Lesgourges exhaled. 'The thieves gave us the safe name, and the combination to open it, while they were stealing the painting.'

'Those flaming assholes.' Bizot spun back to the safe and flashed a broad smile. His gloved fingers seized the dial. With satisfying incremental *ticks*, he turned the dial to the first of seven thirty-fours.

CHAPTER THIRTY

The next morning, the Conservation Room was crowded with bystanders whose nerves were frayed to varying degrees. Harry Wickenden was Earl Grey teabag-eyed, his mustache unusually droopy. He had neglected to tie his left shoelace, which, while dragging along the ground, had acquired new acquaintances, in the form of leaf fragments, white fuzz, and a long black hair. He did not notice any of this, however, nor would he have cared. His mind was ticking, more like a bomb than a clock, sifting through the silt of information he'd acquired during the case.

None of it had prepared him for this confrontation with a freshly stolen Caravaggio painting. He'd immediately telephoned the first person of whom he'd thought, as he knew that the Carabinieri were on the hunt for the painting. Gabriel Coffin. Coffin had contacted the Carabinieri man on the case, someone called Risotto, or something, who had then telephoned Wickenden. Ariosto, that was it. Ariosto said he trusted Coffin to represent the Carabinieri in London. They'd only send over their own men if the authenticity was verified.

It was good, strange fortune for the Carabinieri, Ariosto had said in thickly accented English. He'd had no luck on the search within Italy and, frankly, his hands were full with the recent disappearance of a Giacometti statuette from a Roman town house, and Benvenuto Cellini's famous gold salt cellar, which was thought to be in Italy, after its theft from Vienna's Kunsthistorisches Museum. Ariosto was happy to have the Caravaggio recovered, and he didn't seem to desire an explanation for how it ended up in the National Gallery of Modern Art, in London, buried beneath a newly bought fake Malevich *White on White* that had been stolen from the museum and ransomed back.

He didn't even inquire as to whether the painting had been deemed original by a scholar. That was the first question in Harry's mind, when he heard that it was found beneath a fake Malevich. Who's to say that the Caravaggio wasn't fake, as well? Maybe they'd stumbled on the honors project of a very talented arts student with an inordinate amount of time on his hands. The lesson that Harry had gleaned from this case thus far was never to believe his eyes. Which reminded him of his meeting next Thursday with Dr. Mixter, his optometrist. Which reminded him of his appointment with his chiropodist on the twentieth. Harry shook his head.

This Caravaggio certainly looked real, as far as he could tell, which was not far. It looked to be by the same hand as the pieces he'd seen when his wife dragged him to the National Gallery, in Trafalgar Square. He'd looked up the artist last night, after all the commotion.

299

Yes, Harry considered, that looks like a Caravaggio to me. But what the hell do I know?

'Think it's the real deal, Dr. Coffin?' Harry asked. Gabriel Coffin stood in the room beside him.

Coffin was looking across the room, at Professor Simon Barrow. The professor was dressed in a brown, olive, and red-checked hunting jacket, and black trousers, which made him looked exceedingly top-heavy. Barrow was sweating profusely. His white hair matted at the back of his neck, and he kept both hands rigidly thrust into trouser pockets.

'It's good,' replied Coffin. 'But I prefer to yield to our expert, Professor Barrow, here.'

Also in the room, along with Wickenden, Coffin, and Barrow, stood Elizabeth Van Der Mier. Coffin's eyes rested on her as he tried to read her thoughts. She could not decide whether she preferred to sit or stand. She preferred neither, and would rather have flung herself out the window, it seemed. MUSEUM DIRECTOR AUTO-DEFENESTRATED, Coffin imagined the headline the next day, smiling. That probably sounded preferable to her than facing the board of trustees, for the second emergency meeting within the same week.

Van Der Mier's conversation the night before with Geneviève Delacloche suggested what she'd feared. If Delacloche had suspected that the painting they'd bought from Christie's was a fake all along, then it must have been, mustn't it? That would explain why a Caravaggio was found beneath it.

But then the Malevich Society painting had

300

gone missing in Paris. It didn't seem like there was a connection with this Caravaggio. This couldn't be the Malevich Society painting. Of course not. Delacloche would have recognized it. The missing Malevich Society *White on White* painting had been confirmed authentic long ago. But it was too much for coincidence. Delacloche didn't have any better suggestions about what was going on, but her information thickened the plot and, for some reason, made Van Der Mier feel better. Victims seek company.

'How,' Wickenden whispered, 'did Lord Harkers take the news?'

Elizabeth snapped out of her thoughts. 'Lord Harkness was extremely polite on the phone,' she replied. 'He exhibited an aristocratic restraint that I'd hoped for, but not expected. I imagined him thrusting pins into his thigh, while he calmly listened over the telephone. Or, more likely, thrusting pins into a doll shaped like me. In my experience, Inspector, aristocrats are no kinder nor more understanding than others, they were just better at disguising what they really think.'

Wickenden had already spoken with Barney. The scuttlebutt that perpetually circulated within the Conservation Department had been misleading, it seemed. The in-house conservators had said that they had heard from the conservators at the Tate Britain, that they'd heard from the department at the Wallace Collection museum, that Lord Harkness was hard up for cash and in danger of losing his ancestral home. Apparently not, although now he might be, having forked over £6.3 million with nothing to show for it but Van Der Mier's profuse apologies. It was this tradition of gossip within conservation departments that led to their baptism as conversation departments. Wickenden knew whom to ask. But mustn't always trust what you hear, he reminded himself. And now, it seemed, he could not believe his eyes, either.

Barrow mopped his neck with a purple paisley bandanna, which he returned to his breast pocket only to withdraw again. He leaned in toward the painting, now leaned back.

Thanks to the efforts of the conservators, and the easily removed chemical composition of the top layer of paint, the entire canvas was now exposed. No trace of the fake Malevich remained to mask the dark, brooding tones of the Caravaggio, a feast of chiaroscuro, light emerging from darkness. It drew all eyes: Van Der Mier's, Wickenden's, Barney's, Coffin's. They waited on Barrow's words.

Coffin stood, silent. In many ways, he thought, it was the opposite of the Malevich. An all-white painting is light on top of light, without any hint of shadow or darkness.

'The dimensions are 140 by 94 centimeters. That's 12.4 by 20 centimeters smaller than the listed dimensions of Caravaggio, but I see evidence that the canvas was cut down,' Coffin said.

'Why would they do that?' Van Der Mier asked.

'It's too coincidental to try to smuggle a painting of the exact dimensions of one recently stolen,' replied Coffin. 'It's common practice to trim down stolen paintings. Unfortunately, sometimes the trimming eliminates integral portions of the artwork. It's lucky, in this case, that the periphery of this Caravaggio *Annunciation* did not contain any figures. Just more of the black backdrop. But you can see, the edge is creeping dangerously close to Mary's right shoulder.'

'Does,' began Wickenden slowly, 'that mean that the fake Malevich was painted over this Caravaggio, in order to smuggle it out of Italy?'

Everyone turned to look at him.

'That's brilliant, Harry,' said Coffin.

'Makes sense. Just logic. I mean, that's how I'd smuggle it out of the country. If I gave a damn about owning art.'

'Well, it's a good thing that you don't, Inspector, or else the world's supply of Caravaggios would disappear.' Elizabeth was suddenly impressed.

'Would you like some water, Professor Barrow?' Coffin looked at the red-faced Simon, still huffing in front of the Caravaggio.

'No, no, I'm fine,' he dismissed, his glance darting away. 'And, it's real. It's the original. I'm sure.'

'Then, we'll call the Carabinieri and let them know.' Took the professor long enough, thought Wickenden. He looked at Elizabeth. She didn't quite know what to say, he imagined. This was good news for the church in Rome, and for the Carabinieri, but Van Der Mier mustn't really give a damn, given her situation. Harry was struggling to conceive of how this was related to the stolen Malevich. And if this fake, with the Caravaggio underneath, was the same painting sold through Christie's, then why hadn't Christie's noticed what had been so evident to the museum's experts?

'May I go?' asked Barrow, haltingly. 'Yes,' replied Van Der Mier, 'of course. Thank you for coming.' Barrow abruptly took leave. Coffin,

303

smiling, watched him pass out of sight.

'You know,' complained Elizabeth, 'I thought that we were narrowing things down, answering the pool of questions asked. But, coupled with my conversation with Ms. Delacloche, we've got a flood of new questions. I don't even know where to start.'

'How about, what is the stolen Caravaggio doing under our stolen Malevich?'

'Too right, Dr. Coffin,' agreed Wickenden. 'What are you thinking now, Ms. Van Der Mier?'

'I'm just trying to sort it all out. I can't get over thinking that this is not the painting that we bought from Christie's. Ms. Delacloche and I'd have noticed if there was something wrong with it at the auction. I mean . . . oh, I don't know. If it got switched, then, was it switched between the time I saw it at the auction, and when it was delivered to the museum? Or did the ransomers switch it on us?'

'Which would mean that they're more than just ransomers. They're forgers, as well,' Coffin thought aloud.

'But why would the forgery be painted over an original stolen Caravaggio?' Elizabeth asked.

'I think, either they're totally inept or we've fallen into some larger-scale plan. It's got to be one of the two because, in this case, only coincidence falls between,' replied Wickenden.

'Did anything come out of your conversation with Ms. Delacloche, Inspector Wickenden?' Elizabeth inquired. 'She told me that she'd speak to you, as well.'

'She tried to be helpful, but she doesn't know much of anything. It sounds like the French

304

detective working on her problem, the painting gone missing from her Society, hasn't had any luck, either. Inspector Beezo, or something. She also said that he doesn't speak any English, so I think a meeting with him would be akin to bashing my head against a brick wall.'

'Well, that's encouraging.' Elizabeth sighed.

'Not to worry, ma'am. I'll leave no stone right-side up.'

'That's not much more encouraging.' She sighed again.

*   *   *

The next morning, two officers of the Carabinieri arrived at the museum. They were briefed by Coffin, Wickenden, and Van Der Mier about the events transpired. They left in an armored car with the Caravaggio painting.

Later in the week, the Caravaggio was rehung above the altar of Santa Giuliana in Trastevere. This time it was bolted to the wall, clothed by a sheet of nonreflective, bulletproof alarm glass. Most of the parishioners had not noticed that it had been gone.

*   *   *

'I cannot help but think, Gabriel, that you had something to do with this.' Claudio Ariosto rolled his Italian over the phone line, from his spartan Roman office.

'I wish that I could take credit for it, Claudio.' Coffin was on his mobile phone, in front of the cheese section of the Harrods Food Hall. 'Stinking

Bishop please, half a kilo.'

'Che hai detto?'

'Sorry, Claudio, I was addressing the cheesemonger. You've caught me food shopping, when you called. I was following several leads, one through Vallombroso and two of my own, but this, well, I couldn't have dreamt it up. Just dumb luck that an old friend, Harry Wickenden, was assigned to the case and allowed me to follow his investigation.'

'It's quite something. And, although I must admit that I'm curious, I don't care how it happened. I would love to know, but I recognize a godsend and, as you English say, don't look a gift horse in the mouth. If you . . .'

'. . . Of course, Claudio. If I find out anything further about this, I'll let you know. But I'd guess that it will remain a mystery.'

'As long as I can add it to my "solved" pile, and report to Colonel Pastore that it is all sorted out, that's all that I can ask.'

Coffin paid and turned away from the glassed-in avalanche of cheeses, green Harrods bag in hand. 'I must ask, Claudio. On behalf of Vallombroso . . .'

'. . . I've already spoken to Turin. Although it was not her actions that led to the return of the painting . . .'

'. . . as far as you know.'

'. . . as far as I know. You're being coy, Gabriel.'

'I can't compromise my contacts, but . . .'

'. . . In any event, she has been cleared and is now free, but she is on probation for the remainder of the sentence. We . . .'

'. . . I know the fine print, Claudio. That's good news. I appreciate your help.'

306

'*She* appreciates it, I'm sure. Well, I'll leave you to your cheese, Gabriel. Ciao, e grazie.'

It's time, thought Coffin, as he tucked his phone into his inside breast jacket pocket. Here I am, at last. He stopped moving, as his eyes ran over the shimmering fluorescent sight stretched out before him. He cleared his throat, before he spoke.

'Ten chocolate truffles, please, and two chocolate éclairs.'

*   *   *

'Michelangelo Merisi da Caravaggio was born in the town of Caravaggio, near Milan, in 1571. Yes, Fiona, Milan is where Prada comes from. Now are there any real questions, you sinking bollards?'

Professor Simon Barrow wielded his enthusiasm before a group of his bemused, disaffected, tragically hip, apathetic survey students in a green-velvet-walled room of the National Gallery in London. At least, that was how he thought of them. Thirty-three numbskulls and one professor.

'Apprenticed in 1584 to Milanese painter Simone Peterzano . . . no, you don't need to spell the name correctly to receive full credit, Manolo . . . he moved to Rome in 1588, and worked in the studio of Cavaliere d'Arpino, as a specialist in painting fruit and flowers. In the 1590s, Caravaggio found patronage with wealthy and influential and flamingly homosexual orgiastic cardinals, not that there is anything wrong with that, if that is your cup of tea, including Cardinal Del Monte, his greatest sponsor.

'With the help of his patrons, Caravaggio began to receive important commissions from churches.

307

But his highly naturalistic style, and radical interpretation of the biblical scenes depicted, resulted in the rejection of many of his altarpieces as "indecorous," which basically means that they didn't look the way the commissioners were expecting them to. These rejections proved financially lucrative, as private buyers snatched up Caravaggio's wildly popular paintings for more money than the churches were offering.'

Barrow pranced back and forth in front of a row of dark chiaroscuro oil paintings, all by the artist in question.

'Caravaggio's life was punctuated by encounters with the police, violence, and drama. He not only did not have pupils, unlike most artists of his time, but he threatened to kill those who emulated his style. In May of 1606, Caravaggio killed an opponent in a duel, ostensibly over a game of tennis, although it is more likely a territorial fight between two rival street gangs, of which Caravaggio was a pugnacious member.' Barrow now displayed inept fencing postures to illustrate his story. Some students giggled but none turned away their attentions. 'He was wounded badly in the swordplay involved and fled Rome to avoid prosecution for murder. He worked in Naples, until he was imprisoned for quarreling with a supervisor. He escaped prison and spent time in Malta before moving to Sicily in 1608. When he returned to Naples in 1609, he was attacked by hired thugs and disfigured, his face cut up beyond recognition.

'Expecting a papal pardon for his homicide of 1606, Caravaggio left Naples in June of 1610, only to be arrested, mistakenly, at Port"Ercole . . . yes, bad luck indeed, although throughout it seems as though he was asking for it. Caravaggio once threatened to kill a waiter at his favorite neighborhood bar because he didn't like the way his artichokes were boiled, so he's not the most sympathetic of characters. He was released after this arrest. But while he'd been detained, his only earthly possessions remained on the boat on which he'd been traveling. The boat and his possessions, including some paintings, were now several days' journey farther along. Caravaggio set off on foot to retrieve his belongings but contracted a malignant fever en route and died, never knowing that his pardon had come through, only a short time before.'

Barrow was lost in the story, his face ever redder, his back-and-forth pace quickening, spinning often to gesticulate wildly at the paintings on the wall behind him.

'He should not be pitied, however . . . so wipe that tearful look off your face, Nadja . . . as his lifetime of confrontation was self-inflicted and cultivated by his personality. Caravaggio's creed was inscribed on the hilt of his sword, which he carried, though it was illegal to do so: "Without hope, without fear." Rather, as you tempestuous teenagers might say, "bad-ass," is it not? Though his life was tumultuous, and his art shocking, he was one of the most revolutionary, influential painters in the history of art.'

Barrow had not, at first, noticed that the three dark-suited men now stood at the back of the room in the National Gallery, waiting. They now caught his attention, and his discourse slowed to a halt.

309

'To the next room, you children of the corn! Come on now. There will be plenty of time to download illegal music later on, while you're rolling doobies and watching the television. Nuggets, my children! I have nuggets of knowledge, fragments of wisdom that, when amassed, run the risk of rendering you intelligent. I have them to give to you, for the modest sum of your educational fees and attention. But I suppose that sniffing glue and breasts is a more interesting pastime.'

All of Barrow's students were paying full attention, but this did not seem to dampen his momentum. They came to a stop in front of a large painting that stretched the length of a wall, with two figures in it, painted life-size.

'Fifteen thirty-four. This is *The Ambassadors* by Hans Holbein. Had any of you goobers done the reading, you would know that. But that's like asking a monkey to stop picking his nose and write *Hamlet*. Nathan Donne, are you paying attention!?

'Paintings hold secrets. Why do we study art? Or rather, I should ask, why do I talk art *at* you, under the dismaying misapprehension that anything I say is absorbed? Because I firmly believe that universal truths about the human condition are embedded into great works of art. Whether or not the artist is aware, these are painted passions. History: political, social, artistic, literary, religious, philosophical, psychological, emotional . . . it's all in there. You want love and sex and death? Hell, that's all there is in these paintings! The secrets are caught like beasts in a tar pit, struggling to get out, leaning out to you, the viewers, the students, like buried treasure with the glint of gold just beckoning below the surface. So, you turkeys, take the hand that reaches out to you!'

A voice from the crowd of students called out: 'We are listening! Start teaching us something already!'

'Right. Holbein was the court painter to King Henry VIII of England, the fat one with all the wives. Know why he was a fatty? He had a horrible skin disease the name of which I can't recall, that resulted in nasty scabby things on his legs that made it painful for him to walk. So he had to be carried about, and this lack of exercise caused him to, shall we say, aggrandize. But that's as may be. Holbein was Flemish, as you'll recall, if I'm exceedingly lucky, from past classes on Northern Renaissance painting, so this style should not be unfamiliar. Remember van Eyck? Well this painting, too, is full of disguised symbolism!'

They're still at the back of the room, Barrow noted, but they haven't moved. They're just standing there. What the hell do they want now? Shit shit shit shit shit.

'This painting was commissioned by the two gentlemen portrayed on either side of this two-tiered table full of strange instruments and implements. The fellow on the left was the French political ambassador, and this gentleman on the right was the French religious ambassador, close friends representing France at Henry's court in England. This is, at first glance, a double portrait to commemorate a friendship. But there is much more that is hidden. Look deeper.

'The table at the center of the painting has two tiers. The top tier contains instruments for measuring the heavens: an astrolabe, celestial globe, telescope, and so on. The lower tier contains terrestrial instruments, both of music and of measurement. A terrestrial globe, a piece of music, and what is this bulbous instrument? Yes, Cathal, thank you for your contribution. It is, indeed, a lute. So, the painting is divided into celestial and terrestrial, Heaven and Earth. But that's not the true subject of the painting. That's merely the means of conveyance. Come up close to the painting, and look at the strings of the lute. See? One of the strings is broken. If you played this lute, it would sound off, discordant. Therefore, there is discord on the terrestrial realm. See where I'm going?'

A shout came from the crowd: 'No.'

'Right, well, shut up then. Discord on Earth, peace in the Heavens. We need another clue, maybe. Here it is. This piece of music displayed has been identified as a composition by Martin Luther. Urska, would you care to guess at the subject of this painting, based on the aforementioned clues?'

Urska stared at the painting. She has the loveliest eyes, thought Barrow. Then his glance swung to the back of the room. Shit.

Urska spoke. 'Didn't Henry VIII break from the Catholic church and start the Church of England, or something? So, like, maybe because Luther was breaking from the Catholic church, too, around the same time, then the painting is about the discord on Earth over little details about Christianity, but in the Heavens everything is still okay? The problem is the interpretation of Christianity on Earth.'

Barrow smiled. 'You're, like, absolutely right.

312

Well done! You get a cookie. That is exactly the subject of this painting. But before you all waddle off to eat fast food and smoke those doobies, there is one other trick to this painting. I want you all to look at this white squiggly blurry shape painted below the table, at the bottom center of the painting. Doesn't look like much of anything, does it? Now, I want you all to walk to your right, to the painting's left, and keep your eyes locked on that white shape there.'

The mass of students slowly shifted to their right, curling toward the wall alongside the large painting, eyes focused on the amorphous white mass painted at the bottom center. The formless form at the bottom of the painting slowly morphed—into a perfectly shaped white skull.

'Holy shit,' said Nathan, amid a sea of similar exclamations. 'That is so damn cool.'

'Holy shit, indeed. Eloquently put. This is a little trick called anamorphosis. Holbein is particularly clever, as he toys with the fact that his name means 'hollow bone' or 'skull.' Anamorphosis is a mathematical painter's trick, in which a form is painted in such a way that it may only be seen clearly from one extreme angle. This white blob turns into a perfectly proportioned skull. It is thought that this painting was displayed in a narrow hallway, so it would be approached from the left, an angle from which the skull looks formless. As you walk in front of the painting, then turn back toward it, you can see the skull. It is a memento mori, remembrance that you will die, so you should be good and religious and stuff. So the path of walking past this painting mirrors one's lifespan. Initially death is not considered, but near

313

the end of one's life, death's-head is just over your shoulder, staring at you from behind . . .'

Barrow interrupted himself, as he saw the three suited men break from their station at the back of the room, and walk toward him.

'Uh, I think that's enough for today, students . . . turkeys. I . . . we'll see you next, whenever.'

The students wandered off. Barrow inhaled deeply and took a step toward the three men.

'Gentlemen,' he exhaled, 'how may I . . .'

'It's just this,' said one of them. Barrow was not sure which. An envelope was held out to him. 'For you.'

Barrow looked down at the plump envelope. He swallowed. 'If this is a severed hand, I'll be very disappointed.' They did not smile.

He looked from the faces of the men back down to the envelope. He took it in his reddened, moist hands and pulled open its lips. It was stuffed full of bristling twenty-pound notes. Barrow quick-shut the envelope, and his eyes. He took a deep breath.

'Thank you, gentlemen.'

'With warmest regards and thanks from our mutual employer.' They turned and slowly walked away. Barrow looked around the room and shoved the envelope into his inside breast pocket. No one had seen. He pressed the bulge over his heart with his hand.

Barrow looked over his shoulder at *The Ambassadors* behind him. The skull seemed to stare back. What the hell are you looking at? Barrow thought. He turned away from the painting and moved toward the exit.

Barrow wore his smile like a crown of thorns.

314

CHAPTER THIRTY-ONE

Irma looked up at Harry. He hadn't heard. Then she looked to the phone, as it rang a second time, then to Harry, then back to the phone, then to her plate of shepherd's pie, then to the phone again. She lurched her way out of her chair and shuffled to it.

'Hello? That's right. One moment please, luv.' She cupped the phone to her copious breast. 'Harry, luv, it's for you.'

Harry craned his eyes free from their gaze out the window into the sunset evening and looked long toward his smiling wife. He took the phone. 'Yuh. That's right. What . . . who is this? How did you get this . . . But, I . . . right. Is that so? Hmmm. But . . .' Then just the dial tone.

'Wrong number?' Irma smiled. Harry didn't respond.

'I'll be in the living room,' she continued, as she rolled out of the kitchen.

Ten minutes later, Harry had his coat perched through his left arm, the rest of it dragging along the floor behind him. He tripped over his right sleeve halfway through the living room, where Irma was watching *Coronation Street* and eating salt-and-vinegar crisps. The right corner of her crisped lip rose ever so slightly, as Harry stopped between her and the television.

'So, I get this call from an anonymous source, no idea how he got the number or knows about the case, and he says that he's seen something that we should see, we being me, and I'm going out.' Harry paused. 'You don't look very impressed.'

'I'm just wondering who this fellow was, phoning you up out of the blue like that, and telling you this. Is there some reward?'

'No.'

'Then why would he tell you?'

'Why shouldn't he?'

'But why should he?'

Harry scowled. 'Come on, Irma, maybe he's just a good Samaritan. There are plenty of . . .'

'. . . But didn't you keep this out of the paper, to protect the museum?'

'Yes. What about it?' Harry was struggling to shrug his right sleeve over his right arm, but it resisted. Then he realized that he was standing on the tail of his coat.

'How was he to know about it?' Irma scraped her plate and ran water across it in the sink beneath the dry yellow fluorescent light that clung to the glowing underside of the cupboards, like a radioactive centipede.

'About what?' Harry had extricated his sleeve from beneath his heel and now was having difficulty with the coat's shimmering coffee-colored lining, which hung, a corner ripped out and dragging on the linoleum floor.

'He must have been involved in the investigation, if he knew about it and it was confidential.'

Harry's mustache wiggled, as he glared in Irma's general direction, though not at her.

'And I don't like you going out at night by yourself.'

'Well, you're not coming.'

'I don't want to come. But why can't you take

someone with you?'

Harry looked hurt. His eyes told.

Irma looked away. 'Can't you at least wait until . . .'

Harry spun dramatically, swirling the tail of his coat, now tattered, and brushed through the front door. A moment later, his mustache poked back through the door, followed immediately by the rest of his head.

'You may be right, but I don't have to like it,' he said, before finally effecting egress.

Out in the street, the sour smell of food wrappers and blackened dust and cigarette ends and fish oil radiated up from the still-wet ground, dappled in the smoldering tobacco burn of remaining sunlight. The rain had stopped for the moment, but he was halfway down the block before Harry realized that he'd forgotten his umbrella. I'll be damned if I'm going back in there for it, he thought, as he approached the bus stop.

It would have made far more sense for Harry Wickenden to have taken a cab, but so many years of repeated movements had rendered them automatic. Every morning at 7:20, Harry turned right out of his building and walked to the corner, then turned left for another hundred or so meters, until he reached the bus stop. There were two buses, the 45 and the 29, which would take Harry to his office at New Scotland Yard. But no matter which came first, he always took the 45. Now that Harry was leaving from his home at—he checked his ten-pound gold Rolex watch, 7:45 in the evening, and was not destined for the office, he wasn't quite sure what to do. The 111, like some hunchbacked fire truck, arrived and he boarded.

Harry had a way of boarding buses. The short black man, or was he Indian, thought Harry, did not look at him, but just stood, ticket machine hung and slung before him, in that dark blue woolly sweater. Harry paid him no mind and immediately mounted the precipitous torqued staircase along the bus's inside hindquarters. On his way up, the bus started to move, and he was pressed against the wall, the curling metal handle at the small of his back. At the top of the stairs, he bent his knees against the push-back and walked all the way to the front.

Harry sought the front left top-deck seat. He had once forcibly removed a five-year-old boy from that seat in order to claim it. He particularly liked the seat during rainstorms. The slashing lashes of water against the window, Harry warm and dry within, reminded him of a favorite memory:

Harry, perhaps seven or nine, sat on the gray-carpeted floor, between his mother's ankles, as she sat in the chair above him, his back to her. He stared out the window at an overzealous drainpipe that shuddered out water from the roof above and created a miniature waterfall, just for him, amidst the reverberant rainfall outside, as his mother rolled her fingers through his wheaty hair, along the measure of his scalp, and the sound of the rain, like a million teardrops on the thick glass, and everything was beautiful.

Harry emerged from the moist-leathery bus and stepped onto the pavement. He hailed a cab. The brakes squealed. He got in.

Fifteen minutes later, Harry was standing in a valley of warehouses that looked like dormant

318

moths crouched in neat rows beneath the cotton-mouth sky. As far as he could see in either direction, the identical red-doored, dull gray structures rippled into the distance. A grumble from above the clutch of clouds made Harry wish he'd brought his umbrella. He buttoned his dilapidated trench coat across his Buddha-like belly.

Number 34, he thought, as he looked up at the number glued onto the garage door. It read *33*. He turned around and squinted in the fleeting light. Across from where he stood was Number 34. He took a step, then stopped.

Had he seen it? From the corner of his eye, something had moved. He looked to his right, along the paved road between the warehouse fronts. He saw nothing. Then he noticed the narrow black alleys between each warehouse structure.

He stepped quickly to his right and trotted past two warehouses, glancing along the length of each alley, unable to see through the overcast light and shadows cast by the structures.

Three alleys down, he gave up. Had he seen something? Someone, that is? Periphery is a bottom feeder, but perhaps. He rethought his refusal to carry a mobile phone, as he walked back to number 34.

The massive cargo door, painted the same cool red as every one of its siblings along the rows of depots, was locked. His fingers slipped on his first pull of the water-dropped metal handle. Must be mechanical, he thought. Of course it is, I'm an idiot. Along to his right, the same color as, and perpendicular to, the cargo door, was a personnel

319

entrance.

I'm also going blind, as well, he thought, as he approached it. This had better be legitimate. If this is a wild goose chase, I'm going to . . .

But he didn't need to finish his thought. Harry looked at the handle to the personnel door, brass on red, and noticed a shine in the paint along the edge of the door, by the knob. He grasped the knob. The door swung open with the lightest touch. Now we're on to something.

Harry knelt, the edge of the door facing him. There was a piece of transparent tape blocking the bolt from sliding into place, keeping the door unlocked. The corners of the tape crept around to either side of the door, shining in the chalk-dust light of fading day.

Still kneeling, Wickenden looked to his right, into the depot. It was impenetrably dark, and colder than the outside. Harry stood up and, with a casual air, surveyed behind him. Who am I performing for, he thought? Myself, I suppose. There was still no one along the corridor road. The light misty rain began to fall in earnest. Wickenden reached into his pocket. His fingers felt for his pipe to rub for comfort, but instead found the small tubular plastic bottle. The pills within rattled, as it rolled beneath his fingers. No, he thought, as he shrugged and stepped inside the warehouse.

The steel-wool darkness and drifting light behind threw Harry into poor-postured silhouette against the open doorway. He felt along the wall to the right of the entry. His fingers fumbled over a switch, which he threw.

Nothing happened. Damn it, he thought. He

continued to spider across the cold wall, in search of another switch. His knees bent, as he worked his way down toward the floor. I don't know where the damn light is. Then he kicked something.

A plasticky scattering sound. By the cloud-smothered twilight, he could make out a shape rolling back and forth on the floor. A torch, bloody brilliant. He picked it up and switched it on.

The thin beam illumined, in small portions, a completely empty space. The vacuous warehouse was devoid of machinery, product, even evidence of occupation. As far as his little light could see, pinballing from wall to floor and back again, he had been led to nothingness. The voice on the phone had said that Harry would be interested to see what was in Number 34, that it was pertinent to the museum theft. But was anything here? He played the light around further as he progressed into the dark void.

Then the door slammed shut behind him.

Harry clutched his chest and spun around. Sweat vaulted through his pores and dampened his undershirt in one great flood. There was now no light anywhere, save for the flashlight in his tight, hot hand.

The door could have been blown shut, he thought. But it was heavy. But if there's someone outside, why would they want to . . . am I locked in? Or, he swallowed hard, are they *inside* now, too? He quickly switched off his flashlight, and the darkness was complete.

Well, they can't see me, but I can't tell my ass from my elbow. If there is a *they*. He listened. There was no sound, save the palpable distance to the peripheral walls. Harry's breath came heavy.

321

His heart was beating too loudly. He stood for a minute and heard nothing. Then a minute longer. He switched on his flashlight.

The light skipped into nothingness. Harry chose a direction and began to walk. He was only loosely certain of the location of the door. A flurry of paces brought him to an external wall. He turned and followed it to his right. His light picked up the undulating metal of the wall for many steps, without surcease, before he saw something.

Harry jumped back at first, startled. It looked like a body. Some form beneath a clustered ripple of heavy tan tarpaulin. Harry recoiled and peered out into the darkness beside him. Nothing was moving, not that he could have seen it.

He'd always had a sense that he could *feel* if someone were out there. Like the moments before eyes pry open after sleep, he could sense the copious presence of his wife looking over him, as she liked the way his mustache fluttered like a breezy banner when he snored. But he felt no one out in the void. He did feel a presence, however, beneath the tarpaulin.

What the hell is this, he thought? Nobody's dead. Yet. Harry took a step closer.

It was impossible to say whether the bunched tarp hid a curled-up form, certainly not breathing, or if it was just a trick of the fabric. He leaned over close to the mass on the floor. It smelled of oil and dust and burlap. Harry reached his hand out, still shining the light with the other, toward the material. His fingers clasped round a thick piece. He slowly dragged the tarpaulin toward him, breath quick and mouthy. The rough material caught and clawed to remain in place. Harry

322

pulled harder. It's not a body, he thought, thank God.

Then the tarpaulin slid free, exposing the treasure beneath. A roll of canvas. A painting.

Harry leaned his light farther over. Now what? he thought. It's the . . . oh, you've got to be kidding me . . .

*   *   *

Harry couldn't believe his eyes. No wonder the informant on the phone had told him he'd be interested. He was, but also confused. This didn't make any sense. He couldn't digest what he was staring down. He had just seen it leave for Rome. Now rolled up before him. He knew immediately, just from the portion visible at the top of the roll. The *Annunciation* by Caravaggio. He unrolled it farther.

What the fuck is going on? My brain is too small for this. What had the informant said? Harry pinched the bridge of his nose, as his flashlight flickered. Oh shit, he thought. Right.

He leaned over and wrapped the painting in the tarp. With it cradled in his arm, Wickenden picked up his pace along the inside of the wall. The battery was coughing to fail, and Harry moved faster, trying to keep hold of the rolled canvas under his arm, without pressing so hard as to scrape the paint. Then he saw the door.

Harry dropped the flashlight and twisted the handle. The door eased open, then was caught by the wind and leapt from his grip, slamming a metallic crack against the outside wall.

Outside was lightless. The rain continued soft in

323

the low-hung sealskin sky, and Harry stepped into it, leaning his body over the wrapped artwork in his arms. Where the fuck am I going to find a cab? he thought. And why the fuck am I swearing so much?

He huddled off down the warehouse canyon.

*   *   *

Harry Wickenden stood, soaking wet, dripping a pool of coat-soiled water at his squinching feet, a soggy bloodhound, drooped further in saturation.

The limited overnight staff of the office at Scotland Yard looked on, confused.

'Get me the'—Wickenden sneezed moistly—'Carabinieri. And the museum. Now.'

Within the hour, Elizabeth Van Der Mier and Barney, the conservator, were standing on the third floor of New Scotland Yard, among the identical desks lit by identical crane-necked lamps of the open office. As they entered, Wickenden was on the phone. He gestured to the painting, which rested at a forty-five-degree angle against the back of a chair. Harsh lamplight glared off the skin of limp canvas. Harry cradled the telephone within the fat of his neck.

'. . . never left your sight? Well, that's reassuring, but how do you explain what I'm looking at right now? Is that really the case? I can't . . . well, I understand your position, but . . . right. Well, I will do, yeah. That's right. Fine.'

Harry hung up the black office phone; its corkscrew cord had knotted itself during the conversation. He turned to the newly arrived.

'That was the Carabinieri. But first, what do you

324

make of this?' Eyes had never left the unrolled painting, since entering.

'It's fake, right?' Someone in the office asked, as Barney puttered around the canvas, which lay flat on a desk beneath lamplight. The silence continued.

'Of course it's a bloody fake,' said Van Der Mier. Everyone was quiet.

'It's all right, Ms. Van Der Mier,' Wickenden resumed. 'We're all a little stressed, and none of us like this. But . . . are you certain?'

'Yes, but what the bloody hell is it doing here?' Van Der Mier stood, elbows akimbo across her chest, a scarlet complexion showing through the skin at the back of her neck, where a thin film of shining moisture matted the wisps of hair.

Harry stepped forward. 'That is what I'd like to know.'

'But who was the informant?' Van Der Mier paced, staring at the painting.

'That,' continued Harry, 'is also on my shopping list.' His manner of speech was tortoiselike, as usual, and only served to increase Van Der Mier's irritation, as did Wickenden's staunch refusal to make eye contact with any person he addressed. Harry's mustache ruffled, 'I would still appreciate the word of an *expert.*' He leaned into the last word.

'I'm confused, Inspector. Isn't the original stolen Caravaggio back in the church where it belongs?' Barney asked without looking up from the canvas.

'Funny you should ask. I was just on the phone with our Italian friends. The Carabinieri claim that the original Caravaggio never left their possession

325

between London and Rome, and is currently back in the church of Santa-whatever-the-hell-it's-called, pardon my French, all safe and sound, right? You'll be pleased to know that the Carabinieri have their hands full, and no, they will not send agents back over here to look at this painting that is clearly applicable to the case. Don't bother me with more information, don't confuse me with the facts, the toffee-nosed bastards. They've got so much going on, apparently, that they're very pleased to shift this mess to the "case closed" pile, and that's that. Well, that is not that. That is not fucking anything, pardon my French. I don't know what passes for satisfactory conclusion over there, but they're all fattened up on spaghetti or whatever it is they eat, and I'm stuck with a Caravaggio painting that looks like the original to me, so it must be a pretty damn good copy, which means that it was probably made from the original, which means that this case stinks even more than Denmark, or whatever the hell the metaphor or whatever it is, is.' Harry was short of breath, and he leaned back against a desk to support his irate enthusiasm. 'So what is this, then? I want to talk to Simon Barrel.'

'Barrow,' Barney offered.

'I don't give a flying fuck what his name is, pardon my French. I want an *expert* opinion. I don't know much about art, but I know that this ain't Russian twentieth century, so I'll not accept dismissive angst. Get me Barrow on the phone.'

'I'll call him for you,' said Van Der Mier, as she flipped open her silver mobile phone. She pressed one key, and held the phone to her ear. Wickenden eyed Elizabeth with a glow and half-smile. Was Barrow on her speed dial?

Van Der Mier connected. 'Hello, Professor Barrow? It's Elizabeth Van Der Mier, from the . . . that's right. Listen, we just wanted to confirm your last statement, about the Carav . . . yes, well that's what I thought . . . but the fact is that Inspector Wickenden wanted to . . . no, don't worry. I promise. Thank you, Professor . . .'

Harry had grabbed the phone from her hand. 'If you don't mind, miss.' He pressed it to his own ear.

'Is this Professor Simon Barrel? Yes, Barrow. Good. The fact is that we've got a freshly recovered painting in the office down at New Scotland Yard that looks exactly like the Caravaggio that you authenticated. Now, are you absolutely . . . yes, I understand. Please calm down, Professor. No, you're not implica . . . no. It's just that this looks so good. If you could . . . if you could . . . excuse me, if you could just tell us whether or not this . . . copy, then, was made in the presence of the original, then . . . of course you're not, but we would appreciate your coopera . . . all right, thank you, then. Right, that would be fine.' He folded the phone shut and returned it to its owner, who was not amused. 'Thank you for your cooperation, and the use of your telephone, Miss Van Der Mier. I've got a case to solve. I do not like loose ends. I finish every crossword puzzle I begin, including the Sunday crossword, or I do not sleep at night. And you want me to get a good night's sleep, believe me. Miss Van Der Mier, what do you make of this?'

Elizabeth nested her chin on her fist, which rested on her chest-crossed left arm. 'It's so well done. I don't know if it would stand up to any tests, but it certainly looks . . . Barney, how good is it?'

Barney was still knelt before the canvas, which spread loose on a tabletop. 'It still looks fantastic. But there are a lot of artists who are brilliant copyists. I'd have to get it back to the lab to determine whether this one took the time to get the chemical details right . . . but I think I've solved the mystery for you.'

'How's that?' Wickenden had been pouring two and a half packets of sugar into his flower-patterned favorite tea mug, and was trying to fold the half-empty sugar packet, in order to save it for his next cup. Now he spilled the remaining contents of the packet onto the desk before him.

'What is it?' Elizabeth leaned in.

Barney smiled. 'Everyone was so preoccupied with the painting, and no one thought to look on its back. It's easy to lose the trees for the forest. See?' He turned the canvas around, to reveal a clean bright white removable sticker that read CHRISTIE'S, LOT 34.

'Well I'll be . . . ,' Elizabeth trailed off.

'That's the painting that went missing from that American, Grayson's, flat.' Harry just stood, his sugar-covered hands on his small hips. 'Kirsty!' His secretary looked up. 'Get me Christie's on the phone. Now.'

*　　　*　　　*

'It is so perfect that he's paying you, on top of it all,' Daniela whispered into Gabriel's ear. Then she noticed the waiter, smiling politely, pen in hand.

'We'll both have the poulet des Landes in the

328

truffle sauce,' said Coffin, as the black-vested waiter nodded in approval.

'An excellent choice, sir.'

'Best chicken I've ever had. To call it chicken is like calling Michelangelo's *David* a rock.' The waiter smiled as he withdrew. 'And a very happy birthday to you, amore,' Daniela purred. 'Forty years young . . .'

The Ivy, arguably the most beloved restaurant in the world, buzzed in gentle humming tones, never harsh but ever hot, as the clock neared its smile of the evening. Night tried to peer in through the stained-glass windows, but the immaculate facets of the restaurant kept a sense of insularity that made its celebrity clientele return to its camera-free comforts, and made its plebeian patrons feel patrician.

Coffin turned to the handsome woman beside him at the table for two, her hair, he thought, like fire maple leaves before a setting sun. Daniela wore a black slip dress, with a new sapphire necklace around her gently browned throat. Coffin's eyes were always drawn to the elegance of her clavicle, the sweep of soft bone from shoulder to breastplate that is of unsurpassed beauty in the fairer sex.

'One must find ways of delaying or sublimating one's inevitable midlife crisis.' He smiled. 'Being with you is the best birthday gift I could wish for.'

Gabriel particularly loved the small freckle just above Daniela's upper lip, barely perceptible except in intimacy. He leaned over and kissed this, wispily.

The waiter returned with a bottle of champagne, which he poured into translucent flutes, arresting just before the foam flowed over the edge.

Coffin lifted his glass, and met eyes with the dark-curled creature to his left.

'Congratulazioni, Daniela. Now that you are free of that pesky prison sentence and back in the arms of your beloved, what do you plan to do?'

Vallombroso smiled coyly.

'I mean, besides that.' Gabriel grinned despite himself.

'Well,' she began, 'revenge. But, thanks to you . . . You are quite brilliant, you know.'

'I missed you more . . . more than I would like to admit. Without you, I was . . . Well, I've a mind like a steel sieve. But the important pieces never slip through.'

'Am I a piece, then?'

'You're the queen,' said Gabriel, as he sipped his champagne.

'Is this another of your chess analogies? Last time we spoke, I was the good thief.'

'I'm afraid so. My therapist says that I never got over losing that chess tournament, and I've repressed the desire to actualize my parents' dream of having a chess master for a son.'

'Weren't you ten years old?'

'Yes. My glory days are far behind me. Backgammon is safer, anyway. And I never did trust therapists. Surprising that I go to them so often.'

'They tend to be correct a dismaying percentage of the time,' Daniela mused. 'For instance, they would likely point out the fact that your parents both died on their thirty-fourth wedding anniversary, in your thirty-fourth year, and link it with your fascination with the fact that this tragedy occurred on the third day of April, the fourth month of the year, between three and four in the afternoon.'

'Why do you . . . can we just . . .' Coffin's lips tightened in.

Daniela put her hand on his. 'I'm sorry, Gabriel. But it does no good to . . . I want to help, you know . . . because I love you . . .'

Coffin forced a smile. 'I'm sure you're right, of course, about the . . . It's also your current age, if I recall. Nothing is ever just a coincidence.'

'Except when it is.'

Coffin was quiet. Daniela looked away, around the plush green room. Then she looked back, but not into his eyes.

'What is it about mathematicians, I've often wondered,' she asked, 'and people who are exceptionally good at chess?'

Daniela's eyes flitted now to the waiter, who had rolled a cart up next to their table. He deftly unveiled a plate containing a whole chicken, nearly black, bathed in shaved truffle slices in truffle oil. He slid a knife between breast and bone, the clavicle, thought Gabriel, and laid out the perfect meat on a large white plate.

'I think that it's some combination of logic and forethought. One must anticipate every potential move of every piece on the board, and form a prescient countermove. Adequately obsessive-compulsive. Keeps the mind elastic. Mmm, and don't forget to save room for the sticky toffee pudding.'

The waiter placed the overfilled plates before Daniela and Gabriel, then gracefully left them to

331

dine.

'Chess or no, I always need lots of diagrams with colored arrows to sort out the plot, so don't think too highly of me. It takes real genius to map it all out in one's head.'

Daniela smiled and nodded. 'With regard to revenge . . .'

'What about it?' Gabriel speared another slice from his plate.

'I'm all for the biblical variety,' Daniela said, as she slipped a piece of truffly chicken between her teeth. Gabriel looked up at her, with a smile.

'I know you are.'

'But is satisfaction in biblical law, an eye for an eye, a tooth for a tooth . . .'

'. . . or a . . .'

'. . . or, exactly. Is it an inherent part of human nature, or has human nature evolved to accept it because of its authoritative source and its longevity. If it didn't go back to Hammurabi's Code and . . .'

'. . . Matthew 5:38.'

'. . . and Matthew 5:38. How do you remember this stuff?'

'That one's easy, come on. And I told you. I remember the important things. Your birthday, on the other hand . . .'

'Well, what do you think?'

'What do I think? I think that people are programmed to act in prescribed ways. It takes only observation of individuals, and knowledge of culture and society, to logically conclude courses of action that may then be reacted to.

'I think that there are animal instincts that we're born with, and based on our environment as we

332

live, our instincts are programmed. That's the big secret. If you can gather information about someone's life, through observation and research, and if you can infer how different environments and experiences will affect said person, then you can predict action and reaction.'

'So, you just gave away your secret?'

'I've been lecturing on it for years, but I don't think anyone's really paying attention. Art thief and patron profiling. That's how I catch my prey.' Gabriel punctuated his sentence by dramatically harpooning a piece of meat, then continued.

'But nothing is complete yet. I never laugh maniacally until after I've succeeded. I've seen enough films. Don't count your . . . well, you know.' He took a bite of chicken. His recoiled reaction ejaculated in English: 'This chicken is fucking good, dear God.'

'Shall we speak in English now? I need practice,' Daniela smiled, as she spoke in an English thickly accented. 'I like when you swear. You sound more a real person.'

'Sorry,' he said, with mouth full. 'I like words.'

'But I like you can be silly, too. Wouldn't do to think too much of the time. ' She sipped her champagne. 'Speak of which, I never understood why you like to use those quotations when you're on the job, shall we say. It's rather melodramatic and makes people think . . .'

'That is precisely why I use them. I know how both sides of the game function. Creating a false profile protects the innocent.'

Daniela thought for a moment. 'Very clever. But what makes you think you're so innocent?'

'Me? I'm a saint.'

333

'Not in my bed,' she smiled. 'I'm glad you're not a religious, uh . . .'

'. . . zealot?'

'Zealot.' She took a bite. 'Mmm, this is good for my vocabulary. Zealot . . .' Daniela winked. 'Always think one step ahead.'

'Or more, if possible.'

'So that's why you love your work, is it? The criminal mind is your chess opponent?'

'That's a heavy-handed way of putting it, but I'm sure you're right. If we were to go further, you could say that I do it to impress my parents, after I disappointed them back in my tempestuous youth.'

'I'm sure they sit on a cloud somewhere, very pleased with your performance. I know I am. Vengeance is the sweetest revenge.'

Gabriel started laughing.

'What, Gabriel?'

'Sorry. Your English is marvelous, I often forget that you . . . you can't say "vengeance is the sweetest revenge."'

'Why not?'

'I don't know. It just sounds funny. Vengeance and revenge mean the same thing.'

'Now you're just teasing me.'

'You're right. I've got an even better quotation for you. "There is no vengeance which may be inflicted, as biting and as limitless as regret."'

'Is that another one of your biblical . . .'

'No, made that one up myself.'

'I'm impress.' Daniela lifted and clinked her glass with Gabriel's. 'And this chicken is so fucking good.'

*   *   *

334

'So you see, Mister Grayson, we've not established the connection between the painting you purchased and the recently recovered Caravaggio *Annunciation*. But we have determined that the painting that you *thought* you purchased, the anonymous Suprematist, listed as Christie's lot 34, was a fake. I know this will come as a shock to you, particularly in receiving this information from Scotland Yard. Rest assured that you are under no suspicion. We merely wish to keep you informed, to the degree that we are permitted. An expert has determined that this fake Caravaggio painting that we recently found was actually *beneath* the painting that you bought. Yes, that's right. Someone, presumably the thieves, used chemicals to dissolve the fake Suprematist painting on top, to reveal this fake Caravaggio underneath. No, we can't say why, nor why it was abandoned.

Obviously, this fake Caravaggio was not what they had hoped to find beneath . . . right. I'm afraid I can't say. But the canvas is the same, with the Christie's label and serial number on the back, and there are traces of the Suprematist painting still on top of the Caravaggio.

'It's a complicated mess, really, but I assure you that we're on top of things. Yes. Yes, of course. You see, the case to which I was assigned was another one, about which I've been told not to speak. But I've appropriated part of the stolen Caravaggio case, as I managed to recover the stolen Caravaggio in the midst of my own investigation. It's a long story, but suffice it to say, we appreciate your . . . yes. The point is, Mr. Grayson, that no one claims this fake Caravaggio, so the painting is still technically your property, and it is to be returned to you. I've been in consultation with the people at Christie's, and you did legally purchase the artwork, although I'm afraid it no longer looks as you had hoped. Christie's explained it to me in simple terms, as I'm a bear of little brain, and long words bother me. Yes, from Winnie-the-Pooh, I think. It's just as though you bought a car that you thought was red, and it turned out to have been painted blue underneath . . . I know it sounds funny, but . . . right. Well, I'm not sure when . . . I can't talk about the investigation more than I have, no . . . but the case is considered solved by the ones who pressed charges . . . that's right, the church from which it was stolen, so the case is closed. I'm afraid that I'll have to live with a happy ending for the victims of an unsolved crime. While that conclusion gives me indigestion, it's not my place to complain. Nor to you, sir, you're right . . . The painting will be returned to you shortly. Thank you for your understanding. Right, then.'

Wickenden hung up the phone. He looked down at his right hand, at the tiny piece of graphite from a pencil that had broken under his skin when Frank Scheib had accidentally stabbed him in class, at age seven. It had never extricated itself. He liked to use it as a focal point, whenever thought was required.

Had he just answered his own question? Sometimes having to teach crystallizes thoughts and sifts the gold from the soil. It must have been the thieves who stripped that ugly Suprematist painting off the canvas to reveal the fake Caravaggio. But they must not have been happy

336

with what they found, as they seemed to have abandoned it. So what had they hoped to find instead?

The phone rang. Harry's gaze broke from his pencil wound, and he picked up the phone from his desk.

'Hello? Oh, for God's sake, Irma, I'm thinking. What? Uh, I don't know . . . how much? All right, then, and . . . fine . . .' He fingered the small orange plastic tube in his coat pocket. The pills inside ticked together. He removed his hand from his pocket. '. . . a pint of skim milk, and whole-wheat bread . . . look, I know that you don't like the malted grain . . . I've got work to do, Irma . . . in a little while. At seven, all right? I . . . I . . . you, too.'

He cradled the phone. Where had he left off? Oh, right. Who could the informant have been? Not the thief, surely? What would the thief have had to gain from the police discovering the painting? It could only augment the case and inch the police closer to the capture. There were no untoward fingerprints on the painting or its canvas. Unless it was a red herring. But who would go to all this effort, and after the recovery and return of the stolen original Caravaggio had been announced in all the newspapers? And the informant must have known that the painting would just be returned to the man they stole it from, this Grayson. What the hell had happened?

*   *   *

Bizot and Lesgourges sat on the floor of the latter's apartment. Containers of mostly eaten

337

Chinese food, along with one and a half empty bottles of wine, lay like land mines around them. They leaned against an old black leather couch. The luminescent spire of the Invalides stared in at them through the window and the starlit night outside.

After many moments, Bizot spoke again. 'But I really . . .'

'Bizot,' Lesgourges held up a silencing finger, 'if that Delacloche confirmed that the painting we found in the safe at Galerie Sallenave was the Malevich *White on White* which had been stolen from the Malevich Society, why are you still going on about the case? Isn't your job done, until charges are pressed, if ever they are?'

Bizot thought, as he gazed out the midnight window.

'I keep thinking that there was some clue that we missed . . .'

'. . . we found enough clues, Jean. We followed the treasure hunt and came away with the treasure.'

'That's what bothers me. We followed each clue that was laid out for us, as we were *meant* to. That's the sand that's still in my sock. We were meant to, and we were strung along like puppets.'

'But we decided that they were trying to make a point, not keep the painting,' said Lesgourges.

'That's another pebble in my shoe. They don't like Malevich's idea of spirituality. So, they were trying to make a point. But to whom?'

Lesgourges lit a clove with a spark and crackle. 'What do you mean, *to whom*?'

'I mean,' Bizot tried to stand up for dramatic effect, but thought better of it and remained

338

propped against the couch, on the floor. 'I mean that no one has changed. We kept this out of the press, so the only people who even know that the affair occurred are the police and the Malevich Society. And, rather than yield the public mouthpiece the thieves had wanted, the Malevich Society may not even press charges.'

'But, Jean . . .'

'We're like children, led on until we discover the correct answer in a way that feels like a personal revelation, when we'd never have been allowed to fail.'

They sat in silence once more.

'More shrimp in black bean sauce?' Lesgourges offered. 'No? Well, I'll finish it.' He ate in silence. They both leaned back farther into the couch.

'I've been thinking,' began Lesgourges.

'Always a bad sign.'

'And I did a little research, I don't think I told you. About the number square in Dürer's engraving.' Lesgourges readjusted his posterior. 'It's called a magic square. It's a mathematical term for a group of evenly spaced numbers in which the sum of the horizontal, vertical, and diagonal lines each equal the same number.'

Bizot was impressed. 'Where did you learn all this?'

'The internet.'

'Hmm.'

'This particular one is called a gnomon magic square, because clusters of any four contiguous numbers add up to the same sum. There are eighty-six different combinations of four numbers, in this particular square, all of which add up to thirty-four.'

'That's amazing.'

'It seems that the engraving *Melencolia I* is about the intellectual struggle of a self-conscious genius rationalizing the empiricism of science and the imagination of art in the secular world. Enlightenment science removes the mystical element of faith, and the artist mourns the loss.'

'That doesn't sound . . .'

'. . . I know. That's a direct quotation off . . . off the internet.'

'Hmm,' said Bizot. 'Well, I'm still impressed.'

'It seems that the other two Dürer engravings in the series may be part of the same overall theme, rationalizing the enlightenment of science with the mystical awe inspired by religion and art. *Knight, the Devil, and Death* is about this struggle from a moral standpoint, while *Saint Jerome in His Study* shows it from a religious one. And all on the internet, which they have on computers these days. As my old professor used to say, "Salvation in reading." But I never listened to him.'

'That is all very interesting. But, as Sherlock Holmes used to do, we must put ourselves in the mind of those we wish to catch, to think as they would. And I can't imagine that these destroyers would read up on their art history.'

'They didn't actually destroy anything, Jean . . .'

'No,' Bizot interrupted. 'But if we're dealing with iconoclasts, we're dealing with philistines. They haven't taken the time to understand why the Malevich painting looks the way it does. Not that I profess to understand it, but I know enough to know that a difference of opinion does not grant the right to destroy. They're just reacting to what they read into it, because it goes against their doctrine. They're making a judgment based on the aesthetic, not the internal content, and their judgment is that no one should be allowed to come to their own decision about the painting. They made it disappear.' He paused for breath. 'I don't think there's a deep-seated reason why they chose *Melencolia I* to lead us to the stolen painting.'

'Do you think there is a deeper reason why Dürer chose to use a magic square with the number thirty-four as the key?' Lesgourges stared out the window. 'I read that some scholars think that *Melencolia I* is Dürer's reaction to his mother's death, and that there's some connection between his mother and the number thirty-four. But I can't remember the rest.'

'For thoughtful people, there is a reason for everything. So, yes, I think that Dürer had a reason. But not for these criminals. *Melencolia I* just served their needs, on a superficial level, because it has numbers in it. It's not solving the philosophical puzzle. This is about solving the literal puzzle: *what* we see on the surface, not *how* we read what we see. These people think only skin deep.' He paused. 'And what's with you and all this *reading*? You know I don't approve of you improving yourself.'

Lesgourges said, 'If Sallenave is somehow to blame, or at least connected with the thieves, then how do you explain his art collection? Not just what's for show in the gallery, but in the private apartment?'

Bizot wove the air with his hands. 'This is the art that you're *supposed* to have. If you are a serious and wealthy collector of prints, then you must have Rembrandt and Dürer. I'm not saying that these criminals don't admire an artist's beauty and skill. I'm saying that's all they admire. To look at the Malevich *White on White,* a supreme display of artistic ability does not come immediately to mind. The ignorant would say, "I could do that, the artist displays no skill," and not consider why it was done, or that their antagonistic reaction is exactly what the artist wanted to provoke.'

'Do you think we might be on the wrong track?' Lesgourges asked. 'I mean, altogether?'

They sat in silence.

'Yes.' Silence. 'Anyway, I don't like it,' Bizot continued, his short, fat arms crossed. 'It's too smooth. And I don't like to feel I've been used. There are too many loose ends here, in that there are none.

Everything tied itself up too nicely. The truth is not so clean. They must have made some mistake, and I'm going to find it. This case may be closed, but I'm not finished yet.'

Silence.

'I thought of something else today,' Lesgourges offered, 'not that it matters now. The final clue we needed, *Melencolia I,* which led us to discover that the combination to the safe was thirty-four, dialed seven times . . . Well, the engraving was on the third floor of the building at 47 rue de Jérusalem. Three-four-seven. Do you think that's just a coincidence?'

Bizot looked over to him, then back out the window. 'Nothing, it seems, is ever just a coincidence.'

CHAPTER THIRTY-TWO

Sunlight dipped toward the horizon, over pencil-sketch trees calligraphed onto the impossible blue of the sky, tinged a burnt scarlet. The moon was already aloft, its craterous yin-yang hanging in the premature daylit night.

Lord Malcolm Harkness stared out at the sky from behind the antique warbled glass panes of a window in the study of Harkness Hall. He leaned into a tall brass-studded leather armchair, his back to an immense desk in the bookshelved room. Works of art dotted the ivy-green walls wherever bookshelves ceased momentarily, before winding their way on along the wall several feet farther on.

To the right of his desk, a glass-topped table displayed his family Bible, a rare sixteenth-century printed book, handpainted, the words in Gothicized stretched letters, curdled from black to brown with age. On the edge of his desk, an Art Deco sculpture in the shape of a tiny naked bronze woman held aloft the serpentine neck and colored-glass shade of a Tiffany lamp. A small Hokusai colored woodblock print of a Japanese girl, seated indoors at tea as a rainstorm flashed outside, hung on the wall to the left of the desk. Above, a crystalline chandelier spread an oceanic light over the dusky chamber, and on Harkness's harvest locks and well-cut shoulders.

His land stretched out as far as he could see, until the hill slipped down from its crest, at the tree line, by the clearing where he had played as a child. He thought about the abomination that had crossed his mind too often and led to such sleeplessness. He could not lose this, his ancestral home, his history, his childhood, his generations past, his identity, the reason for his lordship, the evidence of what puissance he possessed, the fruit of the labor of his grandfathers nine times over, his self. It had come dangerously close. But now, all would be well.

He arched angular fingers like buttresses over the bridge of his nose. A thorn still clawed at him, but that was an aesthetic grievance, one he could only afford the luxury to suffer if his primary concerns were sorted. But the foretaste of catastrophe, that he feared was prescience, ingrained a metallic sourness into his mood. Could he not be satisfied that his home and his position were safe? The missing piece bothered him less for want of what he had been promised but did not have. Rather, it was the sense that his puzzle-perfect plan lacked its final piece. A tower was as yet unbuilt, designed but undelivered, which left his fortress penetrable. A rook was missing.

Lord Harkness's fingers combed through his hair, like bleached flax. Rotating his chair away from the nightfall window, he tugged at his ironed-crisp, cuff-linked shirtsleeves, as his eyes fixed on the wall across from his desk. On it hung a frameless painting. It was white on white.

'Still upset, Malcolm?'

An elegant, whitening blond-haired woman walked into the study, wearing only an emerald green slip, a strap of which had crept down from her shoulder. She lithed behind the desk and climbed onto his lap, straddling his legs. She ran her hands along the collar of his pale gray suit

344

jacket.

'I'm sorry, Elizabeth,' he said in his gently tumbled accent. 'I'm just a bit distracted still, because of . . .'

'Forget about him.' She pulled him to her lips by his collar, and sunk her mouth to his. 'Aren't I more distracting?'

He kissed back, only briefly, and with eyes open. His sight wandered to the white-on-white painting across from him, and then fell down to the floor below it, where a blank canvas, covered only in gesso, leaned against the wall.

'You're supposed to kiss back, remember?' She lifted his face away from the canvases, and toward hers, with her soft hands.

'I don't like being tricked.' His warm eyes were always liquid and looked at the brink of tears, even in emotionless moments.

'We don't know if we were tricked.'

'It's either tricked or double-crossed. I pre-prefer the former, because the latter could mean . . . you know what he could . . .'

'But we'd bring him down with us, if he did. All that he can do now is keep us from the Caravaggio. Everything else has gone perfectly.'

'But, I . . .'

She pressed her finger to his lips, and then ran it along them. 'Think about how well we've done, Malcolm. You mustn't fixate on the one thing we haven't, when we have so much. The Caravaggio was merely a dream, a greed, which we weren't meant to have. But you were meant to save your home, and that's done.'

'I suppose that I'm just . . . I'm just scared of him. Look what he's done . . . he's so . . .'

345

'Yes. Look what he's done *for us.* He actualized the plan that you came up with. You put your family heirloom, that original Malevich *White on White,*' she gestured to the painting on the wall, 'up for sale at Christie's. I bought it from you for my museum. You pocketed £6.3 million that the museum paid, and cleared all your debts, and saved this wonderful house, your family estate. Then, as you'd planned, he stole your painting back from my museum for you. And look, now it's hanging in your study, as it had before, plus you've all the money from having sold it. *Your* brilliant plan worked perfectly. Don't forget who is manipulating whom. You are in control. Now I don't want you to obsess about the pipe dream of ours that was, frankly, greedy.'

'Your acting was brilliant throughout, Elizabeth. No one suspected a thing.'

'It didn't require much acting, as I never knew the intricacies of the plan, what would happen next. So I could react organically.'

'Don't discount your per-performance. Covering our relationship was the key subterfuge, and you were . . . magnificent.'

'So why are you still distracted, Malcolm, about this one missing piece?'

'I commissioned him to steal the Caravaggio pa-painting *for me.* Not only do I not have it, I've no idea where it is.' Lord Harkness leaned back in his chair, and rested his hands on Elizabeth's wide-spread hips, as her bare legs draped over his. 'As far as we know, it's just disappeared.'

Elizabeth slowly unbuttoned Harkness's blue and white bespoke Turnbull & Asser dress shirt, slightly worn at the back of the collar. 'You think he's sold it to someone else, out from under you? Is that it?'

Harkness stayed her hand. 'It makes sense, doesn't it? He had such a foolproof pa-plan. Arranging the ransom for my pa-painting that he'd stolen from your museum, then returning a fake Malevich *White on White* with a fake Caravaggio beneath it, and paying an expert to authenticate it as the original, closing the case.'

Elizabeth leaned back on his lap. 'Did you ever learn how he stole it from the museum? I mean, we both know what the police discovered, but . . . I knew he was a forger, but I didn't know that he was a thief, as well.'

'I didn't know that he was a thief, either. He's renowned only for masterminding the scheme, and for his forgeries. Maybe he used someone else to actually break into the museum. Or pe-perhaps he's that much of an athlete, as well. It still amazes me how many of his pa-paintings are hanging in the world's museums, in place of the stolen originals. The Louvre, the Hermitage, the Met, the Uffizi, the Getty is full of them . . . And nobody knows. Maybe he's too damn smart.'

'Look at me, Malcolm. Don't undercut your contribution to the success of this scheme. It was your idea to volunteer to pay the ransom on behalf of the museum. You're a hero now because of it. And all you had to do was to pay yourself the £6.3 million, which you demanded and paid. While he suggested paying an expert to authenticate the fake Caravaggio, it was your clever idea to use Simon Barrow. With his scandal dragging behind him, he was the perfect man for the job.'

Harkness sighed, and glided his fingers over her

347

thighs. 'It was elegant. No one questions Barrow's identification, the museum hands the apparently recovered Caravaggio back to the church from which it was stolen, and the case is closed. The church thinks it has its pa-painting back, the police don't understand, but the case is closed nonetheless, and no one is looking for the Caravaggio that should be on our . . . our . . . bloody wall. But where is it now? He's pa-paved the perfect path for him to take my money up front, then sell the original stolen Caravaggio to someone else, and make even more.'

'And what are we going to do to stop him?' Elizabeth stroked Harkness's hair. 'If we try to expose him, he'll expose us. If you hire some friends of yours to threaten it out of him, he'll expose us. If your friends kill him, then we're no better off, still no Caravaggio. But don't forget that he cannot expose us, without bringing himself down, too. There are only two kings on the board. That's the delicate balance that makes this business relationship function. There's nothing he can do now to harm us, other than depriving us of the Caravaggio. You have your house, you have no debts, and you have your Malevich. We're safe.'

'I just don't like it . . . there's something . . . he's got such a flawless track record, a reputation for pro-professional honesty. Unless we did something to offend . . . or if he thinks we double-crossed him . . .'

'Do you think that it's because we stole that painting from Robert Grayson?' Elizabeth asked.

'That's the only thing I could imagine. But he had pro-promised that the Caravaggio would be underneath the lot 34 painting, which my

348

associates bought for me. And there's nothing but white gesso beneath it.' Harkness looked across the room at the remnants of lot 27, leaning against the wall, just a canvas covered in white gesso. Harkness continued. 'I don't like it when I don't understand something. When you made the fake pro-provenance that allowed lot 27 to be sold through Christie's, he had also asked you to pre-prepare fake provenance for lot 34 for some other deal he was working, on the side. I was suspicious, so I told my men to buy lot 34, too, at the auction. Is that reason enough to . . . It was only when we saw that the Caravaggio was not underneath lot 27, as he'd said it would be, that I had lot 34 stolen from that American, Grayson. But what really bothers me is that there was a *fake* Caravaggio beneath lot 34. That means that he thought that I might try to take it, even though he'd told me not to.'

'Maybe he was punishing you for not trusting him, for dishonesty,' Elizabeth offered.

'Punishing me for dishonesty? But he's a thief!'

'It doesn't matter now. Perhaps there's some code that you failed to follow. Perhaps the only reason for lot 34 was as an ethics test, built into the theft plan.'

'Elizabeth, do you suggest that we're dealing with a violently moral art thief? I . . .'

She kissed him on his forehead. 'Shh. Everything will be okay.' Elizabeth leaned in, and whispered into his ear. 'As far as I'm concerned, Gabriel Coffin can go fuck himself.'

*   *   *

349

On a bright cool cloudless morning, the doorbell rang to Robert Grayson's apartment. Grayson, about to pour skim milk into his muesli cereal, walked to the door, still in slippers and his matching blue bathrobe. A sagging detective appeared outside the wide-swung door.

'Morning, Mr. Grayson. I have something that belongs to you.'

Grayson looked down and saw a thin rectangle of brown paper tied up with string, leaning against the detective's short brown pants leg. He looked back up the leg and met the vacant, wet, red-eyed stare of the detective.

'Inspector Wickenden. I appreciate your bringing it, especially coming down in person like this. I'd invite you in, but . . .'

'No need. I can see I've gotten you out of bed. My apologies. I tend to form personal attachments to my cases, Mr. Grayson, and so I seek to have what I believe is referred to as "closure." This is why I am hand-delivering the goods. I regret to say that, although the victim of this crime, the Roman church of Santa-something, is pleased with the outcome of this now closed case, I am not. Beginning a crossword puzzle, falling asleep, and waking to find it completed is not my idea of satisfaction. But it seems that the powers-that-be are content with miracles, and needn't concern themselves with the how they came about. Then again, we are dealing with a church. It's their full-time job to be content with miracles, and never ask how. A phrase about a mouth and a gift horse comes to mind, but I can't recall how it goes. In any event, I am confronted with an unsolved case, and it will no doubt form a permanent canker

350

reminiscent of gangrene run rampant through my psyche, or at least so says my therapist. For what it's worth, enjoy your painting, and have a nice day.'

Wickenden presented the wrapped painting to Grayson, nodded, and took his leave.

Grayson, package in hand, closed his front door and walked back into his apartment.

'Gen, it's here,' he shouted.

From out of his bedroom, yawning and stretching sleepily, walked Geneviève Delacloche, wearing only Grayson's old oversize navy-blue T-shirt with the words RED SOX printed on it in red.

'Already,' she yawned, 'that was efficient. In France, it would be months before the police sort out all the paperwork.'

'It's all thanks to that very strange detective,' said Grayson, as he laid the package down on his dining table. 'He's like a slowly deflating balloon.'

'Good analogy.' Delacloche kissed him deeply on the lips. Then Grayson pulled off the white hard string, followed by the brown paper. When it was removed, they looked down at it for a long while.

'Well,' Delacloche began. 'It certainly isn't an anonymous Suprematist painting.'

Grayson smiled. 'That's a good thing. That painting I bought was absolutely hideous. But you know that. Nice work. Can't say that I'm much of a Caravaggio fan, but this is very well done. You sure could have fooled me, if you'd told me this was real.'

'I know. Seems a shame, doesn't it?'

'A bit. But only a bit. Are you ready?'

Delacloche winked. 'I've waited so long to get back my family treasure, you'd better believe I'm ready.'

'You've been very patient. And now you look like you're about to receive your lost childhood teddy bear.'

'That's what it feels like. If only Papa were alive to see this returned . . .'

Grayson put his arm around her and kissed her forehead softly. 'I'm sure he's looking down at you right now and smiling.'

Delacloche lifted the canvas from the table and, cradling it in her arms, walked over to the living room. There was a small wooden easel set up in the middle of the room, on which she carefully placed the painting. Grayson retrieved a dark green fishing tackle box from his bedroom. He placed it on the table, next to Delacloche. She opened it and began to sort through the myriad of plastic white-labeled bottles, brushes, and implements inside. She took up a small tuft of cotton, which she dipped into one of the bottles. Grayson looked on, as Delacloche dabbed the soaked cotton onto the fake Caravaggio painting. The apothecary smell floated through the room. Beneath her touch, the paint melted away.

Something white shone beneath.

*   *   *

'Come in, Robert! I've just finished!' Delacloche called out from the living room. Grayson came from out the bedroom, showered and dressed.

'That was fast, babe. You are amazing.' He paused and took a short breath, as he stood at the

352

threshold of the living room. The fake Caravaggio had vanished, traceless. In its place, on the easel, was a *White on White* by Kasimir Malevich.

'It's just as beautiful as I remembered it.' He sighed softly. 'You don't think your Malevich Society will miss it, do you?'

'Not now that I have verified the replacement that was, shall we say, *discovered* by Inspector Bizot in the Galerie Sallenave last week.' Delacloche smiled. 'And poor old Monsieur Sallenave never knew a thing about it.'

'He's not that poor, but he is old.' Grayson smiled. 'Convalescing in his château while we sorted out the police from his Paris apartment. Case closed. Just like clockwork. And the police believed every word you said. That's the funny thing about experts. Everyone believes what they say. No one considers that they . . . that you . . . might have an ulterior motive. I have to admit that I thought we were in trouble when this one was stolen from here as soon as it arrived. Not part of our plan. But it seems he'd anticipated that, as well. Amazing.'

Delacloche turned back to the painting and shook her head. 'I don't see any damage, whatsoever. It's just perfect.'

Grayson pulled out his mobile phone and dialed.

'It's Grayson. We've got it. Perfect condition, everything just as you promised. Even delivered to us by the police, like you said. I wouldn't have believed it if I hadn't been . . . right. Well, I don't know how you do it. You are well worth your price. We can't thank you enough.'

'The pleasure is all mine,' replied the voice of

Gabriel Coffin.

*   *   *

Harry Wickenden lumbered through the electric white sunny day. The air was warm but crisp. Not a cloud broke the celestial blue, sky like the Venetian Lagoon, and the scintillant sun, a knife in the water, just beneath the surface waves. It struck Wickenden like a taunting slap, and his eyes squinted in feeble defense. Perhaps I should buy sunglasses, he thought. Ah, what's the point?

He longed for the gauzy embrace of rain clouds, rain which did not mock him with false joy, the irrational exuberance of uncut blades of sunlight. Perhaps he should buy an umbrella and wade through the bright like a parasoled Victorian lady. But then people would mock him, as if nature's derision were not scorn enough. He wanted to be noticed, surely. Not more, but at all. But not at the cost of dignity.

Did not his profession, his phenomenal success rate, warrant adulation? But he was tucked away in the department, thought undercultured and undercharismatic for promotion and profile. His colleagues did not care for his despondent company, which made him suffer more, which perpetuated their distance, and his disdain: his uraeus, the snake biting its own tail, the self-perpetuating, unbroken circle. He was admired, perhaps, but not loved nor sought. He'd all too often walk past the Red Lion pub, with its perfume of ale and laughter floating out into the evening into his path, but he was never invited in.

And for how long? Harry could not remember

when he had not felt this quiet, infinite weight, this daylight devil, this endless shadow upon him. Surely it had not always been this way. But ever since his little son . . . His bus pulled up to the curb, and he climbed inside. He brushed past the bus attendant, up the quick-curled stairs, along the upper deck, and to the front.

His seat was taken. There was a fat old woman with her groceries piled beside her, wearing a fur-collared overcoat in the heat of the sunlit bus front. Harry sat in the row immediately behind her.

The bus lurched forward. Harry sat sideways, one leg bent onto the seat. He felt his jaw extend forward, and his lower lip lift over and up, but he tried to hold back. What did he have? If work failed, what was left? His thoughts fed fuel to the speeding train of his quivering eyes, his temples beaten by the sunlight streaming in through the huge glass window at the front of the bus, a refracted barrage of white on white, an avalanche of absolute emptiness. The sun was blunted only by the shadow of the abundant old woman seated in the row in front of him. He leaned farther into her shadow.

Harry wiped his precipitous eyes with the back of his hand. He slid his moist palm down his body to wipe it dry, and then into his coat pocket. Inside, he found his blue paisley handkerchief, and something else. He blindly fumbled fingers around a small orange plastic tube, whose contents ticked together inside. Harry stopped moving for a moment. His heavy head leaned against the back of the seat before him. Then he gripped the plastic tube, and pulled his hand out of his pocket.

Held low in his lap, Harry looked down at the tube. It was translucent orange, the form of little pills piled up beneath the fleshy plastic, the oversize white top like a sailor's cap. How many were in there? What would happen if he took them all?

He pushed the meat of his palm onto the cap, and twisted. It made a pink impression in his hand. He poured the contents of the small container into his palm. The pile of happy oval pills, half green, half yellow, seemed to smile up at him. He pushed his finger into the pile and rolled them around with a dirty fingernail.

The bus came to a stop, and the old woman left the front seat. In her absence, the light shattered unbroken through the window and soaked him in its unwanted brilliance. Harry's eyes narrowed. Then he looked back down at the pile of pills. He breathed in, deep and slow. He pinched one pill between two fingers, held it for a moment, then popped it in his mouth and swallowed it down. He turned back to the rest of the yellow—and—greens, so light in his hand, promising weightlessness, a beautiful storm cloud void. Then he tipped them back into their plastic tube—some stuck to his palm—before twisting tight the bright white cap and returning it to his pocket. He sat up straighter and opened his eyes to see the world passing through the great window before him. Through the squinty glint he remained but did not move to the vacant front seat. Perhaps the second seat would do, for now.

When he'd reached his stop, Harry dismounted, first from his reverie, then from the bus. His street looked clean and gleamed, as he began to walk the short distance home, past the Italian restaurant, the coffee shop, the Coach & Horses pub, the fresh—flower stand on the street, the Laundromat ...

Then Harry stopped for a moment. His shoulder rolled back, and his chest pressed forward ever so slightly. He turned and walked back several paces, then cleared his throat.

'Um, excuse me, miss. May . . . may I have, uh, one white carnation, please?'

'Certainly, sir.' A young woman smiled at him. 'Here you are.'

'Thank you.' Harry took the flower between thumb and forefinger. He reached into his back pocket.

'No need,' said the bright young woman.

'Thank you.' Harry mustered a half-smile as he turned to walk home through the harsh sunshine to see his beautiful wife.

CHAPTER THIRTY-THREE

The next morning, the rain smiled faces on weepy windowpanes as Lord Harkness opened his eyes. He stared up at the dark wooden ceiling of the master bedroom in Harkness Hall. Craning his neck backward against the soft of the pillow, he saw, inverted, the rain-bitten day through the foggy-glassed windows.

Elizabeth Van Der Mier, her back turned to him as she lay asleep, arched feline, the lift and fall of her shoulder blades like butterfly wings. Her back shuddered in tender breath. She rolled over and

357

slung a sleepy arm across Harkness's bare chest. She nuzzled in close to his gritty, unshaven neck.

'Good morning,' she sighed.

'Good morning, darling.'

'Must we get up?'

'It's Sunday out. You can sleep as long as you like.'

'As long as I like?' She lifted her head just enough to give him a breathy kiss on the cheek, missing his lips from fatigue, and then she fell back to her pillow.

'It's raining out, anyway. Best to stay where it's safe.' Harkness fluttered his fingers through her long white-blond hair, as he lay on his back, eyes open but, as yet, senseless. Comfort finally won out, and his lids slowly dragged shut. He was asleep again.

Hours later, Harkness was slipping on his burgundy-brown dress shoes over plaid-stockinged feet. He was dressed for a leisurely Sunday in the country: no jacket to cover his immaculate dress shirt, only perhaps a Burberry cardigan. Elizabeth emerged from the shower, a white towel wrapped round her breasts, and hanging to her knees. She leaned her head left and dried her hair with another towel.

In the breakfast room, Harkness sat with the *Financial Times* and a half-eaten croissant with strawberry preserves, and a quarter-full cup of white tea. Elizabeth, at the other end of the table, corrected the proof for an upcoming exhibition, her right hand raised, hovering her teacup inches from lips.

'Do you have a dictionary, Malcolm?'

'In the study, there should be one. What's the

word?'

'How do you spell *perspicacity*?'

'I've no idea, darling.'

'Right. This fellow's spelled it with an *h.*' Elizabeth replaced her teacup, stood, and left the room.

A moment later, her cry filtered through, from several rooms away.

Harkness stood up immediately at the sound, spilling what remained of his tea, and hurried to the study. Elizabeth was in the middle of the room, leaned up against the desk, her left arm across her chest, right hand cupped to mouth. Harkness tried to follow the line of her eyes, down to the floor, against the wall, below the Malevich painting. There was nothing there.

'Where's lot 27, the gessoed canvas?' he asked of no one, knowing the answer. 'But why would he take that from me? There's nothing on it . . .'

Elizabeth could not move. She muttered to herself in shivers. Harkness came to her and placed his arm on her shoulder. She did not respond.

Then he saw it.

There was a note on the floor, where the gessoed canvas had been. It was written on glossy paper, in sharp-scrawled red ink: 'Never judge a book by its frontispiece. Zechariah 5:4, Psalms 23:4.'

He spun to the far corner of the study, to the glass case in which he kept his sixteenth-century family Bible. With stormy steps, he crossed the room and looked down at the case.

It was still locked. The Bible was still inside. His shoulders rolled to ease, but only for a moment, as his eyes focused through the glass, onto the aged, inky Bible below. It was open to the book of Zechariah.

Harkness looked to the note in his hand, then sought chapter 5, verse 4, beneath the glass. *I will bring it forth, saith the Lord, and it shall enter the house of the thief, and into the house of him who sweareth falsely by my name . . .*

That self-righteous, pretentious bastard, thought Harkness, as he clenched his teeth. Why the hell is he doing this? Just because I stole the Grayson painting? He paused for a moment, then looked back at the note. Psalms 23:4, what the . . . wait. I know that line. The only one I do know. *Yea, though I walk through the valley of the shadow of death, I fear no evil* . . . valley of the shadow . . . Vallombro . . . Oh, my God . . . Harkness's fist cupped in front of his open mouth, a mix of admiration, realization, frustration, and anger. So that's how he stole, she did . . . and that's why he's doing this to me, because of what I did to . . .

He looked up at Elizabeth. She was staring at the note clasped in his hand. Then he realized why. Harkness felt his fingers stick along the back of the note. He turned it over in his hands. The note had been written on the back of a photograph—a photograph that showed him and Elizabeth in his bedroom, lying asleep, dressed as they were last night. Harkness tight-shut his eyes. His mind spun from rapid revelations. Never judge a book by its frontispiece? What the hell does . . . and then he realized. His unbroken demeanor slowly splintered, as the full brunt of his own perceptive failure struck him between the eyes.

He crushed the photograph into his talon-fist

360

fingers, and cast it violently to the floor.

'Elizabeth, what . . .'

Elizabeth pressed the lids to her tight-shut eyes. '. . . There's another note,' she whispered. Harkness spun around in white anger.

A piece of paper was pinned to the Malevich *White on White* that hung on his wall. His heart slipped before he saw its contents. Then he approached.

The note contained four red words: *'I'm not real either.'*

'That goddamned . . . But if this is not my family's original Male-vich, then where the hell is it!?'

*　　*　　*

In the Roman church of Santa Giuliana in Trastevere, Father Amoroso gave communion to his small congregation. As the congregants knelt to genuflect and receive the body and blood of Christ, they crossed themselves and looked up at the Caravaggio altarpiece that hung on the wall above the priest.

EPILOGUE

Gabriel Coffin and Daniela Vallombroso drank espresso from tiny brushed-metal cups in their London flat across the street from the British Museum, beneath the ocular window, above the Forum Café.

Gabriel crossed his right leg over his left and set down his empty cup.

'Feel better now?'

'Much, thank you,' Daniela sighed, as she slunk back in her chair. 'Treachery must be punished. Even among thieves.'

'Especially among thieves.'

Daniela's gaze swept to the modern copy of the Dürer engraving *Melencolia I,* framed in silver on the wall, by the table at which they sat. 'Tell me, Gabriel. Do you like abstract art?'

'Not particularly.'

'It occurs to me that you seem to get yourself involved with it rather often, for someone who is a devout formalist.'

Gabriel twisted his cup in his fingers. 'If you're asking whether I'd like to have an abstract painting on my living room wall, the answer is, not particularly. An old professor of mine once said, "If you had a Mondrian in the kitchen, you would burn the soup."'

'What did he mean by that?'

'I've no idea, really, but it's always stuck with me, and somehow seems apt. In the absence of something genuinely profound, always say something quotable, right?'

Daniela laughed, 'I suppose.'

'But if you're asking about work, well, I must admit that I'm inherently lazy, and it's a hell of a lot easier to forge a painting that is all white, than it is to forge a Caravaggio.'

'Hmm. That's a simple answer.'

'The right ones always are. I only paint Caravaggios when I really must, but I can fire off a Malevich. You do what you're good at. Try not to push too hard against the grain, if you can circumnavigate it.'

Vallombroso and Coffin sat in silence for a moment.

'I've been thinking, Gabriel . . .'

'Always a bad sign. I prefer my women as dumb as possible.' He smiled.

'That's because your iron logic is prone to developing fissures.'

'Touché.' Coffin took Daniela's hands in his and looked at her red nails.

'I've been thinking that iconography is a dangerous knowledge,' Daniela continued. 'I'll give you an example. Your study of the language of icons allows you to interpret paintings . . .'

'Yes,' said Coffin, 'you've been to my lectures . . .'

'But if I know that you have this knowledge, then the advantage is mine.'

'Aren't you supposed to be the brawn of this team, not the . . . How is my knowledge a weakness? Knowledge is power. Or so I've read.'

'You've said that iconography is a language. It's the same as learning . . . oh I don't know . . . Italian. If you know that buongiorno means hello, and arrivederci means good-bye, then you are privy to information that was hitherto held secret from you. A piece of the great jigsaw is unlocked and shifted into place, and if you bother to learn another few thousand words, then the puzzle is solved, the language known . . .'

'I'm the one meant to give the boring lectures, Daniela, I . . .'

She raised her finger in polite protest. 'But if I am aware that you have learned that buongiorno means hello, then I can choose to say it when I want you to hear and understand it, or not to say it at all.'

'I don't think . . .'

'It's like painting. If I paint an old man with an hourglass, your knowledge might lead you to think that he represents Time. But what if it's actually a portrait of my grandfather, and the hourglass is arbitrary. Then your knowledge would have led you astray. You can know too much, or at least think too much.'

'Well, um, yes. But no.' Coffin leaned back. 'Nothing is arbitrary, especially in art. If, as you say, you painted the work, but did not intend to incorporate iconography, I would say to you that it was beyond your control.'

'What do you mean, beyond my control? If I didn't put in a symbol, then there isn't a symbol.'

'What would Freud say? Or Roland Barthes, or any of a swarm of art theorists? Whether or not you intended it, cultural, and especially art-historical, awareness has floated through the oxygen you breathe, drawn into your lungs, and will emerge again in anything you create,' said Coffin. 'It doesn't matter whether or not you meant this painting to refer to Time. It simply

365

does, to anyone exposed to culture. If someone speaks in nonsense words that flow from his stream of conscious, but each word happens to be a real one, in Italian for example, then he's still speaking Italian, whether or not he means to, or is even aware of it.'

'I read Barthes and all the rest. There was little else to do when I was . . . visiting Turin. The author loses power the moment his creation is experienced by an audience. Whatever the audience reads into the work is correct, *for that reader*. But what if I know what you will think? That's when your knowledge can be used against you. If I say that a man dressed all in black, carrying a flashlight, tiptoes through a dark house at night, you'll likely think that it's a burglar. But what if the man is a priest, and the electricity has gone out, and the house is his own? Your assumption would have been incorrect. How do we logically deduce? Deduction is based on inference. You take the evidence given, you call upon experience from past examples, and you infer from a combination of this evidence and experience that the past experience will repeat. Evidence: I tell you that a painting shows an old man with an hourglass. Experience: you have seen many such paintings that refer to Time. Inference: paintings of this subject will follow the trend of past examples, and the new painting in question follows the thread of the others you have seen. But I know this about you. I can manipulate your thoughts.'

Coffin sat silent for a moment. 'Why do you bring this up now?'

'The point, Gabriel, is that you and your iconographic paintings, and your logical, observation-based deductions, are dangerously prone to manipulation. And your own knowledge should tell you that, whether or not you were thinking of the connection at the time, there is a reason that you return to the number thirty-four. And that could be used to hunt you down.'

They were quiet for a moment, before she spoke again. 'I worry . . .'

'You needn't.'

'The profiler can be profiled. Be careful. There's only one thing that I believe to be safe.'

Coffin crossed his arms. 'And what's that?'

'Malevich. With *White on White,* iconography is negated. There is nothing but the art, nothing to infer, no piece of evidence, no experience to call on. It just is.'

'But even Malevich is reacting against, and in doing so, he *refers to.* At first, some things were art. In postmodernism, everything is art. The only logical next step is that nothing will be art. A white canvas. But even that would be referring back to art, to Malevich. And Male-vich was referring back. Even in an unprecedented all-white painting, the history of art is lurking, hiding in plain sight, because there's nothing on the canvas to hide behind.'

Daniela leaned in to speak again, but Coffin resumed. 'But your point is well taken. Shall we call it a draw? Two kings on the board?'

Daniela nodded. They sat in each other's arms.

'One final and significant question for you, Dani.'

'Sì?'

'Do you feel better? I mean . . . avenged?'

Daniela paused. 'The man who framed me for

367

arrest during my last job, and got me sent to prison, has been deprived of the painting he loves and which he hired you to steal for him, the Caravaggio. We've also deprived him of his family's greatest treasure, his original Malevich *White on White*. And he has been tricked. The justice may not be biblical, but it is poetic.'

'I'm glad. And we have come out ahead . . . with an unexpected house guest . . .' Gabriel leaned in. 'Shall I?'

'Prego.'

Gabriel rose and walked into the bedroom. On the wall, above the head of the bed, hung a substantial engraving of a Roman ruin, by Giovanni Piranesi. Gabriel glanced at it, then turned with a smile to the painting on the wall opposite it. This painting was a large, heavily chiaroscuro oil on canvas. Two figures seemed to swim in the amorphous black shadowy background. One figure, with its back to the viewer, had bright wings.

It was *Jacob Wrestling the Angel* by Palma il Vecchio. Gabriel recalled the storm-tossed day, wind-beaten watery leaves shaking outside, when he'd bought that painting at auction, nearly twenty years ago.

He moved past it and turned to the third wall of his bedroom, on which hung an enormous ornate Indian tapestry, a wash of saffron, gold, rust, and cinnamon. He slipped his hand into his pocket and withdrew a thin brass key. Coffin lifted the tapestry aside and slid the key into the knobless door hidden beneath it. The door clicked open.

The small secret room fluoresced with a gentle hum, as Coffin switched on the light. Immaculately kept shelves and file cabinets were labeled with the names of chemicals, pigments, samples, reference books, and photographs. A small, round, convex mirror hung opposite the door, on the bare plywood wall that smelled of dust and sour chemicals. The portions of interior wall that were not blocked by cabinets contained pasted cutouts of paintings, newspaper clippings, and art postcards. A framed black-and-white photograph showed Marcel Duchamp playing chess with a naked woman. One painting hung on the wall, frameless, a Rembrandt: shipwreck-bound sailors clung for help on the crest of a storm-tossed sea.

In the middle of the room stood a wooden easel, on which lay a large canvas, blank except for a layer of white gesso. Daniela came up behind Gabriel and stood with her hands on his shoulders, as he sat on a stool, facing the canvas. Beside him, his work table contained a coffee mug full of brushes, all bristle-end up; a glass jar of swabs; and bottles of liquids, labeled in accurate capital letters, which his surgically precise hands manipulated. Coffin applied a sterile cloth, chemically soaked, to the waiting canvas and, with his gentle stroke, he peeled back the liquidy layer of gesso.

His first touch revealed the face of a young woman, her neck craned backward, as if surprised by her lover, who peeks in at her through the tiny window in the gesso wall that hid her secret.

Daniela exhaled. 'Mary's never looked so beautiful.'

'Funny how white obscures. It should be a semantic impossibility,' Gabriel mused. 'Looks rather like she's peering out a snowbound

369

windowpane.'

'She's been buried for a long time. Let's leave her to rest for the moment. We have all the time in the world with her now. She must be tired after all that she's been through.'

'All right. Just give me a moment alone with her.'

Daniela kissed the top of Gabriel's head and left the small room, closing the door behind her.

Coffin turned to the gessoed canvas before him. The little, clean square revealed the face of Mary. She looked tired, and perhaps a little sad, captured in perpetuity, hearing the words of the archangel that imparted the cross onto her fragile, innocent shoulders.

'Don't worry,' he whispered to her. 'I'll protect you.'

He stood and switched off the light.

Before he left the room, Coffin paused and turned back to the painting, nestled in the darkness. One thief was saved. He smiled.

'Trust in thieves.'

ACKNOWLEDGMENTS

All of my friends shape my creative process, and most will hear an echo of our shared experiences in the body of this novel. I hope that these allusions made you smile. But I would like to single out for special thanks those who helped most directly to make this novel what it is.

To David Simon, Michael Marlais, and Veronique Plesch, who made me an art historian. To Boylan and Mills, who taught me that what I write is of a merit greater than I conceived. To my friends and colleagues in the art and police worlds, particularly Bob Wittman, Bob Goldman, Dennis Ahern, Vernon Rapley, Silvia Ciotti, and Gianni Pastore who, through their confidence in me, propelled my voyage upon the uncharted seas of the study of art crime.

To my friends who helped me with their suggestions and edits, especially Sophy Downes and Patrick Tonks. To Katie Williams, for being the first professional to see promise in my work. To Peter Borland, who is an exceptional editor, the best friend a young novel could have. And to Lois Wallace, for taking me in as the youngest member of her legendary and exclusive client list . . . and because she rocks.

*For more information on real art crimes,
and to learn how you can help to solve them,
please go to www.artcrime.info.*